LITTLE FOLLIES

A MYSTERY AT THE MILLENNIUM

CAROLYN KORSMEYER

Black Rose Writing | Texas

The author grants the final approval for this literary material.

First printing

This is a work of fiction. Names, characters, businesses, places, events, and incidents are either the products of the author's imagination or used in a fictitious manner. Any resemblance to actual persons, living or dead, or actual events is purely coincidental.

ISBN: 978-1-68513-105-0
PUBLISHED BY BLACK ROSE WRITING
www.blackrosewriting.com

Printed in the United States of America
Suggested Retail Price (SRP) $23.95

Little Follies is printed in Book Antiqua

*As a planet-friendly publisher, Black Rose Writing does its best to eliminate unnecessary waste to reduce paper usage and energy costs, while never compromising the reading experience. As a result, the final word count vs. page count may not meet common expectations.

Dead flies make the perfumer's ointment give off an evil odor;
so a little folly outweighs wisdom and honor.
–Ecclesiastes

Contents

LITTLE FOLLIES

A MYSTERY AT THE MILLENNIUM

Preface

This story is a work of fiction, though many of the scenes in Krakow are set in actual places. There is one major exception: There is no Radincki Museum, nor to my knowledge was there ever any noble family of that name.

In order to insert a large building into an ancient, crowded city I have taken some liberties with the map, situating the museum at the eastern edge of the Old City just inside the Planty, the park that rings the oldest parts of Krakow and describes the medieval fortified walls. Placing the building there required the Old City to bulge out a distance, permitting the insinuation of an extra Institute behind the Jagiellonian University's Collegium Broscianum.

Other aspects of the plot also straddle fact and fiction. Tadeusz Kosciuszko, the Polish patriot who lent his engineering skills to the American Revolution, was a historical figure, but his friend Andrzej Gorski is a product of imagination. There is a painting attributed to Leonardo da Vinci that I place in the Radincki Museum whose status in the story is ambiguous. As it happens, a painting bearing the same name, *Salvator Mundi* (Savior of the World), was authenticated in 2017 as the work of Leonardo—some years after the plot of *Little Follies* takes place.

It brought $450 million at auction, but the hand of the artist who painted it remains a matter of dispute, a trait that it shares with the painting that figures in this novel.

The story takes place at the turn of the last century, which was also the turn of the millennium. This was a time that engendered all manner of folly both grand and petty, from predictions for the end of the world to panic over Y2K, the fear that at the stroke of midnight, computers across the globe would be unable to compute dates and related factors when the digits of the year apparently reversed from 99 to 00, causing widespread equipment failures. Millennial hysteria was also a fact, although the little follies that beset the characters of this story are invented.

1
A Fly in the Ointment

September, 1999

A patch of surly weather over the Atlantic jolted Adam from an uncomfortable doze into a state of high-alert. The movie flickered, the seat belt command chimed, and plastic glasses scattered into the aisle. Passengers stunned with alcohol and sleeping pills grumbled and shifted in their cramped sleep, while outside in the frigid dark cavorting winds stirred a storm a thousand feet below.

Adam retrieved his book and tried to read, but a sickening drop and a series of bumps sent his book to the floor. He grabbed for Joan's hand — a panicky clutch — but she was wrapped tightly in a cocoon of airline blanket, her head turned toward the window and her face screened by a fall of dark hair. He had declined her offer of a sleeping pill, but now he wanted one — urgently — to calm the excess adrenaline pumping into his bloodstream.

He reached under his companion's feet and snagged the strap of her zipped carry-on. Magazines, maps, water bottles, candy, aspirins, indigestion tablets, directions, a guide book — all jumbled together. Adam plunged his hands into the mess and felt around for the small bottle of sleeping pills. His hunt felt slightly transgressive. He hadn't known Joan long enough to have rummaged through her handbag before, and it was a strangely intimate invasion. The plane pitched sideways, and an envelope with their itinerary and return tickets popped out and landed out of reach.

Disregarding the seatbelt warning, Adam unhooked himself and retrieved the tickets from the aisle. His effort dislodged the little airsickness bag, which disappeared in the dark shadow beneath the seat. He hoped he wouldn't have need of it. He gave up his search for a pill and began replacing everything into the bag, automatically arranging the contents in better order. I wonder if Joan will be a messy roommate, he thought. He both envied and resented her peaceful slumber.

In fact, Joan was not quite asleep. She was hazily aware of Adam's agitation next to her, but she had taken two pills and was deeply relaxed, the jolts of the plane no more to her than the jiggling motion of a car on a bumpy road. She didn't mind the bumps. In her dozy state they seemed like a carnival ride.

She heard Adam's voice raised against the drone of the engines.

"Damn it, Joan! These tickets! I just looked at them again. What have you done?"

She had gotten the tickets at a good price. He had been pleased when she told him. What could be the matter now?

"You booked us home on December 31! I told you not to do that!" His panicky yell rose above the roar.

She kept her eyes closed. It wouldn't do to have an argument before they even began their adventure together. She hoped Adam wouldn't turn out to be a nag.

"You booked these tickets for the last day of the year! The last day of the century!! No wonder they were so cheap. No one in their right mind is flying on that day!" He imagined that dreadful moment when midnight chimed serially across the planet and the last two digits of 1999 reversed direction to 00, consternating computers and dropping aircraft into frozen seas at the turn of the millennium.

How could Joan sleep? He glared at her wrapped figure, the offending tickets in hand. He reached to give her shoulder a shake and demand that she account for the disastrous purchase. Just in time, he remembered her injured arm and withdrew his hand.

The turbulence began to subside, and the plane settled into a steady, rhythmic tremor on its way to calmer air. Adam stuffed the tickets back into the bag and closed the zipper, glad that Joan had slept through his hysterical moment. He would bring up the ticket problem later. He switched off the overhead lamp and let the night settle back around him.

Hours later, as the plane began its morning descent to their final destination, it cast a moving shadow on the outskirts of the city below. Its tiny winged shape flickered over the large castle standing guard above the river, then it circled above the expansive market square where two men sat separately over their morning coffees. Each glanced up as the sun shot a gleam of silver over the fuselage—eye-piercing for passengers in window seats, a twinkle for those on the ground. Both men resumed reading their papers; both would forget their fleeting notice of the descending plane.

The moment when events begin to align and lives will change is seldom noted when it happens.

2

The Other Side of the River

At touchdown a playful gust of wind caught the aircraft, and the pilot could not avert a sharp bump that jounced open two overhead compartments. Joan's first impression of Poland was a somatic bump, a rush of engines, and a crackling *Witamy w Krakowie* over the intercom.

"Welcome to Krakow," said Adam. "Let's hope the luggage is here."

The taxi let them off in front of a vine-covered house set behind a green fence. Joan was slightly disappointed that they had not found accommodation in the older part of the city, but Adam was more than satisfied with the flat on the other side of the river where rents were low and tourists scarce.

Up a long set of stairs there were two large rooms designated as bedroom and sitting room. The old floors were polished boards set in a herringbone pattern that seemed too elegant for the odd collection of newer furniture. Pale laminate cabinets lined the walls, offering storage space they would never fill in the course of their four-month stay. In lieu of closets there were tall, unmatched armoires. Colorful blankets covered the drab upholstery of several couches. Sitting regally amidst these items of recent vintage was a heavy desk with lion's-paw feet topped with an art deco lamp. There was a small bathroom filled with unfamiliar plumbing, and above a dried-up bidet hung a wall-mounted tank that appeared to be a water heater. It emitted a slow hiss when the tap was turned.

They stood back to back in the living room with their bags at their feet, swaying slightly from fatigue and disorientation.

"It's nice," Adam ventured. The stately old desk seemed like a good omen for his work.

Joan unlatched a window and a breeze stirred the long, lace curtains. Fat, late-summer leaves shimmered on the trees, making the world outside look slightly unstable. Their ears still rang from the long plane ride. The floor heaved gently. Perhaps it was warped, or maybe it was the two of them who were unsteady.

"It's nice," he said again.

"Yes, we'll be comfortable enough here," said Joan after a pause. "Especially after we eat and get some sleep."

Her tone did not seem unduly bright, as it might if she were not sincere. Perhaps I should have come alone after all, he thought. What if this turns out to have been a mistake? But how delighted he had been when she agreed to come along. He decided not to mention the return tickets just yet.

Joan turned and gave him a smile. Adam smiled back and extended his arms, and they stood wrapped together for a moment. Hand in hand they slowly walked through the small flat, edging around furniture and suitcases, each thinking: which armoire will be mine? Is that bed wide enough for two? And where, exactly is my space? Together they turned and kissed with willfully reassuring warmth.

"Plenty of room," said Joan.

They stepped into the sunny kitchen. A couch ran along one wall, flanked by stools crowded with potted plants. In the center of the room was a square table and four straight-backed chairs.

There were two plastic bags on the counter and a note on the table.

Adam took the note to the window and slowly began to translate. "Sorry I am not with—no here—sorry I am not here to be with, to meet, to greet—oh, I get it. Sorry I am not here to greet you today."

Joan, suddenly energetic, was one-handedly opening cupboards. "There are certainly enough dishes. All different patterns. This must be the place all the leftover things get put."

"I hope you find everything likeable, um, to your liking."

"I wonder how you light this stove? I'm dying for some coffee. Oh look, there is a new jar of instant here. Do you want some instant coffee? I don't see a regular coffee maker."

"Instant coffee is fine. Can you make it with your bad arm?"

"Yes, it's okay. Better every day. I need to move it to keep the joint loose. Here are some tea bags. Would you rather have tea?"

"There are two beds in one room and three others in. Huh. Can there really be a bed in the kitchen? I guess this couch is a fold-out. Well, we won't lack for places to sleep."

"There are lots of keys in these cupboard locks, but they don't turn. I guess they are used for handles, because there aren't any regular handles."

"I went to the shop for . . . What's that noise?"

"Just water boiling. It makes the kettle rattle. Do you suppose that the water is safe to drink here? There is bottled water in the refrigerator. Might that be a clue that we're not supposed to drink from the tap?"

"The water's probably okay. I think she is saying that she bought us some things."

"I thought you said the landlady knows English. What's her name again?"

"Beata. Be-ah-ta, three syllables. But she wrote the note in Polish. I am supposed to speak it, after all. You should learn it too."

"Bread, milk, butter, cheese—there's lots in the fridge. Oh look, there is a beautiful bird in the tree outside. I wonder if it's a magpie. Aren't there supposed to be magpies here?"

"I will be gone for two days to Warsaw. What's this?"

"Lunch. There is lots of food in the fridge. She did a nice shopping for us already. Wasn't that thoughtful? Did you say coffee or tea?"

Adam sank into one of the chairs and dropped his head in his hands. "If Gorski's handwriting is as bad as hers, I'm sunk."

"Don't worry," said Joan. "You just need some food."

"I want to see how long it takes me to get to the archives from here. On the map it looks far, but I don't think it really is."

"All in good time," said Joan. "We need to unpack and change first. I'm sick of these clothes."

A short time later, half-eaten sandwiches curled drily on the table and Joan and Adam lay asleep sprawled against each other. After lunch it had seemed a good idea to celebrate their arrival in bed, and they had tried all of them—wobbly four-poster, trundle, and fold-out couch—before jet lag overtook desire.

It can't be far to the archives, Adam thought as he drifted into oblivion. On the other side of the river. Just across that bridge.

3

The Archives

Across the river at the edge of the Old City sat the Radincki Museum of Art, Artifacts, and Manuscripts, a rambling stone structure so disproportionately large for its surroundings that it kept the entire vicinity in shade. Centuries of architectural tinkering had expanded the edifice beyond its original design, and it now obtruded onto a street so narrow that cars could barely squeeze past one another.

On the cavernous upper exhibition level, Klementyna Kamynska's sturdy heels clopped slowly across the floor. Daily her footsteps patrolled the exhibits, sharp reports as discrete and precise as gunshots. She wore the same gray skirt, white blouse, and blue blazer that she had worn every day for years. Under the jacket the blouse was beginning to separate at the seams that strained across her thick shoulders, but it was hidden and she hadn't bothered to replace it. Her shoes were resoled every year, for the hard floors—ancient oak in the exhibition rooms, stone in the corridors—took their toll.

Most of the visitors to the museum were tourists who had stayed a bit too long in Krakow and didn't want to trudge up to the Wawel Castle yet again. Once in a while someone would approach her with a question, but the guards on duty rarely spoke. They had found that the surest guardian was silence, for mischief makes noise. Silence and approaching footsteps made even the most casual visitor draw back from touching the furniture or fogging the jewelry cases with their breath. Klementyna marveled that her tedious patrolling could awaken guilt, and in the wasted corners of her mind she was developing a theory about original sin. Sometimes she wished for the entertainment of a thief.

She heard the tall doors groan as they were pulled back for morning visitors. From the upper landing of the grand staircase, Klementyna had a view all the way to the street. She was surprised to see that there were already two people waiting to enter.

Joan and Adam stood at the foot of a bank of stone steps that led up to towering doors decorated with the ornate Radincki crest. The doors were flanked by pilasters of heavy-featured figures, perhaps unnamed deities, perhaps ancestral Radinckis.

"The archive has shorter hours than the rest of the museum," said Adam. "There are even some days the museum is open that the archives are not."

"That's okay," said Joan. "On those days we can play tourist and look around."

"Maybe. But I need to get to work."

Sometimes he felt an absurd urgency to get to Gorski's papers before anyone else found them, although it was unlikely that another scholar would have decided to study the papers of a little-known follower of the great Polish engineer of the American Revolution, Tadeusz Kosciuszko: The forgotten Andrzej Gorski, who (possibly) had stood beside Kosciuszko at the Battle of Saratoga, had (maybe) followed him down the Hudson, and (at a guess) helped to supervise the fortifications at West Point. The extant record was distinctly sketchy, but Adam hoped to fill in the blanks with an article or even a chapter of some future book that would protect his job, his career, and his ultimate desires. This prospect had opened when he learned that the remnants of Gorski's family had donated family records to the Radincki's manuscript collection. He gazed at the edifice looming before him, savoring the moment when he would ascend the steps and enter the archive.

"Go ahead," said Joan, nudging him forward. "I need to catch the bus to Czestochowa. Did I say that right? I mean the place where they have the black Madonna. Sure you don't want to come along? It's only a day's tour. You should look around a little before buckling down."

"No. I want to get to work," said Adam. "Are you sure you need to go there now? Why not relax a bit first and catch up on sleep?"

"All in good time. If I want to reboot my career as a journalist, I need to start collecting copy. See you later. I'll bring you a souvenir."

A quick kiss and she turned and hurried back to busy Grodzka Street, the city map flapping in her hands. Adam watched her go, thinking how pretty she was with her curly hair blowing and her strides energetic, confident and at ease in a strange city where she didn't speak a word of the language. Although her broken elbow was nearly healed, today she wore a protective sling. An injury is handy, she had said with a smile, for getting people to give you their seat. Part of him wished to go sightseeing with her, but the larger part was eager to begin his archival task. He took a deep breath and mounted the stairs.

The Radincki's echoing space was divided into four asymmetrical wings whose rooms were linked by complicated angles and twisting corridors. In two of the wings were displayed furniture, historical artifacts, and luxurious clutter. A third held a painting collection replete with mammoth depictions of mythic and romanticized events in Polish history. Figured prominently among the kneeling knights, plunging horses, and decoratively garbed bishops were nine generations of Radinckis, the noble family that once had called the structure home. The family line had petered out in exile sometime in the previous century, though thanks to a series of compliant artists, images of various Radinckis lived on. They fought heroically at the battle of Legnica, rode beside Jan Sobieski as he liberated Vienna, and were singled out for divine approval with a shaft of light beaming onto a tombstone.

When their necks became stiff from staring up at Radinckis, visitors might meander to a corner of the gallery that held a cluster of work from a group of nineteenth-century artists who had traveled to Paris and brought back the modern styles of that city. Their colorful oils were mounted next to wrinkled sketches of the artists themselves looking self-consciously bohemian. Further along the wall were some older pieces, including one painting optimistically attributed to Leonardo da Vinci—acquired by Count Stanislaw Radincki in the mid eighteenth century as a wedding gift for his wife Katarina—and a couple of Dürer drawings, creased and inexpertly repaired. In the two galleries devoted to furniture and artifacts, the tired tourist could perch on a stone bench and study the fine detail of embroidered vestments hanging on walls or peer into cases of jewelry and gilded housewares.

Adam now saw more of these galleries than he intended, as he immediately became lost on his way to the archives. He asked for directions in his hesitant Polish from a large woman with a square jaw and a sour smell about her jacket. He nodded at her reply but took another wrong turn before locating the wing where the archives were housed. Klementyna noticed his error but shrugged.

Then he had to wait in a cramped anteroom amid metal shelves and stacks of bound reports, his eyes watering from the flickering florescent light overhead. Adam dug out the letter that confirmed the approval of his request to conduct research, and a loose-leafed notebook was consulted with maddening leisure. Yes indeed, he was on record as a visiting scholar, Adam was finally assured. He sighed with relief and picked up his briefcase.

But then there was a document to sign, an agreement about the use of the archives. Adam scanned it quickly. No materials to be removed from the building, no fountain pens, no photocopies. That was too bad; it would be handy to be able to make copies. But the copy machine standing nearby was an obsolete model with a raking scan and a hot smell, clearly damaging to delicate old paper. He quickly signed the bottom and took his copy, intending to examine it more carefully in the evening.

Finally, he was ushered through the next door.

The space opened to a generous set of rooms filled with parallel rows of tall book shelves. The widely-spaced wooden tables were large and solid, the seats numerous and commodious. A few upholstered wingbacks invited the occasional doze. A small adjacent room was outfitted with sink and hotplate so that visitors could make coffee or nibble a snack at a scrupulous distance from the desks spread with books and manuscripts. Lamps bestowed private pools of light on the work of each scholar, and the dimness of recesses gave the impression of endless books, boxes, papers, treasures. Adam drew a deep breath and smiled.

But then they couldn't find the right collection. Instead of the materials on Gorski that he had requested, the fragmentary correspondence of one Andrzej Goranski had been delivered. So befuddled had Adam been, what with the bewildering layout of the place and the remnants of jet lag, that he read through several pages before the absolute irrelevance of these materials became obvious. And then it took him yet more time to explain the error, all in Polish that rapidly progressed from faltering to incompetent. The librarian was used to foreign scholars with their terrible accents, and he patiently took away Goranski's file with a shrug and what Adam took to be an apologetic joke. He soon returned wheeling a trolley loaded with four boxes containing materials from the once influential Gorski family, including the manuscripts, the letters, the journal of Andrzej Gorski, forgotten companion of the heroic Kosciuszko. Adam found a desk and sat down like a hungry man at a laden table.

Another man had quietly arrived during Adam's anxious moments. From a table across the room he watched as the newcomer finally settled down. English, he guessed from his accent, or American. Maybe Canadian. Certainly an academic. No one else would possess a jacket with such belled-out elbows or let his hair grow so shaggy. He shook his own neatly-barbered head and returned to his private task. For an hour he was the only other researcher in the archive, but he sat in shadow and Adam hardly noticed him.

Tentatively, Adam began to separate significant documents from those that pertained only to members of the Gorski family in Warsaw and Paris. The materials were old, many fragmentary, faded, or smudged. With scrupulous care he held the fragile pages and puzzled over the faded writing. When a document was written with a hasty hand or in language that exceeded his decoding skills, he quashed a wave of anxiety and put it aside for later.

For the first time in months he felt truly optimistic that his happenstance discovery a year ago, when he had unearthed some miscataloged microfilm and correlated it with Kosciuszko's Saratoga fortifications, might confirm the role of another Pole among the foreign soldiers of the American Revolution. This well-researched historical territory rarely revealed new findings, so if he were successful in his project, the now utter obscurity of Andrzej Gorski would rise to mere relative dimness in the annals of scholarship. A small step, but his own.

It was hard to explain to another the fervent anticipation with which he opened each old letter, the pleasure of his fingers tracing the creased paper. The faded ink with its peculiar curves and angles seemed a living conduit for the personality behind the handwriting. Adam noticed the haste of a notation dashed with a pen too heavily inked, the trail of faded drops still as impatient as the moment they had sprayed across the page. How shallow would be the record left for historians of the future, he thought, with only featureless computer printouts to analyze.

Nothing resembling the diary that Gorski alluded to in his letters appeared to be here, but in its place Adam had letters, including drafts that were never sent but apparently had served as notes or memoranda. He felt like a clever shadow trailing Gorski and his companions as they followed Kosciuszko up and down the Hudson valley. It was left to him to gather up the fragments of their record and bring their past to light. By afternoon his hands were grimy with a fine gray dust that had sifted into the boxes over years of storage. He found this soil somehow reassuring, as if he had entered into the world of the letters like a miner descending to ore. When he left for the day, blinking in the late sunshine that still filled the city, it took him a moment to adjust to the light and to recognize Joan sitting on the wide stone steps and eating an ice cream cone.

4
Strange Bedfellows

The man who called himself Pawel Radincki had his own table at the archive, or at least he liked to think of it as exclusively his. On its large surface he would unfold the four quadrants of a folio page of heavy rag paper that he had bought in Paris the previous summer. On each visit he would consult a volume or two from the nearby collection of pre-war reference books and old editions of central European histories. After a time he would take his fine-tipped fountain pen, which should not have been used among those documents (pencils only, please!) and add a carefully-printed name to his chart. He imagined that the surrounding scholars were curious, but in fact they paid little heed. Genealogy was a popular pastime these days. It was not uncommon to see someone filling names in the branches of a family tree.

Pawel had watched as Adam fumbled about locating his materials and settling into his research. He had also overheard the archivist's scrupulous questions before he granted a stranger access to rare documents, which made him grateful that he only needed to consult the shelved books in the reading room. He preferred that his purposes in the archive remain vague.

Today Pawel was neatly dressed in a dark suit, a crisp white shirt, and a tie decorated with small red and gold crests. Such finery was hardly necessary for the museum's library, but while examining himself in the mirror that morning, he had decided his appearance needed a little patina. His clothing looked too new, too nouveau, in fact, especially the shoes. They were fine leather, but after a few weeks of walking Krakow's stony streets they would have just the appropriate appearance for a man such as he aimed to be: one used to fine things despite dwindling wealth. Pawel had studied the discernible difference between upstart and aristocrat. Such knowledge was indispensable for the eventual success of his plan.

On the fourth finger of his left hand he wore a heavy gold ring incised with a heraldic design flanked with faceted amber. It also needed a little more wear, but it would take longer to achieve the look of an aged family jewel than it would to scuff up his shoes. He stretched his hand into a patch of sunlight angling through the curtains and admired the ring. There was a tiny wax fragment lodged in the pattern from where he had practiced with a drippy candle to see how the imprint of the seal would look. The sun slanted through the amber and set two small fires ablaze.

Pawel had encountered some frustration launching the plan that had brought him back to Krakow. On the basis of the films noirs that afforded his education in crime, he had presumed that thieves for hire would be easily found by hanging out in dark bars and dropping cryptic hints to men who nursed drinks alone. There were plenty of likely-looking establishments in Paris for such a search; but his first attempt had been seriously misconstrued, requiring a quick exit from a tavern followed by a beefy prostitute offended that his territory was breached. And the second and third efforts had been so opaque that the targets had concluded he was simply drunk. Finally, he enlisted the advice of a pawnbroker acquaintance of his late wife's, whose fund of information indicated that Pawel must have lived in closer proximity to marginally criminal activity than he had realized during the several years of his marriage.

That proximity might have been the most useful thing to have come from the marriage. Not an ideal match though common enough: an older woman attracted to a handsome man, a younger man attracted to the opportunities she afforded. He polished his demeanor under her tutelage; she found him a charming companion, adequate if not spectacular in bed. He hadn't been devastated when she died, and with the money she left he could finally launch the daring scheme that had been growing in his mind for years. He was ready at last.

The pawnbroker had produced a name. In a storage area of the shop, strategically equipped with an imitation Coromandel screen, Pawel peered through the lattice-work at a large man with an unpleasant Canadian accent. His potential employee gave an insubordinate eye-roll at the set up, but Pawel intended to keep his own identity secret. In return, the man he hired gave only one name.

Bodie, he said. Just Bodie.

He left it to Bodie to enlist a second man, preferably someone new enough to the game that a slim payment would satisfy. His legacy did not permit largesse. Pawel had lurked in a doorway in the rain when the two met. The surveillance had been damp but highly satisfying, assuring Pawel that he had the requisite skills for the caper he intended. Thinking of it as a caper lent his plan panache, a drama starring himself as a gentleman thief, like John Robie. The two supporting members of the cast, with their heavy shoulders hunched against the drizzle, would do well enough, thought Pawel. He himself would direct the fine points of the plan.

Bodie and Keith arrived in Krakow by different routes and located adjacent rooms in a shabby establishment just outside the Old Town. Bodie's initial worries about being conspicuous in a strange place turned out to be groundless. Who would have thought that the city would be so full of tourists with their babble of languages, so loaded with artists, students, musicians on street corners, and even the occasional gypsy. Their appearance raised not an eyebrow.

Still, Bodie knew it was a more select crowd that frequented museums, and he insisted that Keith obtain a better wardrobe. The numerous shops were less well-stocked than they appeared at first, having little to sell that wasn't in the window displays. But street vendors with knock-off sporting gear supplied jackets that were clean and new. Bodie was relieved that his younger, greener partner cleaned up well enough, though little could be done about his stream of mindless blather and rubbernecking habits. In addition, Keith was having trouble identifying local prostitutes and had made two violently unwelcome advances to girls who turned out to be university students. Choosing this blundering amateur for a partner might have been a mistake, though after a few days walking the streets it appeared that no one gave them a second look. Bodie began to relax. In Poland he might pass for French, birthplace Marseilles, as one of his passports testified. Things were not so comfortable at present back in Quebec.

The two of them first visited the Radincki Museum just to get a sense of the layout. It might have been wiser to scope out the place later in the day when there were more people around. Bodie wondered if they had experienced a close call when that female guard had turned their way. Her dull gaze beneath heavy brows, like a buffalo turning its head. Keith hadn't noticed, but Bodie had steered them quickly into the next room.

A second preparatory visit was supposed to follow directly, except locating the materials for their project had mandated a train to Katowice with an unpronounceable list of items jotted down by their annoyingly mysterious employer and conveyed to them in an envelope stuck under a bench in the park. Rain had dampened the paper so the list had smudged. Bodie snorted at the unnecessary drama. He was beginning to doubt that their enigmatic employer quite knew what he was doing, and he resolved to investigate more carefully to discover what was really going on. Their stated objectives didn't line up with all the preliminary preparations underway. There must be something else at stake.

He went to the Radincki Museum a third time on his own, but the visit yielded no clue. They were tasked with two jobs, and the combination didn't make sense. The painting was an obvious choice, especially if it was authentic. But that little cabinet was a baffling target. He must be missing something. But he would keep his suspicions to himself. The pay for this job wasn't great. He had only agreed to take it on for lack of immediate alternatives. But if there was a larger prize at stake than they had been told, he intended to get his share.

5

A Café

Joan sat at a small outdoor café at the edge of the Rynek, the large old market square. She was hungry and wanted more than coffee but needed to put together a sentence for the request. She was trying now not to speak English, having quickly followed Adam's lead and begun to refer to certain things in Polish: *Rynek* rather than market square, *sklep* rather than shop, *chleb* rather than bread; *Sukiennice* rather than Market Hall. ("Not soo-keh-nice, Joan," said Adam during the course of one of his periodic tutorials. "Soo-keh-ni-tzeh. And it's RIH-neck with a short 'i' sound. Not like rye bread.") Adam's pronunciation seemed to be pretty good, though he looked baffled occasionally and often filled his conversation with *tak* and *dobrze*, nodding as though he understood: Yes, very good, yes, yes. Useful fillers.

After Adam found his niche in the Radincki archives and became difficult to extract, she stuck her phrase book and maps into her purse and set off on her own to explore. It had been a risk to agree to come with someone she had known so briefly, but she was a risk-taker by nature. The unexpected cancelation of the two courses she was supposed to teach in the coming year, combined with her bicycle accident (caused in part by agitation over the former) might have sent someone else into a bout of despondence. Joan had taken it as a sign that she was due for a change of scene. She dutifully squeezed the little exercise ball every day, optimistic that soon the traumatized nerves in her fingers would repair themselves, and she could return to typing with the ease and speed required of an aspiring journalist. Poland afforded an opportunity for a few feature articles, and maybe the relationship with Adam would become a true commitment. For both of them. The delight he had expressed when she told him she would come, she suspected, was a combination of affection for her and relief that he would have company in a foreign land.

Not that he appeared to need much company; so far her tourist excursions had been conducted alone. She had visited the Wawel Castle twice, admired the tapestries and the paintings, the furniture and jewels and armaments. She climbed the narrow staircase of the cathedral tower and contemplated the bell. She gazed across the river from the ancient ramparts and tried to identify the roof of their flat among the distant tree tops. And she had even attached herself to a group of schoolchildren and visited the lair of the legendary dragon that lay under the castle. On an overcast Tuesday, she had trudged through the streets of Kazimierz. She visited the one functioning synagogue, tiny and austere, walking among ancient tombs and the smashed remnants of gravestones now jigsawed into memorial walls. By herself she had poked through the Czartoryszki collection, and she had taken the long, forlorn bus tour to Auschwitz.

Adam had accompanied her once to the Wawel Cathedral, mainly to descend to its crypt and pay homage at Kosciuszko's tomb. Their relationship was not advancing in any noteworthy way, yet they found each other pleasant company, and the nights were passionate enough. She thought it slightly odd that they seemed to have reached a comfortable plateau with none of the preliminary elation of romance. But Joan did not mind being on her own for a time.

At the moment her attention was absorbed in the work that a crew of men was undertaking on an ancient building on the adjacent street. It was a thick-walled structure with narrow windows and a high pitched roof. The walkway in front had been taken up in chunks that now leaned against the wall, revealing remnants of uneven cobbles. Three men were at work with picks and shovels hacking at the edges of the foundation. From time to time a fourth emerged from the back with a barrow full of bricks and stone. Glassless windows revealed that the ground floor was gutted, though the windows on the upper floor were curtained as though someone still lived within. In the distance she could hear the intermittent roar of a backhoe. Krakow was renewing itself.

There was a startled shout, and one of the workmen vanished. His shovel hovered cartoon-like in the air a second before clattering to the ground, but he himself had slid from view like laundry down a chute. The other two men dropped their tools and dashed to the cavity that had suddenly opened at the foot of the house. Joan found that she had half-risen from her seat in an impulse to rush to help, and that her cup had overturned and the remaining coffee was pooling in the saucer.

But the exclamations echoing out of the hole did not sound urgent, and she sat back feeling self-conscious and a bit foolish.

"Less to carry out, it seems," said a voice beside her. "That cellar must be clear already."

She had not particularly noticed this man before, but as he snapped his newspaper back into neat folds she recognized him as another frequent visitor to the café. "Your coffee is going to run out of the saucer," he said.

Joan sluiced the coffee from the saucer back into the cup. "So he fell into a cellar?" she said.

"Probably, yes. They are excavating and clearing out the old basements of all these buildings. Haven't you noticed all the underground restaurants? Gives a nice antique atmosphere for the tourists."

A nice antique atmosphere had been just what she was enjoying about the city. "Surely not just for tourists," she replied. "I hear mostly Polish spoken in them." She had in fact been in only a few, and the neighboring tables were usually filled with gabbling French and Germans.

"Poles are tourists too. Krakow is their cultural capital. Haven't you noticed all the school groups on tour?"

Haven't you noticed. Haven't you noticed. The man had a finger-wagging tone.

"Why did you speak English to me?"

He pointed to the corner of a map protruding from her jacket pocket, a street plan in English.

And just as Joan was about to conclude that the man was insufferable, he smiled, and his face was lit with such good humor that she found herself smiling back. "I apologize," he said. "I must sound presumptuous speaking to you like that. But you looked so startled."

"I was afraid the man was hurt."

"He might have been, but possibly the cave-in saved them a bit of work. Most of these cellars were filled with debris over the years, and they take a lot of clearing. These chaps might have caught a break. Let's have a look, shall we?"

The man unfolded himself from the low wicker chair. He was very tall and had to duck beneath the rim of the table umbrella. Joan followed him to the edge of the excavation. The work area was casually roped off with a drooping piece of tape. A cloud of brown dust was beginning to settle around a small landslide of dirt slanting underground into a pool of darkness. The man by her side spoke Polish to one of the workmen, who nodded and replied at length, apparently glad of the opportunity to light a cigarette and have a rest.

"Yes, I guessed right," said her companion. "The passage to the cellar in back was blocked from the interior, and they thought it was all filled with debris. But the fellow who fell just now was digging where there was an unexpected gap in the foundation, and he broke through to an area that is quite empty. Fortunately, he landed on packed earth rather than rock."

"Do they ever find interesting artifacts in these renovations?"

"Oh yes. I'm sure they do. All of Krakow is an interesting artifact, don't you think?" He turned back to his table to finish his coffee, and Joan found herself following him.

"Are you German?" she asked. The man's accent was hard to identify.

"Dutch. I've been living here for several years, though. My name is Rudy Vander Lage." He extended his hand and she shook it. He glanced briefly at her left arm, held protectively against her ribs.

"Joan Templeton."

"Here on holiday?"

"No. Here to live for a few months. I came with a friend who is doing some research."

"Lots to see in Krakow. You won't be bored."

And since they had both finished their coffee and were both foreigners, it seemed only natural that they would gather their jackets and leave money for the bill, and then walk out together into the Rynek.

"So all these old buildings have an underground part like that one?" she asked, reluctant to have the conversation end. It was nice to be speaking to someone new.

"Many of them, I suppose. A few of these were quite grand at one time, even qualified as palaces. Lots of church buildings too, convents and such. Plus it's been a center of commerce forever. Of course the street has risen over the years, what with new pavement and all. I suppose what is now completely underground was once half-above." Rudy began fumbling in his pockets absently. A cigarette appeared. "Americans don't smoke anymore, I suppose?"

Joan shook her head. "These cellars. Were they all filled up like the one the workmen are excavating?"

"Only the smaller ones probably. But the buildings are very old and were built up against one another over time. It was inevitable that debris would accumulate. The Communist government didn't encourage renovation and no one had much spare money. That's why there's so much building going on now. Everyone with a street front is leaping into commerce. Great entrepreneurs, the Poles. Overturn a government and start afresh. Here in Krakow, at least in the Old City inside the Planty—you know the Planty? That green park that circles the area? —and in places like Kazimierz, the renovations have to conform to certain standards. Can't risk the tourist trade, naturally. But people are very fond of their history too. There's romance to a place this old."

Silence as they scanned the huge square together. Rudy glanced at his watch.

"I'm afraid I must be off. Perhaps I'll see you again in our favorite coffee bar." He shook her hand again and left with a brief, polite smile.

Joan watched him lope away. He was a handsome man with graying hair swept back from pale eyes and an easy gait that suggested former athleticism. She wondered if he had really needed to go or had devised a gracious way to end the conversation. Perhaps he was, like her, just restless by nature. She decided to try out her Polish at the vegetable market on her way home, for the little refrigerator at the flat was bare.

6

Thieves in Waiting

The two men were back again on Thursday. Klementyna Kamynska took notice because it was not common for tourists to visit the Radincki Museum more than once. Her curiosity mildly piqued, she diverted her slow trajectory in their direction. Their attention was focused with unlikely intensity at a case full of eighteenth-century tableware.

Did they move rather too hastily away to look at the suits of armor lined up along the wall? Klementyna was aware that her approach sometimes prompted visitors to draw back from their scrutiny of some jewelry or hanging vestment or other piece of over-decorated fandango. It amused her to see the effect she wielded without saying a word. She glanced at the case the men had been looking in but saw nothing of special interest.

Klementyna was bored, so with her measured pace she followed them. As she neared, did their voices drop? Possibly, but many people dislike having their every word magnified by the echoes of large rooms. As she passed by the two men, her eyes directed only at her toes, she caught a few words and thought they might have been speaking English. She could understand a bit of that language. English was the common language of the world now, and Klementyna was glad enough to learn it. These days, it was more useful than her school Russian. She thought she'd make another circuit and see if she could understand any of the two men's conversation. It wasn't nosiness exactly, though her presence might have appeared inquisitive to someone who did not comprehend the tedium of her job.

If she had known just a little more English she might have recalled what curiosity did to the cat.

Keith, sweating inside his new jacket, was getting nervous. "Damn it. Here she comes again. That same woman who spotted us the first time."

Bodie shrugged. "Don't worry so much. She won't recognize us. Ignore her."

Klementyna moved past, and the two men peered together at a set of ivory chessmen. As they heard her footfalls recede they moved towards a hallway at the end of the main gallery.

"Don't trot like that, dammit," hissed Bodie. "Just walk. What did I tell you? You've got to be cool. Casual. Don't call attention to yourself." Bodie deliberately strolled, forcing Keith to slow to a jittery amble. They paused before a darkened suit of armor and a rack of long weapons.

"Look how many different kinds of swords there are!" wondered Keith. "What do you suppose they needed them all for?"

"No idea," Bodie said indifferently. He tamped down irritation at Keith's skipping attention span. The man was capable of being distracted by just about anything. Keith continued to study the array, puzzling like an inexperienced diner before a table laid with unfamiliar forks. Bodie moved on and had to pause before his partner noticed he had fallen behind. He was annoyed to see Keith canter up again.

"Just walk!" he hissed. "It's this room here. No one is there now, so we can start the job. But you have to keep an eye out! If you see anyone approaching let me know."

With a quick glance around, they entered a corridor that branched off the main gallery and opened to three small rooms. There the ceiling was lower, and the echoes that magnified every cough, tap, and ping in the main gallery were left behind. Their target was the last small room. It was illuminated only by two stained glass windows set in shallow niches that were lit from behind. They broadcast the gazes of two austere saints who once had occupied a bygone chapel. Keith unzipped his jacket and took several deep breaths to calm his pulse. It was dimmer in here, kind of church-like. He felt uneasy with the saintly faces looking at him in that disapproving manner. They seemed to be assessing him and not much liking what they saw.

Three square display cases housed a miscellaneous assortment of relics retrieved from various palaces long demolished. One case was filled with the kinds of things that would have been discarded if they weren't so old: antique nails that once studded a door, a set of decorative hinges, and a pile of what looked to Keith like petrified bird droppings. (They were in fact ancient wax seals.) The other vitrines contained two pairs of earrings, a flat trencher with a decorated rim, three chains of differing widths, one stirrup, a heavily embroidered shooting glove, and a silver goblet with a fused stem. None of it looked particularly worth stealing.

"I can't believe we're going to all this trouble about this case of crap," he said. "There aren't even any jewels. There is much better stuff in the other room."

Bodie only grunted and knelt on the floor. He was inclined to agree with Keith that this part of their job made little sense. There had to be something else going on. The contents of this particular cabinet couldn't be important enough for all this work. But he would figure out what was really at stake on his own. No need to involve the amateur.

He pulled on a pair of latex gloves. They were tight on his large hands.

"Ours not to reason why. Ours to deliver for a nice chunk of change," he said.

The task had to be done quickly. Most of the ingredients were already prepared, but now at the last minute he opened two small jars, pouring one into the other and mixing carefully with a small swab until the material thickened. A sharp smell arose in the still air.

"Man, that stuff stinks!" said Keith.

"Quiet. It'll disperse soon enough. You just look out for anyone coming this way." Bodie lay on his back and with a wide syringe began to insert gluey gel into the square keyhole on the underside of the old cabinet.

"Maybe I should light a cigarette or something to cover it up," offered Keith. This prompted an exasperated snort from the floor.

"The fastest way to draw attention in a museum is to light a cigarette, asshole. Besides, this stuff's flammable. You light a match here and you'll turn this case into a barbecue. Shut up and keep watch. And listen. Listen for footsteps."

Keith stepped back into the larger gallery and occupied himself with a collection of tables, stepping around them and peering closely as if intending to recommend one to a decorator. The smell was less noticeable out here in the high-ceilinged room, and fortunately the handful of visitors today was not interested in this wing. He jittered nervously and wondered where the toilets were in this huge place. Some of the deep bowls in the case on the far wall were in fact chamber pots, but Keith was not to know this.

Bodie suddenly appeared from behind and startled him.

"Some lookout you are."

They had finished the job just in time, for now they could hear the slow, ominous clop of steps nearing. They scooted into the next exhibit hall. When Klementyna passed, she was bemused to see them deeply absorbed in nineteenth-century ladies' fashion. Maybe their football jackets disguised more effeminate leanings; foreigners were strange birds. In a teasing mood, she made a circuit of the room, approaching them twice, and was amused to see the younger man's eyes dart nervously in her direction.

The two men progressed rather too quickly through the rest of the museum. Keith was convinced their odd activities in the little gallery would be discovered, but Bodie — who was himself more nervous than he appeared — observed that they had caught a break. A cleaner with a large waxing buffer was making his way through the museum. The smell of the wax would cover any trail of chemical odor they might have left.

"See Keith?" he said. "Things are going our way. No need for nerves."

"I'll feel better when we get paid and I'm back on the train. You may be used to this, Bodie, but I'm not."

"Well, be patient. We can't leave for a while."

Outside the wind blew away the last of the smell clinging to his jacket, and Bodie balled up his latex gloves and threw them into a trash can full of crumpled maps and used paper cups. "In the meantime," he suggested, "why don't we visit the castle? I hear they've got a dragon and everything."

He was beginning to get an idea about the real job at hand, the one they weren't being told about. There were lots of those display cases in the museum, and some of them held jewels. I'll bet, he thought, that keys for one cabinet also fit some of the others, including the ones holding gold and jewelry. He vowed to do some more looking around. There might be more money to be had in this job than what they were offered. But no need to share. He was the pro after all.

Keith perked up. A dragon sounded fun.

As Bodie and Keith exited the museum, a far better-dressed man ascended the wide stone stairs. They passed with one-sided recognition, but Pawel Radincki turned his head away just in case. He was fairly certain that neither could recognize him, but the big one had a suspicious face and it was wise to be cautious.

Before entering, he paused before the heavy doors and surveyed the building with a proprietary air, which was then compromised by the necessity of paying the entrance fee. Vague thoughts sustained his sense of ownership while he gained entrance like an ordinary visitor. He made his way up the stairs to the galleries, his gaze sweeping the rooms, nodding with approval at the opulence displayed. He hadn't toured the collection thoroughly since his return, but it hadn't changed much. The walls were still lined with armor, with gold-embroidered ceremonial clothing, and with swords bearing the arms of noble households. There were exhibits of the vestments of bishops and precious altar cloths and cases filled with silver and gilt crosses. Carved baptismal fonts were placed along the walls, remnants of chapels long destroyed. The cabinets in one section were entirely filled with jewelry. Pawel was displeased to find a small exhibit of Jewish Krakow which he hadn't remembered being there. He couldn't identify the items by name, though he recognized the stars and those crowded candlesticks. At least the exhibit was set off from the main rooms and not mixed in with the artifacts from what he regarded as true Poland.

Today he wasn't headed for the archive. His first destination was the picture gallery where hung half the strategy of his grand plan. He nodded at the paintings as if greeting members of his own family—as indeed he reckoned he was. In his jacket pocket was the folded folio of his family tree: Pawel Radincki, last scion of the noble house of Radincki. He kept it close to his heart.

Unfortunately, this name did not match the one on his passport. That was the problem with illegitimacy; it interrupted the chain of patronymics. But once he brought light into the murk of his family history, he was increasingly certain that he would be able to trace a crooked path to some promiscuous Radincki, thereby confirming his descent from nobility.

It was the genealogist in France who had first corroborated this elevated pedigree, implying with the canniness of a fortune teller that it was not inconceivable that he could find evidence of noble lineage. Not inconceivable meant possible; and possible was but a short step to probable, from which there was only one more step to certain. At this point in his imaginings, Pawel's thoughts invariably raced into exhilarating incoherence. He envisioned finding other kin, perhaps even a link to the distinguished Radziwills, though even he had to grant that the kinship between that great princely family and the small, dried-up stream of Radinckis only occurred when they were listed in alphabetical order.

Now that he was back in Krakow and traveling under this name, his rightful if unacknowledged patronymic, he had reverted to the correct spelling. During the five years of his sojourn abroad he had spelled it "Radinski," having discovered away from Poland that the "c" was apt to be pronounced just like the adjacent "k," with unfortunately amusing effects. His own wife, adept with languages, had snorted disloyally. Apparently in English it sounded particularly funny.

He passed a mammoth painting of the battle of Vienna where King Jan Sobieski had so wonderfully defeated the Ottoman Turks with a Count Radincki by his side. The profile of this illustrious figure reassuringly matched his own nose viewed from the left. And the telltale long fingers that resembled his own gripped the very sword that lay in the adjoining gallery.

His last vigil took place before a much smaller picture, and he breathed a sigh of relief to find it hanging there. It had been returned from expert examination only last month. It was surprising that it should already be on display. One would have expected the museum to keep it under wraps until the authentication had been publicly announced. But perhaps that contentious process had been in the works for so long that officials decided the suspense had already dissipated. In any event, here it was for all to see: the gem of that glorious hand, soon to be known throughout the world.

Pawel was a little alarmed to see that the painting had been placed in an additional protective glass-fronted box with a small humidity register tucked into a corner. But on reflection he understood the necessity of this, for the polluted air of Krakow, not to mention the breath of museum visitors, could damage the old paint. Besides, once it was authenticated as one of the few paintings of Leonardo da Vinci, every tourist in Europe would want to come and take a look. At the Louvre the crowds before the *Mona Lisa* prevented close inspection. Here no one disturbed him as he gazed upon the contested masterpiece, *Salvator Mundi*. Pawel caught the painted, slightly unfocused eyes of Christ and looked away.

Was it good or bad luck that the museum had decided to proceed with a formal, public authentication at the very time that Pawel had begun to devise his great plan? It made it both bolder and riskier, and Pawel felt a swell of anxiety. He quelled it with the reassuring thought that it was destiny itself that propelled his schemes. He would just give destiny a little boost.

Pawel glanced around to assure that he was alone and stepped close to the painting, then closer still until his eyes could no longer focus on the fine brush strokes. Then he moved to the side and peered at the edge where the frame met the wall. No audible alarms went off, though it was impossible to tell if any silent sensors had been installed. Still, how likely was it that this item had not been equipped with special protection? He had originally counted on the casual, near nonexistent security that the museum had maintained for years. If there was a new, electronic alarm system in place, the execution of his plan would be more complicated.

He heard the approaching clop of heavy shoes and moved away from the wall. His eyes skimmed the glitter and gleam of old luxuries as he called to mind his experience as a small boy who once ran freely through an empty museum. Somewhere nearby there was a stair to the basement, and somewhere in the basement was a giant fuse box. Could he remember how to reach the utility area? Surely he could. His memory would not play him false. This was his true home, after all. Nothing could stop him now. The signs were auspicious; the time was ripe.

7

Saints and Silver

After several weeks, the ticket-takers in the booth by the museum's entrance recognized Joan when she came to meet Adam at the end of the day, and they kindly admitted her with just a wave of the hand and a smile. She smiled back and whispered *Dziękuję.* Thank you.

Adam would be another half hour at least, so she wandered slowly through the galleries on the way to their meeting place. The museum had become familiar, even a little dull. The same huge pictures loomed over her. The same cases gleamed with jewelry, porcelain, silver, and unidentifiable items rendered mysterious by their remoteness in time. Some labels on the exhibit cabinets provided information in English or German or French, though many were only in Polish, and some had no identifiers at all. She made her way through the larger rooms where most tourists browsed and stepped into the hallway that led from a collection of armaments to a smaller exhibit space. It was usually empty, although today another visitor, a slim, dark-haired man, was exiting from the room as she approached. He caught her eye and gave a brief nod before increasing his pace and hurrying away.

This room had become their habitual place to meet after the archives closed and even Adam felt the need for fresh air and dinner. In the intimate space of the little gallery rested an eclectic assortment of relatively ancient artifacts: a few silver pieces, tableware, small household items. Joan preferred their simpler designs to the elaborate embroideries, inlaid furniture, and jewel-encrusted garments of the later, wealthier periods.

Here there was space enough for only three glass-topped display cases. There was no bench or chair to tempt the weary visitor to linger, so usually Joan was there alone. Two walls were set with backlit stained glass windows from chapels long destroyed, and Saints Bartholomew and Gertruda kept vigil with hieratic severity. Bartholomew's broad forehead was topped by a square hat, and his eyes were cast upward following the direction of his pointing finger. Saint Gertruda looked directly into the room. Her head was turned at a slight angle and her brows and nose were outlined with heavy leaded lines so that she resembled the Queen on a deck of cards. That must be why, Joan thought, she looks so familiar

The middle of the three cases held her favorite object: a gently curving silver bowl. The interior rim was edged with a geometric pattern, and the sides were formed in arched indentations, rather like the rind of a melon. Most intriguing was the thick stem made up of four images fused back to back. A swan with a looping neck, a woman in a drifting gown, an animal peering through a screen of tall grass, and what seemed to be a small dragon, its pointed wings slightly dented. It was harder to see, since it lay against a mirrored surface. The laminated plaque tethered to the cabinet's corner labeled it "Bronislaw's chalice." There was more, but the accompanying description was in Polish.

She thought about taking a photograph. It would have to be quick and furtive, for throughout the museum there were stern signs picturing a camera in a circle with an emphatic red slash across it. No photos. Adam had also complained about a similar prohibition against photoduplication in the archives. Joan tended to be casual about rules that seemed unjustified, so she took out the camera she had lugged around all day and aimed. The flash was blinding as it bounced off the glass, and for a moment Saint Gertruda disappeared in a glare of after-image. Joan switched off the flash and tried again, though the room was so dim she doubted the picture would be clear. This project called for a more old-fashioned approach.

From her cavernous handbag, she took out the notebook she had purchased to record her tours in Krakow and its environs. On a clean page she began to sketch the chalice. Not bad, she thought as the image grew on the paper; good thing the fingers on my right hand still work. As she drew, she called to mind a brief summer of art lessons during the period when she thought she might have a future as a painter, a possibility overtaken by a turn to journalism and a job as a stringer for a newspaper chain.

Joan put away her sketch, wondering idly why the cup attracted her so strongly. She dumped her jacket and bag in a corner and stepped out of her stylish but uncomfortable shoes, bought in a splurge in one of the expensive airport shops before departure. It had been a mistake to wear them this morning on what had turned out to be a fairly extensive walking tour of Tyniec with Beata the landlady, now a welcome friend. Her injured arm ached after the long day of touring, and she gently rubbed her elbow and clenched and unclenched her fist. Two fingers were still stubbornly numb. Then she sat on the floor, straightened her legs, and bent her head to her knees in several leisurely balletic stretches. She was out of the line of sight of Saints Bartholomew and Gertruda, who continued to glower respectively straight up and ahead. All around was silence, so she ventured to lie down briefly flat on her back. The muscles at the base of her spine spasmed, then relaxed. Joan preferred a hard bed, and the sloping mattress she and Adam shared in the flat was not particularly comfortable. In the middle of the night she sometimes moved to the firm couch in the sitting room.

Adam. He was not sleeping well. He worked late into the night, and when he finally slid into bed next to her he shifted and jerked as his muscles released their tension. Joan had repeatedly cajoled him to accompany her on a few side trips, but he always said one of these days but not now. Your work will go better if you relax sometimes, she said. And he said yes but later. And tossed and turned. But when she slipped out of bed to read in the living room, he awoke and called out for her, as if worried she had disappeared.

The undersides of the glass cases were not as well-tended as their polished upper surfaces. Under the central vitrine she could see shredded cobwebs and a smear of chewing gum near the edge. Probably a childish tourist leaving a comment on the exhibit, she thought. A boring place for children. Or was it gum at all? There was a funny smell down here. She scooted further under the case for a closer look. Hardened bits of some kind of glue clustered around a square keyhole rimmed with brass. In fact, the substance seemed to fill the keyhole. Perhaps it was a kind of seal on the lock, double protection for the case. She prodded it with a finger.

Feet appeared by her head.

"Joan? Are you alright? What are you doing on the floor?"

She scrambled upright. "Good lord Adam. I didn't hear you coming. You startled me."

Adam was wearing sneakers, and her ears had been so tuned for the heavy steps of the guards that she had missed his quiet tread. He had a pale, hectic look, and the hair on the left side of his head stood out in the screws that indicated he had been weaving tendrils around his fingers as he wrote. This was a good sign, as tangles on both sides would indicate he had merely been sitting with his head clutched in his hands.

"Let's go, shall we?" he said. "I'm starving." This was also a good sign. Adam seemed to be getting even thinner since they had arrived in Poland. Probably they both were, with all the walking.

"Of course. Let me put on my shoes. But before we go, would you read this for me? There are some interesting things in this case and I want to know more about them. Especially this cup. Isn't it lovely?"

Buoyed by a fairly good day's inroads into Gorski's letters, Adam took the laminated page that hung at the side of the case and scanned the text. He hesitantly translated:

"It's called Bronislaw's Chalice, after a prince who had it cast in the seventeenth century because—um, no, wait a minute. The prince had an earlier cup. This one was made when the first one was melted down to destroy evil."

"An evil cup?"

"I'm not sure about some of these words. It is made of silver from—mined in—central Poland, but melted and, uh, a word I don't know, but it might mean remade. It was used for, for something about salt."

"Maybe it's supposed to hold salt? A fancy salt cellar?"

"Maybe. There is more here. 'Salt was powerful to fight the demon. No, to summon the devil.'"

"Fight or summon? It couldn't do both."

"I'm definitely missing something here. There is also mention of blood. At least I think that's the word. Sometimes the declensions make a word hard to identify."

"Aren't the little figures around the bottom lovely?"

"Yes, they're very pretty. Speaking of salt, let's get some dinner. If you want to know more, why don't you ask someone who works here?"

"Maybe I could ask one of the guards."

As if on cue, slow footfalls neared the annex gallery.

"Maybe, but not now," he added. "I'm too hungry."

Adam replaced the placard, Joan zipped up her jacket, and they left.

8

Convergence

There was a scholar of note visiting the city at the invitation of the Radincki Museum, and to ensure a robust gathering, even the visiting researchers registered at the archives were included among the guests invited to a welcoming reception. Rather to Joan's surprise, Adam had accepted and had left his work for the evening without the reluctance that was keeping him more and more desk-bound. Only six weeks had passed, but he was already worried that he would not be able to complete his research before it was time to return home.

The room was getting crowded. Adam was finding his conversational Polish strained to its limits. An aged librarian turned to him with a question, including him courteously in the larger conversation, and he bent his head to hear. Joan ambled away and studied the ceiling. Its edges were gilt, its center crimson. Patterns of flowers interspersed with the occasional cartouche of a dragon decorated the walls, and everywhere there was the familiar coat of arms of the city — a castle, a gate, a crown. The wood floor had a herringbone pattern not unlike the one in their flat, but most of it was covered by a large, worn Turkish carpet. Drifting around the edges of the crowd, she saw

Adam across the room stooped uncomfortably in conversation with people shorter than he. His head was bobbing with those telltale nods that accompanied his conversational fillers: tak, tak, dobrze, tak. Placeholders for real speech. Poor Adam, she thought fondly. His Polish skills seemed to fly right out of his head when conversing with someone he considered important.

She strolled along the perimeter of the carpet, content to lurk at the margins of the crowd, happily accepting that she could not understand anything being said around her. Therefore when a voice spoke over her shoulder, she was delayed in realizing that someone was actually addressing her in words she could understand.

"It is you, isn't it? The woman with the coffee? Or have I made a mistake?" The words acknowledged the possibility of error, but the man standing behind her looked entirely confident.

"Oh, hello," said Joan, turning. "Yes, it's me. I didn't realize I knew anyone here."

"What brings you to this gathering?"

"My friend is doing research at the Radincki archives," Joan replied. "Everyone registered there was invited, so I came along too. And why are you here?"

"Oh, this sort of soirée is fun from time to time, don't you think? And I know the guest of honor. Distantly anyway. We hail from the same town and used to run into each other occasionally. Haven't seen him yet tonight, though. Surrounded by his hosts, protected from his old pals. Something to drink?"

And although she had been congratulating herself on her solitary contentment, Joan had to grant that it was really nicer to have a conversation and another glass of wine. She felt quite at ease with this man, despite their short acquaintance. So much so that she did not hesitate to say, "You know, this is embarrassing, but I can't recall your name."

"Nor I yours!" said he with a grin. He tossed back his drink and snagged two more from a passing tray. "Let's see. It was something with just one syllable. Let me guess. Jane? No? Janet? Damn it, two syllables. Jean? I'm quite sure there was a J sound. An English J of course, not Polish."

Joan laughed. "You're very close. It's Joan."

"Joan! Of course, Joan. What a difference a vowel makes."

"I've decided that vowels are my favorite letters," confessed Joan. "They are so much easier to say."

"Oh, I don't know. If you add in things like umlauts and diphthongs, they can be just as bloody as consonants. And there are entire Asian languages that seem to cry out for consonants. But I can see why living in Poland would inspire a love of vowels. I'm a vowel man myself. My name has two of them together—uu—you don't have that in English. Oh I forgot: you don't remember it. It's Ruud—that's the part with the double u—Vander Lage. Just call me Rudy. It's easier. Don't you get sick of all the formality around here?"

As if in demonstration of his disregard for formality, Rudy secured her elbow and propelled Joan towards one of the open doors. "I am in desperate need of a smoke. Do keep me company so no one will bother me, won't you? They'll see that I'm deep in conversation with a beautiful foreign lady and will be too polite to interrupt."

Rudy's long legs sliced a path through the crowd. He abruptly halted, paused, and executed a theatrical bow before a man of about his own age, slightly shorter and broader, a handsome florid face glowing from beneath glistening white hair. There were brisk handshakes and a burst of rough sound that Joan took to be Dutch. The entourage that had surrounded the man paused respectfully at this exchange but moved in when Rudy turned to Joan.

"And here he is, the man of the moment, come to enlighten us all. Joan, I would like you to meet my old friend, art expert and historian, Jurgen De Mul." But the man had been whisked away to a more important introduction.

"Ah well, perhaps later," said Rudy, unperturbed. "I'll introduce you another time if you like. Though you might not, he's kind of a bore. Here on an interesting project, however. Expect you've already read about it. Been in the papers all week."

They had reached the doorway, and by luck two people were rising from a stone bench in the vaulted hallway. The casement window opposite was opened wide, and a breeze blew in a few dry leaves. Rudy sat down with a sigh and fished for cigarettes.

"I usually read the *International Herald Tribune*," said Joan. "But I don't know what project you're talking about."

"Of course. Inconvenient you can't read Polish. Bloody difficult language. But they have published pictures too, surely you saw them?"

Pictures of what, she prepared to ask, but Rudy, infused with tobacco and wine, rattled on.

"It's the contested Leonardo da Vinci of course. The one called *Salvator Mundi*. Held by that museum where your friend is doing his work. Been there for years on and off exhibit. For a long time it was thought just to be a knock off of another painting, one in France, I think. Or maybe England. Anyhow, opinion is turning now, and people are thinking perhaps he made more than one. He did that sometimes. At any rate, it was hidden away during the war, then found later hung over some apparatchik's mantle, now it's back on exhibit as a possible second masterpiece to match the girl with the ermine in the Czartoryski. Seen that one have you?'

"I was there just the other —"

"Oh, wait. Maybe it's still on tour. Been loaned to various museums, and I can't remember if it's back in Krakow yet."

"When I was there —"

"That one, *The Lady with the Ermine*, was disputed for a while too, as I recall, but now taken to be quite genuine and given its own display room. Nice picture, mind you, and a very good portrait of the ermine, rather resembles the girl though more rodent-like. You know, it was that picture that taught me that an ermine is just a weasel dressed up for winter. Long and elegant sort of rat, though rather cuddly looking and provides good diagonal line to the composition. I hate this reverence for art, don't you? After all, just an old piece of wood with paint. Might have gone out with the trash, but touched by the hand of the master—ah!—becomes holy. Like magic."

In a brief lull while Rudy paused long enough to light another cigarette from the end of the first, Joan tried speech again. "So this visitor you know, this De Mul. He knows about art?"

"Yes, quite the expert, if rather old-fashioned in his approach. He's a vision person, identifies by style, by overall impression, you know. Fancies himself like Berenson and puts himself above all the modern technical devices, X-rays and chromo-spectrometers and chemical signatures, and what have you. He waits until the tech people are done then sails in with his expert eye. Being Dutch, he rather has to live down the shade of Bredius. Though I've heard that he even defends the old guy, who after all was probably right more than he was wrong, even if it's the wrong judgments over Van Meegeren that will permanently tarnish his reputation. No question of forgery here, of course. The Radincki picture is probably genuine enough, as far as its age is concerned. The technical analysis will no doubt confirm an old wood panel, right paint chemistry, right kind of varnish, flaking and cracking in all the right places. Provenance a bit spotty, but that's not surprising. After all, history isn't a very neat story, is it?"

Joan had only understood a small portion of this ebullient speech, and she found that her head was bobbing at intervals, rather like Adam's with his taks and dobrzes.

"Sorry to rattle on like this," said Rudy. "Terribly rude. Jurgen's here to weigh in on the grand question: is it by the hand of Leonardo da Vinci? Quite a spectacle he'll put on, I'm sure. I plan to be there myself, if only for the theater. Wouldn't miss it. Would you like to come too and watch the show? I expect you'd find it interesting."

"Yes," she said. "I would. Thank you."

I wonder, she thought, if I could write a piece on spec about this painting while I'm here. It might be a good way to get back into the game. Tentatively she tapped her fingers as if trying out a keyboard.

By the time that Adam had extracted himself from his conversation, Joan was still chatting happily on the cold stone bench with Rudy's coat around her shoulders and the smoke from his cigarettes blowing back from the open window into the hallway. Adam announced his presence with a fit of coughing and collapsed on the bench beside them.

"Lord, Joan, where did you go? I've been looking all over for you." His voice was a croak, but any English noise he made at this point was better than more Polish. Joan introduced the two men, and Adam leaned over for a handshake. Joan snuggled next to him for the warmth he carried from the noisy room inside.

"Did you meet the guest of honor?" she asked. "He turns out to be an old friend of Rudy's. He is here to authenticate the Leonardo painting at the Radincki. I don't think I've really looked at it yet. Have you?"

"Time to see it is now," said Rudy, before Adam could reply. He began to repeat his narrative. "It's been off with the tech people all year being cleaned and examined to see if there are any obvious features that would make the attribution impossible. But apparently it's passed the scientists' judgment so they put it back on display, and now it's the turn for the connoisseur." He uttered the last work with a hint of scorn but took the edge off with a smile.

"Part of the painting wing of the museum has been cordoned off all week," rasped Adam, his voice still raw. "They are rearranging it as a viewing space for the announcement. Expecting a splash with the news media and everyone."

"Oh yes. Quite the to-do. But I gather there has been some awkward criticism over the fact that the picture was re-hung before the formal authentication. Takes away a bit of the drama. But nothing to be done about that now."

"It will be embarrassing if it turns out they have to announce that the painting isn't by Leonardo da Vinci after all," said Adam, "So I guess a lot rides on your friend's judgment."

"Oh, he'll put on a good show for sure. It'll be a draw for the tourist dollar. But can't blame them, can you. Everyone's a capitalist now. One year communism, next year the free market. The Poles have done well with the conversion; you've got to admire them for it."

Adam and Joan, who hadn't given the matter much thought, nodded in blank agreement. The conversation took a hairpin turn as Rudy leaned over and asked Adam:

"So I hear you are spending time in the same place — that is, the archives of the Radincki. How did you happen to land there?"

Adam had been answering the same question for the past two hours. But he politely repeated a short version of the path that had brought him to Krakow.

"It all came about by chance. I was reading some of Schuyler's papers at the New York Historical Society last year. He was one of the American generals when Kosciuszko was in New York. I ran across a couple of letters that didn't belong with Schuyler's things, and they sparked my interest. They were from a Pole named Andrzej Gorski to a brother back in Europe, and someone had transcribed and typed up copies years ago. And then at some point the typescript was microfilmed, and then it was filed with a set of materials relevant to Kosciuszko and Schuyler. Gorski was a younger son of what was once an influential family, and some family papers, including his, were donated to the Radincki."

"I see," said Rudy. "Find much of interest?"

"Less than I'd hoped so far."

Very little, in fact. A sore point, but fortunately Rudy wasn't inclined to probe. The night air drifted in from the window, cool and faintly sour with auto exhaust. The spew of Rudy's conversation had at last run its course. Joan was getting sleepy.

And so the evening drew to a close, two long-limbed men at the edges of a bench, a woman in between. Joan leaned her head against Adam's shoulder and felt his own drop against her hair. She glanced to her left and saw that Rudy's head was tipped back against the wall, his hooded eyes directed through the open casement. The moonlight slanting through the window silvered his sharp features and caught the fine moisture gathering under his lids. They might have fallen asleep together in that suddenly still pose, but for the party breaking up and spilling people into the hallway. Rudy leapt to his feet, retrieved his jacket from Joan's shoulders, bowed theatrically to them both, and strode away.

9
Y2K and other troubles

Adam knelt on the floor surrounded by piles of paper. He was barefoot, his hair stood on end, and he was wearing only a tee shirt and boxers because their erratic heater had decided to turn on full blast. It was already late October, and the months available to complete his research were ticking away with alarming speed. So far he had little to show for his efforts, and soon he would be on his way home.

On a flight booked with those return tickets. Adam was no longer trapped in a bouncing plane, and the matter required address.

Joan was getting ready for bed. Nightgown in hand, she passed by on her way to the bathroom.

"Joan. About these tickets. We have to change them."

"What do you mean? What's wrong with them?"

"I didn't want to make a fuss when I first found out. But you made a big mistake here."

Joan dimly remembered some babble issuing from Adam during the trans-Atlantic trip. "What's wrong?"

"The date! Didn't you notice the date?"

"December 31. Yes, I know it's New Year's Eve—the most spectacular New Year's Eve we'll ever have—but I thought we could return in time to go to Jill's party. A plane that leaves in the morning here arrives home by afternoon, well before midnight. And you said you wanted to stay as long we could. Christmas here will be nice, don't you think? Besides, I got a good price."

Adam picked up the morning's *Tribune* and jabbed an agitated finger at a headline: *Y2K Spells Trouble in the Skies*. "How about that? Did you read that? It's only been in the news for two years. Of course you got a good price. It's the one day in the century when no one in their right mind is on an airplane."

"Oh come on, Adam! Don't be ridiculous! No one in their right mind actually thinks there is a problem. Do you really expect the end of the world with the end of the year?"

Adam gritted his teeth. "The end of the world isn't the point! I'm not talking about the Second Coming or the Rapture or the Day of Judgment or Armageddon. Good God, Joan, what do you take me for! Computers figure dates by the two-digit year, and when 1999 turns to 2000, the numbers appear to go backwards. The concern is about widespread failures of anything that uses a computer! Including, maybe, airplanes!"

Joan still refused to become agitated, though her own temper was rising with the heat of the flat. It was not like Adam to be so irritable. And so irrational. At least not like the Adam she thought she knew. Beads of sweat stood out on his forehead, exaggerating the new lines on his face.

"Look, I think you're getting worked up over nothing. You're working too hard, that's what's wrong. You've lost perspective because you're spending too much time at the books. Why don't you take the day off tomorrow and come with me and Beata to visit the salt mine? It's such a waste of time to be in Poland and see nothing of it, don't you think?"

"I am not a tourist," Adam huffed, refusing to be placated. "You go someplace yourself if you have nothing else to do."

The image of herself as a feckless traveler, he a serious scholar with a mission, smoldered between them, ready to flame.

"I appreciate the souvenirs you have collected, Joan. I really do." He gestured to his desk. Propped next to a portrait of Kosciuszko were a hunk of clear amber and a postcard of the Black Madonna. "But these tickets. I really wish you had booked another date."

With an effort, Joan kept her patience. "You are working yourself up over nothing here. Do you really think that airlines haven't figured out how to fly without a computer? There would be no planes at all flying if there were the slightest danger that Y2K is a real concern. Now calm down and come to bed."

Adam had to grant that she was probably right. Still, it would be nice if she were able to share his concern. Not superstition exactly, not even worry. Just, just what? Precaution. Just in case.

"Well, I guess we'll find out, won't we?" he said, attempting grim humor.

It took them both a long time to go to sleep, holding hands, each lying quietly, each pretending to sleep, neither fooled. Each wondering how the next months would play out.

***

Adam awoke as the birds were beginning to quarrel in the trees outside the bedroom window. His heart pounded from the bad dream that had visited him twice before. A specter wearing colonial costume was erecting a scaffold, and waiting nearby was a blindfolded figure. They both were speaking, but Adam could not understand a word until letters glided into his dream like subtitles, a conjunction of m's and l's that sort of resembled Roman numerals but rumbled with the awesome gong of *M-I-L-*

L-E-N-N-I-U-M. The nightmare left behind a sour anxiety that took up residence with the indigestion that now attended every meal.

Adam's queasy insides testified to the state of his research. He perched on a pendulum that swung from optimism to gloom, elation to despair, each swoop taking him further in the opposite direction. The boxes that had promised so much scholarly bounty turned out to contain rather little material from Gorski himself and more from the next generations of his family. He had a scant two months left to discover something worth scholarly analysis, some tidbit of historical insight that would justify his stalled project, scrape out the shallow niche of expertise, and permit him to rest on at least one flimsy, withering laurel leaf of accomplishment. Besides, they were running low on money. The miserly grant that sent him to Poland was not proof against inflation and a strengthening zloty, and the expectation that any American could live like a king in Poland was hardly the case these days. Joan had applied to a small institute as an English teacher, but so far nothing had come of it.

Joan slumbered next to him. The blankets were heaped around her in a cozy twist, and Adam realized that an additional source of his early wakefulness was the fact that he was cold. He tried tugging a few loose from around her, but his anxious stomach twisted into a cramp and prompted him to the bathroom first, and at that point he figured he might as well get ready to go to work. Perhaps the walk to the archives would settle his mind so he could make some headway today.

Joan heard Adam leave. She stayed in bed until she heard the door close downstairs and the gate squeak open, and then she watched at the window as he loped off toward the river. When he turned at the end of the street and headed for the bridge, his pace increased as if he pursued some urgent target—or was pursued himself. Joan went to the bathroom to test for remaining hot water. She was determined to enjoy her trip to Wieliczka with Beata. She had not suggested again that he join them.

The air was chilly and the archives were not open yet. To fill the time, Adam tried the door of a small, ancient church nestled at the edge of the Rynek and was surprised to find it open. In the filtered light from the smudged windows he could see that the cloths on the altar were rumpled like last night's tablecloth, and the sign of recent use made him feel somehow welcome, like the delayed guest of a casual host.

This space bore little resemblance to the simple post-war church of his baptism with its clear, sunny windows and varnished, blond pews, but the items on the altar were the same. That weary head canted against the cross, the arms spread in sacrifice and acceptance. Adam sat for a time, alone but for a custodian who came in wielding a broad broom. The man did not speak lest he disturb the privacy of prayer. The gust of air from the opening door as the dust of the previous day was brushed outside prompted Adam to rise, now stiff from sitting so still. He entered the archives on the heels of the librarian, who made a sour little joke about early-rising scholars. But apparently Adam wasn't the only one who couldn't sleep late, for the tables were soon full of scratchy pencils and rustling papers.

For a time Adam sat inertly before his four document boxes. A pile of notes and pieces of translated text were very slowly growing under his hands, but they were as full of strike-outs as of entire sentences. Rather than getting easier to interpret, Gorski's letters seemed to have become more ambiguous and difficult to read, prompting qualms that perhaps his knowledge of the language was inadequate to the task. Glumly, he had all but decided that what he formerly had thought was a reference to Gorski's diary was in fact just mention of his memories. A simple mistranslation had misled him to hope for something that was never written.

The archive toilets were not conveniently located for someone with Adam's restive stomach, so by the time he rounded the last bend of corridor he was trotting urgently. The toilet sported an old-fashioned overhead tank with a pull chain. These blessedly efficient facilities had escaped the generation of Soviet-manufactured products that had left a trail of loose wall sockets and leaky washing machines all over Poland. A loud torrent of water sucked the rotten effluvia of last night's meal into the sewer. Adam left the stall slightly dizzy, his ears ringing from the echoing flush. In the spotted mirror over the sink his face appeared hollow and grayish. He splashed water on his forehead, obsessive that none touch his lips. The cloth towel roll was out of fresh space, so he shook his hands and waved them in the air, finishing the drying on the back of his trousers. He wished the lightheadedness would pass and began to worry that he was coming down with something.

In the small kitchen alcove he made a cup of tea from one of the tea bags he had added to the communal stash accumulated by visiting scholars too busy or absorbed to break for lunch. He stirred in two teaspoons of sugar thinking he needed some energy. The floor beneath his feet rocked gently. There was an opened box of digestive biscuits that had been left by another researcher recently departed back to England. Adam helped himself to a cautious nibble. Then a bite. Then he crammed the rest in his mouth and realized that he was starving.

Seven digestive biscuits later, Adam found that Gorski's handwriting had become much clearer. The pendulum of scholarship swung back into the light, and for a bright moment it seemed he had a project after all.

10

Bad luck and other troubles

Bodie and Keith had intended to remove the gel mold from the display cabinet as soon as it set. However, anticipation of the upcoming authentication of a work by Leonardo da Vinci had brought more crowds than usual into the Radincki Museum, and visitors overflowed the galleries, even invading the little-used exhibit annex where their surreptitious work had begun. Late on this Friday the museum was near closing, and visitors were finally exiting into a dribbling rain. The rooms were dim, their high overhead lights unable to cheer the darkening afternoon. Streaks of wet smeared the long windows. The rainy light they admitted took the form of a depressing set of glaring rectangles, hard on the eyes yet affording little illumination.

Bodie turned the delay to his own advantage, strolling among the cases of artifacts, paying particular attention to those housed in vitrines of the size and shape of the one that so interested their employer. By the time the crowds thinned, he had identified two likely ones as the true object of their preliminary action. One held a close-packed set of jewelry that, according to a faded label in a language that he could actually read, had been a wedding gift to Katarina Radincki, including a necklace of rubies and diamonds surrounded by matching earrings and a tiara. It was hard to fence historical jewelry, for not only was it well-known, the old-fashioned styles did not sell. But the bigger stones could be cut down nicely and would bring a pretty sum. His second choice was a case of heavily embroidered cloths. He wasn't sure what they were for, but one of them had a fat jewel stuck at its center surrounded by heavy, knotted wire strung with pearls. Hard to see why someone would steal it, but that particular cabinet appeared to be an exact match for the one in the annex, and it was a good bet that the key for one would unlock the other as well.

A plan to make use of this information was beginning to form. He would decide what to do later when it was clear just which target their employer had in his sights. At the very least, he could hold out for an extra subsidy to hold his tongue.

But now it was time to get to work before the guards did a final sweep of the museum before closing. Back in the annex, Bodie knelt beneath the cabinet to pry the gel mold away from the deep lock, while Keith assumed his usual lookout position at the entrance to the small gallery. He hovered in the doorway, shifting from foot to foot.

From their wall niches Saints Bartholomew and Gertruda oversaw Bodie's operation. The mold resisted, and he lay on his back under the cabinet poking gingerly at the lock with his pocket knife, oblivious to divine disapproval. From time to time he swore quietly under his breath, invoking the deity's name in a manner surely displeasing to those glassy saints. It made Keith doubly anxious, but he refrained from comment. Bodie could be touchy. In their early forays to the museum, the place had been nearly empty, but now dozens had decided to visit. Keith had actually heard of Leonardo da Vinci. Everyone else must have too.

"Bodie, damn it. Can't you hurry up?" Keith took darting peeks out into the hall to glance down the long galleries, convinced their luck had run out and they would be discovered this time. "They're closing up. Someone is going to check here and see you down there on the floor."

"This stuff hardened more than it should have. I'm afraid to rush it or it might break. Just be patient and keep watch."

Keith took a circuit of the small room. Accidentally, he met the gaze of Saint Gertruda and quailed. Was there ever a woman so stern? And yet so beautiful. The bulb behind her turned her face a pale gold as if she had swallowed her halo. He could not rid himself of the sense that she resembled someone he knew, with her long face and pale eyes, her defined chin and lips. He stepped back and tried to let the stained glass image focus into memory.

"Watch out!"

Keith stumbled, kicking Bodie's knee and nearly falling.

"Shit! That made me nearly break the edge off. Be careful, damn it! Go back to the hall and keep watch. Just get out of here until I'm done."

But as Keith tiptoed back to the doorway, Bodie summoned him back. "Wait! Hand me the razor tool. I've got to pry this side loose with something thinner than the knife."

Keith picked up the wicked looking razor and handed it over. There was the delicate sound of scraping, and a fine black dust settled over Bodie's face. He tried to strangle a sneeze and sent his neck into a cramp.

Keith stuck his head into the hall and to his horror, from the cavernous distance at the far end of the gallery, he could hear the ominous clop of heavy shoes. They were still far away, but the enormous rooms made every echo sound like a cannon shot.

"Someone's coming!" he squeaked. "Hurry up!!"

"Just about there. Calm down." Bodie was nearly as nervous as Keith, but he was not about to admit it. Nor did he intend to announce that it was the jerk of his sneeze that had loosened the gel plug, nor that the razor had left a distinct gouge in the wood.

The mold was nearly free, and it wiggled tantalizingly in his fingers with only the tip stuck in the furthest crenulation. If only now he could pull it out of the deep lock without breaking off the fancy protrusions that recorded the details of the locking mechanism. Really, it had hardened too much, more than the material was supposed to. Possibly he had mixed the ingredients incorrectly, or maybe the delay in removing it had affected the setting of the gel. But it was useless to speculate at this point.

Keith took a calming breath and stepped into the hall. Where had those footsteps gone? Had he imagined them? He ventured farther and leaned forward, poised like an antenna. Clop, clop. He was not imagining things. But just how far away was the owner of those feet?

And then in an instant there she was. The guard thudded slowly into his line of sight, her heavy, block-like form in stark silhouette against the windows at the far end of the museum. If at that moment Keith had moved back into the annex with his usual jittery dart, things would have been different. But he was mesmerized at the sight of her shape coming clear against the distant windowpanes, and he froze. Like a rabbit in the path of a fox he stood rigid and still, for some primitive instinct advised him that a motionless figure is less likely to be noticed than one that moves. Unfortunately, unlike a rabbit, he had not situated himself beneath a bush to indulge this instinct. It did not occur to him that a matching set of long windows flanked the wall at his back, casting his own form into sharp and unmistakable clarity.

Klementyna regarded the toes of her shoes. It had been a long and tiring day, and she was ready to go home. Sighing, she looked up at the window and studied the rain, and then moved her head from side to side to ease the muscles in her neck. And therefore it was inevitable that her eyes scanned down the hall to the distant end of the gallery, where she saw a man standing like a statue.

It was the duty of the guards to ensure that no visitors lingered at the end of the day. She gave another weary sigh, turned, and began to make her way toward him. If she approached slowly and deliberately, perhaps he would leave before she had to announce the obvious: the museum was closing. In the early years of her job she had relished the authority that permitted her to issue such admonishments. But now it was just the final part of a very long day's work.

Keith did not discern her routine purpose. He only saw that she had caught sight of him and was headed in his direction. His rabbity freeze broke and he leapt back into the little gallery.

"She's coming! That lady guard! The one who saw us before. She's here! And she saw me!"

Bodie had just curled up from his supine position. He still crouched beneath the cabinet and was stowing his knife and the precious gel mold in his pocket. His heart was pounding, but he was taking a moment to gather his composure. He started at Keith's exclamation and bolted to his feet, catching his shoulder on the edge of the glass cabinet with a horrid crunch. Had the vitrine been newer, it might have toppled and crashed, and then they could never have made their exit. But it stood solid as a boulder and did not even rock. A jet of hot pain shot down Bodie's arm, sending him back to his knees.

"Get up! Get up! We've got to get out of here." Keith grabbed at the tools now scattered on the floor and stuffed them into his pockets, oblivious to their sharp edges and the prickles of blood on his hands. "Come on! Get up!"

If there had been enough breath left in his lungs, Bodie would have blasted Keith for his stupid panic, but he had enough to do to keep himself conscious. He struggled up and leaned on Keith's shoulder for support as they hobbled for the stairs.

"Don't look back!" he hissed. But it was too late. Keith's wild face, illuminated by the late, grey glare from the high window, was one that Klementyna Kamynska would surely remember. And that open gape could only mean guilt. Curious, she drew closer.

She recognized the men as the two who had come several times before. They appeared to be leaving together arm and arm. So I was right, she thought with private amusement. Pansies on vacation. With her usual unhurried pace, she arrived at the room where they had been, glanced into the annex, saw nothing amiss, and flipped out the light. Saints Bartholomew and Gertruda dimmed.

The fleeing men stumbled downstairs and struggled to open the tall doors, already pulled shut for the evening. They were heavy and cumbersome, and Bodie could only stand aside and try to remain upright while Keith wrenched one open far enough for them to squeeze through. The cold, rainy wind that swept the stoop was shocking. Keith took great, relieving gulps of air, and Bodie felt his head momentarily clear. The pain in his arm and shoulder was tormenting, but he thought that now he might not pass out. He put his hand in his pocket and was relieved to feel that the little gel mold was safe.

The long stone steps of the museum were slippery with the wet, and darkness was gathering with its peculiar northern speed. Keith scampered down like a goat, but Bodie found he was slowing down. It seemed to him that the stairs were multiplying; little lights were reflecting in the puddles in confusing spangles, and distances were hard to discern. He could not tell just when his foot would meet the steps, which seemed to have grown uneven. With every downward stumble his injured shoulder suffered an excruciating bounce. He made it almost to the bottom before his legs gave out and he collapsed into a puddle, landing on one kneecap and sending a pain up his leg that nearly matched the one in his shoulder. He managed to keep the pocket with the mold on the dry side of his jacket as he crumpled to the ground and felt the dampness soak into his clothing, waiting for his worthless partner to notice him and turn back.

11

Key

On the train north on its way out of Krakow, Pawel Radincki shielded his face by opening wide a newspaper, discouraging other passengers from taking the seat next to him. Little of the news interested him, although he read carefully yet another of the increasingly frequent articles about the coming New Year when the century would turn, marking off another thousand years. The degree of fuss and worry still circulating about whether computers would handle this phenomenon rather amused him. He had no intention of boarding a plane with a midnight flight plan, though it would be interesting to discover if the shrill predictions of equipment failures would take place. However, he knew, as others did not, that the real marvel at the turn of the millennium would be something far more wondrous. If, that is, his plan unfolded smoothly.

For this trip to Warsaw, Pawel reverted to his legitimate name, Pawel Meyer. It was the name on his passport, the one he had married with, and fairly close to the one he was born with though somewhat more Germanic. When he sojourned abroad, he sometimes adjusted it to Paul Meyer. The shorter name came in handy, though Pawel increasingly thought of it as labeling a past self that was receding further and further from his present identity. If all went well, the day would come when he would leave it behind altogether. However, since Meyer was also the name attached to his bank accounts, there was no escaping it for business purposes.

He walked away from the bank a good hour after he had entered it, sweating slightly from the ordeal of the Polish banking system and its numerous kiosks with their triplicate forms and repetitive questions. He had not intended to take out quite so much cash at once, but the long wait and several inquisitive bank officials had prompted the decision to get it over with now. He was alarmed to note that the legacy from his wife had dwindled more than he had thought, but at this point he was committed to the outlay for his two henchmen. From the safe box he removed a bulky item that he kept in its protective wrappings, as well as his accumulated stacks of money. Over the years he had stashed away multiple currencies, though most of the bills were large-denomination American dollars. It was time to be rid of them, as he had heard that the U.S. government was redesigning its currency. Hoarding money obeys its own calendar, like wine. Too long and everything goes sour.

It was a brisk day. The long sleeves of his overcoat hid the fact that his valise was cuffed to his wrist for safekeeping. He didn't dare let it out of his grasp for even a minute, nor did he want to call attention to its contents with an obvious safety device. The chain of the cuffs was fairly light gauge. It wouldn't stop a determined robber equipped with metal cutters, but it was adequate protection against the snatch and grab thief. There were still gypsies at the train station, though their numbers had begun to thin. They were being cleared out because they scared the tourists. They scared him too. Fortunately, he had already purchased his return ticket and would not have to linger long in the terminal.

When Pawel wore his old clothes, he was good at blending into a crowd, and as he walked the streets—not too fast, determined but not intense—nothing indicated to the passer-by that he was carrying an unusual amount of money. His rather delicate good looks and average build were not striking enough to draw attention. He had shaved closely that morning so as to make a decent impression at the bank, but today his shoes were old and down at the heel. He hadn't been able to resist wearing his ring, but he took the precaution of turning the decorative cartouche with its beautiful flanking stones inward to his palm before putting on his gloves. The gloves themselves were ordinary, with leather palms and dull knit uppers in a forgettable grey.

He kept the gloves on when he arrived at his final errand, a locksmith at the edge of the old town. It was awkward managing the payment with only one hand, but fortunately he had the right amount in his pocket. He complimented the man on his work fashioning the unusual key, the one Pawel said he needed for the old library case in his grandmother's house in Lublin, for which he required a new key because it would be such a pity to damage the lovely wooden cabinet. But though it was a good story, the locksmith was not very interested. The man did a fair volume of business with this sort of thing, though this particular key had been unusually intricate and had caused him a vexatious amount of attention. Still, the request was not out of the ordinary. Old furniture and old doors in old houses in old cities often lost their keys, and it was not so rare to have someone come in with a mold of a lock and request a new key.

Pawel reflected that many might consider his plan rather too elaborate. A good set of lock picks would have sufficed to open that display cabinet with no need for a duplicate key. But the groundwork he had commenced was in its own way an end in itself, appropriately extravagant preparation for the grand transformation to come. He paid the locksmith and dropped the key in a crumpled bag, reused in the old frugal Polish way, into his outer pocket. Casually, as if it were not the key to his very future.

12

Tricks of Memory

Finally Adam hit his stride.

For three days he had hardly left the archives. He was at the doors when the building opened and was the last to leave when it closed for the evening. No lunch, only quick breaks for tea and biscuits, or perhaps a sandwich that Joan made for him after breakfast, for she now crammed packets of food into his briefcase with maternal insistence that he eat something. He ate just for fuel, hardly tasting what was in his mouth.

At long last, he had found materials that he could use, a small trove of Gorski's letters that were full of news, flavored with gossip about his colleagues, and that hinted at events to come. And that were — above all and blessedly — readable.

More than readable in fact. Finally his obsessive work had paid off. All at once Adam had come virtually to inhabit Gorski's world, and so intimately that he could anticipate his next words. Gorski and his companions were becoming more familiar to him than the contemporary world outside the walls of the museum library. It seemed that he listened over their shoulders as they tramped on campaign, sometimes in haste and retreat, sometimes striding towards victory. At night as he fell into sleep he could feel the pen in Gorski's hand as he chronicled the events of the day.

It was a heady feeling, very slightly insane, but so exciting that Adam felt electrified. He was there with them during the summer campaign of 1777, there in the heat of central New York, retreating with Kosciuszko from the disaster at Fort Ticonderoga, regrouping at Saratoga, rallying the troops, planning and executing the brilliant fortifications. With Gorski, he wrote home to a brother in July. The sweat of exultation dripping from his own brow had left its mark in the lower corner of one yellowing page, and rather than feeling guilt at this small desecration of an archival relic, Adam felt the sweat to be as much Gorski's as his.

Today we met with the General himself. K. is devoted to the fellow, but I warned him not to be naive. There is division in the Continental army, and not everyone thinks so highly of Gates as a leader. But K. is a loyal man. He insists that I present myself truthfully, despite the unorthodox way I joined the armies of the rebellion.

What unorthodox way? The question made a fleeting trip through Adam's mind; it rang a distant bell, as though something had prompted him to wonder about it before. But he was too busy with the joy of effortless translation to dare pause. He imagined Gorski at Kosciuszko's side as plans were transformed from vision to actuality. Gorski would not have been among those digging and building, of course. He would have stayed by the side of the engineer, his nimble fingers taking discreet notes, perhaps making a suggestion or two. In Adam's imagination, the countenance of Gorski, utterly lost to the present, began to resemble his own. It was, he thought, a boost to his scholarly imagination to be able to identify so closely with the subject of his study.

The weather continues to play us foul. Rain, rain, rising in steam from the horses and soaking through the toughest tent, and the mud up to one's ankles. The swill from the privies makes its way into the streets and the whole encampment stinks.

The words filled his sight, his nose. It was a world he knew, a world he could smell, could almost live again. Sitting at the heavy oak table behind the solid walls of the museum, Adam felt his heart fluttering wildly and realized that his breath was shallow, as though he were on the march towards the Hudson with the hungry, ill-shod colonial troops. He cheered for Gates, reviled the perfidy of Schuyler, always a thorn in Kosciuszko's side. Adam's head was swimming, and as he surfaced into the present he gathered from his giddy symptoms that once again he had forgotten to eat.

He rose from the desk and, staggering slightly, made his way to the kitchen alcove. A strong cup of sugared tea was in order. His pulse still beat rapidly in his throat, and he coughed twice to calm it. When he returned home, perhaps he should get checked out by a doctor as Joan had recently suggested. But despite his bad stomach, his palpitations, and his newly loose waistbands, Adam now felt more alive than he had since he arrived in Poland. The trembling fingers were as much excitement as exhaustion. Revived, he sped back to his desk.

Sometimes it seems the whole hillside will slide into the river. There is fever in the camp, and even K. has come down with the grippe. We were all relieved when the sun came out this morning, and best of all, the wind picked up and blew in some cooler air. It is easier to dig now. And with the better weather will come our success.

Adam too could almost smell the mud, could hear the slow drip of the rain off the trees, could live with Gorski in the damp barracks where those letters had been written. The words sprang off their pages as if spoken in his ear. They were so familiar that he might utter them himself. Yes, he knew they would face illness in the camp, that the weather would play them foul. He was almost afraid to go home at night for fear that this near magical sympathy with the subject of his research might dissipate. Yesterday Joan had joked that he was finally channeling Gorski. He did not dispute it. He wished she could share this moment.

***

At that moment, however, Joan was in the Painting Gallery looking doubtfully at the little picture optimistically attributed to Leonardo da Vinci. To her untutored eye, the composition seemed straightforward and flat compared to his other works, and the painted eyes of Jesus seemed not quite to match. The left one cast very slightly downward. She could not stand close to the work, because a decorative but emphatic barricade had been erected in anticipation of the public announcement of its authenticity.

She looked at her watch. Adam would probably be another two hours in the archive, and it was far too early to head for the restaurant. The sound of clopping footsteps reminded her of the questions she had about the silver cup in the annex gallery. Maybe this guard making her methodical rounds could tell her something about the Bronislaw Chalice. The footsteps continued down the hall and Joan followed, framing an inquiry in Polish in her head and hoping that the woman spoke a little English. She caught up with Klementyna Kamynska just outside the annex gallery.

"Przepraszam Panią," she ventured. Klementyna's broad back paused, then turned in slow surprise as she registered the address. She recognized the woman behind her as a frequent museum visitor.

"Pardon me," Joan switched languages. "Do you perhaps speak English? I have a question about an item just here. Perhaps you can help me." She gestured to the left.

Klementyna nodded. "Perhaps," she said in a rusty voice that hadn't spoken for a while. "But I speak not much."

Joan smiled her appreciation and led her to the vitrine holding the chalice. Neither of them noticed that a slim, dark haired man had hastily departed down the corridor as they approached the room

"Ah. The cup," Klementyna said. "It is one of my favorite."

"Mine too!" said Joan.

As it happened, Klementyna knew nothing beyond what was on the printed placard. She frowned carefully as she attempted to translate it into her slow English, and the description of the chalice still sounded as weird as it had when Adam had read the card. A cup made from silver melted down from an ancient artifact. A ceremony of salt and blood. A demon. In the end Klementyna gave a skeptical shrug and smiled.

"Old legend," she commented, proud that she knew the English word.

Joan was pleased at the exchange and the tenuous connection it built between her and the taciturn guard. She still didn't fathom the purpose of the chalice, but legends are all the more intriguing for being vague. She thanked Klementyna, managing Polish now, and was rewarded by an unpracticed smile.

***

Down the hall in the archive, Adam continued reading Gorski's letters with exhilarated intensity. He was afraid to lift his eyes lest he break the spell of comprehension. Now Gorski was interrupting his record of the campaign to comment on the weather, comparing it to the seasons of his homeland.

How I miss my country. When I was a child, my grandmother used to sing to me of summer, so welcome after the cold grip of the dark winter. It was a song, she said, that was sung when the magpies appeared in the fields.

The magpies. The handsome birds Joan had seen from their window on the first day here, wheeling above the trees, whooshing to the ground, calling to one another as they flew.

He could hear the song of Gorski's childhood, hummed in an old woman's slightly tuneless voice: "The sun's rays are early and warm. They catch the morning blooms." Adam's eyes sped along the page, translating so swiftly his pencil could not keep up.

Sleep on, little one.

Hush, you screeching magpies —

Wait. This could not be.

Adam stared at the page. His lips silently repeated the song over and over. Surely this was too much. Impossible.

Could he so thoroughly have entered Gorski's mind that he anticipated his grandmother's song?

But the words were familiar. He didn't know the tune, but the lyrics. How could he know them already?

Had his obsession transmogrified him into Gorski himself?

Was he insane?

Fate would have been kinder to Adam if at that moment he had indeed been struck insane. Vacantly drooling, bereft of reason. After a suspended moment, the pendulum swung back with all its weight. He uttered an audible groan and dropped his head to the table with a skull-bruising clunk. For a moment it appeared possible that he had dropped dead. Anxious eyes swept the room, checked with each other to see if help should be summoned, but before anyone could make polite inquiries of this alarming behavior, Adam dashed from the table and headed for the toilets.

Heads bent once more, pencils scratched across note pads, keyboards softly clicked. This American really needed to get his guts in order.

Sometimes when one is particularly appalled, a calm descends. Adam returned to his table, and though his head hurt and his hands were unsteady, his stomach just simmered slightly like a sea after a storm, each successive wave smaller than the last. Methodically, he paged through the batch of letters from this box, the one that contained the arresting correspondence that had captivated him for the last days. The one that was supposed to have contained the germs of his breakthrough discovery.

And he saw now what his excitement had obscured.

The file was in far better order than the others had been. That order, which at first had seemed a stroke of luck, now looked suspicious. These letters were arranged chronologically, and they were all aligned in one direction so that no adjustment was needed to bring them into a readable position. These papers had not lain here undisturbed for as long as the others, and the neatness of their arrangement, he now realized, bespoke an earlier scholarly hand. Someone else had gone through the box and put everything to rights. There was a division of the papers into dated sections, and the materials were grouped according to the places where Gorski had been when these letters were written.

In short, someone else had got here first.

Adam's special feeling of sympathy with Gorski, that sense that what he read was so familiar that he had virtually entered the head of the writer, obviously had a source that was neither occult nor the result of extraordinary sympathetic communion.

He had read it all before.

As in slow motion, Adam settled on a page, opened his briefcase, consulted his notes, closed the folder, and sat motionless. He had indeed read it all before.

These were the letters he had found on microfilm the previous year. He had read these very ones, transcribed and typewritten, a year ago in the archives in New York. At the time his Polish had been slower, the occasions he could devote to reading more interrupted. And the words rendered in microfilmed typescript had seemed to carry a less personal voice than the handwritten missives. Here in Krakow, his love of manuscripts and the individual hand that wrote them had taken over, and it had not occurred to him that he should first correlate the materials he had already studied with these supposedly unexamined documents.

In fact, it had not occurred to him to take the perfectly obvious first step for any research: Situate your known materials in relation to the unknown ones to be studied.

And what a price he was paying. So much wasted time, so much lost time.

Drained of energy, Adam fought despair, crashing down from the elation of the last delirious days. Archives are strange and chancy places. They promise much and hide more. At the moment he was one of their heartless accidents.

The afternoon light was slanting low through the window when he roused himself sufficiently to replace the letters in the third box. Quietly he secured the lid and returned it to the librarian, who looked at him sharply, started to say something, then simply bid good night.

He left the archive and walked so inattentively that he got lost and had to double back to find the bridge across the river to home. Under its traffic-ridden arch the oily water was smooth. The uplit walls of the Wawel were reflected in a fairyland castle on a surface tinged with sunset. Swans glided with grace and periodically upended themselves in a clownish display of tail feathers as they nibbled at something polluted beneath. The air stank of diesel exhaust. Belatedly, Adam recalled that he had arranged to meet Joan for dinner, but the time had passed in such a dismal blur that he couldn't figure out where she might now be. Finally, he trudged back to the flat.

13

Renata

Several months after her death, Rudy had begun regular visits to his wife's grave. He never laid flowers or said a prayer; it was more like dropping by for a chat.

Her gravestone sat on a rise of the hill beside a small, nondescript bush that had escaped the gravedigger's spade and flourished in the two years since she was buried. From there Rudy could see across the river. On sunny days the water shimmered against its far banks, long slopes of green where fishermen lounged in the distance. On grey, still days, the river might have been paved it was so flat and placid. Above the water, flocks of birds wheeled like drifts of cinders. He lit a cigarette, hoping the nicotine would disperse the remnants of a hangover, folded his coat into a cushion, and sat down with something between a sigh and a grunt. It wouldn't take long before the damp would penetrate his joints and he would rise stiff and sore, and then he would think how old he was getting. But it was peaceful here, and he needed some peace.

The ember at the end of his cigarette blew away in the breeze and landed between his feet. Rudy rubbed it out with his heel. There was still half a cigarette left, and he relit it with difficulty, using the gravestone as a windbreak. At its base he could see several cigarette ends from his last visit subsiding damply into the earth.

Recollection was stirred by the look of the ground around the stone, perhaps the nearness of it or the smell of crumpled grass. Or perhaps something beneath actual notice, one of those invisible triggers of memory that cause the mind to leap. He saw another grave in another cemetery far away and long ago, where he loitered at the edge of the departing crowd of mourners at his father's funeral, escaping the sympathies and handshakes of neighbors and friends. Across the rough grass there walked a young woman, one hand outstretched, the other holding a brimmed hat firmly against her hair.

"I came to thank him," she said. "But now he is gone. So I must thank you in his stead."

It was Renata. He grasped her hand wordlessly. She thought his voice was gone in grief for his father, but he was simply speechless at the sight of her. So pale and slim, her blond hair almost colorless against her navy blue jacket. To another man she might have appeared plain, but to him she was like a fine drawing, every line precise and true.

At first Rudy's mother wanted to give them the Amsterdam flat and move into a small place by herself. But there wasn't enough money to spare nor space to find in the postwar city, so the three shared the large set of rooms comfortably enough, at least until the children were born. Over dinner they came together to eat at the oval table under the portrait of Rudy's father, a man with a long face, a thin smile, and a tilt to his shoulders.

From the time he was a child, Rudy had known something of his father's actions during the occupation. He was old enough to remember streets full of uniformed men, his father coming and going at odd hours, and his mother sitting in the dark peering through a slit between the shade and the window frame.

Sometimes the word "hero" was uttered. That was how Renata had first heard the man described who spirited her Jewish grandparents out of Amsterdam under the very noses of the Gestapo. It was he whom Renata thanked in the person of his son, and it was the son who reaped the benefits of her gratitude.

Renata was a woman of deep passions and contagious energies. During the occasional rough times when their marriage faltered, for it had not been smooth sailing between the two, Rudy sometimes wondered if it was in fact a version of his father she had intended to marry. A generation had seemingly diluted the hero in Rudy, and especially in the early years of their marriage he felt the lack. But later, as he saw the outwardly happier marriages of friends crumble while their own prickly union stayed stalwart, he came to know that Renata had made no mistake, nor had he. From that understanding grew something deeper than he had imagined love could be.

As their children grew older and more independent, there rose in his wife the mounting desire to visit the city of her grandmother's birth. Two generations before in Krakow, a musical family had produced an accomplished and ambitious pianist. She had toured young, and on her professional travels she had met a man who offered her more than music. She finally emigrated and married in Holland, and the rest of her family stayed behind. Renata's family was no longer Jewish, and she had been a teenager before she fully grasped the chain of choice and accident that had saved her grandmother and taken the others. She marveled with horror at the sheer, random chance of being alive.

And then, with their sons grown and money secure enough, Renata and Rudy had come here. Renata had an old address, but though they walked up and down the streets with many maps, they could not find the house. She wept with frustration, convinced that the numbers had been changed by squatters. And then, finally, they found an ancient neighbor who recalled the family and could point out where the home had been. A crumbled pile of bricks, long plundered for salvage.

That might have sent another woman home. But Renata wanted to stay, and at that time their stable Dutch currency translated into wealth. They found a commodious flat in reasonably good repair, and in time Rudy attached himself to the ancient university. They found Polish difficult but not impossible and added it to the store of the other languages that, being Dutch, had become their own by dint of necessity. Eventually, Renata conducted tours of Auschwitz for increasing numbers of tourists from Holland and Belgium and South Africa, all of whose English or French or German was probably adequate, but who preferred to withstand the experience of that bleak place in the shelter of their own language.

Rudy and Renata had moved to Poland in tumultuous times. The government staggered and resisted under the pressure for reforms, and the atmosphere of the university was charged with the sparks of a student underground. By accident, Rudy found himself a hero's role after all, as early one morning, he spotted a student of his limping with exhaustion, clutching under his jacket an armful of *samizdat* flyers. He brought him home and gave him something to eat, and in so doing saved him from a police sweep of the area. Word of the rescue spread, and despite modest disclaimers on Rudy's part, his reputation was established as a courageous friend of the student movement. The risk to him was so much less than to his students that he was abashed at the appreciation he received.

Their separate dedications gave Rudy and Renata a spur of excitement at a time in their lives when they might have been expected to slow down. They grew closer with shared energies for causes bigger than themselves, but at the same time also separate, for they faced different directions: she the past and its sorrows, he the unfolding future.

And now it was two years since Renata had died, almost two years to the day. They had been in Krakow, how long? Rudy had to stop and think, and it took him a few moments to recall what year it now was. 1999. Impossible to forget the end of a millennium, yet he had been so thoroughly absorbed in recollection that he had nearly done so. Sometimes the past drew him into memories so distorted by nostalgia that the vanished years seemed sweeter than they truly had been. He was beginning to suffer bouts of insomnia. Listening every hour to the thin music of the hejnal played by the trumpeter from St. Mary's steeple, he tried to think of the ancient hymn as a reminder of the comforting peace of God. The centuries over which the hejnal had been played were witness to the rise and fall of generations.

How heartless that the death of the aged is less mourned than the death of the young, so that on learning that someone has died one asks his age, and if the age is enough, the sorrow diminishes. But the loss is the same, is it not? Rudy took to keeping Marcus Aurelius' melancholy journal by his bed: *No one can shed another life than this which he is living, nor live another life than this which he is shedding, so that the longest and the shortest life come to the same thing.* In the middle of the night those calm, bleak words afforded comfort, and after reading them he could sleep.

The chill of the earth had reached his lower back. Rudy boosted himself upright with the aid of the gravestone and stood tentatively while the blood resumed its course to his cramped feet. He lit another cigarette and made his way home as the light began to fade and the birds settled in the tree branches for the night. The river first lightened against the fading afternoon, then darkened to its evening black, flowing northward deep and cold.

14

The Find

After great pain, a formal feeling comes.

It was a line of poetry that kept running through Adam's mind. Not a line from Gorski this time, rocketing delusively around his head like the product of shared consciousness. But something Joan once had quoted to him shortly after they had met. Shakespeare maybe. Perhaps one of the sonnets.

He was, he thought, feeling formal. A calm despair had taken him over, replacing both anxiety and desperation. At least his hands no longer shook. And he had even managed breakfast. At this moment much formal feeling was needed so that he could assess what might be retrieved from his faltering research project.

Not Shakespeare. Someone else. More modern. Maybe Merton?

He considered again the materials he had traveled so far to examine: four long boxes that contained among their historical detritus the extant manuscripts of Andrzej Gorski. Surely the trip hadn't been a complete waste. He had a few lines of new text to play with, a few quotes to support some minor revisions of the historical record. Perhaps there were more petty fragments that he could reap from his disappointing scholarly expedition. That despondent task was all that remained before abandoning the purpose of his visit and playing tourist with Joan. He wondered how much it would cost to turn in his plane ticket and go home early. That would have the added benefit of avoiding Y2K anxieties when the millennium turned its digits forward. But how horrible to arrive back home early and with nothing to show.

Neither Shakespeare nor Merton. Sylvia Plath?

No. Emily Dickinson. That's who it was. Joan's favorite. She had quoted him the whole poem, but he could only remember parts of it.

After great pain, a formal feeling comes.
The Nerves sit ceremonious, like tombs.

The poem danced at the border of memory. He could only recollect its cadence. But maybe even that was mistaken, and some unmatching rhythm was marching around his skull. His memory was not proving very reliable.

He sat up straighter and reached for a box, pulled it to him, and lifted the lid. Two other researchers at nearby tables, who had been casting furtive, worried glances at his still figure, relaxed and went back to their work.

This was the first box he had examined back in September. Many of the materials were letters exchanged among younger generations of the Gorski family. There were also some printed documents, but they said little that Adam didn't already know. But just to make sure, he went through a ritual check, the tedious thoroughness an end in itself. He turned over every page, consulted his notes, even jotted a few lines about matters that he had skipped before when it had seemed that such small points would be irrelevant compared to the wealth of information still to come. After two careful, monotonous hours, he replaced the lid and put the box back on the cart.

Box number two was the one that contained those deceptively wonderful letters. The ones that he had discovered belatedly he had already read on microfilm. Though it was painful to open it again, he made himself page through the well-ordered file. If he had paid more deliberate attention to the research he had already done and correlated his notes with their archival sources, he never would have made such a stupid mistake. It took some effort to cling to the formal feeling before reaching the bottom of the box, but Adam persevered until he was positive that there was nothing else there. This box too was carefully closed and placed on the wheeled cart.

Box number three, oddly, was almost entirely taken up with old posters advertising the two-hundredth anniversary of Kosciuszko's journey to America. He had looked through it before and found no original documents, but now he set everything out on the big table and looked again. They were interesting in themselves, but there was no mention of the men in Kosciuszko's company. Adam dutifully took a few notes on points that might someday add flair to a comment in an article, one of those breezy asides like "two centuries later this event would be remembered differently," and then a break to the personal voice as he reported running across old posters in Poland. He hoped he would have the opportunity to make such a statement, and in a feeble bubble of optimism he even crafted a likely sentence. But then he closed this box too and placed it with its companions on the cart.

He knew the fourth box to be nearly empty. Unlike the others, this container was made from ordinary cardboard, not the acid-free material required for archival storage. An irregular line ran around the bottom of the box marking a dark, ancient stain, indicating water damage at some point in the past. Perhaps a window neglectfully left open to a storm had let in a spurt of rain that had run along a shelf and pooled under this box, soaking it and creeping into its interior. It smelled musty, a good deal worse than the foxing that was common on old paper materials. Adam speculated that whatever undamaged materials had remained after the small flood must have been removed when the accident was discovered, and that whoever had done so had left the rest to dry out. And then perhaps someone else had put the lid back on the box and thoughtlessly reshelved it.

The cardboard sides of this box were warped from the old dampness. The water stain wavered just above a thin stack of papers at the bottom of the box. They were virtually glued together, and Adam had to stand and lean into the box to pry up their edges. Ancient mold spores flew into his nose, and he indulged in a fit of sneezing. He retreated into a wad of tissues and issued a general apology to the room at large. The room was almost empty today. The two other readers nodded and smiled sympathetically, familiar themselves with attacks from mildew and dust.

The papers retrieved were so gummed-together that Adam knew he could not separate the pages without professional assistance, if indeed anyone could pry apart layers so thoroughly melded that they resembled plaster. It was unlikely to be worth the effort. The handwriting on the top page was almost completely washed away, and ink stains had bled along the edges and through the thin stack, suggesting that whatever had been written was probably blurred beyond recognition. Still, he laid the ruined lump aside for future study. He had eight weeks left before he was scheduled to depart, assuming he didn't give up right now and leave early. He might as well spend the time picking at the edges of a matted wad of paper.

He was about to replace the contents and put the lid back on the box when he noticed that its cardboard bottom wasn't the same color as the sides. It was stained with damp like the rest, but the texture was different. And it was not assembled with the same sort of seams as were the top and sides. He took a closer look.

It wasn't part of the container at all but some kind of folder that appeared jammed into the box. It had been pressed flat at the bottom of the pile and then apparently stuck in place by the warping of the sides. Probably it too was pasted together like the papers he had just retrieved, but maybe he could get it out.

Adam's fingernails were not long enough to get a purchase on the edge. He needed something sharp like the paper knife on the archivist's desk. He sidled up and removed it somewhat furtively while the man was making himself a cup of coffee. A perfectly legitimate tool for his job, but at the moment he didn't feel up to explaining the need to pry apart a portion of the library's historical collection. He slid its thin tip carefully into one corner, then another, then along the edge. Very slowly, the old paper separated from the cardboard box, emitting a soft, scratchy sigh. As he removed the item, Adam could see that it wasn't a folder after all but a large, makeshift envelope constructed from a page of heavy-gauge paper folded and secured on three sides. The fourth edge had once been closed with a tie of some sort, and fragments of bleached ribbon unstuck from the paper and fluttered to the table as Adam slid the knife between the edges of the top of the envelope. The heavy paper crackled apart, reluctant to separate after so many years. A fine dust exhaled from the narrow opening. He squinted into the interior.

The envelope contained a dark, dirty-looking object. It smelled even funnier than the rest of the box. Adam hesitated, sniffing cautiously and suppressing another round of sneezes. Then he set it down and took several filtered breaths through the tissue of his handkerchief, cleansing his nose the way a gourmet might cleanse his palate between courses. He readied his senses. Then he sniffed, and sniffed again. He inserted a probing finger and felt along the edges. It felt, it felt like . . .

CAROLYN KORSMEYER   83

Oilcloth. Old oilcloth. Old-fashioned protection against damp.

He inserted his whole hand into the narrow opening and felt the flat side of the stiff fabric, formerly supple and waterproof.

Something inside here had been considered — by someone long ago — to be worth preserving.

Adam set the envelope on the table again and carefully brushed off his hands. His palms were suddenly damp. He had lost the formal feeling altogether now, and an incautious excitement began to flicker. Slowly, holding his breath, he coaxed the dark rectangle free from its paper protection and placed it before him on the table. The object inside the oilcloth was too firm to be a collection of unbound paper. It was small and rectangular, but not rigid enough to be a published book. Above, all, it was something that might have escaped the obliterating water damage of the rest of the box.

The archive was closing, and the two other researchers were gathering up their belongings ready to depart for the day. He nodded at them distractedly as they made their way to the door, attempting to sustain a casual demeanor. Soon the archivist would bustle around and start shutting off the lights.

The oilcloth had lost its original flexibility, and its stiff edges did not want to come apart. But Adam persevered, worrying the material until it began to tear. At any other time that ripping noise would have caused him to stop his efforts and seek some assistance. But his capacity for due caution was used up. Although his brain knew that another day quietly lying in its wrappings would not alter whatever was there to be discovered, his damaged heart, not to mention his mangled stomach, demanded immediate satisfaction.

At last, he slid his fingers into the folds and touched the edges of a slim book. Boldly he thrust both hands into the dark wrap and enlarged its opening. With finger and thumb carefully clamped on the top corners, he pulled out the object, hardly daring to breath. Could it be? Could it possibly be?

In his hands he held a small, leather-bound book. The cover, once a smooth dark brown, was powdery and cracked, the corners blunted and disintegrating. It had the feel of old dirt, compact and dry like earth. Between the covers were bound together thin papers compressed to somewhat less than half an inch thick.

Miraculously, the pages were not glued together by damp. Adam teased open the first several, holding his breath as they separated with faint crackles. The cramped writing was only slightly faded, its outlines unblurred. Pages and pages of writing—dates, names, places—all recorded in that familiar, brotherly hand.

It was Gorski's missing diary.

15

All Saints

The dark came early now. A waning half-moon hung low in the sky, a smudged glow above the city lights. It was cold, but the weather seemed to bother no one in the throngs that made their way through the streets, around churches, and into the cemeteries of Krakow. Adam and Joan followed Beata up paths snaking among the tombstones. Another glow, yellow and soft, was rising around them as families gathered around graves, some marked by stones old and stained, others by new monuments with crisp incised lettering. Beata, leading the way, spoke over her shoulder.

"My family is further in at the top of the hill. It is well that it isn't raining. Sometimes in bad weather the candles go out, but you can see that some have these little umbrellas just in case."

The candles set on the gravestones were large wax pillars poured into deep glass containers and intended for long burning on this one night. Many had small metal parasols stuck in the wax to protect the wicks.

"Last night was Hallowe'en at home," said Joan, dropping behind their landlady and taking Adam's hand. "Kids were out trick or treating."

"I like this better," said Adam after a pause. Joan wondered if the pause indicated that he found her comment frivolous. Of late, she seemed to be the only one making an effort in the relationship. Alternately hurt and irritated, she chatted through the silences that now fell between them.

But she misread his pause. Tonight Adam was feeling so at peace with the world that her words simply took time to register. Every time he thought of Gorski's diary he was awash with pleasure. The anticipation of what he might read there was so joyous that he still savored just being on the brink of discovery. He had not told Joan yet what he had found. Not precisely at least. Only that he had come upon an interesting batch of papers. Keeping the diary to himself for a while prolonged the excitement of the find. Long ago when he was a child, he had found an arrowhead lying at the edge of a river. He had peered at it for a moment before the distinctive edges came into focus against the rocky shore. Then he had picked it up and, thrilled to the bone, had replaced it in the same spot over and over, finding it again and again and relishing the electricity of discovery.

Joan stumbled on the dark path. The growing crowd of tiny flames cast disorienting pools of shadow underfoot. Adam put his arm around her shoulders and guided her around the turn. He hadn't meant to be brusque. "Beata's getting too far ahead. We don't want to lose her in the dark."

They toiled up the hill. The headstones that remained candleless and dark seemed forlorn and abandoned. Perhaps whole families had died out or moved away and there was no one left to remember All Saints' Eve. Beata came to a stop near the top of a rise. She paused and greeted two people, familiar neighbors from past visits. Hands were shaken, and Adam and Joan were introduced. But the attention was on the graves and those who lay beneath. Beata set two candles on adjacent gravestones and placed between them a bouquet of chrysanthemums tied with loose ribbon. The flowers had sat in water all afternoon, but water was hard to carry uphill, and they had skipped the long line at the spigot. Now the damp stems were all that would sustain the blooms for the next few days.

"I always bring real flowers," she said. "Of course, they don't last very long. Many people prefer plastic these days. A month from now there will be lots of plastic still blooming. But I like the real ones. And they shouldn't last long, should they? Everything dies."

Beata stepped back and regarded the graves of her parents. She was silent a minute, then crossed herself and bowed her head. After a moment Adam did the same. Joan loitered uncomfortably, slightly taken aback at Adam's gesture. She was remembering that she had never visited her father's grave. There had been the funeral and the burial, and later she had helped to choose a headstone. But she had never gone back to the town where he had set up a new life after her parents divorced, and now, surrounded by an entire city remembering its dead, she wondered that she hadn't.

Joan discreetly turned away and surveyed the large cemetery. Flickers of light spangled the hillside. A lifting wind sloughed through bare branches, and above the windy trees came the thin, sweet notes of the trumpeter playing the hejnal from St. Mary's steeple.

"I would like to stay just a little while here," said Beata. "You can walk around. I'll catch up with you."

They strolled in the dark under a benignant moon that had shed its veil of cloud. Joan felt the cold of the earth through her shoes. Adam walking next to her was warm, and she slid her hand through his arm. More and more candles were lit until their small pools of light joined, and there was a film of illumination above the dark paths. It caught in their eyes and all but obscured their feet. Joan began to feel pleasantly disoriented, as if she were floating.

A voice spoke out of the dark.

"You again! So soon!"

Rudy stood at the side of the path, a book of spent matches in his hand. His unbuttoned coat flapped open; the cold seemed nothing to him. They greeted him, Joan with a smile, Adam with belated recognition.

"Quite a sight, isn't it?" said Rudy, gesturing down the slope.

"I've never seen anything like it before," said Joan. "It's a nice tradition, All Saints. Did you light a candle?"

"Yes. My wife is buried in this cemetery. Just here in fact."

The gravestone next to him was taller and narrower than the others. On its flat top was a jar holding a wide, still flame. Its light sent shadows over the incised inscription: *Renata Joon Vander Lage 1938-1997*, and then some words below that they could not read. There was a cross over her name, and below it, a small Star of David. Rudy ran his fingers lightly over the incised letters. "Probably the only one here in both Dutch and Polish. But maybe not. Lots of different people have lived here over the years."

"But it's unusual, isn't it," said Joan, "to have both a cross and a Jewish star on the same stone?" Adam's sharp fingers poked disapproval for her nosy question.

"Probably," said Rudy. "But she was both baptized and, according to traditional reckoning, Jewish too. A grandmother, her mother's mother. There had been conversions in the family, but she converted back. Well, not formally, as it turned out. Ran out of time. She was raised Christian, but I had the star added too. I guess you might say that she identified as Jewish at the end. Horrible term, isn't it? Identified as. She simply was. It wouldn't have been up to her at all to identify as anything but Jewish, had that part of her family not moved to Holland. That's why she felt she had to come back."

He had fallen into step with them. As they made their way along the narrow path, Adam dropped back. Three abreast didn't fit with all the mingling people.

"We're here with our landlady," said Joan. "Perhaps we could all go for coffee. Would you like to join us?" Joan sensed that Rudy might be lonely.

"Thanks, but no. I am engaged later and must get home." The engagement was a private one with a bottle of whiskey, but Rudy wasn't feeling sociable tonight. At a branching path he issued a brief bow to them both. Joan wondered if he was aware of the faint comedy he tended to play, or if it was just an inadvertent effect of his own physical style. He started to make off down the path, then turned back.

"I say, don't forget this coming Friday if you want to see the show. Should be interesting. It's the event of the season. Mustn't miss it. I'll look for you there."

And after this rapid series of clipped sentences he was off, the edges of his coat flapping. Beata caught up with them just before the conversation ended.

"Show?" she asked.

"I guess he means the announcement about the painting in the museum," said Adam. "He talked about it before. He knows the man who will give us the expert assessment."

"Oh yes. Of course. The painting by Leonardo da Vinci. This is very exciting and important. We have been waiting for a decision now for some time. There have been lots of people who were convinced that the painting is by Leonardo. But then of course there were others who just thought that the Radincki Museum was trying to compete with the Czartoryszki. I think the news is likely to be good, don't you? Or there wouldn't be such a fuss. And then it will bring more tourists to town and that will be good."

Despite these enthusiastic sentiments, Beata didn't seem as interested in the subject as she might have been, and on their way home before they reached the flat she bid them an early good night and slipped into a church. Light spilled from the open doors.

Adam looked rather wistfully inside at the throngs on their knees.

"There is a nice feeling of unity here, don't you think? With everyone believing the same thing and doing the same things, and all going to light candles like this? At least for tonight."

"Do you want to go inside too?"

He stood silently, a stone in the stream of churchgoers entering the building. "Maybe another time."

But Joan was thinking that perhaps he meant: Maybe alone. He had crossed himself. How little she knew him after all. They went home in silence.

***

In a small cemetery in a village now touched by the creeping expansion of the city, Pawel Radincki wrapped his scarf around the lower part of his face. It was risky coming here, as there were families buried nearby whose younger members might know him. But he felt compelled to come. He was relieved to see that he did not recognize the people nearby. Fastidiously he spread a large handkerchief on the ground and knelt before a low headstone. For some minutes he was still, his eyes staring so intensely at the grave before him that they lost focus. Then they filled with tears and he bowed his head.

Pawel's mother had been dead for nearly two decades. How he missed her. In his youth he had felt that no one would ever love him so much, and as he grew older, he knew for certain how true this was. Even after he married he knew. A wife's love is fine, or he supposed it would have been had he married another woman. But a mother's love is unconditional. Forever. Heavenly.

He placed his candle on her grave. But the stone had shifted since he was last here, and its surface was not level. The glass container slid and he caught it before it fell. It took him a little while to find a flat rock—perhaps the broken edge of another gravestone—and to place it before her grave like a small altar. Lower to the ground and protected from the light wind, the candle burned steady and strong, and he felt his mother's spirit draw near.

From the pocket of his jacket he removed a small paper bag. Tilting it carefully, he glanced around to be sure he was not seen and sprinkled a circle of salt around the candle. In its flickering flame, the tiny crystals glinted. Then he crossed himself twice, once in the conventional manner of the church and second— safely obscured by the cover of the night—in a swirling gesture that finished with a sweep across his heart. Then he folded his hands and lowered his lids until only the candlelight entered his eyes. He steadied his breath until the rhythm matched the wind and his pulse slowed. He began to pray, and as the night deepened he waited to hear her voice.

16

Treasures

Joan had planned to meet Adam just outside the Painting Gallery, but he was nowhere in sight. From the arched entryway she could see two television cameras on wheeled scaffolds and a number of men with video recorders balanced on their shoulders. A podium bristling with microphones was set up at the far end of the room in front of a large screen. There was excitement in the air as the Radincki Museum prepared for what promised to be an occasion to put them on the map, no longer in the shadow of the Czartoryski or the Wawel. They had taken a chance with this public event, and hopes were high.

"Przepraszam, Panią!" said a voice behind her with the impatient tone of someone who has spoken more than once. A suggestive push propelled Joan into the gallery. A man with yet another television camera was backing into the room attended by two intent young women carrying cables. They were followed by a group of well-dressed men and women. At their center was the art expert she recognized from the reception three weeks before. A general jostling and realignment of cameras indicated that the proceedings were about to commence.

By now Joan was all too familiar with the Painting Gallery. The huge canvases that crowded the walls presented a jumbled assemblage of nobles, knights, and clergy. A rearing horse, the froth on his mouth rendered with precise detail, perpetually failed to throw its heroically glaring rider. Cloudy gates parted to let the sun shine approvingly upon distant battlefield carnage. A personage clad in regal rose and gold addressed a collection of soldiers and farmers. And behind her what could only be a stampede thundered towards the viewer. The little painting that was the center of attention today was completely hidden from sight by the crowd.

"Ah, there you are!" said a voice behind her. "I was looking for you outside. I'm glad you came. Where is Adam? Is he here?" Rudy was at her elbow.

"I thought he would be, but I haven't seen him."

"Impossible to see anything at all from this corner. Let's move up a bit, shall we?" Rudy took her elbow and exercised his peculiar ability to slice through crowds. More people pressed into the room until they were squeezed together with the indifferent intimacy of passengers on a crowded bus. At her back Joan could feel the scratchy wool of Rudy's jacket and smell a not unpleasant combination of after-shave and beer. Lateral jostling threatened to separate them, and he clamped his hands over her shoulders. She cradled her injured elbow against the pressure of the crowd. Rudy noticed the gesture and positioned his hands protectively.

There was an ear-splitting squeal from the sound system. As one the crowd put their hands to their ears and groaned, then laughed. Another squeal, then a tentative knocking against the mouthpiece, then comic silence as a man mouthed soundlessly into the microphone. There was fiddling with wires. The microphone emitted a hollow exhale, then a series of quacks. A man in a squarely tailored suit gave an exaggerated shrug and broadcast bonhomie.

"Ex-KGB," muttered Rudy into her hair.

"What? Here? How do you know?"

"Just a comment about style. Men that thick around the middle should never button their jackets."

"I didn't expect sartorial opinion from you." If she tilted her head back, Joan could see the side of his jaw.

"Clothes hang better when they don't encounter bulges. My wife always said so, and I had no reason to disbelieve her. She dressed very well."

A wuthering noise from the sound system was making conversation difficult, but mention of his wife seemed to invite further inquiry. Joan aimed her words at his ear.

"How long has your wife been gone?" Joan couldn't remember if she could see the dates on the tombstone in the light of the flickering candles.

"She died two years ago. Wanted to be buried here in Krakow rather than back in Holland. Our children wished to take her home, but it was her decision and I honored it. Decided to stay for a while afterwards, as you can see."

The words were matter of fact, the tone melancholy. Joan leaned against him slightly and felt his hands tighten.

Someone at the front stepped onto a low platform and held up her hands for quiet. An obedient hush descended and, all of a sudden, it was underway. In Polish. Joan looked up at Rudy for enlightenment and saw that he was studying a set of portraits on the wall nearest them. She whispered, "What's going on?"

"This woman is introducing the Curator of Painting, who is introducing the Museum Director, who will read the report of the Scientific Investigation Committee. There is a lot of gratitude being expressed, appropriate thanks to various people. Don't worry. When the findings are presented there will be translations. After all, the foreign press is here."

Rudy was right. After three separate and apparently prefatory sets of remarks were delivered, two people positioned themselves next to one another at the podium: a man and a woman. The man read slowly from a sheaf of papers. He paused frequently to permit his words to be translated. English was the chosen language on the assumption that it was now Europe's lingua franca.

The Museum Director presented the analysis of the technical team which had examined the painting, and their investigation was detailed and recondite. He was pleased to report that the team of experts hired by the Museum had determined that the painting known as *Salvator Mundi*, having been subject to the most up-to-date tests for genuineness of historical materials, was confirmed as an artifact from the late Renaissance. They had examined the wood of the panel and found it to be poplar of the sort used in Italy in the fifteenth and sixteenth centuries. It had been smoothed using tools consistent with the period. X-ray analysis had discovered a row of hand-forged nails along one side, suggesting that at some point the facing edge had been cut down. Infrared photography revealed portions of a preliminary sketch that had been erased and corrected. There were scattered traces of egg tempura, but the primary medium was oil. Spectroscopic examination revealed paints consistent with the pigments in use by painters of the time, namely both woad and lapis blue, yellow ochre, rose madder, and lead white. Traces of zinc white, Prussian blue, and cadmium yellow indicated later retouching on probably two occasions. The more modern pigments were confined to the upper surface of the paint and did not compromise the determination of age. On the original layer of paint no modern synthetic pigments were found either by microchemical testing or by chromospectroscopy. The finish exhibited consistent overall craqueleure that was unlikely to have been produced by anything but age.

The room was getting warm. The audience stood in disciplined and respectful silence. Joan's feet began to hurt as the speaker proceeded from the scientific analysis into a complicated narrative of the painting's provenance. There were gaps in the history of the ownership of the piece, but no more than with other works that issued from the prolific workshops of Renaissance Italy.

Finally, the summary conclusion: the results of the laboratory analysis of the *Salvator Mundi* revealed nothing inconsistent with the painting's origin in Italy in the latter half of the fifteenth century or the beginning of the sixteenth. Nothing that would rule out the possibility that the identity of the artist could be Leonardo da Vinci.

It was the negative determination they had hoped for. And while the conclusion might have been expected given the build-up for the event and the length of time spent by reading the summary, there was a lifting of spirits and scattered applause for the report.

"Now," hissed Rudy, "for the show."

***

Adam was not present at the event that occupied the rest of the Radincki Museum for the simple reason that he had accidentally gotten locked in the archive.

He had every intention of joining Joan at one o'clock as they planned. Even he thought it would be interesting to be present at the confirmation—for surely that is what was to come—of a newly authenticated painting by Leonardo da Vinci. Furthermore, the librarian had announced that he would close up the archive for two hours in the afternoon so that everyone could devote their attention to this important event, since he was sure that they would all prefer to be there for the special occasion. Five heads nodded, including Adam's. Three people arranged their work on the tables so that when the event was over they could return for an hour or so more study; two announced they would cut their day short. Adam was one of the former three, but he was the only one who trotted off to the bathroom before exiting for the Painting Gallery. And the archivist, seeing the tables neatly arranged and vacated, had locked the door on the assumption that everyone had left.

So when Adam made his way to the door, he found that he could not pass beyond the barren anteroom. The door was soundly closed and apparently bolted. He turned the knob left and right. He leaned into the frame, then pulled. He jiggled the lock. He put his shoulder to the door in a tooth-jarring lunge. But while these actions delivered by a strong man might have had an effect on a modern hollow-core door, the antique structure of the Radincki Museum could have withstood the assault of King Kong.

Much as he loved libraries, Adam didn't fancy being locked in one. Especially on a Friday when the librarian was unlikely to return before Tuesday morning. How long would it take Joan to figure out where he was? Would his cell phone work here? Unlikely, since it was sitting on the charger by his bed at home. If he yelled from a window, would anyone come rescue him? Although as a rule a rational man, the emotional upheavals since his arrival in Poland had undermined his equanimity. His heart pounded and his breath was short. What if he fell ill? How long would the oxygen last in here? Might he suffocate before anyone returned? That thought was too hysterical even for him, and he calmed slightly. The museum was not hermetically sealed, and even if it were, it would take a panting army to exhaust all its oxygen in the space of a weekend.

There was a bathroom, thank goodness. Plenty of water therefore. And perhaps his fellow scholars would forgive him if he ate all the little snacks stored in the alcove.

Adam's panic subsided and he began to feel a little silly. His imprisonment was sure to be quite temporary. No more than two hours. The librarian had said quite clearly that the archives would be closed just during the announcement about the painting. The open books and the carts standing around were evidence that their users were intending to return in just a short while.

It was too bad to miss the proceedings now underway in the Painting Gallery. But it wouldn't do any good to keep pounding away on this door. The worst he had to fear was being discovered to be extremely foolish. Embarrassment might make one squirm, but it wasn't fatal.

Well, he might as well get some work done.

Adam settled back into his chair. His back was beginning to feel molded to its curves. When he had first started work at the archives, he had been pleasantly surprised at the comfort of the old library chairs. Now this one was virtually a part of his body. He bent over the little diary and squinted at the faded writing.

Gorski's diary. What a find. And what a pity it had taken him so long to realize that it was here. Sitting right on the cart among all the other useless stuff he had wasted so much time over. It was a gem. And it was excruciatingly hard to read.

Quite apart from the fact that he was reading in a language that he knew only imperfectly, and that the style was antique and full of the author's idiosyncratic abbreviations. And that some of it was written in French. And indeed, blessedly, some in English, though he had puzzled over two lines of English trying to make sense of them in Polish before he realized that Gorski had shifted languages and was reporting a conversation among colonial Americans. Quite apart from the ordinary difficulties of reading someone else's scribbles, was the fact that the diary was in places terribly faded, and on a number of pages some of the lines were crossed out and minuscule writing inserted above them. Often Gorski had written on both sides of a page, and ink from one side bled through onto the other, leaving specks that were easily confused with the accent marks that littered written Polish. Paper had been scarce in Gorski's day, and no one wasted it. The diary would have been hard even for a native speaker to decode. For Adam, it seemed to stretch as an endless project.

And he was running out of time.

At first he had just tried to translate the text. And then after two painstaking pages he realized that he probably would need to refine the translation repeatedly at leisure later on. It crossed his mind that the entire thing might be worth a definitive edition, perhaps a special issue of a journal entirely devoted to bringing this text to the larger scholarly community. That possibility raised a hopeful glow and visions of academic honor. But it was a task for the future. And it would require that he keep a complete text to study at length.

So Adam decided to transcribe the entire diary in its original language and then translate it in sections as he progressed. It had taken the better part of three days to come to this determination. At first he attempted the transcription on his computer, but he found that it was more cumbersome to move between original and translation on the screen than on paper, not to mention the tedium of finding the appropriate accent marks on an Anglophone program. So he bought a large, clean notebook with wide lines and a spiral binding, and by hand he carefully wrote the Polish on the right side and a tentative English version on the left. Already he had filled thirty pages. And there were many more to go.

The light scratch of his pencil against paper was the only sound in the room. His panicky episode on discovering the locked door had receded, replaced by a cozy sort of calm.

One more page completed. Adam put down his pencil and stretched his fingers. So many more pages to go, and how many days left? Holidays looming ahead, and all those wasted weekends. Not to mention the idiosyncratic days when the archive was closed but the museum open.

An uncharacteristically immoral idea danced into his brain. It was so tempting. And really so innocent.

There was the copier behind the librarian's table. It was still switched on. Adam raised his head and looked at it, then forced his eyes back to the page. He looked up again and felt the surrounding silence. The wicked little thought returned.

Photocopying old documents was not approved. The raking light of the machine hastened fading and deterioration. He had already inquired rather casually if he might make a few copies, though he had not been specific about the materials. The response had been emphatic. A copy of the contract was extracted and waved, and Adam nodded at his signature. No escape clause there.

As yet, Adam had not told even the archivist of his remarkable find. He felt justifiably possessive of the diary, for it had already cost him a good deal of anxiety. He did not intend to announce its existence until he had completed his examination. So perhaps the need for copies had not been made quite clear enough, although probably no reason would have been sufficient to the mind of the pleasant but rather fussy librarian. Adam might apply to see if microfilming were possible, he was reminded, but that of course might exceed his time in Krakow. And indeed it would, so Adam had dropped the subject as if it were no matter and returned to the antique tradition of pencil and paper. He would order a microfilm copy at the end of his stay, but he didn't want to relinquish the journal now for that process. So he was anchored to the archive table trying to decipher the devilish text at a maddeningly slow pace,

But there the copier stood, an industrial cube emitting its idle whirr. And here was Gorski's diary, which no one had even seen for decades, maybe even a century. How much damage could one little copy do? Surely none at all.

If everyone reasoned that way, said his conscience, then there would be no protection for valuable documents. That is why there are no exceptions.

No exceptions. It's the rule. The principle.

Adam had been told more than once that his conscience was his scourge. You never met a rule you wouldn't obey, his older sister used to say in exasperation. Bend a little. Use your own judgment. Adam had been the only one among his boyhood friends who refused to smuggle home-popped popcorn into the movies, the only teenager who didn't have a fake ID. He had once spent ten minutes at a broken stop light at a cross roads in the middle of the night with no other car in sight. Because the light was red.

At this moment his conscience was sounding like a gong: *wrong, wrong, wrong, wrong, wrong*. But every strike of the gong sounded more faintly.

With a copy he could work at home in the evenings and on the weekends. He could finish his work. Maybe he could even take home a whole copy! The idea that he might return home with an entire copy of Gorski's diary was too tempting for even his robust principles.

Adam slithered around the librarian's desk and examined the machine. He found he was moving quietly as if there were nearby ears. The weakening tug of his conscience was discomforting, but the situation had also become furtively exciting. He wasn't very good with machines, but this copier looked pretty standard. He went back to his table and picked up the diary, opening it carefully as far as he could without damaging the fragile binding. He returned to the copier and positioned the diary on the glass. He didn't put down the top for fear of splitting the spine. He pressed a button. Nothing happened. He pressed another. There was a buzz of fan. Then a light, then the top of the whole apparatus slid across and back. Where was the copied page? Adam searched both sides of the machine before he found a thin slot at the bottom. The page was blank.

He tried again: position the book, press the button, watch it slide over the scorching lamp. The pages all were blank. He tried again. Still blank. Or, no. Not quite blank. Just incredibly faint.

He looked for an icon that indicated it might darken the print. He pressed several more buttons. The page came out grey this time. A uniform grey. He tried again, risking the top down this time. Now the page was black. Something was wrong. He experimented with a typed page from the desk. This one came out fine, if rather faint. Then he tried again with the diary. Apparently the old ink on the flimsy pages was simply too faded to photocopy clearly. Plus the ink cartridge in the machine probably needed replacing, a feat quite beyond him.

Having made the decision to violate his conscience in the first place, Adam was now exasperated that his immoral venture was not succeeding. If he was going to do something wrong, at least it ought to be effective. He located a section of the diary where the ink was less faded and tried to copy those pages. Mild success. He tried a few more. Readable, if just barely. Perhaps he could deal with these at home. A few pages this weekend would help. Anything would help. He flipped through the diary and located the darkest and least smudged spots and ran them through the copier. To his delight, he found several pages that contained diagrams of, what were they? Sketches of fortifications perhaps, and some kind of large, spiky machine. What a pleasure to have pictures to study rather than all those ambiguous letters. He copied these too, working faster now.

The two hours were nearly up. Adam retrieved all the pages he had copied and checked the copier to be sure he had left nothing around that betrayed his intrusion. He considered replenishing the stack of paper with the amount that he had used, but he was reluctant to open any of the bins. The machine felt warm under his hands and would need some time to cool off lest it betray its recent use. He crumpled the failed blank sheets and put them at the bottom of a waste basket in the far corner of the reading room below some other trash, and he placed his furtively copied pages in the zippered lining of his briefcase. He looked around again and assured himself that all looked undisturbed. Then he took his place at the table and resumed work with a casual, studious air. The little book was still warm from the photocopy lamp.

17
The Savior of the World

Jurgen de Mul took the podium. His white hair gleamed like silver, his dark suit was expertly tailored. Over his shoulder the projection screen came to life and the familiar picture of the Czartoryski Museum's *Lady with an Ermine* appeared. After a brief silence during which he swept the crowd with a pleasant smile, he positioned a pair of reading glasses on his nose and began to speak. This time the order of translation was reversed. De Mul's English was precise and confident, accented with a light combination of Dutch and Oxbridge.

"The pioneer art connoisseur of the beginning of our dwindling century, Bernard Berenson, once said of Leonardo da Vinci: 'Nothing that he touched but turned into a thing of eternal beauty'." Jurgen de Mul paused while his opening sentence was translated into Polish. The picture behind him switched to the Louvre's *Madonna of the Rocks*.

"So great is his importance in the history of painting, that we tend to forget these days that Leonardo was a not a dedicated painter at all. He liked to sketch and has left us numerous drawings." Several of these appeared on the screen in rapid succession. "But his restless, brilliant mind was more taken up with inventions and anatomy, with eclectic learning and technology." There were slides of the Vitruvian Man, of a cartoonish flying machine, of bones and muscles, and of an eerie fetus inside a spherical womb.

"When Leonardo did paint, he often did not finish his work. We can only imagine the treasures that we might have today if he had possessed the patience. Ah, but when he did bring his work to completion — or nearly to completion — what a result!"

Mona Lisa smiled from the screen.

But she was shown without much comment and immediately replaced with Ginevra di Benci. De Mul was drawing attention to the modeling of eyelids and mouths. More images blinked by, some paintings, some drawings. The room was getting even warmer. The slide show paused with a blank screen.

"Ladies and Gentlemen, you have now just seen a host of his famous drawings, but only seventeen of Leonardo's paintings. And according to the most recent — and admittedly conservative — scholarly estimate, that is the sum total of extant paintings from the hand of this incomparable master. You have seen them all."

He surveyed the crowd and raised his shoulders. "Or have you? Is there yet one more picture that we might add to the oeuvre of Leonardo da Vinci?"

On screen there appeared the image of the Radincki's *Salvator Mundi*, enlarged many times and glowing with the halo of the slide projector lamp.

"As you might know, *Salvator Mundi* was a popular theme in European painting from the Middle Ages through the Renaissance." Several icon-like images appeared on screen. "It features the image of Christ as the Savior of the World, but a world rendered just as a simple sphere. It is tempting today to imagine that this is a representation of the planet Earth. Although Aristotle speculated that the Earth was round, it was commonly assumed in medieval Europe that it was flat, with edges rimmed by oceans that spilled into the steamy abysses of hell. People were beginning to change their minds by the fifteenth and sixteenth centuries, for of course the great navigators proceeded on the correct assumption that the Earth is a sphere. But it is still unlikely that the sphere in this picture represents our planet. Rather, the sphere was viewed as the perfect geometrical three-dimensional shape, and hence it represents the entirety of God's creation."

De Mul paused to sip from a glass of water. The translator took a little while to finish her segment of text.

"This particular panel has long been attributed by tradition to Leonardo da Vinci, although experts have disputed that possibility and many simply dismissed it altogether. It is the task of today to determine — is this attribution correct?"

De Mul paused again, letting anticipation build.

"As you might have already heard, if this is indeed by Leonardo, it could be his second painting on this theme, for there is another in a private collection, although there are also many doubters about the attribution of that work."

Apparently not everyone was aware of this complication, and an anxious murmur eddied through the crowd.

"Unfortunately, I do not have an image of this other *Salvator Mundi* for you to view, but if you were to see it, you would note a very similar composition. This is not surprising, since the very theme was repeated in standard ways for several centuries: a frontal view of Christ with an upraised hand. A relatively simple composition, rather more icon-like than Leonardo, that compositional innovator, is likely to have designed, all things being equal."

Rudy grumbled into Joan's ear. "I bet he could have gotten a slide of that other picture if he had tried. But why spoil the impact with another? Especially if it's better than the one here."

De Mul turned a page of his text and continued.

"But the existence of a second painting on the theme of the world's savior should not concern us at all on this occasion, for as we know, Leonardo was quite capable of rendering two paintings on the same subject." The two famous versions of the *Madonna of the Rocks* appeared on screen side by side.

"In fact, to my mind, the possible existence of a second picture might even be used to confirm the identity of both. That, however, is a project for other scholars to puzzle over. Let us now consider the panel that now resides in the Radincki collection."

The screen switched again to the Radincki's *Salvator Mundi*. The translator was getting breathless, and De Mul paused again to let the Polish catch up with the English.

"You have just heard the detailed report of the study of the physical object of the painting — its material vehicle as one might say. We know its provenance is interrupted, which is not unusual for paintings of this age. And we have learned beyond a doubt that there is nothing in the physical composition of this little panel that would forestall attribution to Leonardo. So the question remains, what of the artist? What hand created this image of the Savior of the World? What can we say about the immaterial, even the spiritual, entity that is the work of art itself?" Rapid Polish translated these words with almost ecstatic rapidity.

"Is this the hand of the greatest genius of the Renaissance? Or is it just another of the many pictures that are left to us from the prolific workshops of Italy?"

The shining head turned and regarded the screen for a long moment. The silence stretched.

"Drama," muttered Rudy.

The red eye of a laser pointer began to dance over the screen. "Here, we might note the treatment of the hair, not as curly as Ginevra's nor as ragged as the angel of Verrocchio's *Baptism of Christ*, an image that the young Leonardo probably contributed when he trained in Verrocchio's workshop. And consider the sleeves of this voluminous, even cumbersome robe. This is the kind of painting that any apprentice might have done. We know from his early work with Verrocchio that from the beginning Leonardo handled drapery with more flow and especially with more sense of the body beneath."

De Mul let a flutter of anxious comment palpate through the crowd. He raised the pointer once more.

"But then there is the face." Circles of red danced around the head of Christ.

"Here we see those signature heavy eyelids, and the eyes themselves looking out with that slightly world-weary expression. The expression is not as mocking as Mona Lisa's famous smile, nor as blankly passive as Ginevra di Benci's. In fact, the eyes show the intelligence and alertness of Krakow's own Cecelia Gallerani."

There was a murmur of appreciation as *The Lady with the Ermine* flashed briefly on screen next to the *Salvator Mundi*. Then the panel resumed center stage.

"Actually, to me the eyes are out of focus," Joan whispered. Rudy grunted in agreement.

"Here we see those long lips, thin at the edges, well-defined at the center, their exquisite shadows creating an expression both wise and kind. And in the visage of Christ there is also surely sorrow, that indescribable mixture of emotions that one might expect in the divine made human. The face itself hints of a master hand, although perhaps a master yet young and learning his craft."

Another murmur washed through the crowd.

"And now let us consider the hands. The orb cradled in the left hand is very fine, but the way the fingers curve around it — not perhaps the most realistic depiction. And indeed one would think that an expert anatomist would not have made such a crude job of the knuckles here, and here. And surely the thumb looks too short for the fingers." The laser light jiggled across the screen inviting agreement from the audience. Heads nodded.

"However, the raised hand is another matter. The palm is narrow, the fingers long and fine. It is hard even to imagine two such different hands on the same person, is it not? Compare the raised hand of the *Salvator Mundi* with this painting, so familiar to you all." Cecilia Gallerani appeared again on screen, her long fingers lightly stroking her pet ermine. "Can you not see how similar are the right hands in these two paintings?"

There was a wave of assent as heads nodded again. De Mul continued, his momentum building.

"And then there is this enigmatic area in the upper right quadrant. As you can see it is thinly painted. The ground shows through, and we can even discern the grain of the wood, though poplar is very fine-grained. As you heard before from the report of the scientific committee, there are only traces left of the preliminary sketch of the figure to be found by x-rays. And there are faint hints of background sketching up here where the paint is so thin. Let us look more closely."

A detail, vastly enlarged, appeared on the screen. Much vertical smudging and what looked like static. There was a perplexed silence.

"You might not see much here."

"Nothing at all in fact," grumbled Rudy.

"But let me remind you of something that Leonardo himself once recommended in his *Treatise on Painting*. He said that one ought to study uneven surfaces such as damp walls or stained cloth, then to let the eye play over them until one could discover in the shapes and shadows a landscape — mountains, trees, hills, flowers."

Mona Lisa appeared again, and Ginevra di Benci, followed by the exquisite details of the backgrounds over their respective shoulders.

"Now, look again at this section of the Radincki panel. I suggest that something along the lines of the following might have been intended to fill this corner." And now the laser pointer traced some clearer marks, and there was another slide, and another, and soon the audience gasped as the inarticulate surface of the panel receded and was filled with a tiny landscape of a distant hillside with a meandering river snaking into the background. De Mul turned back to the audience with a bit of a shrug. "Of course, these latter details are conjectural reconstruction. I have indulged in a bit of imagination, for which I hope you will forgive me."

The reconstructed background was replaced with the true image of the entire painting once more. But the thrill of the miraculously appearing landscape lingered. De Mul adjusted his spectacles and paused, sweeping the crowd with his gaze.

"I conclude, ladies and gentleman, that the *Salvator Mundi*," a pause for silence, "was painted by at least two hands, possibly three. We cannot put a name to all of them, nor can we be sure which made the first marks on the panel, for it is the nature of painting that issues from a workshop to have more than one creator. But portions of the face, most of the right hand, and perhaps the hint of the background, do indeed appear to be the work of Leonardo da Vinci."

There was applause. It petered out, as when the audience at a symphony concert mistakes the end of a movement for the finale. The Polish translation stopped. The translator looked at Jurgen de Mul as if expecting more.

"Hmm," said Rudy. "Just appear to be?"

De Mul removed his glasses and folded them into a pocket. But he had one more line to deliver before leaving the podium. He raised his head and took a breath, and with his deepened voice there was an expression of the utmost sobriety. "The historical attribution of the Radincki panel of the subject known as *Salvator Mundi* is therefore confirmed. At least a part of this painting can be authenticated as the work of Leonardo da Vinci."

Now there was sustained applause and cheering that racketed off the high ceiling. De Mul stepped down from the podium. Courteously, he shook the hand of the translator, then the museum director, then the other officials. Members of the audience closest to the front surged forward to stand in line before the little panel that had patiently awaited the imprimatur just delivered. The rest jammed the doorway on their way to the stairs.

"Well," said Joan as the press of bodies relaxed and she could turn to face Rudy. "What do you think?"

Rudy nodded slowly. "Very good show, on the whole. Extremely clever. And a very smart diagnosis. Many hands, but only one name. Very useful for the museum, don't you think?"

"Useful? That sounds rather skeptical."

"Not at all. But just think, if he had named the other hands, they would have to assign the painting to more than one artist by name. This way, it is Leonardo plus a couple of insignificant unknowns who will simply be forgotten. Hence, an authentic Leonardo, even if he can be supposed to have painted only bits and pieces of the whole thing. Very happy conclusion all around. Jurgen did them well. Let's go out and get a drink shall we?"

Joan scanned the crowd for Adam, but it was still impossible to see very far. He was probably back at work already anyway. She was annoyed that he hadn't met her as planned. She decided she deserved a drink.

"Okay, but a quick one," she said.

"Excellent," said Rudy, his mind turning to beer.

***

As the crowd made its way out of the Painting Gallery, their exit revealed a slender, well-dressed man leaning against a corner of the room. For most of the previous hour, Pawel Radincki had managed to perch on the protruding edge of a molding, there to remain securely held in place by the bodies jammed in front of him. Consequently, he had a fairly good view of the proceedings and, like Rudy, was mulling over the choice of words delivered by the authoritative consultant. It had seemed for a time that authentication was doubtful. All those other hands, all those badly painted sections. But on reflection, things were really turning out quite well for his purposes. He made his way slowly out of the Painting Gallery, strolling past a chattering crush at the staircase. He turned down a corridor toward the small room at its end, seeking a private moment with the true object of his desire.

Bronislaw's chalice. His chalice. Tarnish enhanced the relief design and deepened its patina. The enigmatic patterns on its edge sang to him their secret incantation and the promise they held. He brushed the glass case lightly with his hand. The nerves in his fingers tingled as though they might reach through the glass to touch the object itself.

And then he thought better of the gesture and rubbed the glass over again with his sleeve. Careless, that. Fingerprints. He would have plenty of time later to touch. For now, just looking would have to suffice. He gazed at the chalice, caressing it with his eyes, taking in how the silver curved, the delicate precision of the four figures, the seductively mysterious symbols.

A sliver of doubt jabbed across his mind. That graceful bowl looked shallower than he had recalled, and those figures at the base—they were not quite how he had remembered. The replica that he had commissioned now seemed less exact than he had reckoned it would be. It should have been a relatively simple task to re-make an old silver cup that he had found in a provincial antique shop and purchased because it reminded him of something. Only later had he recalled the object that had triggered his memory, and it had been a revelation—as if

Bronislaw's chalice had itself called out to him, planting the seeds for his great scheme.

But now he could see some discrepancies between the reshaped bowl that lay hidden in his flat and the original it mimicked. Pawel felt his pulse quicken with anxiety. The match was close enough, he assured himself. The dissimilarities were small, and all that was needed was a reasonable facsimile, since no one would notice that the cabinet had been disturbed — the brilliance of his new key. The substitute, itself antique, would suffice. Surely his plan would not founder at this stage.

He drew a steady, deep breath. The portents were right. He was master of his destiny. He would not fail.

He turned to go and was startled to see that there was a woman watching him from the hallway. A large, squarely built woman wearing the uniform of the museum guards. He gave her a short nod and made to pass her. And then she spoke.

"It's Pawel, isn't it? Little Pawel? Pawel Meyer?" Her tone was eager and friendly.

Pawel Radincki was confused. He had no idea who she was, and he was somewhat affronted that a guard would address him by his Christian name. And then the second name registered: Meyer. She had called him Pawel Meyer. That was dangerous. How could anyone know him by that name any longer? He pretended not to have heard and sustained his aloof expression, but she maneuvered herself so that she blocked his path.

"I thought I recognized you when you were here the other day," she persisted. "Don't you remember me? You must be Anna's son. She was my friend when she worked here. You must remember, don't you? When you used to come with your mother sometimes I gave you sweets. Remember now?"

And then Pawel knew who she was, and his confusion and resentment were shot through with fear. He willed his eyes blank and assumed his haughtiest demeanor.

"You must be mistaken madam," he said with quashing chill. "My mother's name was not Anna. You have taken me for someone else." His mother, he was certain, would forgive this disloyal statement. She would read his heart.

The woman was staring at him, hesitantly now. The certainty was fading from her expression. Perhaps she was wrong. But no, surely that was the same face. Longer now that the boy had grown up. But it was the same.

"I beg your pardon, sir. I thought I knew you." But her tone was less than contrite. She stepped back and a flush began to work its way up her thick neck. Rather than apologetic, she looked truculent.

Pawel gave her a short, dismissive bow and turned towards the stairs. Although the blood thudded in his ears, he walked purposively out of the museum at a leisurely pace, as though the incident were as trivial as he wanted it to be. He willed himself not to hurry, and he paused on the landing just outside the building's entrance to take a long, studied look at his watch as though consulting for his next appointment. Then with controlled theatricality he looked around and raised his hand at a person in the street below, calling out a name and heading into the crowd. Nobody noticed that he hailed no one in particular and fell into step beside a stranger.

As he strode away he dared a glance up at the high windows of the museum. There, quite clearly, he could see Klementyna Kamynska still watching.

18

Forking Paths

Joan and Rudy were not the only ones desiring a celebratory drink. The restaurant was crowded, and the two of them were jammed together at a narrow table placed hard by a window. Rudy went to the bar, ordered four beers at once, and waded back through the crowd holding high two mugs in each hand. He took a deep draught and suppressed a belch. Delicious. Nothing outscored Polish beer. Well, maybe Ukrainian, but both were superior to Dutch. A disloyal thought, but his own.

Joan was frowning over a discarded newspaper picturing a blurry photo of the now famous Leonardo painting under an indecipherable headline. "How many languages do you speak, anyway?"

Rudy had to think. "Depends how much fluency you require. Four quite well. Six if you lower your standards a bit. And I can read a couple of others. No sense trying to make your way in the world with Dutch alone, you know. We all learn other languages from an early age. I already read that article you're holding. Nothing you didn't just hear."

Joan suddenly leaned forward and kissed his cheek. Rudy was so surprised that he started back, bumping his head on a post. "Thanks so much for being with me there in the museum, Rudy," she said with unexpected feeling. "It made it so much more interesting."

"My pleasure." He was both pleased and rattled. He turned to his beer and then was startled again as a blurry face thrust itself into view before him. A man was staring through the window inches away. Rudy took a napkin and cleared the steam from the glass. Adam. Rudy waved and then pointed towards the door with a jabbing finger.

Adam shouldered through the crowd. "I never would have found you if I hadn't seen you through the window," he said. "Lucky you were sitting so close. I thought you would still be at the museum."

"Well, I thought you would be in the gallery," said Joan. "Where were you anyway?"

Adam had formulated an amusing anecdote to account for his absence, but Joan was looking more than a little irritated. He squeezed his chair between them in a welter of competing feelings: Resentment (Joan could have waited for me); Embarrassment (what an idiot to get locked in the archive); and Incredulity. He wasn't sure if his eyes had deceived him, but from outside it had appeared that she was kissing Rudy. Oh, surely not. The window was smeary with steam. He must have misperceived.

Rudy pushed one of the beers in his direction. Adam sipped warily, noticing that Rudy was still rather handsome. In his youth he must have turned heads. But he did not appear flustered as a man with a guilty conscience might have been.

"Sorry you missed the show," said Rudy. "Foregone conclusion, of course. A new Leonardo painting! Quite the event. The experts droned on a lot, but on the whole it was rather entertaining."

"I had a bit of a mishap and couldn't make it."

"Nothing serious, I hope."

"No. Not serious at all. More like ludicrous." Adam now told his well-crafted, amusing version of being locked in the archive, omitting his moments of panic and his stealthy criminality at the copy machine. He was gratified when Rudy laughed appreciatively and followed with an account of his own about once getting stuck in an airplane toilet. Adam laughed heartily in turn, the shared embarrassment putting him at ease. Joan smiled, her irritation receding.

Adam drained his glass. There was another full mug on the counter and he reached for that one too. Rudy watched the level of what he had imagined would be his welcome second begin to drop. He was thinking of that kiss. The sudden warmth of Joan's mouth against his cheek had unsettled him. In different circumstances it might have been promising, but he suspected that this had been only a friendly, passionless kiss. Rudy could feel himself slipping towards his own private gloom.

Maybe Joan had just been reaching for her purse, thought Adam. No kiss at all. Surely Rudy did not represent competition for Joan's affection. He is just a friend. Oh, and so much older. Too old.

The three of them gave up trying to talk in the increasing noise of the crowd and finished their beers in silence, each lost in thought. The lines at the toilets were too long to wait. They bid each other good night, shook hands in a resolutely friendly manner, and set off in their different directions for home.

I'd better not take so much for granted, mused Adam as he and Joan trudged toward the bridge. Things have shifted since we arrived. Was that really a kiss? Oh, what does it matter? People kiss all the time. A friendly gesture. His thoughts returned to Gorski and the diary and his surreptitiously copied pages, and a pang of conscience surfaced. He still hadn't told

Joan about the diary, and he didn't want to confess the improper copying.

He decided that there was no need to clutter her attention at the moment by disclosing the fresh news of his own discoveries. And in fact what had he found? The faded journal of an unimportant man. What was that in comparison to a work by Leonardo da Vinci? He was both annoyed that his small discovery was overshadowed and relieved that he could hide in that shadow for a while longer, keeping his find and his furtive actions to himself.

"I'm really glad you came here with me, Joan," said Adam. "Sometimes it still surprises me that you did."

"Well, I was kind of surprised to be asked," she replied, a little taken aback by this declaration, "but I'm glad I came too."

"I'm sorry that we've had so little time together. I think you've seen more of Poland than I have."

"Most certainly I have!"

"But I really appreciate it that you've left me to my work." Joan's ironic expression told him that he had wrongfooted his expression of gratitude. "That didn't come out right. I mean, that you have understood why I have to spend so much time working."

"Well, frankly, I don't understand completely. This is a wonderful place. Don't you think you would understand your man Gorski better if you were to know more about his country?"

Adam felt a qualm, and his now chronic anxiety rose. He pushed it down.

Joan continued: "You should have come with me to see at least a few things, like the huge salt mine at Wieliczka. It's a strange place. Unbelievably extensive and full of carvings. There's even a whole chapel carved from salt."

"I know. I've seen the pictures. And you brought me that souvenir." A little salt carving of a dragon now sat on his desk. He told himself he could read about such places.

"I'll go with you again, if you want. Come on, just one day?"

"Maybe. I'll think about it."

Of course, he would not come.

19

Cloak and Dagger

It was warm in the old restaurant bar. Pawel Radincki settled against the worn velvet cushions of his high-backed chair and slowly savored his coffee. He was fond of this place with its prewar ambiance of faded elegance and leisure. It possessed the kind of atmosphere where one could imagine that displaced aristocrats, film stars, and café society intellectuals might gather for a relaxing evening over a drink listening to music. Or at least they might have done so in Paris in 1927. He had placed his order in Polish with a faint French accent, as he imagined that the gentry of the last century might have spoken.

Near the bar a man in a dinner jacket played a gleaming grand piano, its lid lowered to muffle the sound and to provide a space for a vase of trembling red roses. The rack of glasses over the bar glittered. There were candles on the tables in etched glass lanterns, and the high ceiling was lit by four branched crystal chandeliers with dozens of tiny lamps. A few of them had burnt out. This did not bother Pawel, for he now considered the desire for perfection a sign of nouveau riche anxiety. The true aristocrat with his distinguished pedigree honors age and cares little for trifles. The subdued strains of one of Chopin's slower preludes drifted across the room.

Usually Bodie was on time. Pawel knew he must be nearby, because his coat (a badly chosen jacket with a sports insignia) was draped over the seat behind him, and there was a half-drunk beer flattening on the table. Although so far Bodie had done everything according to plan and without undue questioning, Pawel wouldn't put it past him to lurk around and try to catch a glimpse of the face of the man who had hired him. Pawel was getting warm, but he kept his jacket on because its padded shoulders effectively disguised his own shape. The ring with its carefully designed crest was again turned to face his palm. Pawel opened his hand just far enough to let the candlelight glimmer through the amber. He had been rubbing the gold with fine abrasives to dull the gleam of the new finish. Now it spoke of ages it had never seen.

He reached for the salt cellar and removed it from its rack next to a matching bottle of pepper and a lidded bowl of sugar. Idly he tapped the contents around the glass shaker, watching the white grains shift smoothly, sensuously, rippling in soft patterns as he tilted the container back and forth. A little spilled onto the table. He tossed a pinch over his left shoulder, though he disguised the act to seem as if he were flicking crumbs from his lapel.

Salt. Even ordinary table salt. It had such an innocent, domestic whiteness. Here on this table, it was just an ordinary object in a container matched by hundreds, thousands, of others. Once so precious it was guarded, salt had become utterly routine. How easy to forget its power. To forget its ubiquity in the earth, in the sea. In the blood.

Just looking at the tiny glimmering grains in the glass shaker, Pawel could conjure the taste of salt on his tongue, the taste of larger crystals, harsh and sharp. The sensuous memory made him young again, remembering the Friday evenings when his grandmother sprinkled salt in every corner of their tiny cottage, then lined up the members of her family and placed a small bit of salt on each of their tongues. When it dissolved on his chapped lips it stung.

"This will scare away the demons!" she would say. And then she crossed herself twice, the second time in that peculiar swirling pattern, and mumbled a verse quickly, indistinctly. She assured them it was not a prayer, just an old custom.

He recalled the murmured incantation: *In fire I bloom, in water I flow, in blood I abide and avail.*

Perhaps it was only the few old women like his grandmother who remembered the ancient power of salt. Little Pawel had pestered her to teach him her prayers, but she insisted they weren't prayers at all and he should listen to the priest.

In fire I bloom. In water I flow,

In his hit-or-miss student days, for he was largely self-educated, he had found a few books that shed some light on ancient salt rituals. Still later he stumbled upon alchemical texts. The symbols of Paracelsus had been revelatory. His wonderful ring featured one for salt, a circle divided by a horizontal line. Signifying one of the three primes, a basic element of transformation. Signifying just about anything he wanted it to, in fact. Including the ritual that the legendary Prince Bronislaw had employed so effectively with a charmed cup—first cast from silver that, it was said, was mined by demons, then destroyed in fire and reborn in art.

In blood I abide and avail.

It was his friend in Paris, the fellow exile and self-anointed heir to the throne of Ruthenia, who planted the idea that he needed a family crest for his ring. The King of Ruthenia had his own: a cockatrice mounted over a complicated set of quarterings. Somewhere in their conversations it had occurred to Pawel that the Radincki crest—his version of it—should feature the sign for salt. He played with a set of symbols appropriate for a declining family whose power was waning and whose offshoots died in increasing obscurity. Into this heraldic mishmash he wove the sign for salt. Pawel smiled as he imagined how the King of Ruthenia would soon react to the results of his carefully designed plan.

The thought reminded him of the absent Bodie.

Pawel set down the salt shaker and glanced around the room. He had let his attention wander. Dangerous, this lapse of vigilance.

He felt rather than saw Bodie slide into the seat behind him, and he worried that the man had been watching as he played with the salt shaker. Neither said anything until the waitress came and inquired after their needs. No food, but Pawel nodded for more coffee. Bodie ordered another beer. They were the only two men seated on this narrow side of the room.

"Vous êtes en retard."

By turning his head and speaking towards the window, Pawel could hide the movement of his lips. His voice slid across the glass to the man seated behind him.

"I was here on time," said Bodie. "But I had to go for a piss. It doesn't matter. No one noticed, did they?"

Pawel didn't care for his subordinate declaring what did and what did not matter. He lowered his voice to a sterner register.

"You had better watch the clock for the next stage of the proceedings. If you are late at any point, you will risk the operation."

"Nothing to worry about."

They spoke in French. Bodie's Quebecois accent grated on his Paris-habituated ears, but Pawel's English was not good enough to sustain the pose of a suave businessman, one with connections to the anonymous personage who supposedly was the mastermind behind the task before them.

The waitress came with a large glass of beer and set it in front of Bodie. Pawel watched the man's reflection relayed through an odd set of angles from one dark window to another window set in the adjacent wall. He had discovered this peculiar viewing strategy by accident some weeks ago, and it had signaled to him the perfect meeting place where he could see the other man without himself being scrutinized. He watched Bodie reach for the beer awkwardly with his left hand. The liquid slopped over the edge of the glass a little. Was that left? With the multiple reflections, it was hard to tell the left from the right side of the image, but surely that wasn't the hand that Pawel had watched Bodie use earlier when he had unfolded and counted the first wad of bills.

"What happened to your hand?" he asked.

Bodie seemed unsurprised that his employer could see his clumsy left-handed manipulations.

"It's my shoulder. Badly bruised."

"And how did that happen?"

"Didn't Keith tell you when he gave you the mold of that lock? I stood up too fast under that cabinet when we went to extract the impression. Hit my shoulder getting up. Hurt like hell. Thanks for your concern." The irony fell flat.

"I hope it won't hinder the rest of the operation," said Pawel. "You will need your muscles."

"No problem. And anyhow, Keith has muscles to spare. Most of them in his head." He waited to hear a responsive laugh, but Pawel wasn't in the mood for wit.

"Here is the rest of the plan," said Pawel. "Do exactly as I say and your part of the operation will be complete."

Pawel had distilled his instructions to the simplest, minimal steps. He repeated them three times until Bodie said yes, yes, he understood. As a signal that their exchange was complete, Pawel readied himself to leave, though he would not in fact depart until the other was safely out of sight.

But then Bodie added: "Listen, I'm not too clear about something."

Pawel had expected more demands for money. He had an answer ready. But he was not prepared for what was to come.

"Did Keith tell you what happened when I had this accident? That we were seen?"

No, Keith had not. At least, not so that Pawel had understood. That brief exchange had taken place in rapid, stuttering English that Pawel had not followed very well. Keith lacked the aplomb of his artful partner, and his nervous stammer had attracted attention in the restaurant. In conformity with Bodie's instructions, Keith spoke to the man behind him without turning around. Unlike Bodie, however, he had sat upright staring straight ahead, so he appeared to be dementedly talking to himself. Pawel had cut the conversation short. At least, Keith had managed to pass the key mold to the table behind him with sufficient stealth, and with that precious object in his possession, Pawel had not been in the mood to pay attention to much else. In retrospect that was an error, for apparently he had missed something important.

"Tell me again," said Pawel, mustering a cold, commanding tone. "In detail."

After Bodie finished, there was a long and unpleasant pause during which Pawel felt dread upwelling. That woman, the intrusive museum guard who had recognized him — or thought she had — was now a double threat. Their inopportune meeting, her tenacious memory. The disowned past intruded dreadfully into his future.

"So, is this a problem?" asked Bodie, uncomfortable at the silence behind him. "I mean, the next part of the operation isn't connected, right?"

Pawel was choked with dismay. Anxiety washed through him and mixed with fury. It would be wrong to be halted in his tracks at this point. Unjust. He could not be stopped by this inconvenient woman. He hoped that his denial when she identified him had been persuasive, but she hadn't looked convinced. How could she have recognized him after all these years? *How could she!*

But she had. And she had stood at the window watching him.

And now she knew something else about that particular exhibit. Something that very soon could jeopardize all of his hard work. That could stand in the way of his rightful destiny.

In a welter of consternation he tried to imagine how to placate her. To remove her from Krakow. To buy her silence. Or to silence her another way. He was not sure he had the stomach for an absolute solution. But Bodie, perhaps Bodie did.

Pawel felt a stir of hope born of terrible opportunity.

"I mean, we'll be in another part of the museum, won't we," Bodie added, feigning nonchalance.

"And are you quite sure you were never seen in the Painting Gallery as well?" When Pawel found his voice he was surprised how calm he sounded. "If she saw you in one place she might have recognized you in the other."

Bodie could not be sure. The guards who tramped the halls of the museum all dressed alike, and there were several heavyset, middle aged women among them. Or maybe there was just the one and he hadn't bothered to mark her features. Even as he tried to reassure Pawel, he realized that he and Keith might have been more careless than they had thought. Doubt crept into his voice.

Pawel was thinking very fast. The next stages of his plan were still incomplete, and over the past few days he had begun to recognize that there might be some gaps in his scheme, some pitfalls that he had not anticipated. And only one of them was the possibility that someone would recognize him from the old days — from another life altogether.

"I mean, I just thought you ought to know." Bodie continued, still straining for a casual tone. "Keith isn't the brightest lad. I wanted to make sure that you knew all the details. But perhaps it wasn't worth mentioning." Bodie made as if to go, gulping the last of his beer, glancing at the check, starting to rise.

Pawel's thoughts still weltered in disorder, but although he was not quite ready to speak, a decision had to be made.

"Sit down." He was pleased at how authoritative and stern the words sounded.

Bodie sat.

"In fact, this changes everything," Pawel said. "I'm afraid you have added to your tasks. There is one more thing that you must now do. And soon."

20

Best Laid Plans

There were to be three thefts from the Radincki Museum, but only one of them would make the news.

Ever since the authentication of the Leonardo panel, the museum had been swarming with visitors. There were queues waiting for the doors to open in the mornings, and late in the day, a tired line of people descended the long steps. A print run of reproductions and postcards had to be quickly reordered for the gift shop. By the Florianska Gate, the street artists added their own renditions of the *Salvator Mundi* to their repertoires, and tourists bought them while the paint was still sticky.

The papers ran the full text of the press release from the museum in a special issue, plus a long interview with Jurgen de Mul by an enterprising reporter who had followed him to the airport for a few final remarks. Only the very attentive or the perennially skeptical would have wondered if perhaps the distinguished expert's opinions were hedged with overtones of caution.

"I wonder if he's having second thoughts," mused Rudy. He noted with a dash of envy that Jurgen's photograph made him look at least ten years younger than Rudy knew him to be.

"He certainly sounded positive enough," said Joan. They were having coffee today just inside the door of the little café at the corner of the Rynek. A brisk wind was blowing a misty rain sideways, and the outdoor area was closed. She shivered.

"Don't you ever get cold?" She asked somewhat peevishly.

"What? Oh, well, move over here if it's too chilly there by the door." He still frowned at the paper.

"You're certainly puzzling over that article a long time. What else does it say?"

"Nothing much. You got the gist. Here, take this section with you. Are you still thinking of writing a piece about the authentication? No? Well, perhaps enough has been written already. Adam can read the text to you if you want a more precise translation. He's the Polish expert." He extracted the pages with the interview and handed them to Joan.

"Adam doesn't consider himself much of an expert these days, I'm afraid," Joan sighed, folding the paper into a square and slipping it into her bag. "I feel sorry for him. In fact, I'm worried. Except for the other night when we had an unusually nice evening, he's done little but sit in that library since we got here. He might as well have never left home."

"So his work isn't going well? I thought he sounded excited about it the last time we spoke."

"He has finally found a set of papers that interest him and that he thinks could be important. But it is taking him a very long time to read them, and I think he is making himself ill. I haven't been able to persuade him to take a real break for a long time, and he gets irritated when I suggest it."

Joan added some grains of sugar to the dregs at the bottom of her cup and stirred them slowly into a sweet sludge. She was sad that Adam's companionship had retreated again after a brief renewal. Perhaps it was his work that preoccupied him, but she was fairly certain that he was also having second thoughts about his feelings for her. Her own feelings were also shifting. She had looked forward to a sojourn in Poland with him, but Adam showed little interest in accompanying her on her tours, even on the weekends when he could not sequester himself in the archives. Her adventurous spirit even seemed to annoy him these days. The next few weeks could be difficult.

"That's too bad. Krakow is a wonderful place. A pity to spend it all in books. Oh, damn!" Rudy shot his wrist out of his jacket and looked at his watch with annoyance. "Speaking of books, I have a lecture coming up. I'm filling in for a colleague. Afraid I have to go."

"See you later," said Joan. She watched Rudy lope out into the rain, the remainder of his folded newspaper a makeshift umbrella, and thought how much younger he seemed than Adam these days.

***

At that very moment Adam, tucked into his usual table by the window on the top floor of the archives, had put down his pencil and was rubbing the top knuckle of his third finger. In the last two months it had developed a hard edge where the thickening callus was squeezed towards the nail by his tense and constant writing. It made his finger look arthritic, a flash forward to the way it might become in later years.

What is more his back hurt, and when he stood up he was aware of a stoop in his posture. The previous day while walking home, he had glanced at a shop window just as the light fell against the surface, making it a perfect mirror of the passing crowd. There he thought he saw his father. Startled, he looked around to locate the familiar face, only belatedly realizing that it was his own image reflected there.

Joan is right, he thought. I really need to get out of here for a while. Perhaps this coming weekend they could take a walk and visit a museum. A different museum, that is. He was heartily sick of the Radincki. Or there might be a chamber concert at one of the churches.

Joan. He still thought she might be a woman he could love, but in the past few weeks he had begun to feel that despite living together for almost three months, he knew her less well than he ought. Can one love without truly knowing a person? Whatever the nature of his feelings, their exploration would have to be postponed.

For there was this troublesome diary. The slender journal appeared to cover less than a year, but he had managed to get through only about a quarter of it, including some eye-straining work with the contraband copied pages he had taken home. As he feared, they had been of limited help. The photocopy he had coaxed from the temperamental machine was much harder to decode than the original. Not only were the copies uneven and faint, the machine had picked up particles of dust and printed them as though they were accent marks and letter components, completely scrambling some of the words. His pulse began to flutter as he counted the few weeks remaining for his work.

The museum was open all weekend to let tourists gawk at that painting. How unreasonable that the archive was closed on Saturday and Sunday. And then the whole place was shut tight on Monday in that ridiculous practice of museums. Adam forgot for a moment his resolve to take a break and fumed with frustration at the thought of the empty three days ahead of him. Once more he bent his head over the little book and picked up his pencil. His finger protested, his back hurt. On one of those dreary winter mornings long ago, Gorski himself might have written under even more trying circumstances. The thought was some comfort.

***

Pawel Radincki carefully timed his appearance among the swarm of visitors that came to see the Leonardo panel. It was his second visit since the authentication, and he hoped that he would not be noticed. His confidence had been shaken by the guard and her unfortunate memory, but he told himself that if he were to let someone so insignificant alter his movements, he would not be worthy of the man—the personage—he hoped to become.

In time, the museum planned to house the painting in a room all its own. But that renovation lay in the future, and the panel still hung in the large gallery. Between the theatrical ascension of a saint and a landscape with horses fleeing a distant battle, the *Salvator Mundi* glowed under its special light. Four brass standards and a velvet rope barrier erected in front of the painting bestowed the look of an altar—an accidental but appropriate effect.

With its large protective frame and climate control monitor, the picture looked heavy. Pawel estimated it weighed at least twenty kilos, maybe a good deal more, depending on the composition of the backing. He hoped that he was right about the mountings and that Bodie had secured appropriate tools. The man's bruised shoulder was a problem but not one that Pawel was in any position to address. Keith was there to do the heavy lifting.

The crowd was impatient this morning. Pawel inserted himself at the side of the cluster and took advantage of the surging press of viewers to feign a stumble and reach out across the velvet barrier to catch his balance, thrusting his hand against the wall near the picture. He recovered his equilibrium and stood upright immediately as if chagrined at his clumsiness. The crowd backed up respectfully, suddenly aware of the admonishing gaze of Christ. A man next to him apologized for the accidental push, and Pawel graciously smiled. My fault entirely, he assured. Such a crush, isn't it?

No alarms had gone off when he steadied himself against the wall. If there was to be an electronic security system sensitive to proximity, it was still in the planning stages. Still, he would have to guess which circuit to disable in the antiquated electrical box just in case there were hidden wires. When it was his turn to shuffle into the optimum viewing position, Pawel admired the panel with carefully posed serenity. So far, so good.

He then strolled through the high galleries, stopping to admire various items before leaving for the day. His heart was thudding rather uncomfortably, and he kept checking to make sure that the annoying guard was not in his vicinity. He had remembered her name: Klementyna Kamynska. Some fragment of the past had surfaced, and he recollected her bulky frame standing by his mother as the latter moved her mop over the floors of the museum. All grownups look more or less the same to a child, and before she had made her unwelcome approach, he could not have picked this woman from a crowd. Yet clearly she did remember him.

When his grandmother was not available to look after him, little Pawel had sometimes scampered around the huge halls as his mother cleaned. It had all been so long ago. Another lifetime. No one should have recognized that little boy in the man today. He had remade himself. That was the injustice. He was a different man today from the long-ago boy. She should not have known him at all.

Maybe, he thought with faint hope, just maybe the guard who had spotted Bodie and Keith during their clumsy exit wasn't Kamynska at all. Bodie's description certainly sounded like her, but all these uniformed women looked similar. His stomach turned at the thought of the trouble she could cause.

It was risky, but on his way out Pawel could not resist paying a furtive visit to the annex gallery. As he approached the hallway, a woman exited. She gave him a nod, and he nodded back courteously. Then alone, he gazed at the Bronislaw chalice with more avidity than he would have liked to be witnessed. He noted again that the copy he had ready at home was not as exact as he had thought it would be, but surely no one would notice the substitution of such a minor item in the museum's vast collection anyway. Not with everything else that would be going on. Not for a very long time at least. For a certainty no one would notice.

But who would have anticipated that Klementyna Kamynska would recognize him? And moreover, that she would have seen him here — in this very gallery before this very object. Of all the acres of artifacts housed in the Radincki Museum, what nasty twist of fortune had dictated that she confront him here? And would her adhesive memory direct suspicion to a part of the museum that ought to be entirely overlooked when the drama of his great plan was enacted?

The time was short. She absolutely must be dealt with before too long. He hoped he had been quite clear about this to Bodie, though he was having difficulty recalling exactly what he had said.

***

The museum was closing, along with the archives. The few remaining scholars stowed away their materials on their assigned carts, and the librarian bid them goodbye as he wheeled everything back into the labyrinthine recesses of the storage area. Adam snapped his briefcase shut and wished him a good evening.

Gorski's diary had slid almost invisibly between his papers. The bulk that it added to the briefcase was imperceptible.

He could hardly believe he was doing this. His head felt tight, as though the air inside a balloon were pressing its container to the breaking point. His feet walking down the corridor to the exit were unusually far away. Right, left, right, left. So remote. The very breath of his lungs seemed locked at the top of his chest.

As he passed through the tall doors and out into the darkening afternoon, Adam felt as he had once long ago when exploring a cave. The space was tighter than anticipated, and at one terrible juncture he had squeezed through an opening so narrow it took his breath away. The recollection of that moment skittered across his mind as he exited the museum and made his way down the steps to the pavement. He hoped to feel the same expanding relief that he had when he escaped from the cave, but his heart was pounding terribly.

He would return it, of course. There was no question of theft. No question. He just needed a little more time with it.

But his knees began to wobble as he reached the street, and there were tiny lights dancing across his vision. The familiar pain clenched below his ribs, and Adam knew that he wouldn't make it home in this state. He turned abruptly to the right and trotted in increasing discomfort up Grodzka Street and into the Rynek. He just made it down the stairs to the men's restroom in the Sukiennice before vomiting out the thin stream of sour bile left from breakfast. He sat for several minutes on the toilet as his bowels emptied in gushes of diarrhea, and he wondered unhappily if this humiliating ailment was a just punishment for what he was becoming.

21

Rightful Heir

Pawel Meyer had come by his obsession with the Radincki Museum from an early age, for he had grown up with tales of a distant great-grandmother seduced by a dissolute nobleman and had embroidered a sketchy family legend into a genealogy. His fevered imagination was further bolstered when he learned that he had been conceived within the mighty precincts of the museum. The furtive act that brought him into being had taken place in one of the many sleeping chambers now open to visitors, and there was a bed on display in that room whose four posts of carved ebony supported hangings of velvet and gold-threaded silk. On the equally venerable Turkey carpet, Pawel's mother had met her lover, who removed the trousers of his guard's uniform and tossed them over a gilded chair before kneeling for a quick and chilly coupling with the cleaning woman.

Pawel had been fifteen when his mother, ill in body and beginning to wander in her mind, had taken him with her for a final round of mopping as her employment with the museum drew to its close. She had pointed out the bedroom to him, adding to his fantasy and planting the seed of a lifelong yearning. Pawel had gazed with wonder at the place of his conception (or slightly above the exact place, as he fixed his eyes upon the bed rather than the carpet) and felt within him the stirrings of a reclaimable identity.

As a child his slender frame had separated him from his robust cousins, providing hopeful evidence of an ancestor whose aristocratic genes had surfaced in his own delicate physique. His grandmother had once referred to him as a changeling, and although she intended derision, he was secretly pleased. It was only after his mother had been dead for some years that Pawel found himself in a position to pursue the possibility that his origins were something other than they seemed. A lucky sojourn as a dance partner on a Baltic cruise ship smoothed out the rougher edges of his manners, and before he was much more than twenty, he presented a suave, near courtly, appearance. Older women found him charming, a trait that had netted him his wife. Like an intelligent sponge, Pawel absorbed what he needed from the styles of others.

His mother had been brutally honest about his paternity in the belief that a boy ought to know his father, even if the father might not be too cheated in missing out on knowledge of his son. Therefore, Pawel harbored no illusions about his immediate family. He sought instead to fill in the blanks of a more distant and romantic past, pressing beyond the obvious to discover some deeper connection to the museum. That his mother had been a poorly paid member of the cleaning staff was of little consequence. There must be a bond stronger than that. Or so he convinced himself, and in her frail dotage she came to agree, conjuring likely progenitors that became more and more real with each indulgence in fantasy. Pawel imaginatively identified one of the more disreputable Radinckis, a dandy of the previous century, as the probable ancestor who had conducted a liaison with a great-great-grandmother, ultimately to produce the remaining scion of a once-noble family: Himself.

Additional evidence of connection with the former palace was a key that came to him on his mother's death. A large, iron key with a crenulated head, a decoratively grooved shank, and a looped finial. It was ancient, heavy, and mysterious, and Pawel kept it in a velvet-lined box under his silk ties. It fit the door to the Radincki Museum that had permitted his mother entry for Sunday night cleaning, not to mention her illicit romance; and after she died, no one on the museum staff thought to ask for it back. That door had fallen out of use and was now all but hidden behind a large utility bin positioned to receive building detritus during one of the renovations undertaken before the change of government. In the tumult of the 1980s, interest in such expenditures had waned, and the large receptacle became a fixture that, because it was so massive, was seldom emptied. A zealously incompetent repair of an overhanging eave had left the door even more obscured, and it was a safe bet that Pawel was the only one now who even remembered its existence.

***

It was a moonless night and densely dark behind the museum, for the huge building blocked the lights from the street, and the adjacent section of the Planty was edged by remnants of the old fortified wall. Though the rain had stopped, a mist was rising from the river and turning the air opaque.

The three men arrived punctually and according to plan. All wore black; all were masked. The masks were at Pawel's insistence, for in addition to being stylistically de rigueur for the occasion, he did not want his henchmen to be able to recognize him in the future. Bodie and Keith itched beneath their woolen ski masks, while Pawel sported a fancy-dress affair that the King of Bohemia might have worn at his first meeting with Sherlock Holmes. Pawel was the slimmest and had no difficulty slipping behind the bin. Bodie and Keith jammed themselves beside him, for only there were they completely hidden from sight.

The beam from Pawel's pen light was narrow and strong. He handed it to Bodie while he manipulated the ancient key. The lock was stiff, although he had been priming it with oil for the last few weeks. After some minutes of strenuous effort the bolt slid back with a small thud. There was some frantic pulling impeded by the narrow space until Pawel recalled that the tall door opened inward. Still, it required Keith's solid shoulder against the heavy wood, its planks blackened with age and braced with iron straps, before it could be persuaded to open. The hinges protested with a shuddering scrape, and all three froze in silence to listen for inquisitive footsteps. Fine particles of rust sifted down around the door jamb.

"All clear," whispered Pawel. "The guard's room is on the other side. Come on."

He entered the building, virtually black inside, pausing only to place a well-worn suitcase near the wall. With his back to the others, he removed an object and secreted it beneath his light jacket before either could see what he held. They would not notice the bulge in the dark. He closed the case, stood, and gestured towards it with a pointing finger. Bodie nodded. Then they were off.

Pawel led the way with his pen light dancing along their crooked path, followed by Bodie, then Keith, who, unable to understand their terse French exchanges, simply trotted behind. Keith was both excited and numb, and his breath was shallow in his throat. It was not his first experience of breaking and entering, but the scale of this job was far larger than anything he had attempted before. He did not admit how nervous he was. Bodie got testy with such confessions.

Pawel, who had spent his childhood exploring the labyrinthine halls of the museum, led them quickly to the second floor. Bodie tried to keep track of the many turns, the two or three half stairs, and the seemingly purposeless doors that they went through. In spite of the fact that he had memorized the map of the exit strategy, he began to worry about finding his way back.

The top of the last staircase opened to a long landing rimmed with doors and high transoms. At this point the two henchmen were commanded to wait, and Pawel disappeared down a staircase. And then it was so easy, so absurdly easy, to locate the ancient fuses and one new circuit breaker amidst the dusty tangle of wiring. Pawel hoped that it controlled only the new security system—assuming there was one—and that the lights in the guards' room would not go out as well. He threw the switch and scampered back upstairs. All was quiet.

The night lights of the museum were dim. Bodie and Keith stepped cautiously into the room. Pawel tapped them on the shoulders and pointed at his watch. He had estimated the guard's surprisingly casual rounds would give them three-quarters of an hour, but he did not say that to the other two men. Twenty minutes maximum, he had said, fifteen until the distracting moment he had planned. So work fast and be prepared.

And then, after signaling with an upraised hand and a stab of his finger, Pawel disappeared back down the stairs. Bodie and Keith were on their own.

Bodie figured he was heading to one of those cases full of jewelry with a key made from that pestiferous gel mold. The jewels of princes, the gems of bishops. Whoever had owned those treasures, Bodie was sure they were now destined for a high-class fence. There was no time to follow, but he would return before long and see just what was missing. Amateur, he thought, to think he could fool me. But his scoffing train of thought was overridden by the job at hand.

The two men skulked along the walls until they arrived at the small painting with its special lighting. The face of Christ gazed at them, his hand upraised, his smile knowing and nasty. Keith felt a chill run down his spine. Strange how some pictures looked at you. This one appeared ready to speak.

"I don't like this," he began, but he was hushed with a sharp punch from Bodie, who made a zipping motion with his hand across his mouth, and then a more ominous slicing motion across his neck. This caused Keith to remember the additional job that they might now have to do. His throat constricted. Maybe it won't come to that, he thought hopefully.

Bodie lifted the felt bag from Keith's shoulder and laid it carefully on the floor. The tools were wrapped to keep them from clanking, but from now on they would have to take extra caution. The silence of the gallery was their enemy; it would magnify the smallest clink.

Bodie located the tools to release the locking bolts and took them out of the bag. While Keith stood to one side bracing the heavy glass case, Bodie jimmied the bolts from the edges. Each corner gave up its fastener with surprising speed, and he put the freed hardware in his pockets. But the painting was still secure. He raised his eyebrows at Keith, who tested the solidity of the connection with the external frame and shook his head. Bodie shone the pen light around the edges and saw that he had missed four additional bolts, more recessed and exceedingly awkward to reach. His sore shoulder protested, and he spent a precious minute positioning himself correctly so that he could insert the proper tool. He glanced at his watch. Eleven minutes had already passed.

**

Pawel Radincki flitted through the dark, narrow basement rooms to another stair just below the gallery annex. Like a shadow, light-footed and fleet, like he had finally come home, he raced in breathless, exhilarated silence. He felt electric, so full of energy that he might carry the whole museum away. He turned quickly, and his hip connected sharply with a stair rail, but it would be morning before he would feel the bruise. He flew up the steps, opened the last door, and paused, anticipating the moment so fervently that he had to quell the desire to delay and savor it. A glance at his watch confirmed the need for speed.

He entered the little gallery where Saints Bartholomew and Gertruda held vigil. Light from a street lamp cast its faint beam through the window of the outer hall. He positioned himself under the end of the vitrine and inserted the small key, so skillfully replicated by the Warsaw locksmith, into the underside of the glass case. He had been unable to test this part of the operation, and he held his breath.

The lock resisted him. His fingers played with it, cajoling, caressing, pleading. Surely he would not be halted at this final moment. It was difficult to find the right place where the tiny bolts would separate, and his hands were sweating in their leather gloves. He did not want to remove them, but finally he took off the right glove and wiped his hand on his trousers. He took care to touch nothing but the key, and he commenced the delicate insertion again. Perhaps the mold had not caught the lock properly, or maybe the locksmith had made a small error. But it was impossible that his quest be halted here on the brink of success. Impossible. He found himself praying, raising his eyes in supplication to Saint Gertruda.

From that day forever forth, she would be the recipient of his candles. The key turned with a little whisper of acceptance, and he scooted out from under the cabinet and raised the lid.

He almost wept as he lifted the chalice and held it cradled in his hands. He removed the replica from the inner pocket of his jacket—remembering just in time to put on his right glove again—and placed it inside the vitrine. It felt lighter than the original, Even in the dim light, Pawel could see that the figures of the stem did not precisely match the original. But the discrepancies did not worry him greatly any longer, for he reminded himself once more that this item was a minor possession of the museum. He was confident that the substitution would never be noticed.

That is, never be noticed unless someone associated the other theft, currently in progress, with an unexplained occurrence in this gallery. He willed the image of Klementyna Kamynska out of his mind.

Pawel carefully lowered the lid of the vitrine, and with equal precision he relocked the case. The key and the lock now seemed to know each other, and the lock slid shut without protest. He placed the chalice inside his jacket with the stem cradled snugly under his arm, and he hurriedly retraced his steps. The chalice warmed against his body, and Pawel had an exalted image of his heart's blood filling it with welcome.

As soon it would.

He was but a shadow by the door but Bodie saw him. All but the center bolt fastening the painting had been removed. Pawel raised his hand and pointed at his watch and then disappeared down the staircase silent as a hare.

At two o'clock precisely when the night was darkest and the trumpeter of St. Mary's had just begun his hourly hymn, there was a burst of noise in the street outside the Radincki Museum, followed by an extended series of pops like a string of firecrackers. The two guards on duty ran to the windows to investigate, and then they hurried outside to see what might lie beyond the little cloud of thick smoke. They never heard the sunder of wire and plaster as the *Salvator Mundi* relinquished its final locking mounts, tilted, and dove away from the wall.

"Jesus this is heavy!" exclaimed Keith in a throat-scraping exhalation.

Bodie's injured shoulder nearly gave out as he tried to hold up his side and keep the protective frame from crashing to the floor with its precious contents. They rested the picture against the wall while he picked up the tools and stowed them in his padded jacket. They worked quickly, and for once it was Keith who shushed the grunts of pain emitted by his companion. Bodie just managed to recall the dizzying set of exit instructions. The picture was far heavier than it looked, and his shoulder ached. But they made it to the basement after only one wrong turn that required brief backtracking. The little panel was removed from the heavy protective frame. Keith was clumsy, and the casing cracked under pressure from the crowbar at its edge, scattering wicked shards of glass. The painting slid into the suitcase still standing by the door, and the smile of the world's savior disappeared under a pile of socks and pajamas.

When they opened the door and stuck their heads out cautiously, a figure separated from the dark shape of the dumpster. Pawel slid behind them, and they heard the key turn again in the heavy iron lock. Without a word, Pawel took the suitcase, turned, and melted into the night. Bodie and Keith removed their masks and cut across a shadowed section of the Planty, and by the time they reached the large street beyond, they strolled like tourists having a late amble through town. Bodie lit a cigarette and tried to ignore his shoulder. He had to growl at Keith, who was inclined to hurry. Undue speed at the stage of the game would only give them away. Behind them, they heard a clutch of police investigating the small explosions in the garbage can at the side of the museum entrance. They couldn't understand what was being said, but the voices did not sound unduly concerned. It was safe to surmise that the theft had not yet been discovered.

Pawel heard them too. Without his mask but with his collar raised over his chin—not unusual on a chilly night—he walked like a man with no purpose other than to return home after a weekend out of town. The suitcase knocked against his knees, now shaky after the intensity of the last hour, but the chalice was warm next to his chest. It was bulky and awkward under his jacket, but Pawel felt secure in the thought that it was rightly his. Finally. His breathing was even and normal again, and the mist that was gathering more densely over the city emboldened him to double back and pass near enough to the museum to catch a few sentences before the police dispersed. He was pleased to note that students were being targeted as the likely pranksters. A sharp gunpowder smell mingled with the acrid scent of the damp city.

The guards returned to their stations. The museum was quiet again. The damp chill outside was penetrating the large halls, though their small sitting room was reasonably warm. They settled back wearily into their chairs. One brewed a new pot of coffee, the other riffled though a newspaper. Their comments about the incident were brief. Students were sometimes a rowdy lot, but they rarely caused serious damage. At least not since the government had changed. They looked at the clock: still almost four hours until the morning shift arrived. The incident had jogged a memory, and the older guard began to regale the younger one with tales of the Solidarity movement in the region. The younger man had heard most of this before, but he was a kind person and listened with polite interest.

It is hard to say what triggered their suspicions, but as one sipped coffee and the other stood to relieve a kink in his back, they suddenly looked at each other with simultaneous alarm, pausing for a long moment while thoughts clattered into place. Together, they ran to the Painting Gallery. In the low lights that afforded nighttime illumination, at first it seemed undisturbed. Then they switched on the long bank of overheads, and one by one the wide-rimmed lamps spread their glow. They hurried to the area that had been enshrined with special cordons, and there they stared aghast, too appalled to speak.

The escutcheons with the velvet ropes that should have stood before the *Salvator Mundi* had been neatly set to one side. And between the ascension of Saint Barbara and the Battle of Vienna, there was now only a blank wall pocked with ragged holes and a few splinters and plaster chips resting quietly on the floor.

22

The Wicked Flee

Krakow awoke to filthy smog. Polluted air collided with the vapor rising from the Vistula to produce a thick blanket of eye-stinging haze. The lights on the walls above Wawel hill had become mere smudges in the murk, matched with fainter reflected blurs in the river. By nightfall the immense castle would be utterly invisible.

But no fog however dense could hide the confusion boiling around the Radincki Museum. As Adam drew near, he could see an unusually large cluster of guards by the door. And not just guards; he also noticed the uniforms of police. He clutched his briefcase and felt his insides swoop as if he had dived off a precipice. It was impossible, yet it seemed he was discovered already. Gorski's diary shouted out from his briefcase: *Thief! Thief!* He hesitated in the middle of the street, caught somewhere between fleeing and confessing. At that moment he might casually have left the way other people were doing, shrugging their shoulders or looking mildly annoyed before leaving for another destination. But Adam remained frozen in place, fearing that if he moved, his suddenly liquid bowels might pour out and pool at his feet. Only a small part of his brain was alert enough to wonder at the improbability that an entire police force had been mustered for the theft of an obscure archival item. One of the guards was approaching him. Adam awaited him with helpless dread. The wicked flee when no man pursueth, but when someone does pursue, the wicked sometimes stand rooted to the spot.

"The museum is closed today, sir. I'm afraid you can't enter."

Closed? Adam stared dumbly. His hands cramped around his briefcase in a white-knuckled clutch. It was Tuesday, and he didn't think it was a holiday. He looked up the stairs. The tall doors stood open, but they were blocked by four guards in uniform. The man evidently thought he did not understand Polish, so he tried again in English: "Today no. Closed. Sorry." Then he turned to speak to someone else.

"Dlaczego?" Adam attempted. Why? But the sounds caught in his throat. He managed to move his feet, though his shoes felt gummy and inclined to stick between the cobblestones. He stumbled back to Grodzka Street. The fog seemed less dense here, although as he looked towards the Rynek, the flow of hurrying people rapidly dimmed and faded.

There were more men in uniform coming towards him carrying coffee in paper cups. As they approached, their faces became clearer, and Adam thought he recognized one of the museum guards. He fought another impulse to run, but his sense of being pursued was ebbing, replaced with a strong need to know what he was up against. He drew breath.

"Przepraszam Pana, dlaczego muzeum jest zamknięte?"

The guard hesitated, but then he recognized the American man who passed him daily in the hallway on his way to the museum's library wing. Adam's courteous good mornings now stood him in good stead. The theft hadn't been announced yet, and although it wasn't his place to do so, the guard indulged himself by passing on the terrible news.

Adam's shocked face was eloquent. The guard nodded gravely at him and hastened to catch up with his colleagues on their way back to work. The Leonardo panel stolen. Anyone would be dismayed.

Had he waited longer, however, he would have had a harder time decoding the expressions that passed across Adam's face.

There had been a theft.

Well, yes. Adam already knew that.

The painting by Leonardo da Vinci was stolen.

Oh.

The *Leonardo* stolen?

Not Gorski's diary but that little painting? All that fuss and now it was missing?

What a blessing!

Oh, of course no. How terrible.

But what luck! The diary was still his private guilty secret. Like a prisoner reprieved on the eve of execution, Adam was virtually lifted off his feet with relief.

He collapsed on a chair in a café and ordered a coffee. There was so much adrenaline stewing in his stomach that caffeine was the last thing he needed, but it was the easiest thing to order. And so common for the morning, unlike the vodka that he really wanted. When the coffee arrived, he had to wait until it was nearly cold before he could hold the cup without spilling.

His thoughts were assembling in more order now. His own theft—*borrowing*—had not been noticed yet. Maybe the painting's theft had even bought him greater opportunity to work on the diary at home. He still had time to rectify his misdeed, to finish with his work and replace the diary in the archive. In fact, he now vowed, he would do so as soon as possible and just work nonstop at the library until he was done. How foolish it had been to imagine that he might profit from violating the rules, and now fate had dealt him a sharp but merciful lesson. A close call, a narrow escape. And a lucky break thanks to this stolen painting. With all the fuss, no one would think of him.

But as his mind calmed it occurred to him that this other theft might not be so much a reprieve as another problem. The museum would surely now be closed for a time. Perhaps not for long, but when it opened, security might well be tightened. Adam had first intended to carry the diary back and forth for a few weeks, working both at home and in the archives until the pages gave up their secrets. He was a familiar figure now and passed through the doors and along the hallways without anything more than polite nods of greeting. But would that continue? Would he be able to slip the slim leather volume back into the archive, or would he be caught red-handed with it in his possession? Adam weighed the odds, deciding that the sooner he acted the better. He would enter as usual as though nothing were wrong. The archive surely would not be a focus of scrutiny. Trying to quell his anxiety, he began to walk home. The damp quickly penetrated his coat, and he became chilled to the bone, his hand locked around the handle of his briefcase, his movements mechanical, the soles of his feet numb against the uneven pressure of the cobbles.

***

From a high window in the museum, Klementyna Kamynska gazed down at the crowd filling the narrow street. Many had come to see the painting, and more were gathering as the word spread of its theft. This would certainly put the Radincki Museum on the map.

She had not been the only employee to wonder why the museum had not increased its security beyond that one electronic sensor, which evidently had been easily silenced.

There were criticisms and accusations flying around now, and she was glad that those decisions had been taken by officials way above her level of responsibility.

She watched two security guards on the street below change positions at a post by the steps. Some of the cleaning staff were outside having a smoke. And there was a familiar face. Little Pawel Meyer, all grown up now and pretending not to recognize her. Klementyna leaned closer to the window. She was sure it was he. What a snob he was to act as if he didn't know her. It might be fun to make him admit it.

On sunny mornings, the light glanced off the upper windows of the museum, preventing a clear view inside. But today the heavy mist blurring the air oddly had the opposite effect. The dim light of the interior set the items near the windows in clear relief, including the outline of a large woman. When Pawel raised his eyes for the kind of glance a passerby might cast on a scene of confusion, he met the gaze of Klementyna Kamynska. Startled, he stared at her in dismay.

It had been a mistake to come, but he could not resist. Now as this ominous form gazed down at him, he berated himself his carelessness. Perhaps he was mistaken, perhaps he was seeing things. He ventured another look up at the window. He did not look away fast enough, and as he turned to go, she caught his eye and gave a wicked, knowing smile.

Now it was clear what had to be done. And soon. He had to summon Bodie and make sure he understood.

As it happened, Bodie had his own cause for alarm. From a doorway niche he too watched the milling crowds that filled the street. Keith had marked how the eyes of paintings can seem to follow one. When the eyes watching you come from a person looking out a window, they too can seem to follow one. Even if they are looking at someone else. Bodie saw the eyes turn his way and in them he saw recognition. This can't be, he told himself. You're imagining things. But then his terrible qualm was confirmed by a nasty smile.

She knows, thought Bodie. That woman guard. She knows, and now she sees. Damn Keith. Damn him to bottomless hell. This is the last time I work with amateurs.

23

The Fog

On her frequent solitary walks, Joan had taken to resting in churches. No one seemed to care if one entered for prayer or confession or a service, to look curiously around, or just to sit quietly and think.

Today she sat in an ancient church dedicated to Saint Andrew. Before her rose a huge ironwork grill through which she could see a long aisle leading to the altar, permitting a glimpse of the divine while barring approach. The fog outside obscured any light that might have struggled through the narrow windows, and the feeble glow from the chandeliers was dispersed in vapor that permeated the space. From time to time the heavy door opened, causing the votives to flicker.

She had hoped that the atmosphere of meditation would help her unsettled mood. She was beset with a peculiar combination of aggravation and guilt. How convenient it had been to latch onto Adam's travels after the accident and her broken elbow, especially after her teaching contract for the fall had not materialized. She had turned the ill-luck into an opportunity to travel and had skipped continents with a man whom she found attractive and good company, but now who seemed to have drifted into a world apart. The romance that might have bloomed had instead dissipated, replaced with worry. She closed her eyes and willed herself calm. This is what prayer is for. Be still.

She was tired from several nights of poor sleep, and there was an interval when she wondered if she had fallen into a doze. Joan opened her eyes with a jerk and found that she was kneeling with her palms pressed against her face. She was freezing. She got up to leave and discovered that in the interim when her eyes were closed, others had entered the church. There was a kneeling man at the end of the row, and she had to make a circuit around the aisle so as not to disturb him. As she opened the door, more fog entered in a ghostly cloud.

***

The kneeling man was not so much praying as intoning a plea for divine intervention. Over and over he whispered: *Please, please, please*.

Keith couldn't finish the supplication. Guidance was not what he sought, for he knew what he would do. Like a soldier obeying a command, like a puppet without will, he knew that he would do as he was told. It fell to him to do it because it was his fault that it was necessary in the first place. Bodie had finally convinced him of that, and besides he was marooned in a foreign country where he knew no one else, and Bodie had the rest of the money and wouldn't turn it over until the awful deed was done. He would have to go along. But this was absolutely the last time, and he shot a prayer diagonally to the saint standing in the corner of the church with a promise: if you let me do this and it goes off okay, I won't ever sin again. Never. Not ever. Just let this be over. Or let it not happen at all. Please. Please. Please. Keith rocked back and forth. His final supplication was the wish that it be suddenly tomorrow with the dreadful night ahead already past.

He felt the row of seats shift as someone moved, and he opened his eyes. He hoped that he had not called attention to himself or accidentally spoken aloud. A woman was gathering her coat about her and leaving. So locked in his own mind had he been that Keith was startled to discover that another person had prayed alongside him. It was no comfort. No one else's troubles could weigh as heavily as his. He sat back, feeling the loneliness of sin.

As Joan crossed in front of him, he raised his head and caught a glimpse of her face. He gasped. She looked familiar to him: that crisply drawn profile, that long-lidded eye. It was she! That saint from the museum! Here in church, not in the museum sitting in her window. She must have followed him. She must have heard his prayer.

Could it be a sign? Was this the divine signal that he awaited? Could Saint Gertrude herself be offering him solace? Or was she warning him away? He struggled to his feet, his knees stiff and clumsy. It seemed that no one else had seen his vision, for all other eyes were downcast.

He left the church and sought to follow her, but the fog had swallowed her path. Keith cast his eyes heavenward, but above him there was only the denseness of cloud.

***

Pedestrians hurried home, their feet slipping on the damp pavement, its skin of dirt and automotive oil turned treacherously greasy. Traffic slowed. The swans clustered nearer the riverbank, their graceful white shapes standing out with odd clarity in the wispy murk.

"The fog's in our favor," said Bodie. "Just make sure you don't lose her. A quick blow and an easy tip into the water, and we're done."

Keith didn't answer. He was choking on dread. The nausea that he had tried to pass off as a hangover returned.

"I'm not sure I can do this, Bodie. I don't feel so good. I think I'm gonna puke."

Bodie took his time answering. He knew that the silence would weigh so heavily on Keith that he would in time answer his own question. Predictably, he spoke again.

"This wasn't part of our job. We don't have to do this. We can leave. We can forfeit the rest of the money. Why can't we just leave?" The boyish voice rose to an irritating whine, quavering as if Keith were on the brink of tears.

Bodie drew a slow breath and exhaled an admonishing hiss. "Keith, listen to me. You really think we can just walk off and no one will follow? You think that this guy will let us go that easily? I'm telling you, this isn't a man to cross. I have more experience with this, believe me." Bodie's voice was cold.

Keith still balked. "But this is different. This is worse. This might be unforgivable. Unforgivable."

Bodie turned toward the window. He didn't feel the least sympathy for Keith, nor did he care that much about the woman he was set to murder. Pity did not number among his sentiments. He only wanted the job done right—and quickly.

"It's all up to you, buddy. Thanks to you, I can't be the one to do it." He cradled his arm. The wince was not exaggerated, for a crippling pain shot from shoulder to fingers. He had opted not to see a doctor, a decision that might not have been wise. His fingers were swollen and now streaked with purple.

"I know. It's partly—okay, it's all—my fault. I know that. But I just don't think that I can do it. I'm not a good person, God knows. But I'm not a, not a . . ." He could not even say the word that named what he was not.

"And who put in for being found out so soon, Keith buddy?" said Bodie with a quiet, casual tone. "No one expected this would be necessary. And whose fault was that? Well, I know that we had a spot of bad luck there, but you're the one who called attention to us at the museum. You don't want to get caught, do you? You gotta deal with the situation you caused. Don't make me sorry I picked you for the job."

Bodie peered at the younger man to see if the threatening tone of that last utterance had registered. "And we're late already with this job. We don't want to mess with the boss. Don't assume you can disappear and he won't follow. He's got connections, and he's pretty pissed. Just do this and we'll get out."

Bodie always assumed there had to be connections. Pawel had played that part of his role well. Allusions to a powerful circle of professional art thieves made so much sense that Bodie had never doubted their existence. It was they, Pawel intimated, who also insisted on the elimination of an inconvenient witness.

"I know," said Keith dully. He felt caught, almost without will.

Bodie hoped that his stern tone would calm down his partner so that he would stop pacing and griping and running to the can. Later on he'd rip his throat out if he continued this whining. But Bodie was glad it wasn't he who had to do the job. He had an alibi planned, just in case. He would shortly be heading to a sports bar to display himself. And besides, there was this horrible shoulder mishap. Bodie dismissed the idea that his relief was simply craven. The fantasy of tossing the large woman into the water was entirely satisfying.

"But remember," said Bodie, "you gotta make it look like an accident. And like I said, the fog's your friend tonight. No one is going to suspect you, or me, or anyone else." Bodie exhaled and stubbed out his cigarette. The room was almost as obscure from his incessant smoking as from the early dark of the ebbing afternoon. "It's time you got going. She'll be leaving work soon. If you lose her in this fog, then we're in for more trouble."

"I thought the fog was our friend," muttered Keith. But he left the room and went into the murky evening like a man entering swampy water. He trudged along the long street that led to the castle, taking up position at the corner of the side street where the museum sat in its heavy opulence. There he waited for Klementyna Kamynska to leave work and head for her home across the river.

***

By the time Klementyna emerged, the fog was so dense that he fell into step close behind her with little fear of being noticed. It was almost a relief to be moving. Now that the horrid deed was underway, Keith only wanted it finished.

He kept Klementyna ahead just far enough that he could see the long ends of her coat floating out of the haze. The pavement below his feet felt slippery, and he was cold to the bone. Trucks and cars and buses growled by him, giants emerging from the murk then retreating in a muffle as they crossed the bridge. There was only a little foot traffic. The few pedestrians on their way home walked rapidly and purposively with their heads lowered into their coat collars. Keith's high muffler and low cap looked quite normal and not the wrongdoer's disguise they also provided. He had little worry that anyone would take note of him. For once in his disreputable life, Keith was bothered not by the thought that he might be caught but by the utter wrongness of what he was about to do.

Thanks to a gap in the street lamps, at the height of the bridge there was a pool of shadow that turned the fog even murkier. It was there that Keith made his move. He took a deep, ragged breath. The sour taste of the smog scoured his throat. Then with three long strides he was behind her. Klementyna was a large woman, tall enough that the guard railing was little higher than her waist. Keith figured he would give a quick twist of the neck or a knock on the skull, and then a heave over the side would permit the cold river to finish her off.

He was a short man but heavily muscled, and it should have been easy to boost her quickly over the railing. However, she was heavier than he had counted on, and he had already expended so much anxious energy that he feared he would not have the strength to pitch her over. In truth, the real barrier he faced was that Keith did not have the heart of a murderer. When he felt her struggle in a startled surge of resistance, the intimate contact between killer and victim was overwhelming. He felt her muscles, the bones of her jaw under his hand; he smelt the damp odor of her wool coat, the sour reek of her hair. It was she he held in his grip, she who demanded release. She whose fear and shock radiated through him. He remembered the first time he caught a fish—that slippery, frantic squirming in his hands, his reluctance to squeeze tight enough to quell it. The fish had slid from his hands back into the lake. Now he desperately wanted just to run away, leaving her to think that she was the near-victim of a mugging. Had anyone been watching, that is likely what they would have thought. Some man trying to snatch a purse in the fog. His attempt at twisting her neck in that neat snap that one sees at the movies was made difficult by her thick scarf and the fact that she was taller than he, but even more difficult by the fact that he fervently did not want to do it. He succeeded only in cutting off her ability to scream, and they swayed in an awkward two-step at the zenith of the bridge, he wishing her into the water and out of his life, she alarmed and struggling and filled with the strength of terror.

It is hard to say who would have won the dance. Possibly she would have broken free and run, or filled her lungs with air and screamed for help. Possibly he would have succeeded in sending them both over the railing to take their chances in the filthy water below. Possibly, more than possibly, he would have given up. But in the end their fate was decided by another.

In the darkest patch of shadow, in the heaviest veil of fog, Keith and Klementyna's struggle was interrupted by a terrible blow. Keith's shoulder was jammed so hard into its own socket that his arm went numb, his head slammed into the railing with a force that shook his teeth, and his legs shot out from under him as he fell heavily on his back. Before the pain reached his brain he was aware of a weight lifting off him, and he heard a rasping screech finally released from the constricted throat. Then a wave of agony hit him. Keith lost consciousness before he heard the splash.

The unseen cyclist flew sideways into traffic, his bicycle skidding down the walk along the railing. It bounced crazily across the curb, ricocheted, and was smashed back by the wheels of a truck, finally landing in a tangle of metal at the base of the bridge. There was a screaming of brakes and a dizzy blur of red lights as cars skidded to avoid the cyclist's falling body. In the fog it was difficult for the line of traffic to anticipate the sudden halt, and when the police arrived, they came upon a twenty car pile-up of mostly bent fenders and aggravated drivers. The ambulance came in a swirl of lights and collected a near dead cyclist and an unconscious pedestrian. It would be days before anyone realized that there had been a third victim in the fog.

24
The Best of a Bad Situation

Contrary to Adam's fears, the Radincki Museum did not remain closed to visitors for long. There were several days of consternation during which the two night guards were suspended and anyone who had ever worked for the museum was summoned for questioning by the authorities. Those authorities included a congested array of local police, an art theft team from Interpol, and various independent experts on the international trade in stolen artifacts.

Prior to reopening, the museum was examined from basement to rafters. The broken glass and the painting's protective frame were discovered by a disused door, which was quickly sealed against further access. Only after confirming that the Leonardo panel was not still secreted someplace inside the building awaiting a second stage of removal, did the police and their advisors permit visitors to return. Fortunately for his fragile peace of mind, Adam did not yet know that even the archives were scoured inch by inch and inventoried before being cleared for use. The absence of Gorski's little diary was not noticed. Indeed, it could not have been, for the only living person who knew of its existence was sitting at home behind closed curtains staring red-eyed at its pages, riven with an intense desire to finish his task and an incapacitating guilt that froze his fingers into cramps. Her annoyance with him turning to concern, Joan borrowed a thermometer from Beata and took his temperature. It was normal. But everything else about him was ill.

***

The museum Director wrung her hands about the anticipated loss of visitors to one of Krakow's less popular museums, whose new and spectacular claim for attention had been so quickly snatched from their grasp. She was anxious that operations return to normal as soon as possible, although what normal might be from now on was not clear. Of particular difficulty in a semblance of business as usual was the crime scene, still an expanse of damaged wall and a smudged floor. It had been examined thoroughly and repeatedly, but the authorities still requested holding off repairs. The museum had all but decided to keep the large Painting Gallery closed, when a young assistant curator had a flash of twisted brilliance and turned the crisis into something close to an asset.

Andrzej Rogowicz, temporarily dubbed Assistant Curator of Special Information Exhibits, assembled a team of his old university friends, and within a few days of hectic work they produced a succinct video of the recent history of the *Salvator Mundi*. A series of images of familiar works by Leonardo da Vinci opened the show, and then the distinguished figure of Dr. Jurgen de Mul authenticated the picture with highlights from his recently recorded speech. It concluded with a dramatic flourish as Andrzej himself wrapped up the events of the last several days with a suspenseful comparison of the recent robbery with other famous art thefts, including that of the *Mona Lisa* in 1911, stressing the similarities between the Louvre robbery and the apparent method of the Radincki thieves.

The video ran on a loop broadcast from two monitors positioned on either side of what was now transformed into something like a shrine. A large cordoned-off area that incorporated the original escutcheons reverently marked the space of the absent painting, directing attention to the empty wall and its shredded bolt-holes. On the dusty floor a few large footprints were just visible. They were in fact the prints of a guard who had examined the wall before being told to watch his step, but the implication that they might have been left by the thief was not disputed. To top it off, two of the better reproductions painted by the artists at the Florianska Gate were bought and positioned on easels flanking the monitors. They bore the captions—in four languages—"Who will save the Savior of the World?" Near blasphemous, some grumbled, but so catchy it was left to stand.

Although the high season for tourism was long over, the theft appeared to have swelled the numbers of visitors to the city. It had to be admitted, in the short run there was profit as well as loss in the wake of the spectacular robbery. The flow of visitors held steady, and Andrzej Rogowicz was complimented and vaguely promised a promotion. In fact, his supply of ideas to capitalize on the theft was so enthusiastic that two of the international experts quietly opened files on him, wondering if perhaps the theft had been an inside job whose instigator was unwisely showing his hand.

For the time being, museum visitors were all required to check their coats at the door, and any purses or briefcases they carried were searched by hand before their owners were permitted to enter. Rogowicz and his team provided entertainment for those waiting in the tedious lines with illustrated information on boards mounted along the wall, so that by the time visitors entered the Painting Gallery, they felt as if they had been at an enlightening tutorial rather than a security checkpoint. The Director breathed a sigh of relief. This sort of stunt couldn't go on for very long before it became tiresome, but for the moment it appeared to be a successful way to save both face and revenue.

The researchers who worked in the archives were included in this new routine, to which they acquiesced with cooperative good humor. Only one of them was seriously inconvenienced.

Adam attempted once to return to the archives with Gorski's diary, but he didn't dare hand over his briefcase for inspection. He might simply have broken his routine and worked steadily at home, but his anxiety level was unbearably high there. He resumed work at the library just to pore over the transcriptions from the diary text he had written in his notebook. In the evenings he returned to the contraband original, dutifully copying Gorski's difficult text, sometimes with a hand so unsteady that he could hardly read it the next day when, with dictionary and sharpened pencil, he sat by the high window at the archives and attempted to render it into sensible English.

The old saying: a burden shared is a burden halved, did not occur to him. Had he spoken of his theft to Joan, his guilty conscience might not have swollen so out of proportion to his crime. But he did not. Shame or a simple, stunning lack of energy stopped him from that obvious communication.

Joan saw that he suffered, and she thought she understood why. They were drifting apart, the short relationship already foundering, and she both regretted this and resented him for his tunnel vision. She saw a mirror of her own dissatisfaction in his weary face, and their purposes seemed to diverge more and more. She too might have spoken but did not. If she had, she would have realized that she grasped only part of his trouble, and not even the most tormenting part. But she too was silent.

The other principals in the Radincki thefts followed up with their own strategies. Bodie showered and shaved and dressed in a fresh and sober shirt. His shoulder was still extremely sore, but he left the sling behind as he ventured again to the museum one morning, intent to discover what their masked employer had really been up to while they removed the painting. He took nothing with him and encountered no trouble with security. He was startled to see the corridor of information boards about the theft, and he made himself read them carefully, schooling his features into an expression of interest rather than alarm.

He avoided the Painting Gallery, being more interested to check out the jewel cases he had identified as the true targets for robbery. But to his surprise, nothing seemed to be missing. The buckets of jewels were undisturbed, the embroidered clothes still moldered in their cases. He looked around more extensively but could see no change in any of the display cases. Even in the annex where they had spent so much time with the lock mold, every item in the vitrines was still in place.

Unsatisfied, he returned to his rented room and sat smoking until his pack ran out. Perhaps the painting was the only target after all. But if so, what had they been doing with the cabinet lock?

It didn't make sense.

Something else was going on. Something important enough to require doing away with that guard who had seen them near the little exhibit room. It was hard to believe that she had linked Keith's strange behavior with the spectacular theft of the painting. The more Bodie studied the situation, the less it added up. If he was to reap any additional reward from this affair, he had to find out more.

Reluctant to remain in the flat and tired of sitting in cold churches, Joan too wandered back to the museum. The familiar place made her think of the closeness that she and Adam had so recently shared, and she lingered there alternately nursing sadness and resentment. She saved for last her favorite little annex with its window saints and ancient silver.

She felt herself relax as she entered. Old things bestow calm. They announce the insignificance of individual woes. We last longer than you do, they say. Forget about your little grievances. They will soon be over. If Rudy had been present, he might have quoted Marcus Aurelius about the ineluctable cycles of time: *Many grains of incense on the same altar; one was cast earlier, the other later, but it makes no difference.*

Had he uttered that quotation when entering the annex, however, both of them would have recognized that Marcus Aurelius probably had something different in mind than the precise items in a historical museum, where there is a considerable difference between the one cast earlier and the one cast later.

Joan stood before the central case for some moments in a kind of suspended doubt. It took her a while to come to terms with what lay before her eyes.

There was the Bronislaw chalice just where it belonged. Or at least there was a silver bowl in the place where the chalice had lain. But something was different. It did not beguile her as it once had. Its lively figures did not make her fingers itch to touch them. Disappointed, she thought perhaps she had grown weary of the object, but then she looked more closely. Something was definitely wrong.

Memory is faulty. She knew that. But surely the chalice looked different now. Had it been cleaned, perhaps? No, the tarnish that heightened the relief was still there. It was the images themselves that were not quite right. The swan in its nest of reeds was too small. And the bowl. The silver rim appeared thinner, and the bowl was somewhat shallower than she recalled.

Joan felt a peculiar dizziness swirl around her skull. She was tired, and she was upset about Adam. Perhaps she was not seeing things correctly. She closed her eyes and opened them again. But the chalice still looked wrong. She circled the room slowly, pausing before the faintly lit images of Saints Gertruda and Bartholomew. They looked the same; their gazes were just as she remembered. The stirrup and the wax seals looked the same; so did the earrings and the necklace in the adjacent case. But the chalice looked different. She wished she could put her finger on exactly why, on something definite that would prove she was not simply misremembering.

And then all at once she knew. The dragon figure now faced upward, and the woman with the long hair lay against the mirror.

She dashed into the larger gallery and inquired of puzzled guards until she was directed to an administrative wing. Andrzej Rogowicz was still in his office when he heard rapid footsteps approaching. A woman appeared in the doorway breathing hard and spoke to him in English. "Come with me," she commanded. "Quickly please. I think there was another theft."

25

Suspicions

Andrzej felt duty bound to report Joan's suspicions to his superiors, although he believed she was probably mistaken and had simply misremembered the position of the chalice. There was only one Leonardo. He didn't care deeply about the fate of the old silver cup.

His older colleagues did not share his insouciance. The very idea that another item might be missing from the collection presented a delicate hazard. The theft of a work of art by a great Renaissance master puts an institution on the map. Losing an obscure artifact by a complete unknown makes that institution look careless. Couple the two together, and it raises questions about what else might also have gone astray. They had just checked high and low for one painting. This was not the time to undertake a full inventory of everything on display. Not to mention all the things in storage. If word got out that something else might be missing, rumor control could get complicated.

Stern cautions were advanced, and Andrzej Rogowicz was ordered to put a stop to Joan's tongue. All present were issued a definitive command by the Director not to broadcast this new accusation. This directive was aimed with special emphasis to

Andrzej, just in case he discovered an urge to put on another show. In fact, the latter needed little quelling, since he couldn't remember even having noticed the Bronislaw chalice before. Besides, a second stolen piece distracted from the drama of the major one.

To do them justice, most of them were motivated by genuine skepticism rather than protectiveness. There was no real evidence that anything had been taken at all. Just the inexpert impression of some tourist. The item in question was in a locked case, whose intact glass indicated it had not been disturbed. Although none could recall the last time they had examined the chalice, the one there now looked pretty much like they remembered, and why trust the word of some casual visitor? Also, it was not an object of great consequence. Though a genuine artifact dating from the late seventeenth century, the bogus aura that surrounded it was a product of legend: silver melted down and recast from an older chalice that had been used in magical rites. If there had been a theft, it was more perplexing than dire.

There was yet another factor that contributed to the assessment of their present situation, and this one trumped all the other considerations. One of their security guards was missing. Her absence had been noted the day after the theft, though in the fluster and bustle of the time it had not been pursued. "She is perhaps home sick," a colleague had speculated. "Her throat was hurting, and the terrible fog probably made it worse." The head of staff made a note to follow up on this and put it aside.

But then there was a visit from the sister of Klementyna Kamynska, a similarly bulky, insistent woman who would not leave until someone listened to her: Her sister is never sick, she declared. Never. She had gone to her sister's flat three times, finally locating the spare key and letting herself in. The stove was cold and dusty, and the cat was hungry, its litterbox overflowing.

It transpired that Klementyna Kamynska had not been heard from since the day after the robbery. Since the night of the fog. This pregnant fact was reported to the investigating authorities, who seized on the guard as a possible suspect. Official attention veered in her direction. Her sister was closely questioned about any new acquaintances she might have made recently, but she had nothing to add. Kamynska had worked for the Radincki Museum for over thirty years. In all that time she had been an unremarkable but reliable employee.

However, she knew the museum inside and out. And the collection. She had opportunity, and anyone wanting money would have motive. And with help she would have the means. The museum staff was sworn to secrecy, and the attention of the investigation swerved towards Klementyna Kamynska. At the very least, she was needed for questioning.

At the behest of his superiors, Andrzej told Joan the minimum amount of information to assure her that her suspicions about the chalice were being taken with due seriousness. He alluded to suspicions of a possible thief and showed her a photograph of the guard who regularly patrolled the hallways. Joan recognized her; they had exchanged a nod or pleasantry or two, and once Joan had asked her about—about the very object that was now missing! No, no, not the painting. The chalice. A favorite of both of theirs, as it happened. And twice they had passed each other on the same bridge across the river. With a shock, Joan realized that she and the guard might be neighbors.

Joan was frustrated that so few believed that the chalice had also been taken, but she was regarded as a nosy interloper and not taken seriously. Andrzej Rogowicz brushed off her continued questions. Adam advised her that she had to respect the museum's request for silence on this matter; he did not add that he didn't want any attention directed to him either, given his own illicit action. Aggravated that even Adam did not take her seriously, Joan stopped insisting but privately intended to pursue her own inquiries. It marked yet one more subject that fell into the growing silence between them.

The official investigators themselves, though they dutifully followed up on the absence of the guard, were far from convinced that Kamynska was a leading suspect. A guard might be an ideal inside accomplice. But anyone who could plan to steal a painting by Leonardo da Vinci would be most unlikely to forget to provide for her cat. Klementyna's flat—tiny kitchen with hotplate, living room with a fold-out bed, and a shared bath—was sealed off for thorough searching. Her sister was permitted to take the cat home with her. An unlucky policeman carefully sifted through the litter box for clues before releasing it, too, into her custody.

***

The cold broke for a day and the sun shone.

The Vistula was flat as glass. The fishermen with their long lines returned to its banks, sitting on newspapers and drinking beer. Dogs loped along the embankment, ducks waited for bread crusts, and the swans upended themselves in the water searching for food, tail feathers poking raggedly into the air. In the short respite before impending winter, children played on the higher ground, old people walked, young mothers pushed strollers, and bicyclers sped along the upper path, oblivious to the fate of one of their own on that recent foggy night.

Joan walked home across the bridge admiring the loveliness of everything spread out before her. To her left rose the Wawel hill, and above her wheeled crowds of jackdaws, their clacking cries rising high above. She took a deep breath of blessedly fresh air, for in a bout of high pressure Krakow was less polluted than usual, and a lungful of river air was refreshing. Still, she would not want to eat a fish that swam in that murky flow. The fishermen never seemed to hook anything, and she wondered if there were any fish in those dark waters to catch. Not a fisherman herself, she did not understand that just sitting with pole and line was satisfying enough.

But today it seemed that one of them had caught something. His pole suddenly bent in a sharp curve, and he stood with both heels dug into the bank. His companion set his own pole aside and came over to watch. The line must have snapped, for suddenly the man staggered back and sat down hard, and the pole rocketed upwards and vibrated back and forth in his hands. The other man began to laugh. Perhaps he was drunk.

But then there were more men gathering on the riverbank, leaning and pointing out over the water. Several others ran to the scene. One of them waded into the freezing water. It was deeper than he reckoned, for soon he was wet to the armpits. He returned to the bank slowly and with obvious effort, visibly shivering, and with his hands gripping something that he tried to heave to the surface. Two more splashed forward to help haul to shore the object in his grasp. The cluster of men grew larger. Then one of them broke away and ran uphill to the newspaper kiosk by the bridge, where there was a urine-scented booth with a public telephone.

A police car drew up, lights flashing, and from downriver a tug boat set out with a mournful whistle. Joan drifted to the small crowd at the railing of the bridge. People peered down at the water with curiosity, then with horror, then with the avid expression of those who cannot look away.

It was at first hard to distinguish Klementyna Kamynska from a knotted pile of old clothes. The transition from life to lifeless seemed to have stamped a heartless symmetry on her square body, so that it was difficult to tell back from front. The mud in her hair was caked so thickly that she seemed to be wearing a caul. Her shoes were gone, her stockings rent so that the water streaked through them in stripes. When she was turned on her back the mud fell away, and all could see her swollen face and half-mast eyes and the drowned mouth still open in a fruitless search for air.

Why Joan recognized her she could not say. Certainly the face now hardly resembled the woman she had seen pacing the museum halls. But there was a certain proportion of head to neck, of neck to shoulders, of shoulders to waist that she had learnt from watching the guard walk back and forth through galleries. Whatever the trigger to memory, Joan knew at once who the woman was. And she told the crowd, she told the police, she told the paramedics loading the body onto a stretcher. And no one understood her.

Later at the flat she could not get warm. Adam wrapped her in blankets and sat her before the space heater. He made a cup of scalding tea and stirred in three spoonsful of sugar, and he held it to her lips because her hands shook so hard. Her teeth chattered against the rim of the cup and liquid dribbled down her chin. Finally he helped her to bed and lay beside her under the covers, holding her close. It was dark before he felt the shivering subside and heard her breathing become steady. Carefully he slid his arm from beneath her ribs and tucked the blankets snugly around her. He closed the bedroom door softly and sat at his desk, working quietly by lamplight as she slept.

A week later a shoe washed up beneath the bridge. The heel was worn. No one thought to tell the police.

26

Daughter of Time

"I've looked up your artifact and got the opinion of a colleague who knows something about the legend behind it," reported Rudy. They were sitting in his flat surrounded by comfortable clutter. The book-lined room served as both living room and study, and from the crushed cushions, afghans, and stacked papers, it was evident that he spent most of his time here before the fire.

"As you already know, the story is that the chalice was cast from the silver of some magical cup made much earlier. When the silver was melted down, the first cup lost its form, naturally. But somehow the magic got transferred, the magic that helped this Bronislaw character conjure up a helpful demon. Actually, the story is vague as to whether he used the first cup and then cast the other, fancier one as a kind of gesture to the demon, or whether the second one was made much later. There is more than one version of the legend."

"The label in the museum calls him a prince. Wouldn't there be a clearer picture of a prince in the historical record?"

"Well, according to my colleague, there are some doubts that he even existed. Like King Arthur, you know. He could be more legend than fact. But he was quite an obscure fellow. If he existed at all."

"But there is his chalice."

"Well, there is this silver dish. Might be a chalice. More like a bowl, if you ask me, but 'chalice' sounds nicer. There is an oblique mention of a person who might have been Bronislaw in Drogultz's history, but most of the stories about him date from much later, adding to the speculation that they are mostly legend. In any event, it seems that Bronislaw, whose mother was Lithuanian, was a somewhat reluctant convert to Christianity. It came rather late to these parts, you know. Leading religion of Poland since the tenth century, but there were pockets of the older religions practiced for some time after that. And Lithuania remained pagan—or what Christians labeled pagan—until later. Anyhow, there were a number of fly-by-night sects that popped up as Christianity was taking root, and Bronislaw belonged to one of them. They might have been called the Brotherhood of the Salt, but Tomasz—that's my colleague—thinks that's a spurious name of later date. What is apparent is that they had ties to the mining community at Wieliczka, where the salt is mined. Ever been there? Impressive place. You ought to go, you and Adam."

"I've been there, but I went alone. Adam said there was something about salt in the description of the bowl at the museum. But he couldn't make a lot of sense out of it."

"Well, that might be because there isn't a lot of sense to be made. It's tempting to see old beliefs as harboring ancient wisdom, but of course they're just as likely to be as silly as the cults that arise today. Like those Californians who thought they would be rescued by a comet. Makes quite a lot more sense for an antique Pole to believe in the power of salt than for a twentieth century American to castrate himself waiting for a space ship. Of course, all this waiting for the millennium seems to be accelerating the deterioration of the intellect all round. You're not from California by any chance are you?"

"No." Joan sensed Rudy veering off on a tangent. "Let's get back to the salt. What does it have to do with the chalice?"

"One possible interpretation of the base of the chalice is that those four figures that you drew so prettily are all sitting on a lump of the stuff. See? It even shows up in your sketch, even though you probably didn't know what you were drawing so it is just a shape. But the base and also the rim are decorated with these little circular designs. And according to Tomasz, those might be the alchemical symbols for salt."

Joan examined the images in her notebook that she had sketched during her first month in Krakow. It seemed as if she had drawn them far longer ago.

"I thought they were just decorations. I'm pretty sure that they are accurate, but I was paying more attention to the figures on the stem. They were harder to draw, and I could never see the one that lay against the mirror very clearly. Actually, I took a couple of photos too, but they aren't much clearer than the sketches. I couldn't find an angle that was free from reflection off the glass case."

Rudy studied the drawings. "One interpretation is that they represent directions. See this woman floating in the river? Stands to reason it is the Vistula, or the Wisła as they say here. It flows north, so this might be a directional point. And the one opposite that you had trouble drawing is a dragon. Lots of dragons scattered around the iconography of medieval Europe, so it's hard to tell Saint George's adversary from the dragon beneath the Wawel. Could be either I guess, but the locale suggests the Krakow dragon. If that's south, then the other two represent east and west."

"But we've lost track of the salt." Joan pondered the sketch. "Or maybe we haven't. If salt is so important, maybe that is why the four directions are placed over it. It could symbolize the earth itself. Does that make sense?"

"That's probably as good a hypothesis as any. Anyhow, Tomasz says that salt figured prominently in the story of the chalice because salt was believed to have the power to summon and to repel evil forces."

"That's what Adam read on the display placard, but I thought it was a mistake. How can salt do both those things? Summon and repel? Surely it would do one or the other."

"Now there's the inappropriately logical mind at work." Rudy got up and poured Joan more tea from the flowered pot on the table between them. He had lit a fire and a sharp but pleasant scent of wood smoke drifted into the room. Joan relaxed further into the cushions and propped up her feet, which were beginning to regain feeling after her cold walk into town. Rudy stood by the fireplace, unconsciously striking his lecture pose, and continued.

"Traditionally, salt is regarded as a protection from evil. That makes sense given its actual preservative powers, you know; it keeps things from spoiling. But the idea is that salt can summon and repel because it is a powerful substance. He who wields the salt — properly of course, with all the requisite mumbo-jumbo and ritual — releases its power, and it can either ward off spirits or bring them forth. Usually the salt gets combined with something equally potent, like the blood of a virgin or a murder victim. Timing is important too. Bronislaw's sect put quite a premium on Sylwester, the turn of the new year, when they held their special rituals. Pretty heady stuff, if you buy it."

"How big was this sect?"

"No idea at all. Possibly local. I had never heard of it before, though of course there is no particular reason why I should have, being a philosopher. My bailiwick is more focused on reason, or what at least appears to be rational belief."

"What does this have to do with the chalice? Is it like the Holy Grail?"

"Oh good lord no! Nothing like that at all. And of course all this business about the rituals of salt and the demons could be just modern fancy. For all one knows the thing was used for soup. A lot of care was taken with it though, so it might have been a special wedding gift, or a tribute to a dignitary, or all sorts of things. It's much more exciting to imagine conjuring up demons to do your bidding, vanquish enemies and all that. Maybe someone did attribute such a function to it, in which case I think we can safely assume that it didn't work. But legends grow up afterwards, and one became attached to this bowl. But you know, veritas isn't always filia temporis."

"What does that mean?"

"Sorry. My old Latin teacher liked to instruct by means of aphorisms. Veritas est filia temporis. Truth is the daughter of time. Only it isn't. Not necessarily. It sounds good, like Murder will out. But who knows how many murderers have gotten away with the deed. And certainly time obscures a lot of truth." Rudy paused to sip his tea, his long fingers daintily folded around the handle of the China teacup.

"And you said there were stories about Bronislaw attached to the chalice?"

"Yes. One in particular that seems to be at the core of all the accounts." Rudy put down his cup and tented his fingers. "It seems that one day young Bronislaw found himself in a tight spot. He was fleeing from enemies of some sort, maybe Tartars. He had this old silver cup with him; probably stole it. At any rate, it was winter and the Vistula was choppy with ice but not frozen enough to cross. Bronislaw found himself at the edge of the river, wounded and bleeding, with the enemy hot on his heels. He also was, for some reason, unbearably thirsty. So he scooped up a bit of river for a drink from the silver cup, crossed himself with his bloody hands, and uttered a prayer for deliverance. And a demon appeared before him and did him a great favor. He flung up a bridge of salt across the river."

"Salt!"

"Yes. The salt was strong enough to support Bronislaw and his horse as they crossed to the other side. When the enemy arrived and saw Bronislaw escaping they tried to pursue across the bridge too. But it dissolved midway and fell apart, and they were vanquished, drowned in the river."

"So the chalice has magic powers?"

"Well, the thing in the museum isn't the cup from that story. It's not old enough. But somewhere along the line, the notion arose that his magic cup was melted down and cast into its new and more decorative form, and after many years it landed in the Radincki Museum. Quite a tall tale."

A log fell in the fire and a plume of sparks went up the chimney.

Joan nibbled the edge of an almond cookie. She didn't care for almond, but Rudy did, and he had bought them today especially for her. Rudy put down the sheaf of papers he had been consulting and rubbed his eyes. He was good company today.

"That's an interesting story, but I still don't see why the bowl was worth stealing," she said. "It doesn't seem all that valuable, except for its history and the story attached to it. If that guard was really murdered as her sister thinks, that is a very high premium for an old silver cup, no matter how romantic the legend. The price is too high. It doesn't make sense."

Rudy studied her for a minute. He leaned forward and topped up her teacup. "If you don't like those biscuits, don't feel obliged to eat them."

"They're yummy. I'm just getting full." Joan put the rest of the cookie in her mouth and swallowed it with a gulp of tea. "The museum people aren't sure that what is lying there now was taken at all, you know. I've been trying to convince them, but they are more interested in the stolen painting."

Outside there was the muffled sound of traffic accumulating at the end of the day. Rudy poked at the fire, stirring the embers until a small flame revived.

"Why are you pursuing this, Joan? It should be no surprise that the museum is more interested in the theft of the Leonardo than with your chalice. The painting is, after all, their most famous possession. Or it was. And for a frustratingly short time. You on the other hand are occupied with the possible loss of a minor antiquity. A curiosity of course. But a priority? What do you imagine is going on?"

Joan frowned."I just think that it is very curious that two items would have been stolen at the same time. It must have been the same time, don't you think? It strains belief to think that after many years of calm, there would be two independent robberies so close together."

"If, in fact, the chalice was stolen at all. It is very hard to keep the exact image of an object in one's mind, you know. It would be no shame to discover that you were wrong."

That was the challenge—her trust in her own memory. Over the past two days, even Joan had suffered doubts about her judgment, but now she was sure.

"I am quite certain that a different chalice is sitting there now. I kept a set of notes as a kind of travel journal when we first arrived. You see them here. They aren't very good, but they confirm my memory of what it looked like. So do the photos, unfocused as they are. I know that it is not the same thing. And also positive that it was repositioned. And the museum people refuse even to examine the artifact that is now in the case."

"They will," Rudy assured her. "Eventually. At the moment the painting is top priority. But when that business is settled, someone will turn their attention to your chalice."

Joan stared at him. "Surely you don't believe that. As you said, the chalice isn't that valuable. They have a bigger problem. Much bigger."

Rudy smiled. "Okay, maybe it won't be pursued with the same vigor. And maybe the record will remain confused. But the question still stands: why are you so interested?"

"Because it simply interests me," said Joan truculently. She had almost too many reasons. "And it was one of my favorite things to look at. I guess I feel a bit proprietary. And since no one else is worried about the chalice, that job falls to me. I am a journalist of sorts, though I was sidelined temporarily by my broken elbow. I've had features in a couple of magazines that have liked my work. I'm going to write up the history and — I'm convinced — the theft of the chalice on spec. Loads are now being written about the *Salvator Mundi* and the theft, but the chalice hasn't received any attention, so that's my subject."

"What do you mean 'on speck'?"

"Speculation. It means that editors won't promise to print the story, but at least they'll read it and maybe like it."

"So that's your main reason?"

"Yes." And then she added more slowly, "And also, you know, because I saw the museum guard being pulled from the river."

Rudy waited.

"It was horrible, of course. Anyone would feel that. But I had just seen her a few days before, and we had actually spoken. Twice. Once in the museum when I asked about the chalice. And once, almost, on the street. We passed on the bridge, that very bridge, and I said czien dobry, and she nodded and sort of smiled."

Rudy did not speak. Joan's voice had dropped, and she seemed to be struggling with her thoughts. How pretty she is, thought Rudy. And with a pang: lucky Adam.

"And again, I had gotten into the habit of waiting for Adam in that small exhibit room. It is so quiet and peaceful. And the bowl was — is — very lovely. I was making a sketch of it just to have something to do while I was waiting. That's why I'm so sure that it's gone. So why am I interested? Because in a strange way I feel connected. I could turn my back, but the connection would break."

Bells rang faintly through the closed windows. The hour was being marked.

Joan drew a deep breath. "I didn't have a very good reason for coming here, you know," she confessed. "I've already told you some of the circumstances. I had a stupid accident on a bike and broke my elbow, which made it hard to use a keyboard for a while. But also, I was supposed to teach two journalism courses at an extension of the college where Adam works, but the program was cancelled at the last minute. So there I was with no job and an injured arm. It seemed like a sign. Adam and I had begun what seemed like a promising relationship, so when he asked, I decided to make a clean break and come to Poland with him. It was a series of chance events rather than a thoughtful decision."

She bent her head to the teacup, conscious of Rudy's keen gaze. He turned and looked out the window, his eyes tracing an arc of birds flying by. She could see their small shadows darting across his face, lit by the sun just before it took its evening dip behind the rooftops.

"Choice is sometimes another name for chance," he said.

It took Joan a moment to speak. "Is that a quote from someone?"

"I think it is. Can't recall just who at the moment, but I'm sure I read it somewhere."

"One of your Stoics? Or Spinoza?"

"Unlikely. They were determinists. They didn't attribute much choice to human life, and they weren't big on chance either. It must have been someone else. But it seems true to me. The choices we make are framed by chance, including the unforeseen circumstances we find ourselves in at any given moment. It fits my own life, as it happens."

Joan let the thought settle.

"But you ask a very important question," Rudy resumed their former discussion. "Why go to the trouble of stealing this particular item? As you say, it is not especially valuable. In fact, in the adjacent room there is a case full of jewelry worth a king's ransom. Ha! In fact, some of it was a king's ransom!"

Rudy would have been surprised to learn that Bodie had thought the same.

"But you have put your finger on the key question: why that item? Why all the bother for an old silver cup? Or bowl, or goblet, or chalice, whatever name you choose. What could make it a particular target of theft. Did the guard tell you anything about it, by the way?"

"No. Nothing more than what was on the plaque. But she said she liked it." That shared liking had forged a tenuous bond between them. "Who would steal such a thing? And why go to the trouble of disguising the theft with a substitute chalice?"

"Good questions. I suppose that the only person who would construct such elaborate plans would be someone who is also interested in the attached legend. Someone who wanted it enough to plan a peculiarly elaborate theft," said Rudy. "But why also kill a guard? It's hard to see the necessity. Perhaps, indeed, her death was an accident."

"That's not what her sister thinks."

"I know. It must be very hard for her."

"You know, there is something else," said Joan. "I forgot to mention this. But the case where the chalice was kept wasn't broken. Therefore, it had to have been unlocked by someone who had a key."

"Really? I didn't know that. I guess I wasn't sure how those cases were secured, or if they were locked at all."

"They are. From the bottom. A little keyhole on the bottom of the case releases a lock, and the other side of the glass is hinged."

"How do you know?"

"I noticed it one day when I was lying on the floor."

"Ah. Lying on the floor. Good vantage, that."

The next minute was filled with sudden hilarity, leaving Joan feeling limp and Rudy rummaging for a whisky.

"Drink?" he managed.

But the sun was already setting on the short November day. Above the pointed tops of houses, the jackdaws whirled around the steeples. Here twilight seemed to last but a moment, and soon it would be dark. Joan imagined stepping into the cold air, seeing stars appear above the Rynek, making her way back home across the bridge. The bridge. She felt a twinge of apprehension.

"Thanks, but no. I need to be getting home." She began to gather up her coat and put on her boots. "Actually, I forgot to mention the main reason I came by."

"What was that?" Rudy held her coat, disappointed at the loss of her company.

"I came to ask you to come to Thanksgiving dinner."

"Thanksgiving?" For a moment the word meant nothing. Rudy was still in the moment of laughter, wanting a drink.

"It's an American holiday. I thought — Adam and I thought — that we would celebrate it here, even though no one else does. It will be a small dinner, just us and our landlady. But it would be nice if you could come too. Please."

Rudy smiled. "Of course I shall! With pleasure. I remember Thanksgiving now. Even went to a dinner once when I visited the States. When was that? A long time ago. I seem to recall that it is always one day of the week, but I can't remember which one."

Joan smiled back. "Thursday. Always Thursday. The last one in November."

As Joan headed for the door, Rudy voiced another thought.

"You know, I can think of one more reason that someone would go to all the trouble to steal the Bronislaw chalice," he said. "And it's probably not a reason that the authorities will bear in mind."

"I know," said Joan. "Only one." She put on her gloves and looped her handbag across her shoulder. Then she turned to face him and said only half mockingly, "Maybe someone wants to summon a demon."

27

Giving Thanks

Pawel Radincki would have bristled at Joan's offhand remark. One should not joke about summoning demons.

He had prepared a place for the chalice.

His flat was an irregular segment of the upper story of an old building, which had been altered over the years by renovations designed to divide large spaces into small apartments. Between kitchen and bedroom such redesign had miscalculated, and previous residents had used a narrow spot with a slanting dormer for storage. When Pawel had moved in, he discovered scattered mouse droppings caught in dense clots of dust.

After obsessive cleaning and slathering several coats of paint onto the walls, Pawel had fitted a heavy curtain over the opening. When lifted, it revealed a dark niche transformed into a place of mystery. A low, inlaid table sat at the center, topped by a velvet cloth and heavy silver candle holders. Their flames illumined a few pieces of aged China on which a faded coat of arms could just be discerned. Although a lingering fingerhold on rationality still prevailed over his ambitious fantasy, that coat of arms seemed more and more to match the one on his ring. In the shallow drawer of the table Pawel kept his ever-expanding family tree and several old sepia photographs, so creased and worn that by now they could have been anyone, including the great-great-grandparents that figured in Pawel's imagination.

Peasant son or bastard noble, Pawel was a lover of beauty, for his childhood amid the luxurious detritus of the Radincki Museum had made its mark upon his soul. In his carefully arranged flat, there was beauty. Not simple prettiness, which he held to be an overrated surface quality, but the kind of deep beauty that only objects of age and power attain. Old silver, rich cloth, a small, decorative table.

And now, in the center of this beauty, the Bronislaw chalice.

In the candlelight, the quadrant of designs on the stem came to life. The long hair of the woman flowed in waves, mingling in eddies of the cradling water; the slender wings of the swan arched above its fragile neck; the wolf's face peered between tall stands of grass; and the dragon with its bat-like wings breathed power. The tiny figures conjured a whole world, supporting the swell of the bowl above. He spent an hour on his knees just gazing at it.

Before it he murmured the fabulous incantation. *In fire I bloom, in water I flow, in blood I abide and avail.*

After he had determined that these were indeed the correct words, distilled from his memory and confirmed by arcane and inventive research, he wrote them out with a quilled pen dipped in black ink, using one of his heavy linen papers. The written words were not needed, for he knew them by heart, but their presence in the drawer beneath the chalice rooted the ravishing object in its proper place.

The power of words. The power of place and time. Of objects, salt, and blood. His own power soon to come. The next step in his great plan would be uncomfortable, involving as it did the letting of blood, but the outcome overrode any pain required on the journey to the coveted end.

In the meantime, Pawel had to handle the next move with extreme caution. Although it was in fact the very hub of his great plan, as the time neared he found that there were still quite a few details that he hadn't thoroughly worked out. So carried away had he been with the execution of the thefts—John Robie himself would have been proud—that he had not entirely figured out how to behave when the famous painting was returned to its rightful owners. Increasingly, this part of his scheme appeared to be rather badly conceived. What if it cast suspicion on him? What if the authorities raised too many questions? Could he actually be in danger of police detention, or even arrest? That was an outcome that occurred to him woefully belatedly.

And now, horribly, the Kamynska woman's body had been found. He scrutinized the papers and read every word of the published police report. So far there was no hint of foul play. Nor should there be, he assured himself. An accident. A tragic accident. Fortune—destiny!—had intervened with a set of accidents. Not only the woman crushed and thrown over the bridge but also her assailant badly injured. The unfortunate Keith, seemingly only another hapless victim of the crash. And that cyclist, still unconscious and in the hospital. All were proof that fate had interceded on his behalf. What seemed accidents to others were in fact the forces of destiny at work.

He wished that Bodie and Keith had been able to leave Poland as they had planned, but the latter's injuries had delayed their departure. Loose ends. Dangerous.

On the last Thursday of November, Pawel awakened before dawn with his heart racing, worried about the imminent phase of his scheme. He quailed at the attention the next days would bring. Left to himself, he might have revised the plan, bided his time, and devised a less dramatic way to handle that inconvenient painting. But the machinery was in place and could not now be stopped. The wheels were in motion.

Before the cheval mirror with its delicately carved frame he dressed in clothes that signaled the casual glamour of the previous generation: a loose cashmere sweater, pleated slacks, leather shoes. His hair was just slightly too long, as if he was overdue at the barber but too careless of his appearance to bother getting it trimmed yet. His signet ring gleamed on his finger. He reminded himself not to look at it, for it should by now be so familiar that he hardly noticed it. Now all he had to do was wait. He closed his eyes and uttered a little prayer to Saint Gertruda.

***

A breathy sound of gas exhaled from the oven. In Poland it did not have the rank smell that it was given at home, so it took a while before Joan realized how much had already dispersed into the kitchen. She opened the window and fanned with a towel until she judged it had safely dissipated. This was her first foray with the oven in the flat. Previously she had cooked only foods that could be prepared on the top of the stove. The tilted back burners were small but held a reliable temperature once they managed to bring pots to a simmer. The left front was good only if one remembered to use the wide skillet, because one side of the flame shot erratically high if the pan was too small. And the right front had to be watched carefully, for one of the edges of the burner was broken, and a pot had once slid to the floor with a hot splash.

She made another attempt to light the oven. There was a small explosion and a puff of smoke. She tried again. Blue flame spread and then evaporated. A pile of spent matches collected by her feet. She called downstairs.

"It's freezing in here!" said Beata, entering the kitchen. "Is the heat broken again?"

"No. It's fine. I just opened the window. I can't figure out how to light the oven."

"Ah. Yes. The oven. It can be a bit difficult."

Beata bent to the task. Another small explosion.

"See, it keeps doing that. I've used up nearly all the matches, and when I light the gas it all goes up in a bang, but the oven doesn't stay lit."

Beata adjusted the knob. The cold air from the window made them both shiver, but Joan didn't dare close it yet.

"Let's try not turning it on so far. There might be uneven pressure in the line," ventured Beata. There was the sound of expiration that ended with a puff and a blue flame that reached across the oven like dragon's breath. But this time it retreated beneath the bottom grill and glowed with licks of yellow. The two women stood back and waited hopefully. Small eddies of warmth emanated from the oven.

"It seems to be lit now. But perhaps you had better keep the window open just for a while," said Beata, recalling the advice from a service man two years ago that the old stove ought to be replaced. "I am so much looking forward to dinner tonight."

"Can I offer you some coffee?" said Joan, hoping the answer would be no. She was already behind with Thanksgiving preparation.

"That would be very nice," said Beata, thinking she ought to superintend the stove for a little while, just in case. "But only if you let me help you. What are these? Pies? What is in them? Really? How unusual."

They sat with coffee while the oven heated. It seemed to be behaving itself, so Joan closed the window. The room warmed comfortably. With no temperature gauge, Joan had to guess when to put in her two pies, one of them lumpy with apples and nuts. She had been unable to locate pumpkin, but the yams were approximately the right color. Beata was eyeing them doubtfully. The conversation veered away from dinner.

"I see you were brave and went to the hairdresser," said Beata. "That color suits you very well."

Joan's hair was now a striking auburn with slight hints of purple.

"Believe it or not," she said, "I'm a natural redhead. Not quite this color of red. I'm not sure that anyone is naturally this color."

"It's a very Polish color." Beata nodded with approval. "I knew you could do it. Your Polish must be getting very good."

"I just went with the phrase book and pointed to the right sentences," Joan said rather proudly. "But it worked. The hairdresser was very nice about pretending to understand what I said."

"And what does Adam think of it?"

"He'll get used to it." Adam had not in fact noticed her hair.

"Where is he? At the museum?"

"No, he's at the market picking up a few more things. We're going to cook together."

"Very nice to have a man to help in the kitchen," said Beata. "That must be an American way. What is that smell? Should the pies smell like that?"

Joan ran to the oven. The edges of her carefully rolled pie crusts were alarmingly dark already.

"Perhaps the heat is just a little too high. But if you cut off the edges the rest will still be good, I'm sure."

In the end Beata took the pies down to her own kitchen to finish baking, and Joan was left to stuff a pale and elderly chicken, its sheer size qualifying it as a substitute turkey. As she crammed its slippery interior with onions, stale bread, and celery, she hoped the oven would sustain a high enough temperature to cook it.

Giblet gravy, thought Joan. I wonder how you make it. The innards of the chicken sagged on the table. She wasn't used to having feet come with the bird.

Adam came in with an armful of groceries.

"Something smells good. Well, maybe not quite good yet. What burnt?"

"Nothing burnt," Joan replied. "It just took a while to light the oven. Did you find cranberries?"

"Not exactly."

They set to work together. Everything looks better once it is cooked, thought Joan.

***

At the building where Pawel Radincki had his flat, a bulky, rectangular package was heaved from a truck and placed outside the door. More postage was due, and the delivery man rang the bell impatiently. He had to ring twice and knock loudly before anyone responded, and two downstairs neighbors poked their heads into the hall to investigate the fuss. They continued to peer as the elegant upstairs tenant made his leisurely way down two floors and answered the door with a polite inquiry. They listened avidly to the exchange.

Pan Radincki was audibly perplexed. He was not expecting a package. How very odd. And how much was due? One of his neighbors, an elderly woman keenly interested in the building's normally dull activities, ventured into the hall and inspected the package. She observed that while the street address and the first name of the addressee were clear, the surname and the postal code were somewhat blurred.

"This must be the place," insisted the delivery man. "There is no such street at any other part of the city."

Pawel shrugged and went back upstairs for the appropriate money due. He signed the delivery slip. Both neighbors were now standing by. This was not precisely the scenario he had envisioned, but suddenly a huge hole in his plan occurred to him, one so obvious it was staggering. He needed witnesses. Reliable ones, and right away. In this unanticipated quandary he started to lift the package to take it upstairs, and then put it down again.

"It is rather heavy," he said. "I wonder what it could be?"

The delivery man turned back from the door as if expecting to be asked to haul the parcel upstairs, perhaps for a gratuity, as its recipient looked to be well-heeled.

"What do you suppose it is?" said Pawel again. The neighbors drew closer.

"Perhaps if you opened it here you could leave some of the weight behind," said the man.

"Right," said the woman. "No sense taking up trash only to bring it down again."

"And one can always reuse the paper and the string," mused Pawel. His neighbors were of the generation that still squirreled away such things.

"Indeed one can. I, for example, must send my grandchildren presents soon."

Pawel hesitated. He had not expected an audience at this stage of the game, but what a blessing that they were here. He had selected a busy but under-staffed office in Nowa Huta for the surreptitious dispatch, and there he had striven to look as far from his own dapper self as possible. But now public light was about to blaze upon him, and he was beset with anxiety at the impending scorch. How could he not have anticipated the need for witnesses? They were precisely what had been missing from his plan. And here were three at the ready, as though destiny itself had again stepped in and saved him from his oversight.

"Then I might as well open it here," said Pawel decisively. "I shall open it carefully so that you may have the wrappings, proszę Pani." He gave a short, courteous bow to the woman.

He took a small pen knife from his pocket, and as the delivery man held the corners of the large parcel to keep it from toppling and the two neighbors looked on, he cut the string.

There were no words adequate for what they discovered when the packing materials fell away.

Adam cleared off his desk, a wide library table with carved legs, and moved it to the center of the living room for the feast. Joan had anticipated an objection to any plan that might dislodge Gorski, but he had put up little fuss and had moved his work into one of the cabinets. Had she been paying more notice, she might have detected a whiff of furtiveness in this agreeable speed, but her attention was focused on the demands of the meal and their first dinner party in the flat. A colorful bedspread was discovered on one of the high shelves, and when folded in half it made for a cheerful tablecloth. She found four matching plates and arranged a full set of flatware at each place, along with four almost-matching napkins.

As evening fell the lamplight and candles illuminated the room. Although when entering the flat one had to pass the kitchen and its wreckage of pots, pans, and bags of garbage, once in the main room, the Thanksgiving feast appeared orderly and festive. The room was full of the smells of the season: deep, savory, roasting odors.

Beata was early, Rudy was late. Adam couldn't think of anything to say, and Joan fussed over vegetables cooked too soon and the muscular chicken that gave evidence of remaining raw in the center. Fortunately, there was lots of cheese, and when Rudy finally arrived he carried a bag full of clanking bottles and discharged a barrage of conversation already primed by beer on the way. They sat down and toasted the holiday, and just as it was time to eat Joan remembered she hadn't made gravy. There was a mass trip to the kitchen and many cooks spoiling the broth as she struggled with a spattering pan of fat and lumps of flour.

"Whisk it a little faster."

"Perhaps milk should be added to make the color come out right?"

"Did you use all the pan drippings?"

"What about a splash of whiskey?" That suggestion from Rudy, who executed it with a flourish that raised a respondent flame from the burner.

Joan removed her apron and with greasy hands smoothed her newly red hair, curling fuzzily from the steamy kitchen. She summoned everyone to the table, and the feast commenced.

***

Across the river, the dramatic delivery had been reported. A bevy of officials from the Radincki Museum left their suppers to converge on the site, and photographers and reporters surged in their wake.

***

The four of them, Joan, Adam, Beata, and Rudy, had reached that stage of a meal where everyone is full but sheer greed propels eating. They all agreed that the Thanksgiving meal was delicious, although the chicken-cum-turkey had required strenuous chewing and the combination of orange peel and grape jelly that Joan had imagined might make a substitute cranberry sauce had been a mistake. Luckily, the gravy, in spite of its communal preparation, was both flavorful and plentiful.

The bottle of vodka that Rudy had brought was half-empty, as were two bottles of wine. He gestured in the direction of another bottle, and Beata protested in that tone of voice that indicates she expects another glass to be poured immediately.

"One is never too full for champagne," declared Rudy. The fat cork popped loudly and flew across the room. "Besides, it settles the stomach and prepares the system for those delicious pies that Joan has baked."

Adam hiccupped and apologized blurrily. He could not remember the last time he had eaten so much. He felt good. But the bubbly champagne was setting up a series of belches he found impossible to quell, though Beata's immoderate peals of laughter effectively hid his eruptive noises. Rudy was clowning in his usual way and didn't appear to be drunk at all. Or perhaps he just didn't appear much different from the way he always did. Joan looked flushed and happy and relaxed, free for a moment from the memory of the river and its terrible bounty. Joan looked . . . Joan looked . . . different. Adam squinted at her. Perhaps it was the candlelight, but she appeared definitely different from the way he remembered she ought to look. He couldn't quite put his finger on it.

"In vino veritas," declared Rudy. It appeared to be the concluding comment to some story that Adam had missed.

"In vino delusitas more like it," mumbled Adam, thinking with one part of his brain that he had been witty. But he elected not to pursue a linguistic game, since his tongue was under less than complete control. It was a pleasant sensation rimmed with digestive unease, but the latter was so habitual a condition these days that he hardly noted it. His surroundings, however, now were definitely different from usual. And it wasn't just Joan.

"The room is tilting, and there are interesting colors coming from the edges of the room. Blue under the windows and a sort of orange by the door," Adam reported. He gazed at the objects in the room with a kind of curious admiration. "Candles," he said. "Napkins. Carpet." The others glanced around for evidence of blue and orange.

"Orange? That had better not mean that something is burning," said Joan. She took a plate in either hand and went into the kitchen, emerging with pies which she set on the table to be admired before being cut.

"Pies," said Adam. "Dinner."

"Such a wonderful meal, Joan," said Beata. "I have heard about Thanksgiving before but this is the first traditional dinner I have ever had."

"It isn't quite as traditional as it would have been if we had been at home," said Joan once again. She had been apologizing for various culinary mishaps off and on all evening. "I couldn't get all the usual ingredients."

"Thanksgiving. Dinner. Turkey," Adam chanted.

"Not a turkey at all . . ."

"Admirable Joan!" Rudy broke in. "In fact, altogether delicious. And when you think about it, how remarkable that you have found replacements for everything missing. That largish chicken for a turkey, for example. And those orange potatoes for pies. Better for those of us who deplore the American habit of eating pumpkin. And the sauce . . ." He trailed off. It was hard to know what to say about the sauce. He carried on. "And your pies look delicious. A fine finish to the meal. And I believe Adam also lent a hand to the feast?"

They all looked at Adam, whose eyelids were rising and falling in long, leisurely blinks.

"I believe I have drunk rather more than I thought," said Beata as though noticing Adam had awakened a suspicion about herself.

"Perhaps we all have," said Joan. "Shall I make coffee?"

"Surely not yet," said Rudy. "It is, after all, a celebration. Besides, it is a mistake to think that alcohol always breeds delusion," he continued with his precise, intoxicated speech. By the time he became actually drunk he would sound like knives. "If one goes too far, then of course it does. But I always find that there is a lovely balance just before one is actually drunk when petty details fall away and one notices things that are truly important."

"Perhaps we aren't quite ready for pie yet, then," said Joan. "After all, we don't want to lose our balance."

Her guests were more or less sprawled with champagne glasses balanced on their chests. They showed no interest in yet another course of dinner but were unprepared to make the effort to leave the table. Adam was frowning at her, staring fixedly.

"I told you there were new colors in the room," he said. "And Joan you are a new color yourself. Look in the mirror!"

Joan lurched to her feet and hurried to the hallway to inspect her reflection in the mirror over the telephone.

"I think I'm the usual color. Perhaps you've had enough champagne."

"No I'm quite sure. Look again. Your hair has turned magenta!"

Peals of laughter from Beata and a pivoting peer from Rudy.

"I had my hair done on Tuesday, Adam," said Joan. "You didn't notice until now, that's all. You aren't hallucinating. Congratulations on the use of 'magenta' by the way. I think of it as aubergine." Belatedly, she recalled that she had bought a large eggplant to serve with dinner but had forgotten to cook it.

"I think it looks splendid," said Beata. "You men! So late to notice a woman's hair. Joan is becoming quite adept at Polish. She went by herself to the hairdressers. I am quite proud."

"There now, you see?" said Rudy, to whom the new hair color was also a revelation. "This is just what I mean. Adam didn't notice Joan's hair until he was relaxed with an infusion of alcohol. Now he is in the state of mind to pay attention to things that are important. Just at that balance point where one sees afresh, Joan's new hair came into focus."

Joan considered again making coffee, but she didn't want to do anything that might be interpreted as a signal that she wanted their guests to leave.

Beata held out her glass and Rudy tipped in the remainder of the champagne.

"Shall I open another bottle?"

"I think that was the last one."

"No, no, there is another. Always must have one on hand, you know, in case of emergencies. And it is always an emergency to run out. Or so I do believe."

Joan wanted to go to sleep on the couch right now. Alert conversation seemed beyond her.

"Vacuum!" she suddenly exclaimed.

"Already? The floor is quite clean," said Beata.

"No. Not vacuum cleaner. The word. There are two u's together in it, just like Dutch."

All eyes turned to Rudy for enlightenment. For a moment he looked baffled, and then the memory slotted into place.

"Right you are, Joan! Not unique to Dutch after all. But I think that word is a rare exception, is it not?"

This made little general sense, but neither Beata nor Adam felt like pursuing it. Joan's moment of alertness receded. Perhaps if she just closed her eyes for a brief moment the others wouldn't notice. She eased her shoes off and sat mermaid style at the edge of the couch nearest the table. Adam stretched his feet across the chair she had vacated, and Beata scooted closer to Rudy. Adam is right, Joan thought, there are new colors in the room. And it is so nice and warm.

She wasn't aware of dropping off, but there was a gap in time during which she must have entered a brief doze. Something happened in the interim, for when her eyes opened again the three others were pointed like retrievers toward the corner of the room. Adam's eyes were not entirely focused, and he frowned terribly in the effort to look awake. Beata had her hands clasped over her heart, and Rudy's eyebrows were shot to the top of his head.

The radio was no longer playing waltzes. It was issuing a stream of excited speech.

"What are they saying?" she inquired. The others shushed her.

"Extraordinary!"

"How wonderful!"

"What can it mean?"

Rudy got up and twiddled knobs on the small television set in the corner. The news popped on, along with a photograph of the *Salvator Mundi*. The announcer was speaking in excited tones.

Rudy is right, thought Adam in surprise. I must have reached a balance. I can understand everything. Everything. I'm not even sure what language he is speaking. But how vivid everything is. The room with its colorful auras had achieved a stunning clarity.

Good God, thought Rudy. This will bring Jurgen back in a hurry. I wonder what he'll say this time.

"What is it? What is going on?" Joan didn't have the energy to do more than peer at the television from an oblique angle.

Beata translated breathlessly, a beat behind the chaotic announcement.

The police were called to a Krakow residence today to investigate the delivery of a mysterious package to a tenant of the building. Pan Pawel Meyer-Radincki was surprised to find a large parcel addressed to him that was owed postage. He opened it with his neighbors looking on and discovered the painting that all Poland has sought for the last many days.

At first he thought it was a joke and that someone had mailed him one of the reproductions that have been painted since Leonardo da Vinci's Salvador Mundi, owned by the Radincki Museum, was authenticated three weeks ago. But the painting looked old, and he called the police. Authorities from the Museum have tentatively identified the panel, though they have asked the Dutch scholar who authenticated it to return to Krakow to inspect it again.

"I knew it," said Rudy.

In the meantime, the painting has been locked in one of the museum's vaults. It will be back on display as soon as possible with extra security in place so that the public can resume enjoyment of this masterpiece.

An idea intruding into Adam's consciousness was beginning to take a wonderful shape. The Leonardo panel was back.

Restored to its rightful owner. No longer would the museum need all that extra security. No more briefcases checked. No more searches in and out. Now he could return Gorski's diary! No one would ever know what he had done. The weight of the stolen diary fell away, and he felt he might float with relief. He was dizzy with the thought that he would again be free, his guilt behind him.

The television camera had shifted to a jouncing shot of a slender, dark-haired man standing before a brick building. He was wearing a nicely-cut jacket and a cream colored scarf. The wind blew his hair back from his face. He appeared to be somewhat reluctantly making a statement into a collection of microphones thrust forward. The wind caught in the microphones and wuthered through his words.

I am as surprised and baffled as you are, he was saying. *I can't imagine why this would have been mailed to me. It makes no sense at all. But I am as happy as any Pole can be that this precious item can be returned to its rightful owner.*

The man turned to go, but the reporters had more questions, this time about his name.

A mere coincidence, of course. His gesture was dismissive and modest. *Indeed, probably a family legend. Perhaps it prompted someone to mail it to this address. Perhaps they thought it would be returned safely. As it has.*

And the slender gentleman smiled graciously and made his exit indoors.

"How absolutely wonderful!" said Beata.

"I understand everything," said Adam.

"Was that the only thing returned?" asked Joan. "What about the chalice. Did they say anything about the chalice?"

"Now this is very good news," declared Rudy. "It calls for a drink! And of course, pies."

28

Afterthoughts

Bilious and hungover, Joan struggled into the cold kitchen and made herself the strongest cup of coffee she thought she could stomach. The dirty dishes from last night were piled in the sink and the stove was stacked with sticky pans. A spill of gravy ignited briefly under the coffee pot, broadcasting a resentful flare and the stench of burnt chicken.

Her head pounded, but the thought of swallowing even so small an object as an aspirin was too much for her tortured stomach. Muscles ached, stomach churned, head throbbed.

The revelation that the stolen painting had been returned had only slightly penetrated her consciousness last night, but she had dreamed about it, seemingly for hours, and awoke feeling dreadful. How much had they all drunk? Glass after glass of wine marched across her memory.

Hair of the dog that bit you skimmed across her mind.

Might as well try. She figured she couldn't feel any worse.

Rudy's bottle of vodka stood on the desk, its cap off, the spirits evaporating into the morning. Joan reached out a trembling hand and poured a dash into someone's empty wine glass. The fume of alcohol seemed clean and refreshing, rather like mouthwash, and she downed the shot in one hopeful swallow.

Thirty seconds later she was retching over the toilet, and after an unpleasant session during which the hair of the dog behaved like a giant fur ball, she raised her head and discovered that she felt marginally better, well enough to crawl to the shower. Hot needles scoured her skin, and the steam rising from the cold tiles released a smell of gravy from her hair. She reached for the shampoo. Lather streaked down her body, swirled around her feet and into the drain.

The shower wasn't nearly long enough, but the hot water ran out and sent her shivering into a thin towel, apparently the only one not in the laundry. She was momentarily alarmed at the sight of the strange woman in the mirror with the dripping purple hair, but then she recollected her trip to the hairdresser. She tiptoed into the bedroom and dressed in clothes retrieved here and there from the floor. She didn't want to disturb Adam, who was sunk in slumber, his head canted back over a pillow, jaw slack, arms flat by his sides, feet poking from the blanket and pointing east and west. She hovered maternally by the bed to make sure he was still breathing, tugged the blanket over his toes, and returned to the living room to gather her thoughts.

Beyond the startling announcement last night, she couldn't recall a single detail. The television had shown the *Salvator Mundi*, a police spokesman, a museum official, and then jiggling footage of some man on his doorstep. Joan had the vague idea that this person might have found the picture, but it was hard to sort through the recollection of an event she hadn't completely understood.

I wonder if the silver chalice was also returned, she thought. Maybe no one has thought to check. Why am I the only one who cares about that? Her sense of duty to the object, a kind of proprietary feeling, returned. Joan savored it for a while, acknowledged its slight irrationality, but also felt her mission intensifying. I will find out what happened, she thought. No one else will bother. This is my story to tell.

***

Pawel Meyer—on the very brink of being officially Pawel Radincki—was inventing his post-theft tactics on the fly, for his original strategy was faltering in face of the ballooning attention he had attracted. The blurry address of the momentous package had been determined by the officials who impounded the wrapping to hyphenate his birth name with that of the museum's noble founders, which indeed was just as he had planned. However, when he first conceived of this stage of the operation, he hadn't reckoned on the anxiety, the heart-thumping trepidation, the moments of sheer panic, that would attend the raking spotlight of official interest. Therefore, rather than granting the fact of his ancestry with the discreet modesty that he had originally planned, Pawel found himself denying its accuracy. With mannered grace, his collar pulled up to mask the pulse jumping in his neck, he rejected any relation between himself and the defunct aristocratic family.

Despite his hope to use this occasion to insinuate his noble connection, he found he could not bring himself to utter so bold a statement in public. In the privacy of daydreams, pleasant illusion invigorated with hearty bouts of fantasy had convinced him of his lineage. But Pawel was not completely delusional, not yet. And this imaginary world could be sustained only in private or in the shared puffed-up company of his like-minded friend, the King of Ruthenia. Now with a public face to maintain, it was much safer to deflect attention to some unknown lunatic who sent the package to him. Thus did he try to repair the flaws that had become apparent in his great plan and attempt to slither away from the surprisingly unwelcome attention.

But then, oddly, he found that the very denial served his original ends. For delivered with casual firmness, his disclaimers prompted the conviction that there was truth in the association of his lowly name with the house of Radincki. Discovering this unexpected effect, he practiced a sober shake of the head, followed by a smile and raised shoulders, and from time to time a weary sigh. These assembled gestures were designed to indicate tacit disclosure of some sorry event of the past. If someone were to conclude that he was protecting the reputation of a distant great-grandmother seduced and abandoned — well, who was he to deny it? His spoken words continued to refuse, even to deride, the allegations of a noble connection. His demeanor indicated assent.

When yet another batch of photographers approached him that evening as he returned from a walk by the river, Pawel hesitated then nodded graciously. He shrugged his coat collar higher against the cold in the style that Cary Grant wore in *Caprice*, leaned against the railing, and aimed a slight smile at the lens. Behind him the overcast sky was suffused with light from the warming fires of the Rynek fair. The camera flash created sharp shadows in the foreground, casting his narrow frame in dramatic relief.

This new tactic inspired another. In the dark of night, with his curtains drawn carefully and his desk lamp heavily shaded, Pawel studied his folio genealogy. From the supply of old paper bought from that convenient Paris bookseller whose overflowing shelves of antique junk contained a forger's paradise, he selected a discolored sheet. With diluted ink flowing from the nib of an aged fountain pen, he sketched the name of a great-great-grandmother and noted a few Radincki scions. The following week he might make a quick trip to the archives to slip the papers into one of the more obscure histories of Poland. In the meantime, to the inquiries from reporters and the ominously inquisitive investigating authorities, he would continue to suggest politely that the overheated imagination of the mysterious personage who returned the Leonardo was misguided beyond his comprehension.

And of course, he refused the reward the museum had hurriedly assembled for return of their most famous possession. A noble spirit could do no less.

29

New Problems

Adam did not make it back to the archives until the Tuesday following the dramatic return of the Leonardo panel. He, too, had required some time before the gastronomic ravages of Thanksgiving receded, but even in the throes of a wicked hangover he felt reprieved. During the minutes when he drifted into consciousness just long enough to stagger to the bathroom, slake a raging thirst, and deal with a throbbing headache, his discomfort had been palliated by the news from the radio report. He was buoyed by the confidence that soon the museum would return to its casual security practices, and that he would at last be able to rid himself of the purloined diary. Indigestion and hangover were eclipsed by relief.

Tuesday brought a terrible shock.

Adam arrived at the Radincki Museum with a spring in his step and a bulging briefcase, ready to resume his scholarly life on the upright path. But it was only to find even more guards posted at the entrance. Instead of a perfunctory frisk of the possessions and persons who streamed back to see the famous painting—even more famous now after its astonishing recent theft and return—there were double lines and slow, deliberate searches. Each handbag, each backpack, each coat pocket was scrutinized, and gaining entrance was slow-going.

Adam turned back, dizzy with dismay. The diary festered in his briefcase, guiltily lurking between innocent folders and a newspaper. Why all the security now when the painting was recovered? What purpose could it possibly serve?

He paced the streets for an hour, returning every now and then to the museum to see if the searches were still ongoing, but finally he gave up. When he went back to the flat, it was all he could do to continue copying the Polish text into his notebook, let alone struggle with the translation. There were only a few more weeks left of his stay, and with the upcoming holidays the museum would be closed even more frequently than usual. Therefore, dwindling opportunities to return the purloined manuscript, maybe none at all with the upheaval caused by the spectacular theft. He looked over the brink of his personal precipice and saw disaster.

Gorski's diary promised to provide the foundation for a good batch of scholarly articles, for it provided a close account of a few weeks in the life of the great Kosciuszko as he traveled on campaign with the armies of the American rebels. In addition, Adam harbored hopes of producing a translation of the entire diary, a slim manuscript of interest to some university press to which he would contribute an introduction and copious notes. And above all, he felt something like a friendship, even kinship, with this long-ago man. He felt he owed it to Andrzej Gorski to bring his existence to light. To recover for a few interested readers the existence of a person who had lived beside a famous man but had himself died forgotten. A silly debt perhaps. But he would feel he had failed the man as well as himself if he could not finish his work with the diary and make it known.

But the diary would do him no good at all if he could not return it to its rightful home. He could not refer to it even in the most obscure footnote if there were no original manuscript in the

Radincki archives to be checked by the scrupulous and the suspicious. If he could not return it, there was no surety against the charge that he had simply invented Andrzej Gorski's record of events from start to finish.

And of course if he went home with the diary itself, he would be either condemned to keep it secret for the rest of his life or charged with theft.

He had to figure out a way to return it. To slip it past the guards and the security checks, back to the shelves where he fervently wished he had let it lie.

It was Joan who discovered the reason for the intensified search procedures. She patiently went through the entrance line and wormed her way into the office of Andrzej Rogowicz to ask him for his opinion about the return of the panel. She found him sitting in his office before a flickering computer screen and surrounded with poster board and marking pens. He was preparing new wall plaques that described the history of attempts to steal the *Mona Lisa*. He barely acknowledged her presence.

"You need a definite article there," said Joan, reading the text for the English version over his shoulder. "You have to say '*the* earlier theft,' not just 'earlier theft'."

"Thank you." Andrzej moved his cursor and added the word.

"And another one here, and then here you need to say '*an*' accident."

Andrzej pushed back from his desk, grazing her knees and creasing a pile of poster board. "All those extra little words make good English impossible!" he exclaimed in irritation. "I have studied your language for fifteen years, and I still can't make any sense over them. A! An! The! Totally unnecessary! And why do they get called articles anyway? What does that mean? What is article?"

"*An* article," said Joan.

He glared. "I am very busy, as you can see."

"Why is your screen flickering like that?"

"Probably there is too much power being used. We are all working very hard. We are all very busy and don't have time to chat."

Joan persisted."Why don't you let me help with this text? In the meantime you can talk to me about the returned picture."

She scooted another chair in front of his computer before he could answer. In truth, he was glad of the opportunity to rest his eyes.

"Thank you. I've been doing this since early this morning."

"Did they search you too when you entered? I would have thought that the security checks would be less intense now rather than more. It took me half an hour to get in."

Andrzej stood and stretched. His crumpled shirt escaped from his loose belt and two pens fell out of his pockets. "Actually, Joan, you are sort of responsible for this situation."

"Me!"

Andrzej explained. Although no one at the museum was convinced of Joan's story that the Bronislaw chalice was really missing and replaced with a replica, no one was entirely certain that it was not either. At first, the energies of the entire museum staff had been devoted to the immediate emergency represented by the theft of the painting, and the question about the old silver item had been put off. But now that the panel had been returned—not discovered after official investigation, not liberated from thieves, but simply returned by post—profound and disturbing suspicions were aroused that someone was making a deliberate mockery of the Radincki Museum. It would be an additional embarrassment if an obscure cup had also been taken and substituted with a replica. Perhaps the purpose of the theft was to test its lax security, really no worse than many other museums, Andrzej hastened to add. But there was continued criticism about the early display of the painting as well as about the ease with which the newly-installed electronic security had been disabled.

"I wondered about that," said Joan.

"Well, you were not alone. It was probably budgetary decision, but now no one will take responsibility."

With strong enjoinders for secrecy, Andrzej continued with the story: The museum was beginning to consider the dreadful possibility that someone aimed to cast doubt on the authenticity of its whole collection. The *Salvator Mundi* was a Leonardo of hitherto dubious attribution. They had gained instant celebrity with its dramatic authentication. But that authentication could be rescinded, and in fact there was a rising tide of art critical disagreement already. The distinguished Dutch scholar was presently on his way back to Krakow and might take a second look and change his mind.

It would be disastrous if the genuineness of other items of the museum were cast into doubt as well. The Director had alerted postal authorities and delivery services to be on the lookout for oddly addressed parcels. And in addition, on the off chance that someone was engaging in a large game of snatch-and-replace that might employ miscreants disguised as visitors, the security that was posted both on entrance and on exit was stricter than ever.

"But Joan, you absolutely must not repeat this," Andrzej repeated. "You must promise me that." He was surprised that he had told her so much, but the American woman was easy to talk to.

"No, of course not. I'll keep it to myself," Joan assured him. An idea began to form. It was a bit farfetched, but Andrzej might be just the person to try it out on.

"You know, there is another possibility," she ventured. "Have you thought that perhaps the painting was stolen as a cover for the other theft?"

"Cover?"

"To distract attention. Maybe the thief never intended to keep the painting. He—or she I suppose—was after the chalice all along. But maybe he figured that it would never be missed with all the fuss over the Leonardo. So he stole the famous painting but never intended to keep it. It was only a cover, a way to hide, taking the silver chalice."

As she uttered these words, all at once Joan was sure she was right. She leapt to her feet with mounting excitement.

"Think about it! This is the only kind of story that makes any sense of these events. Why steal a painting and immediately return it? Doesn't it stand to reason that there was another motive at work?"

Andrzej was not convinced. "That sort of thing might happen, but it doesn't make sense with chalice," he said, puncturing Joan's elation. "In fact, one of the senior curators already thought of the possibility, and everyone is looking around museum to see what else might have been taken. But if someone went to trouble of stealing the painting in order to get something else—as cover as you say—they should have stolen something more valuable. So we are looking for what else could be gone."

Joan ignored the missing articles and considered this objection. "There is an awful lot here in the museum. Can they really check on every single thing?"

Andrzej sighed. "Not easily. Because of course there are going to be some items that are mislabeled, or misattributed, or even fakes. Some we already suspect. But that is true in every large, old collection. Even greatest museums have falsely attributed objects. Any museum authority knows this. But the public doesn't. If other errors are found, then the Director fears that the whole collection will be in doubt. It is a terrible worry!"

Joan nodded. "But it is missing, the first one I saw. I'm sure of it," she persisted. "Why would anyone go to the trouble of stealing something that is so worthless?"

"Not worthless. I didn't say that. But hardly worth stealing. Not like the painting."

"No, I guess not," Joan conceded.

It wasn't the time to bring up the possibility that the legend of the chalice provided a motive. That would only be convincing if the thief truly wanted to summon a demon. And who would believe that?

30

Pursuits

Like a chain and its weakest link, a crime is only as strong as its frailest participant, and where there are two or three, one is bound to be more fragile than the others.

Pawel had enlisted the help of Bodie on the advice of one of the shadier acquaintances of his late wife, a man whose long relationship with the pawnshops of Europe would have been accurately described as a fence, although he had avoided conviction under that sobriquet for all of his long and disreputable life. And Bodie had brought in the rookie Keith, a man he had met under circumstances that had made Keith appear less afflicted with a conscience than turned out to be the case.

Keith, still limping and sore from his encounter on the bridge, had been missing all day. Though Bodie methodically visited the various taverns and cafés that they frequented, he had failed to find him. Bodie could care less about the wellbeing of that young man, but he was quite concerned about his inability to keep his mouth shut. At first his yipping babble had been merely an annoyance that could be put off on youthful nerves and relatively low brain power. But after the bridge incident (Bodie thought of Klementyna Kamynska's murder as an "incident"), Keith showed all his weaknesses. He relived the event over and over, always getting stuck at the point where the utterly unpredictable recklessness of a cyclist had completed the act — perhaps just at the moment when Keith might have faltered and let her go. Now Keith would never know if he himself would have finished the job or backed off and saved his soul. The indeterminacy tormented him. What if, what if, he said. If only, if only. Such a tiny word: If. Minute but engulfing.

In an unpracticed attempt at sensitivity, Bodie suggested that Keith might think of the accident as the hand of God. Probably the impact from the bicyclist had dealt the fatal blow, after all, not the plunge into the river. Bodie was a practical man. Had he, like Keith, literally gotten away with murder, he would have been triumphant. But Keith was flailing with guilt for an action that, in Bodie's flexible assessment, might not even have been his fault at all. Fate had taken a hand, he insisted. You didn't do it. Not the final push, the one that sent her over the railing. In fact, you were as much victim of the accident as she. Or that guy on the bicycle. But Keith had a hard time taking that view of things. He was like a man drowning in shallow water who refused to put his feet down. Last night he had dreamed and wailed in his sleep.

Worst of all, he was attracting attention with his wild, bruised face and the fraying sling on his arm. Heads turned as he walked down the street, his gait askew and his eyes burning. Bodie had to get him out of Krakow. They both needed to make their exit. But they also needed their final payment. Damned if he would leave now without squeezing the last dime out of it all. Keith himself seemed to have forgotten about the money, but Bodie hadn't. He chafed that they had to wait for a summons from their highhanded employer to meet again. He was briefly tempted to forget the final payment and take off by himself, but he feared Keith would break completely and confess everything without his constraining presence. But Keith wouldn't leave. His fragile conscience rooted him here. He babbled about forgiveness and wouldn't leave until he got it.

Bodie decided to take matters into his own hands.

Though Krakow is a large city, its ancient center is small, bounded by the Planty, a vaguely circular park that once described the walled perimeter of earlier times. If Bodie cast his net across the whole city, there was no chance of tracking down their employer. How stupid he had looked in that prancy little mask, which didn't even cover his chin. Style had trumped prudence, and Bodie thought that he might recognize him. So he trod the now familiar streets of the Old Town, confident that his quarry would turn up again in territory where they had already met.

There were lots of places to sit in the vicinity of the town center. Bodie positioned himself at the end of a bar from which he could look out over the Rynek. He still had not figured out why they had spent all that time in the small room of the museum making a cast of the lock of that cabinet. Presumably their employer had used it to make a key. If Bodie had directed that job, he would have simply cut the glass top off the case. He couldn't figure out why the key was needed in the first place. And anyhow, it hadn't been used, at least not yet. The only thing stolen was the painting. All those fancy jewels lying around were still in their cases.

And now the painting was back at the museum. It didn't make sense. Nothing made sense.

The bar was subdued today. Most of the patrons were men like him drinking alone. A television mounted in the corner broadcast sports programs interspersed with news. He could follow the sports, but the news was in Polish, and he could only guess what it reported.

He had been at this very bar several nights ago when the news broke that the stolen painting had been discovered. That had been a surprise. But it seemed the painting had just somehow been returned. He had puzzled over the report and tried to pick up the thread of news. Everyone in the little bar was riveted on the screen and had left their tables to come closer. Some of the patrons were foreigners who had asked questions in English, and he strained to hear the answers. All he could figure out was that a package had been opened by someone who alerted the authorities.

Obviously, something had gone wrong. The painting must have been intercepted on its way to whoever had commissioned the theft. But whatever had misfired, it wasn't Bodie's fault. He had followed instructions down to the last detail and had done the job he was paid for. But the return of the painting worried him, for if the delivery had gone badly their employer might have already absconded without dispensing the extra payment.

Above all, it wasn't safe to stay now that the woman's body had been found. They had to collect their money and get out of town. If he could convince Keith to go. If he could even find him.

***

Keith had spent the morning in the one place Bodie did not think to check: sitting in church. A cold, quiet place where his thoughts had room to move around. Sometimes they formed prayers that filled his head and made him dizzy. He was exhausted from a night of terrible dreams, nightmares that clawed at him and refused to let him wake. Finally he had struggled out of bed and left the room while the morning was still dark. Such a dark place, Poland. Especially now that the shortest day of the year approached. Keith longed for someplace south where the sun would warm his soul. A place where he might be forgiven.

It took him three tries to find the right church. They all looked similar to him with their clutter of statues, and all the streets looked the same too. Was there nothing that ran straight in this city? But finally he located the ancient place where she had appeared to him. He entered and lit a candle, then two, then three.

He took a seat on one of the straight wooden chairs and folded his hands, waiting for Saint Gertruda to appear.

***

There was that painting again. The news channel wouldn't let it alone. In fact, the broadcast over the bar seemed to be recapitulating the museum theft. Bodie moved away from the window so he could see the screen with less reflection. Christ's raised hand gestured from the television. Wouldn't it be a joke if the painting turned out to be a fake after all. He could still feel its weight against his injured shoulder. And now the camera panned through the museum with its damaged wall where the bolts had been pried away. And then the Leonardo panel came into view again hanging in its new place of honor on an adjacent wall. Bodie couldn't figure why they didn't just clean up the original spot and put it there again rather than leave the vacant gap that reminded everyone of the theft. A repaired wall would give him slightly more assurance that the investigation was finished.

But these matters weren't now the center of his attention, which was suddenly riveted on the figure of a man being interviewed. From the splicing of scenes he determined that this was old footage that was part of the narrative of events surrounding the theft, and now he realized that he had missed part of the earlier broadcast.

This man had a familiar look about him. Bodie switched seats again and drew closer to the screen. When the man turned away from the reporters his slim shoulders stood out against the front of the building, and suspicion dawned. That studied movement, that turn of the head and that practiced grace. Mentally, Bodie matched the figure to the silhouette of the man who had led them through the twisting corridors of the museum. It had been dark, but from time to time they had passed banks of tall windows, and the light from the streets had shone in with a grey gleam outlining the man ahead, that slim build, narrow shoulders, girlish waist. Or such was his recollection. It wasn't evidence enough. Many men were slight like this one. He wished he could be sure.

And then he was. The man turned again and extended a hand towards the camera, making what Bodie would have recognized as a deprecating gesture had he been able to follow the speech. And there were his hands. That ring.

Bodie summoned up the image of the three of them just before they slid through the hidden door of the Radincki Museum. All of them had put on gloves. A snotty directive, as if Bodie and Keith didn't know about fingerprints. And their leader had paused to twist a ring to the inside of his hand so that his leather glove could fit over the jewel. Bodie had been holding the light, and he recollected how two amber glints like small cat's eyes swiveled toward the palm of his hand.

He risked a question in English to the bartender.

"That man. Who is he?"

The bartender's English was more suited for drink orders than for museum discourse, but one of the fellow beer drinkers supplemented his account. It seems that this man on television had received the missing painting, which was posted to him anonymously. Quite mysterious why it was sent to him. Confusion of names perhaps, but some think he is actually a descendent of the Radincki family. He denies it, but you never know. An upright citizen, in any event, because he is refusing the reward money.

And the screen switched to resume broadcast of a soccer game. Bodie stayed and watched while he finished his beer and let this new information fall into place.

So the painting wasn't intercepted after all. It went right to the man who had stolen it, and he just gave it back. Bodie thought he might recognize the street front where the man had been interviewed during the broadcast. It looked familiar. It probably wasn't very far away.

On his way back to his room Bodie sought out a newspaper that covered the news of the week, one that included pictures. It took him a while at a smelly kiosk with an impatient proprietor. He bought two papers and scanned the incomprehensible pages until he found a long article surrounding a photo of the painting. And then another photo of a slender man standing on a narrow set of steps. With the patience of a scholar Bodie pored over it carefully, running his eyes over each indecipherable word until he found one he knew: *Ulica*. Street. A named street. Then he got out his city map. He was confident now, knowing that his quarry was in his sights.

**

Pawel favored sitting in corners. At the restaurant where he had chosen to have a late lunch, he sat with his back to the door on the far end of the wall, hoping to avoid yet another camera. The reporters had been relentless, though their attention was finally waning. But when a shadow crossed his table and a man appeared in front of him, he was at first politely resigned to field more questions.

But it wasn't a reporter. It was a large man whose long legs made him cant his knees sideways as, presumptuously, he took a seat at the small table. Pawel raised his head with a frown. Then his stomach lurched. He fleetingly considered pretending not to know his visitor, though it was quickly clear that tactic would be unwise. He simply regarded him, speechless, hoping that his pounding heart would calm before he had to speak.

"So you refused the reward," said Bodie after a pause that went on for just as long as he desired. He spoke the mandated French. Mr. Pawel Meyer or Radincki or whoever the hell he was had gone satisfyingly pale. How easy it had been to wait outside his apartment and follow him here.

"What idiot refuses a reward? A rich one, I figure. One who can afford to pay us what we are owed. And even more, what we deserve." Bodie had crafted his opening statement carefully.

With a supreme effort Pawel entered his zone of superiority and sipped delicately at the rim of an empty coffee cup. He was thinking very hard.

"Do keep your voice down," he said repressively, pitching his voice low. "And for goodness sake, appear friendly. We don't want to attract attention."

Bodie passed his hand over his eyes as if to erase his glare. Pawel noticed the stubble on his chin with disapproval.

"The pay for this job hasn't been so good, you know," Bodie continued in a lower voice. "Keith and I deserve more. Especially for the extra job. No one signed up for murder. We're not leaving until we get more money."

Pawel knew it was critical that he not lose control of the conversation. "May I offer you a drink?" he asked. "Something to eat?"

He nodded to a passing waiter and Bodie ordered a beer. Pawel translated the French into Polish, an unnecessary courtesy for the waiter, who knew the word for beer in eight languages. But he was buying time.

"I suppose I should inquire how you located me," he said. The question appeared casual, but Pawel was worried that in spite of all his caution, he might have left behind some betraying clue.

"I recognized you from the TV," said Bodie.

He did not elaborate, leaving Pawel to wonder if those clever reflections at their rendezvous restaurant had rendered him as visible to Bodie as the latter was to him.

"You can run, but you can't hide." This nasty thought was expressed in English, but the meaning was clear enough.

"It is not a question of running. As I explained long ago," Pawel said, "it is crucial that no suspicion fall on me for the theft. If I am implicated in any way whatsoever, then so will you be. And you don't want that. You don't want questions raised about my recent associations, especially those with a less than clean police record, such as yourself."

It was a lucky guess, but accurate. "Well, if you want to cut loose from your 'recent associations,' as I suppose you mean Keith and me, then all you have to do is pay us the rest and we'll be out of here."

"And I shall do so. As promised. But at the moment the funds are not ready to hand."

Bodie raised his eyebrows skeptically. The beer appeared and he took a long swallow, all the time watching Pawel over the rim. Bodie didn't believe for a minute that he didn't have the money.

"Why not just take the reward?"

Pawel folded his napkin and leaned forward to speak quietly but intensely. "I cannot profit in any way from the theft. To take the reward under the circumstances in which the painting was returned would be to profit. It is quite impossible. Out of the question."

And then Bodie asked the obvious question.

"Then why did you go to all this trouble? Why steal the thing at all? What do you get from this anyway?"

Pawel sat back. "That," he said with lofty and dismissive condescension, "is none of your concern. The theft of the painting and its return will have consequences many years ahead. But none of it will touch you. Your work is finished."

Bodie persisted. "How about the key to that other cabinet? The one that injured my shoulder, by the way. Don't forget that. What was all that about?"

"Again, it does not concern you," said Pawel with a shrug. Then brilliantly added, "Or even me, that one." A clever ploy, he thought. His extemporizing was going rather well. Bodie had no doubts that there were superior criminal forces behind the theft.

Bodie was quiet. The answers didn't satisfy him, but he really didn't care what the motive was so long as his own profit was secure. He had always supposed that there were more participants in the theft, higher-ups whom Pawel had not disclosed. Presumably, the reasoning for the theft and its quick recovery made sense to them, not to mention tampering with that stupid lock when the key made from it hadn't been used to open anything.

"We deserve more than we got. A lot more. The job was bigger than planned. And both Keith and I got hurt." Keith's body was healing. It was his mind that was disintegrating, but Bodie kept that to himself.

Pawel was silent. He gazed out the window with apparent calm, mentally assessing both his bank account and the calendar. He desperately wanted both Bodie and Keith out of the country, out of his sight, out of his life. He was done with them.

"You have indeed confronted some unforeseen difficulties," he granted.

"Damn right."

"I am sorry that Keith was hurt. Of course, his actions have aroused no suspicion at all. You are both quite in the clear with regard to the unfortunate necessity."

"That's a fancy way of putting it."

"But accurate." There was a long pause while both assessed their relative positions. Bodie could make quite a lot of trouble for Pawel, but he couldn't figure out how to do so without at the same time making just as much for himself. It was rather a stand-off. But it appeared that there was less urgency than he had feared. He risked ceding his upper hand by asking a question.

"What do you mean, we're in the clear?" He shifted in his seat. It was the first time his demeanor had been less than menacing. Pawel, alert to advantage, permitted himself a superior shake of the head.

"Didn't you hear? No. Of course you would not be understanding the papers. The police believe that the woman, the museum guard, was the victim of an accident. The fog, you know. Easy to lose your way and your footing. And then there was the automobile accident with the bicycle, which they believe contributed to her fall. Several cars hit the guard rail, and one of those must have knocked her over unconscious into the water. They have closed the case."

Pawel reported this outcome as though the matter were of little significance to him personally, though he still felt an exalted relief that Klementyna Kamynska was out of his life by means of the fortuitous crash. Destiny had taken a hand once more—another auspicious portent.

Bodie too was relieved. Maybe this news would settle Keith down. If the authorities had judged the death accidental, then who was he to dispute them?

"Even so we still demand more," he said. "You're so rich you don't need a reward, I guess. But I do. We do. You are not done with the payment."

There was a pause while the waitress brought Pawel a plate of food: cutlets with potatoes and green beans. She looked inquiringly at Bodie, who shook his head.

Pawel picked up his fork. "I am prepared," he announced with an air of generosity, "to compensate you for your extended stay and extra effort. Not by very much, mind you. I have exhausted my resources for this project. And I don't want to bring my own superiors into this; that would be risky for both of us." Another brilliant ploy, he thought. That comment should keep Bodie from demanding too much. He continued, "But next week I should be able to give you another payment, say two thousand American dollars. That is quite a nice bonus for you. Meet me here in one week precisely. But after that you must be on your way."

"Two thousand isn't much. It's only a thousand apiece. Chump change."

Pawel reassessed. "I meant two thousand apiece, of course. It is the best I can do. And it is better than nothing. You have already been paid handsomely remember."

That was true.

"Okay, one week," Bodie conceded. It would be double for him anyhow, for it took only a moment to decide that he would keep the entire extra pay for himself. Keith need never know.

Bodie wanted to see the last of his pitiful partner. As soon as they were out of Poland he would make his crooked way home. Too bad that the need for misdirection would use up some of the cash with extra fares, but it was more important to cover his tracks and leave both Keith and the Savior of the World far behind. He was glad that he had revealed his real name neither to Keith nor to the strange man who was now fussily cutting his cutlet into delicate slices.

It was too much to watch. He drained his glass and left.

31

Saint Joan

Saint Gertruda did not make an appearance in the church, though Keith prayed for her to come and sat patiently for a long time. He was disappointed but not surprised. It was not up to him to command the presence of a saint. After a kneeling nap that was as much the result of his lingering concussion as his disturbed night's sleep, he stiffly left and wandered back to the place where first he had seen her.

The security lines at the Radincki Museum were not yet long, though Keith was given a particularly thorough search, because with his bruised face and wrinkled clothing he looked more like a derelict seeking warmth than a patron of history or the arts. But he had the entrance fee. In fact, as he rummaged in his pockets for the correct amount, he inadvertently revealed a wad of his share of Pawel's first payment, duly noted by the woman at the kiosk. Finally, he was passed through the check point with a guarded smile, which he managed to return. He had caught a glimpse of himself in the window reflection. His first visit was to the cloakroom, where he splashed his face with water and straightened his clothing. He noted that the guards were keeping an eye on him, so he strolled quietly through the galleries on his best behavior until finally they seemed to relax.

He found himself in the Painting Gallery by accident, for it was the last place he intended to visit. It looked different in the light of day, even larger and a lot more cluttered. He was momentarily disoriented when he saw the bare wall still showing the damage that he and Bodie had caused during the removal of the painting. And then he was even more confused when he saw that very painting hanging nearby. How could that be? Were there two of them?

It certainly looked the same: the figure of Jesus with his hand held up as if in greeting. Or perhaps in blessing. Or maybe he was about to point. To point right at the thief who stole him! That slight smile, did it mock? Keith stepped sideways, but the heavy-lidded eyes continued to search him out.

A nearby security guard took a step forward out of concern for the newly hung masterpiece, so cleverly placed beside the scene of its theft (another of Andrzej's ideas). Keith made himself turn slowly away to inspect the pictures along another wall. He was remembering Bodie's advice: a rapid retreat signals guilt. Hang around until they get used to you. Keith left the gallery to sit for a time on one of the benches in front of a wall filled with weapons displayed in fan-spreads of swords and spears. From his pocket he took out the museum floor plan he'd been given with his entrance ticket and pretended to study it. He knew perfectly well where he had to go. He just needed a little time to summon the strength.

He heard voices coming from the stairs, and three people passed by him and headed towards the smaller galleries. Keith kept his head down. He couldn't lower it very far before his bruised skull started to throb. It had made it hard to pray properly when visiting the church. Maybe that is why Saint Gertruda hadn't arrived when he asked for her.

A distance behind him he could hear the slow, clopping footsteps of a security guard, and for a moment time reversed. His heart stopped as he remembered the dreaded footfalls of the guard who had spied him and Bodie engaged in their furtive labors. But this was someone else. Not that woman. It could never be that woman. He had stopped her steps forever. Keith stood and took a deep breath. His only salvation lay in Saint Gertruda. He set off toward the annex gallery to seek her counsel.

His wish was granted, for there she was right in front of him. Not in her window niche but there in the middle of the room. She knelt beside the cabinet that he and Bodie had monkeyed with. It seemed an odd place for a saint to perch.

Before Keith could fall to his knees and join her in prayer, he realized that she was not alone. A young man was crouching with his head half way under the cabinet.

"You see what I mean?" said Saint Gertruda. And Keith understood her words. Perhaps one always understands saints when they speak, but Keith was also pretty sure that she was speaking English. His head was aching very badly.

"The lock is scratched," she continued. "And it looks like there was some kind of goop stuck around it. I'm pretty sure that it was tampered with a little while ago because I noticed a funny smell earlier, some kind of chemical odor."

And then the saint turned and saw Keith, and her face changed. The long brows raised, the pale eyes lit, and her mouth parted as if about to speak. Keith read the expression as disapproval and warning.

He realized with dismay what she must be doing there. Showing someone what Bodie and he had done with the lock. That apparently pointless cast. And she must also know of that other, that terrible, that unspeakable thing that he had done. She knew his guilt. She knew his sin.

Would she betray him? Had she summoned him to this place to render him up to the police? No, not that. It couldn't be that, for she remained silent, saying nothing to the man under the cabinet.

What then? She must be warning him away. Yes. She was warning him. His protector, his fairy godmother, his very own saint.

Keith obeyed. He fled the room with a prayer of thanks in his heart and a terrible conviction that he would never get out of Poland. His penance might be to stay here forever in the service of Saint Gertruda, for he had committed a sin, and without her forgiveness he could never leave.

***

Joan had turned at a noise at the door and was shocked to see a man with a face so damaged that at first she wondered if it was painted. There was a deep welt along his jaw. One eye was swollen and purple surrounded with streaks of green. But perhaps worst of all was the ghastly pallor that underlay the discolorations. He was looking at her with an alarming expression: fervent, shocked. Then he bolted away and disappeared down the hall.

It all happened so fast that Joan wondered momentarily if she had imagined him. The light was odd in this little gallery. Perhaps a reflection from the stained glass niches had somehow been cast across his features, turning the flesh shades of rose and blue. The moment of startle passed, and she directed her attention back to the vitrine that once held the Bronislaw chalice.

"Do you see what I mean?" she said. "Don't you think that this lock has been tampered with?"

"Perhaps," said Andrzej. He didn't sound convinced. And then he did something unexpected. "Shall we take a closer look?"

He fished a ring of keys from his pocket and chose a thin key with a dog-legged square tip. He slid back under the vitrine and fiddled with the lock until the glass top released. He stood, reached into the case, and lifted the chalice.

"Shouldn't we be worried about fingerprints?"

"It's already been checked. The surface was clean. If anyone touched it recently, there is no way to know."

Surprised and pleased at the opportunity, Joan cradled the chalice in her hands with the bowl resting against her palms. She lifted it and looked closely at the figures around the stem. The woman with the long hair stood back to back against a dragon with pointy, folded wings. On the other sides a swan drifted among water weeds and a wolf peered out of a screen of tall grass. The figures still looked slightly wrong, but she had lost the precise image of what they had been before.

"Joan, surely you can see that it is not likely that this would have been a target for thieves," said Andrzej. "It really is not an object of great value. In fact, this bowl was placed with the older items in these cases mainly because somewhere along the way a strange story arose about its magic powers. But that doesn't add much to its value."

Joan didn't reply. After a minute, Andrzej took the chalice from her and replaced it carefully back in the vitrine, positioning it over the mirror so the figures at the back could be seen. Now the swan was uppermost and the wolf faced the mirror.

"I am sorry if you are disappointed," he said.

Joan forced a smile. "Not disappointed, no. But I still think you should investigate the lock, which has obviously been tampered with. Suppose someone made a duplicate key?"

Andrzej shrugged. "Who knows? But I shall report the suspicion to my superiors, you can be sure." They shook hands and he disappeared down to the hall to the offices. Hopefully, he had satisfied this woman's curiosity and she would stop fretting about the chalice.

In his hasty exit, Keith had blundered down an unfamiliar hallway and into a room that overlooked a little courtyard formed by the space between jutting sections of the museum. He found it a heaven-sent mistake, for now he gazed through two sets of windows and witnessed a ritual that confirmed his conviction that he was in thrall to Saint Gertruda.

The living saint stood just before the niche where her glass image glowed. Her finely-drawn brows lifted. Slender arms reached out, and a silver bowl was placed in her spread fingers. Saint Gertruda held the offering before her, quite still. Then she lifted it above her head—a gesture to God. And she lowered it again. She turned slightly towards the window, and it seemed to Keith that she signaled him, knowing that he stood looking on.

Keith was transfixed, comforted, then alarmed. He wasn't certain if the saint was protecting or threatening him. He held his breath to see what she would do now. Through the two windows he saw Saint Gertruda turn her back and step out of his line of sight. Her message must be finished. He wished he could figure out just what it was.

32

Reassessments

Bodie had walked the circuit of the Planty twice. His feet were cold in his heavy shoes. He cut through the park and was passing the Radincki Museum when Keith stumbled down the steps. He caught up with him on the street.

"I've been looking for you all day!" he growled, "Where the hell have you been?"

Keith didn't answer at first. He looked blankly at Bodie with hardly a sign of recognition and made as if to walk away from him. Bodie grabbed his elbow.

"What's the matter buddy? Where have you been? Why are you back here of all places?" At the scene of the crime, you asshole, he thought. But he kept his voice casual and friendly. When Keith finally spoke, it was in a voice so low and toneless he could hardly be heard.

"I saw her," said Keith. "I keep seeing her everywhere. Maybe she is following me. I can't get away. But when I look for her she isn't there."

"What the hell are you talking about? Here, don't walk so fast. You're bumping into people."

They had to get out of this crowd; people were giving them odd looks. There was a bar somewhere nearby that he remembered was quiet. Only when they were seated at a small table in the back corner away from the window did he permit Keith to speak again. The bar was blessedly warm. Keith had been shivering, and the sudden heat sent him into shudders. There was a radiator behind him, and he scooted his chair back and canted against it.

"Now what's this all about?" asked Bodie, modulating his impatience and trying to sound friendly. "Who are you following? Are you in trouble with some woman?"

Keith felt in desperate need of a friend to share his burden, and this fierce and unlikable man might have to do. He shook his head emphatically.

"No. You've got it all wrong. It's not just a woman." How could he put this so Bodie would understand? "It's not an ordinary woman, I'm sure she's not. She's a saint. Or maybe an angel. I saw her first in the museum in the little place where we made the lock mold. First she was just in the window, you saw her there too. But now she has been following me around. She came to me in church. But then when I tried to find her again she disappeared. And then she was in the museum just now in the same place, but she was with someone else so I couldn't talk to her. And she knows—Bodie, she knows what I did! I know that she knows. And I don't know what she wants me to do."

Bodie was stunned. He sat back and scrutinized his miserable partner. This was worse than he had imagined. Could there really be something to worry about here? Was someone really on to their activities? Surely Keith had enough brains to keep his mouth shut. But he had been in such bad shape since the episode on the bridge that his state of mind was hard to judge. Bodie knew himself just well enough to realize that sympathy was not his strong suit. He had to be very careful. There might be a lot at stake here. He cleared his throat and spoke evenly.

"Calm down. Start at the beginning and tell me what you mean. No, wait. I'll get us something to drink."

He rose to get them beers, but to his horror Keith's bruised eyes filled with tears and his lower lip began to fold back like a fearful child's.

"Whoa there friend!" he said heartily. "You just sit there a minute and warm up. No need to get all stirred up."

Great Christ, tears! Bodie permitted himself a private eyeroll as he hurried to the bar and requested two brandies. And in a burst of insight he also ordered two bowls of thick soup he could see sitting in a large pot in the small kitchen behind the counter. The food came quickly, and Keith, suddenly hit with hunger, bent to eat like a starving animal.

"Relax, buddy," said Bodie. "All you need is a little food. Now eat up and tell me everything. No, not yet. Get some soup in you first and then a little brandy. Here you can have mine too; I'm not that hungry. Eat. Then you can tell me everything. Everything."

***

Around the corner from Bodie and Keith, Joan and Andrzej were sitting over coffee and the remains of a lunch so late it would count for dinner.

"Thank you for opening the exhibit case for me," said Joan. "I truly appreciate it. It was very nice of you." She suspected rightly that Andrzej wasn't supposed to talk further with her, but matters were still not settled.

"But I still think that the chalice now on display is not the one I first saw two months ago," Joan insisted. "There is simply no doubt in my mind. When I sketched the chalice, the dragon was facing the mirror. I know because it was harder to draw than the other figures. And I snapped a few photos. They aren't very good because I couldn't avoid reflections off the glass, but they do confirm that the chalice was repositioned. When you opened the cabinet today, the dragon lay on top. So someone took the thing that was there before and put another thing in its place. And no matter how insignificant you think the chalice was, it was taken. And it could still be a cover for the theft of the Leonardo painting."

"Which is now returned."

"Yes, which is now returned." She sighed. "But aren't you the slightest bit curious about why?"

Andrzej gazed through the window at the crowded square. Through the glass a small brass band could be heard. They were playing American Christmas music. He wondered if Joan would notice, or if Americans were too used to the ubiquity of their own culture to pay it any mind.

"The Director fears that someone is playing games with the museum, Joan," he finally said. "And you have to realize that it is game with very high points for us."

"Stakes?" Joan suggested.

"Stakes. High stakes. And most important, it could be a dangerous game." Andrzej looked into her eyes, such an unusual blue. With their pale clarity, they reminded him oddly of the eyes of some northern dogs bred on the steppes. The frazzled fur around the hood of the jacket she wore today enhanced this impression. "Joan, I think you should be careful about spreading your suspicions too far. You don't want to put yourself in danger, as others perhaps have already." He hoped that didn't sound farfetched, but Joan was looking stubborn.

Her expression changed to perplexity. "Like the guard? You mean the woman who died on the bridge?"

"Possibly," Andrzej nodded. He didn't want to go overboard with his warning. As far as he knew, the museum guard had probably died by accident, though her death was still a puzzle given that it happened so close to the robbery. He had been instructed to discourage Joan from pursuing yet another missing item from the Radincki collection, and perhaps an appeal to her own safety would be effective. Moreover, he found that he was sincere in his warning. Stealing a painting by Leonardo da Vinci made sense. Sending it back did not. The seemingly motiveless thefts and returns were hard to comprehend, and Andrzej didn't like the fact that he could not understand the motive of this thief. The lack of reason behind it all might signal a danger proportionately unaccountable.

For her part, Joan was having a hard time seeing much personal risk in her inquisitive pursuit. Who besides Andrzej and the museum staff would know about it? They just want me out of their hair, she thought. I am an annoyance.

She assumed an appreciative smile. "I promise I'll be cautious, Andrzej," she said. "Even though I don't think I am myself in any danger, you have given me much to think about."

Somehow, he was not reassured.

33
Prayer and Meditation

Joan had first come to the Church of Saint Francis with Adam for a concert. The high vaulted ceiling and thick stone walls provided glorious sound, and the itinerant chamber group played sublime passages of Vivaldi, Bach, and Palestrina. They performed under a series of arches set beneath a soaring ceiling painted twilight blue and spangled with gold stars like the night heavens.

Today she had returned to get out of the wind that was whipping off the river. The building was barely heated, and she still shivered. Several tourists wandered around admiring the opulently painted walls. The churches of Krakow claimed ancient pedigrees, but thanks to periodic fires they had been rebuilt several times over. Here the splendid walls were covered with rich Art Nouveau designs in jewel-like hues. Though comparatively new, they possessed a tapestry-like quality, and their dark glory lent a medieval flavor to the atmosphere. Despite all the renovation over centuries, from time to time Joan stumbled on patches of ancient stone. She found herself reaching to touch those old walls to ground herself in time, to locate one fleeting life on its journey through enduring places. Not a worshipful person, she yet took comfort in being one among thousands to have passed through this space seeking reassurance or peace.

A tall scaffolding in plastic sheeting covered work being done on one wall. She saw that the uprights were barely stripped trees, entire trunks pressed into service with their branches peremptorily torn away. Noble families long forgotten lay beneath the stones at her feet, their coffins stacked in the crypt below, their names, once incised in marble for eternity, now worn blank by the feet of the pious and the curious. Each side altar held a cross, paintings of Biblical scenes, statues of hovering cherubs, long-faced saints. There were reliquaries with mystifying holy artifacts — splintered bone, ragged cloth, the stain of long-dried blood. The more devout prayed in the pews or knelt on the stone floor huddled in a clutch of still devotion. The thick air of worship was to Joan the most foreign of all the foreignness of Poland. She held it in awe laced with a small thread of contempt. It seemed to her abject, superstitious, primitive. Yet she felt a grudging envy too. Prayer with that degree of fervor was a blessing in itself, a respite from the divided mind of the ordinary day.

She tugged the hood of her jacket over her head. The cloaking style of the hood blended with the clerical dress of the young monks who moved in and out of the church with the ease of a householder. From beneath her head covering she glimpsed children gently pressed to their knees by praying parents, women slipping into confessionals, men in work clothes who genuflected stiffly, crossed themselves, and moved to a prayer bench. Off to the sides were banks of burning votive candles.

Joan sometimes felt that she had been driven from the faith of her youth by the sheer blandness of the friendly God preached about by the liberal ministers of her community. They sang about walking with Jesus as if casual conversation with a divinity were no more than an encounter on the street. The informal deity that resided in that bright, Protestant light had in the end just let her go like a weak hand losing its grip. Whatever was true of the intense Catholicism here, surely it was not bland.

These churches with their dim interiors quieted her mind as she pondered Adam and the circumstances that had sundered their growing bond. He was so withdrawn now, his attention entirely inward. Unlike the early weeks when he would come home from the archives either complaining about the paucity of materials or excited to have discovered an interesting text, these days he was not inclined to discuss his work at all. Gorski had been a virtual third occupant of the flat for two months, but now his name was hardly spoken.

Andrzej's unexpected warning intruded on this sea of thoughts. At first, it had seemed an absurd concern, but now she was not so sure. Her earlier distress over the death of Klementyna Kamynska had been all but eclipsed in the excitement of the returned Leonardo and by her conviction that there had been another theft. And now she had to reckon with the possibility that these events were connected more intimately than they had first appeared, and that—strangely—she herself might be one of the links that bound them together.

What, actually, was the proper sequence of the events that had unfolded?

First, the Leonardo panel had been stolen.

No, that wasn't first. First was her notice of the chalice. It had taken her fancy sufficiently that she had photographed it and sketched it in her diary, observantly recording the very details that were discrepant with the artifact now on display.

And then there was that peculiar odor she had noticed and the gummy residue on the bottom of the vitrine. She couldn't remember when she had observed that. Perhaps shortly after she had started sketching. No traces of odor now remained, and Andrzej had not been persuaded that the lock was tampered with, despite the scratch that she pointed out. As he remarked, there was no way of knowing how long it had been there.

Then there was the business with the painting. First it was authenticated. Then it was stolen. Then it was returned.

No, before it was returned the museum guard had died.

For a time it had seemed that Klementyna Kamynska had been a party to the theft. But then her drowned body had been pulled from the river. And shortly thereafter, that odd man had received the painting by a puzzling delivery. The sequence of events made little sense, and Joan was almost persuaded that the woman's death must not play a part in this pattern at all. In fact, it disrupted it. There was no reason to kill someone after a successful theft, especially of an object that was about to be sent back. The Kamynska death was probably an accident after all, just as the authorities had concluded.

There was another mystery that could not be set aside: the return of the painting. One would have expected it might be sold to a wealthy art lover with a covert collection. Or that it might be held for ransom. Or perhaps tracked down by a team of investigators. But the mode of return was perplexingly casual, almost as if the thief had simply changed his mind. Inconceivable.

Joan returned to her earlier insight: the only way to arrange these events into a pattern of any consequence was to shift the Leonardo away from the center of attention and focus on the second theft: the Bronislaw chalice.

Which evidently had little value or importance. The thief, therefore, was not an expert or a collector, not someone aiming at a lucrative market. Someone just who wanted it for himself because . . . Why? Could it possibly be because, as she and Rudy had so flippantly speculated, he believed the legend attached to it? In that case, the thief would be someone who, for obscure reasons, not to mention an almost unbelievable dose of superstition, had wanted to raise a demon badly enough to risk an absurdly complicated theft.

The image of Pawel Meyer—or Radincki—floated into her mind. It was hard to attach such a crazy and dramatic motive to that fussy little man in the news, but he was another discordant figure in these events. He had seemed completely sane and reasonable in the broadcast reports. No hint of the occult about him. Surely it was ludicrous to think that Pawel might be the one in the middle of all this activity. If he was the one behind all this mystery, Andrzej's warning might be put aside.

On the other hand, if he were a pawn in someone else's game, that was another story.

Would Klementyna Kamynska fit into that expanded pattern? Was she one of the thieves, perhaps whom the others had come to mistrust? Or was she simply a bystander who had seen too much?

Perhaps like Joan herself. Maybe Andrzej was right.

How could Joan be perceived as a threat? What had she seen? What did she know?

Nothing about the painting. But quite a lot about the missing chalice. In fact, Andrzej's warning actually confirmed the connection between the two thefts. So if she was really in danger, she must be right about the chalice. She called to mind the day that she had approached the guard with her question and they had walked together to the small gallery—in full view of anyone who might be concerned to keep the theft of the chalice secret. Who might therefore imagine that she had taken undue and dangerous notice of an otherwise insignificant object. I knew it, she thought, wishing that being right did not come with this sudden dose of alarm.

It was perhaps a good thing that they would be leaving Poland soon. It would be safer. But it galled to think that she might leave before all these questions were resolved. Before she fulfilled her plan to write an article about the chalice, to solve its mystery. To resume her former occupation with a flourish. Time was against her.

The door continued to open and close as visitors came and went. In a gust of cold air a man entered, his dark wool coat dusted with snow. With a heavy tread he moved towards the altar. His hood slid back, revealing a face white and taut with strain. So gaunt and haunted was his expression that it took Joan a moment to recognize Adam. Puzzled, she began to rise to greet him, but something in his mien halted her, and she remained seated, not hidden precisely, but rendered anonymous as one bundled up figure among many in a dim church.

Adam would not have seen her even had she moved. His face was blank, his eyes fixed, and he stood in the aisle and stared for a long while at the distant altar. Then he slowly turned and crossed to one of the chapels on the far side, passing a row of confessionals until he stopped before a marble saint and an array of burning candles. Joan stood in time to witness him fall to his knees and bury his face in his hands.

34

More Problems

Pawel spotted Bodie across the street as he left his flat. He pretended to have forgotten something and scampered back up the steps. But he was only buying time, for now that Bodie had identified him, he would lurk outside indefinitely. Pawel watched from behind his curtains for a few minutes to see if the man would grow tired of waiting. But to his chagrin, Bodie scanned the upper windows of the building until by some insubordinate instinct he located just the one from which Pawel peered. He pretended to adjust the curtain and shot an imperious glare down two stories to the street. Bodie lit a cigarette, watching him all the while, and pointed with a jabbing finger towards the Rynek.

It seemed pointless to try further avoidance maneuvers. Bodie's many lawless skills included a particular deftness at locating people and staying on their tail. Resigned, Pawel walked at a brisk pace towards the Rynek as if on his way to attend to some urgent holiday shopping.

Bodie was already seated at a table in the window at one of the cafés, and he had been so bold as to order two mugs of mulled wine. He tapped the window and raised his hand in a beckoning command.

"Flavor of the season," he remarked as Pawel took his seat opposite. Then scornfully, "Glad you could accept my invitation." He was forgetting that they habitually conversed in French. This was careless; these days many people around understood English.

"Nous sommes sur un terrain brûlant," Pawel remarked stuffily. "We should not be meeting in such a public place."

"Je vais le risquer," Bodie replied, reverting to the appropriate tongue. "We have more to worry about than being seen together." But in a burst of belated caution he spoke around the rim of his heavy mug, a ceramic cup in Christmas red with reindeer prancing around the rim. He tipped the mug and drained the strong, spiced wine. It was hotter than expected and burned his throat halfway down his chest. He could not quell a series of strangled coughs.

Pawel sipped his punch decorously. The spicy heat nipped at his nostrils, inflamed from an incipient cold. He spoke in a patronizing tone. "I told you I needed a week to get the money. You are too impatient. It will be another few days."

"I know that. I wouldn't have approached you about so routine a matter." The hot alcohol had scoured Bodie's throat, and his voice was raw. "We have another problem."

"Problem?" Pawel glanced at his companion, allowing his eyes only to graze across the other man's face before settling on the bustling square outside and its cheery scene of holiday merriment. "Do explain yourself."

"It seems that someone else knows of our little caper, as you call it. And it appears that she also knows about what happened afterwards on the bridge." Bodie was meanly pleased to see Pawel's face cloud with appalled disbelief.

It took Bodie several minutes to report the danger that some woman—maybe an American, Keith wasn't sure—might now pose to the secrecy of their activities. His recital was interrupted by the necessity of speaking around menus and refilled mugs of Christmas punch. He was pretty sure that Keith had exaggerated the situation, but it was too risky to dismiss.

"Keith doesn't know what's up. He thinks this woman is a saint who is punishing him for what he did. Or maybe he thinks she's protecting him. He can't decide whose side she is on. But crazy as he is, he seems to be right that she knows something that she shouldn't."

Pawel felt the ground slowly cave in beneath his feet. The wine was strong but it alone could not be blamed for the vertiginous dread that filled him now. "Perhaps this young man is simply deluded," he remarked. A saint. Good lord. "It was a mistake to bring on so unstable an accomplice. You should have been more careful."

Bodie ignored the admonishment. "That's as may be. But regardless, something needs to be done."

"And you suggest?"

Bodie gave up the pretense of surreptitious conversation and leaned his elbows on the table. "My first choice is just to get the hell out of here as soon as possible. Pull up stakes and leave you both behind. What would you think of that? Would save you an extra payment, that would."

Pawel played with a dribble of wine on the side of his mug. He lost control of its downward track, and it stained the linen napkin with a spreading pale redness.

"That would not be a convenient solution," he replied.

"No. I didn't think so."

Pawel folded his napkin and shifted his chair back. He was trying very hard to consider this ominous news inconsequential. "I shall have to think carefully about this," he said. "I believe you are probably overreacting. And certainly the unfortunate Keith is suffering from a delusion of some sort. Your first job will be to calm him."

"You haven't seen him recently, have you? He looks a mess."

"I have not. Nor do I intend to. He is your business. Take care of it."

"And the woman?"

The woman. He leaned forward again, elbows on the table positioned carefully away from the drippy mugs. He was wearing a new jacket. "What do you know about her?"

"Not much. Keith sometimes calls her Saint Gertrude. Gertruda, I guess you would say. Apparently she speaks English. To Keith she sounds like an American, but then he also thinks that she is speaking directly from God, so I suppose she could talk to him in any language she chooses."

Saint Gertruda! That austere image in the window niche. Pawel had sent a prayer in her direction himself. He had a terrible thought that with the impending millennium, perhaps invisible beings might be readying a celestial conflict over his fate. He quelled the idea. Keith was a madman. Surely that was all.

"And you take all this seriously?"

"I know it sounds crazy. But he has seen her several times. And the last time was in the museum in that little room where you wanted a mold of the cabinet keyhole. She seems to have had someone open the case to look at the things inside."

Pawel was having trouble separating material evidence from spiritual clues. It was one thing to find someone inquiring about the painting, so public an object of concern. But why would anyone be interested in the cabinet in that room? No one other than himself should know about the theft of the chalice. Not even Keith and Bodie had guessed his substitution. If the Kamynska woman had suspected, she was well out of the way. But then there was that time he had seen her walking with someone else towards the small gallery. Surely not. It simply could not be that there was yet one more person who considered the chalice worth notice. He felt perspiration gather along his ribs but he kept his face blank. He didn't want Bodie thinking very hard about that part of their job.

"That is a trivial affair," he said breezily. "If she is not wondering about the painting, she surely has no suspicions that concern us."

But Bodie noticed that Pawel had looked stunned at his last announcement. His hands were shaky. The fancy ring, slightly loose, trembled on his finger.

After a pause Pawel rose to go. "I doubt that she really poses a threat," he said. "But I shall evaluate the situation and get back to you. In three days I'll have your final payment. At that point I shall make a decision."

He left. Bodie was surprised at his aplomb. Had he been facing the window, he would have seen Pawel break into a trot on his way home, suddenly feeling the mulled wine slosh ominously upwards.

Bodie ordered another drink and frowned into the steaming cup. This Radincki person wasn't as smart as he thought. The time might come when Bodie would have to make the decisions for all three of them. And damn it, Pawel had stuck him with the bill.

35

Adam Falls Ill

"Proszę Pani," said a small woman wearing a museum identification badge, "Your husband has been taken ill. Please come with me."

Apparently she had known to come directly to the little gallery where Joan stood staring into the vitrine that held the ersatz chalice. Today she had accompanied Adam to the museum, and he would have guessed that she might be here. He had not spoken of his distraught visit to the church, nor had Joan told him of her presence there. Under their present circumstances, it seemed an unpardonable intrusion to have witnessed his anguished prostration.

Joan had again been comparing her sketches to the chalice. She closed her notebook and tucked it into her bag, so thoroughly searched on entrance that the contents were still jumbled.

She had been in the archives only twice before. On the far side of the room an open briefcase and a disorderly pile of papers sat on a table by the window. Adam was slumped in a chair. A hovering fellow scholar stood over him awkwardly with a cup of water.

"Sorry everyone," said Adam with a poor attempt at a smile. "I just became rather dizzy for a moment. I'm sorry to bother everyone like this."

Joan began to stuff his papers into the briefcase. They were uncharacteristically scattered, some on the floor, some on the adjacent chair. Adam feebly protested that she was mixing up the order, but she ignored him. "I'm taking you home. We'll call a cab."

"Madam, you are forgetting those over there." The man with the water gestured to a few more sheets of paper on the window ledge, secured precariously beneath the edge of the heavy curtain. Joan reached over and snared them, shoving them into the briefcase. It was entirely unlike Adam to be so messy. He must have been sitting there for hours shuffling things around haphazardly as he became more and more ill.

At the far end of the room, Pawel Radincki turned his back and knelt to study the lower shelves of a long-defunct journal series. He had experienced momentary alarm when he saw Joan enter the room, because oddly, he thought he recognized her. He was relieved to see that she was heading for someone else. He did not care to be noticed near to the place where he had just deftly secreted his scraps of invented genealogy. Fortunately, her attention was entirely taken up with the man who had so spectacularly collapsed on his way back from the lavatory.

While other occupants of the room were focused on the ministrations she was meting out to Adam, he made a quiet exit. He had overheard Adam asking someone to go find a woman in one of the small galleries, so he forbade himself from checking on the room where he had deposited the substitute chalice.

And then suddenly his conversation with Bodie fell into place.

Could it be that—

No. Impossible. But yes, maybe . . . .

Could *this* be the woman that Bodie had spoken of? The woman who knew of the thefts? She was American. And she obviously knew the museum. And apparently she had been in his—*his*—gallery. And yes, he did recognize her, for he had twice seen her exiting from that very room as he made his entrance. And maybe she was the person who had accompanied Klementyna Kamynska to look at the chalice. And if he knew who she was, it was possible that she knew him!

It came to him with dreadful certainty that too many pieces fit together for mere coincidence. She must be the person who was plaguing Keith. The one, for some reason, he called a saint. But surely it was impossible that she had connected the Leonardo panel with the activities in the smaller gallery. And she could not possibly have noticed the substitution of the chalice. Keith thought she knew of his crime, his sin. But what could she know about the death of the guard? Could she have been on the bridge that night? Maybe she was there in the fog, unseen. A witness. Worst of all, anyone who had kept up with the news would also know about him: Pawel Radincki, the receiver of the stolen painting. It seemed incredible that in spite of all his precautions and secret scheming, someone could have managed to link together the separate parts of his great strategy.

Pawel was so staggered by this realization that he stopped dead in the street, roused only by a screech of brakes. He stumbled to the sidewalk and into the Planty, taking refuge on a hard bench behind tall bushes now stripped of their last leaves. His vision was full of dancing spots, and the breath was shallow in his chest.

How could it be? After all his care to keep the separate elements of his plan apart, how could this one person—a stranger, a happenstance witness—how could she have put them together? Reason told him that indeed she could not have. That he was diving into an anxiety as crazy as Keith's. But she was in too many places for it to be accidental: the gallery where the chalice lay, the archive. How could mere coincidence account for that combination of facts?

And then it also dawned on him why Keith might think she was a saint. Her dark, thin brows and pale eyes and the long oval of her face. Her features strangely resembled the illuminated Saint Gertruda in the room with Bronislaw's chalice.

What terrible timing! He only needed a little more time. Less than three weeks. Pawel tried to assemble his thoughts by remembering the date: there were only—what was it—fifteen, sixteen more days? That was all the time he needed.

Would it be enough? Or would Saint Gertruda—Pawel found himself adopting Keith's way of identifying her— interfere with his great plan on the very brink of the millennium?

It was a risk he couldn't take. Not after all his efforts. Something had to be done. He set out to look for Bodie.

**

Adam recovered sufficiently to stand. He felt exceedingly foolish, and he exaggerated his weakness a little to sustain the impression that his collapse warranted all this attention. He was beginning to suspect that he had just suffered a spectacular anxiety attack, which would be an embarrassing cause for all this fuss. It would be better to have some actual illness to justify such an exhibition. As he gathered himself together and rose to his feet, he looked around and began to pat his pockets.

"Did you pick up my wallet and house keys, Joan? They aren't in my pockets anymore."

"No, but I'm sure they're in your coat."

But they weren't. The librarian and the man with the glass of water still held aimlessly in his hand cast their eyes on various surfaces, and in polite repetition the others in the room also made to look around in vague gestures of helpfulness.

"Could you have left them at home?"

"No. I'm sure I had them."

"Well, we'll have to find them later."

Adam sat heavily again. "I still feel rather dizzy. Perhaps I should go to the—oh. I know where they are. I took them out of my pockets in the bathroom looking for some medicine to calm my stomach. They must be there. On the sink or the windowsill."

The woman who had brought Joan to the archive still hovered nearby, but she hadn't understood their low-pitched English. She looked blank at Joan's inquiry for directions to the restrooms, then understood the common phonemes for "toilet." Joan followed her beyond the work tables along a sort of goat track among boxes and shelves and trolleys stacked with papers.

It was a rather small room that had apparently been carved out of space originally part of the larger area. There were two toilet stalls and a wide sink. Wallpaper of elaborate peacock design was comically uncoordinated with the metal doors of the cubicles. The tiled floor appeared new. Joan located Adam's wallet and keys by following a trail of the used tissues that had fallen from his pockets as he rummaged for a pack of antacids. They sat on the deep sill of a large casement window. As Joan retrieved them, she felt the cold air seeping around the frame. This was evidently the method by which the bathroom was ventilated, for these windows were not locked against winter. In fact, the latch was pointed up so that the interior window could be swung inward, and an outer casement stood slightly open. She noticed a bright tail of rag dangling from the bottom of the outer frame and wondered if some summer kite had come to grief against the glass. Then she decided that it was deliberately attached to provide a makeshift grip for someone inside reaching out to pull the window shut.

She was taking her time, allowing Adam a bit more space for recovery. She was also curious to explore the recesses of this odd building where he had spent most of his time since their arrival. Apparently he had spent a good deal of it in this very place tending to his deteriorating stomach. What a shame if his most lingering memories of Poland should be of a toilet.

Outside the window a few ragged leaves danced at the ends of heavy branches, and when she leaned into the sill she could see that a tall tree had grown undisturbed despite the proximity of an adjacent structure. It must have taken root unnoticed and gradually grown too large for manageable removal, for it had a thick, twisted trunk and its branches had grown in parallel swathes so that it opened like a huge fan jammed between the buildings. Joan wondered which direction she was looking. Although she had traipsed to the museum from many of the surrounding streets, the view outside this window didn't look familiar.

There was a tap on the door and a hesitant inquiry. Joan left the room and smiled at the anxious woman, who apparently felt pressed into service as a sort of hostess. Joan thanked her for her assistance with her best phrase-book Polish.

Adam was on his feet and ready to go, looking sheepish but reasonably recovered. Joan held his jacket for him and picked up his briefcase. As they made their exit he leaned on her shoulder in a gesture so passive that she was alarmed. He seemed more than weak. It was as if he could hardly muster the motivation to walk downstairs.

She rifled through his wallet to pay the cab and then found the right key from his ring to let them into the flat. He sat at the kitchen table while she heated a can of soup. He dutifully swallowed as much as he could. After that he headed for bed, but his defenses were sufficiently breached, and Joan sat by the bed and would not let him sleep until he told her what was wrong.

And only then did Adam confess the whole sorry saga of Gorski's diary. He recounted the story in a voice so flat and affectless that it was almost more worrisome than if he had displayed the distress that was afflicting him.

I took it to work on at home, he said, even though I should not have. And then I had to keep it because it would have been found at the security checks. And now it has me trapped, because it is my only discovery, my only purpose for being here, but if I can't put it back it will be all wasted. All wasted. And my time here has almost run out.

Later Joan would wonder at the state of her own moral universe, for it took her some while to absorb the reasons for Adam's profound sense of guilt and defeat. His transgression appeared so minor. She recalled his abject prostration at the church and realized how little she had understood.

"I'm sorry I didn't know, Adam. I thought that you were upset with me."

"With you? Why?" But he was perplexed for only a short while. "Oh. I see what you mean. It hasn't worked out very well for us, has it? But no. It is the diary that has been worrying me." His hand raised as if to reach for hers, but it fell back weakly against the blanket.

Gorski's diary. Not her so much. Perhaps not her at all. Joan was only secondary to his worries. Adam was tortured by guilt. She was fleetingly chagrined that she herself hadn't been the object of his distress, but she shook that off to deal with the immediate predicament.

With no thievery intended, the worst that he could be accused of was breaking a rule. It was not a moral wrong, or if so it was only a little one. And it was certainly not, she thought, such a major crime—at least not yet. At the moment it was more of a logistical problem. But Adam would not see it that way. His moral sense was incapacitating.

With a wave of intense pity, she uttered assurances and smoothed his forehead.

Your intent was never to steal, never to cheat, only to borrow.

Your error was in the choice of place to read the work, not in reading it.

You are a good man. You are a good scholar.

The good scholar needs the diary returned. The good man can't do it.

But I can.

36

The Sins of Adam

At least one of Adam's inchoate wishes had been granted: He was truly ill, besieged by temperature spikes and bouts of shaking. He sipped soup and refused medical attention, claiming—with surprising correctness—that he was actually feeling better. During the times when his fever abated, he got up and continued his careful transcription of the Polish text of the diary into his notebook. His weariness made him slow, but he was buoyed up by the idea that Joan would find a solution, and soon the diary would be back where it belonged.

Joan was not sure why he trusted her confident assertion that she could return the diary when he himself had failed to do so. Perhaps he was just too tired to worry any longer. At first, she proposed simply to march into the museum with the small book, reporting that she had accidentally picked it up when she collected Adam from the archive when he became ill. Her guileless demeanor would deflect criticism. She would apologize, express dismay at the breach of practice she had inadvertently committed, and take the blame away from Adam.

Adam had pondered that plan for a while. It seemed a somewhat craven device but it might well work. Then he panicked. He staggered from bed and called Joan back from the door just as she was on her way out.

"Wait! Come back! You can't do that after all!"

Joan hurried back, concerned that his fever had risen precipitously.

"What's wrong? Why can't I? If it's to be done, it should be done right away."

"I just thought of something else. This diary was not known to be in the archive at all. It wasn't among the items listed on the box. It was stuck at the bottom of one of the boxes in an envelope that looked just like the cardboard carton."

"So? I'll tell them that it was there after all."

Adam stumbled to a chair and collected his thoughts. He dearly wanted Joan's plan—so simple, so direct, so almost honest—to work. But there was something wrong with it.

"The problem is . . ." He struggled to get the ideas straight. His fever was rising and his thoughts were muddled. "The problem is that they did a check of the boxes in use after the painting was stolen. Before it was returned. I didn't find out about that until yesterday when I tried to go back to work there. One of the other researchers told me. He was annoyed because his materials had been put out of order."

"Why would they do that?"

"Apparently there was suspicion that the stolen painting might be somewhere still in the building. Some famous art theft happened that way. The thieves kept a painting in the museum itself after it was first taken, and they only removed it later."

"So they searched the archives for a painting? Are you sure?"

"I'm not sure of anything anymore!" Adam wailed, his hands clutching his head. "But it is what I was told. The boxes on those carts that we all use. Some of them are large enough for a small painting. So they checked. They checked through everything and listed the contents. Or maybe the check was random, I'm not sure. But if they checked mine and you return the diary now, they will know that you couldn't have taken it yourself. They will know that I had it all along."

Joan considered this worry inflated beyond all reason. But at the moment she was more concerned about Adam's patchily flushed face and rapid breathing. She administered more aspirin and brought him a cool towel.

"Please," he begged, on the brink of tears. "Please don't do it that way."

"Okay, I won't. Don't worry. I'll find another way. I will. Now get some sleep." She sat by his bed until he drifted off and his restless hands relaxed.

Her second plan was almost as direct, for she was pretty sure that the security checkpoints were not as thorough as Adam imagined. By this time it was likely, she thought, that the guards would give her bag no more than a cursory glance. Probably Adam's fear of discovery while passing through the admissions area was vastly exaggerated.

Of course, then she had to figure out how to replace the diary in the archive itself. A story of a lost item that she was there to retrieve ought to suffice, she thought. She would go to the table where Adam had worked, rummage on her hands and knees, and deposit the diary on the floor as though it had been dropped. Or perhaps slip it under the heavy curtains on the window sill. Maybe she would even discover it and return it to the archivist, at the same time showing him her successful retrieval of, say, Adam's favorite pen. It might be an oddity if the diary were not listed on whatever security check had really been conducted, but it would just be assumed that it had been overlooked. There would be no suspicion that it had ever left the archive.

That plan might have worked. She might have slid through the security line without arousing the slightest suspicion. But on the day that she intended to execute the return, there was an altercation at the entrance checkpoint.

It was early afternoon, but the man was already drunk. The guard who politely asked him to turn out his pockets recoiled at the sour breath overlaid with vodka and noticed that his hands were unsteady as he displayed the detritus deposited in his jacket. The matches were common since many people smoke. And it might be that a person would carry around a candle. But when asked to check those items at the desk before proceeding, Keith balked.

I need them, he insisted. I must light a candle to Saint Gertrude. She is upstairs waiting for me.

Light a candle? Here? Out of the question!

There were raised voices and a clash of languages. A phalanx of security arrived and Keith was asked to leave. Dejected, he turned, and his glance fell upon Joan, who was standing in line four persons back. His eyes widened in horror.

"She is already here for me!" he wailed, and he fell to his knees.

Regrettably, his attempt at worshipful prostration was interpreted as falling down drunk. It took three men to remove him from the disconcerted crowd.

Joan turned back too. There was far too much fuss for her to try to pass through casually now. She had barely registered the fact that the troublesome man was looking particularly at her, so busy was she reassessing her plan. Frowning at her watch as if she had just remembered a prior appointment, she shouldered back to the street.

Adam's concerns might not be so exaggerated after all. With the guards on special alert from this incident, Joan quailed at what they might say if they discovered in her possession an old, leather-bound journal written in a language that she manifestly could not read. The flaw in her scheme opened wide, and she flinched at her close call.

She had to find another way.

Joan spent an hour reassessing her options. She sat with a coffee and studied her well-worn city map and the Radincki floor plan given out to visitors on entrance. Not too surprisingly, the two did not match precisely. Their scales were at odds and their details differed. The museum sat amid a crowded cluster of other structures: a church and an adjacent convent, a portion of the ancient wall of the Planty, and the end of a long string of buildings taken over by the university. The map omitted much of this detail and indicated only streets. In contrast, the museum floor plan sketched only those areas of the building open for visitors.

Joan hoped that some portion of what was not apparent on the map might afford an opportunity for a quiet back entry to the museum. She was fairly certain that the entrances themselves were not outfitted with electronic security, for there had been much criticism of this fact when it was learned that the Leonardo painting had been guarded with a single, easily disarmed device.

A fine, winter rain had started to fall, and under the cover of an umbrella Joan squelched through puddles to make a circuit of the Radincki Museum. The main door was set in the grand front of the building, the stairs descending to an abrupt halt at the sidewalk. At the back sat a large bin overflowing with packing materials wilting in the wet. The building jutted and turned in an idiosyncratic set of angles, the result of generations of revisions to the structure. There were doors aplenty, but all appeared to be locked or covered over with crusted gates that had not been used for years. One back entrance stood open, but when she approached, she could see two maintenance men in the doorway sitting out of the rain and chatting over cigarettes.

Twice around the building and Joan was getting discouraged. By the time she returned home, Adam was asleep, and she was too tired to fix herself dinner. She hung her damp clothes in the shower and lay under a blanket on the couch, feeling discouraged. Maybe she would just have to brave the security line after all.

Had she been less preoccupied, she might have noticed that a man had followed her home and was even now standing on the street outside. The next morning Beata was perplexed to find a candle stuck on her mailbox, the wax melted into a solid splotch and greasy with rain.

37

Blood Ritual

The ritual would commence at midnight.

After a day poring over his star charts and checking on the phases of the moon, Pawel was fairly sure that the blood had to be collected tonight.

His plan was at a particularly delicate stage. The powers he intended to summon had not left precise instructions about what they required. Months ago the indeterminacy surrounding the ritual had appeared abstruse and exciting. Now that he had reached the point where the magical rite was at hand, the absence of detailed directions was alarmingly chancy.

The notes he had taken after a consultation with a fortune-teller indicated tonight was the night, but of course he had not been able to tell her exactly what he had in mind. Just enough to get an expert opinion about blood rites. Timing was very important. Midnight was a point of clear agreement. Magic often requires midnight, a median point, darkness, the sorcery of liminal periods.

And the dark of the moon. He had missed the true dark and had suffered a moment of panic when he checked the calendar and discovered that the next time the moon was fully obscured it would be too late. But two of his books suggested that a sliver of new moon was even better than full dark. A sliver of moon cast a glowing crescent. Oblique and sharp, like a sly, side glance.

Like the blade of a knife.

So it would be tonight.

In fire I bloom. In water I flow. In blood I abide and avail.

Pawel knelt before the chalice. The only light in the flat was cast by the tall candles at its sides. They glowed without flicker, strong and insistent. Pawel was naked. In a stronger light he might have appeared scrawny, but here in the warmth of his secret niche, the radiance of the small fires gilded his chest and emphasized his fine bones and smooth muscles. He had shaved carefully for the ritual and checked his appearance in the bathroom mirror. He was clean. Vestiges of rationality retreated under a barrage of avid hope, superstition, and lifelong desire.

On his finger was the ring. In his hand was the knife. Before him was the chalice. Awaiting his heart's blood.

Pawel now confronted a problem. He hadn't experimented with this part of the ritual before, and he wasn't sure exactly how to let out just a bit of blood from his heart without emptying the entire vessel. Magic rituals such as this one were easier if the heart belonged to someone else. Since there was a protective rib cage in the way, Pawel reasoned, heart's blood might not refer to blood coming directly from that organ. Some region sufficiently near the heart would surely satisfy the powers at work. After pondering his chest in the bathroom mirror, he had settled on a place just below his left nipple and marked it in pen with a small *x*. That *x* was now starting to run with perspiration, and Pawel had to take a corner from his altar cloth and blot away the sweat. He took a deep breath, held the knife point close to his skin, and closed his eyes.

Prick.

The pain made him gasp. He opened his eyes, sure he would face a cascade of gore. But only one droplet of red appeared on his skin.

He tried again, attempting a deeper wound.

This time his shaking hand accidentally sliced rather than pierced and he was rewarded with a crimson rivulet. He leaned over the chalice and coaxed the run-off into its bowl. The blood formed a tiny pool and showed signs of wanting to congeal against the cool surface of the silver.

Not enough.

Pawel was getting annoyed. He had imagined plunging the knife point deep into his chest, at least to rib depth — actually not very deep in a man as slim as he. But imagination requires less mettle than action. He admonished himself that only a moment of discomfort stood in his way. A noble heart does not mind shedding its blood in valor. He shut his eyes again and executed a mighty jab. This time he hit a more enthusiastic capillary. The mess on the floor was considerable, but at least there was sufficient blood in the chalice for the next stage of the ritual. The vital stage. The final one. The culmination of his plan.

But that stage could not take place for another two weeks. Quelling a sense of anticlimax, Pawel found himself a bandaid. Then he carefully poured the fruits of his labor into a lovely crystal vial with a silver stopper selected specially for the occasion. He placed it in a cardboard box to shield the contents from the light, and he put it in his small refrigerator on the shelf below a wedge of cheese and a bottle of orange juice. Sitting there amidst his weekly provisions, Pawel's heart's blood lost none of its magical aura. His moment was at hand.

He set himself to clean the dribbles of blood from the floor. He would have liked to wash the chalice in the cleansing waters of the Wisła, but that was far too risky. He settled for a candlelit rinse at the kitchen sink.

38

Joan's Plan

Joan dreamed of kites. Kites with long tails flying in a brilliant sky, their strings diving down to an earth so far away that the children who held them were but specks. She worried that an airplane would suck a kite into one of its jets, and Adam would blame Y2K for the crash. The dream turned scary and she woke up.

Morning mist still covered the river. Adam's forehead was cool, his breathing slow and deep. She waited until the sky began to lighten, then dressed quietly and left him a note on the kitchen table. Tiptoeing down the stairs, she entered the street and hurried into town. From the bridge the castle appeared in dreamy sfumato, as if Leonardo himself had rendered it in paint. Here and there Joan skidded on patches of slick sheen, a combination of motor oil and congealing ice. Treacherous skins of water pooled as the sun rose higher and the mist dispersed.

She was in search of a kite tail. And of a tree. For on awakening, Joan realized that her peregrinations around the Radincki Museum had not been complete. She had encountered no fan-shaped tree, no behemoth growing between buildings, no large trunk with arching, heavy branches close to the archive windows. Close to one particular window from which hung a scrap of crimson fabric. Somehow she had missed a section of the building, one with a side that must therefore be obscured from the street and passing eyes.

But she could not locate her error. Up one street and down another, even along footpaths between buildings, there seemed to be no access to the area she had glimpsed out the archives' bathroom window.

Chilly and frustrated, Joan retreated to the warmth of a café and spread out her map. With fingers clumsy from the cold she moved aside a little vase of flowers—silk at this time of year—and the caddy of salt and pepper to make room for the awkward unfolding. The waitress, used to disoriented tourists, thought nothing of it. Joan drank her first coffee quickly and ordered another. Polish coffee was good, but there was never enough of it. Small, elegant portions for sipping pleasure, not the great American vats one needed to sustain concentration.

Consulting the museum map, Joan located the place where she thought the archives ought to be. She marked the correct side and oriented the plan to coordinate with the street map. But the city map showed no way to approach that portion of the museum from a street. Indeed, it placed the museum and its adjacent building shoulder-to-shoulder, as if they had come over the years to squeeze out the space between them. She knew from looking out the bathroom window that could not be. The map simply must ignore a space where no one would want to go. Over the years an accumulation of remodeling must have formed an accidental courtyard lying behind walls that now belonged to other buildings. Behind one of those walls there was a tree, and above the tree was a window with a red rag tied to it. And beyond that lay the object of her search.

"Good morning, Joan. What are you doing at my doorstep?"

It was Rudy, looking rather subdued and proper in a jacket and tie.

"What do you mean? This isn't where you live." Joan stood before a solid brick building trying to decode the sign carved on the lintel above the door.

"No, but it's where I work. You haven't been here before, have you?"

"This is your Institute?"

"Yes, or at least the Institute is among the various things here. This part of the university has many functions, some administrative, some academic. My office is on the top floor. Would you like to come up?"

"I would!"

Bemused at her enthusiasm, Rudy escorted her up the steps.

"There is an elevator, but it is slow. I prefer stairs in any case. Less claustrophobic. And they keep you in shape."

To prove this point Rudy was striving to speak naturally as they climbed, but little breathy puffs broke through his conversation.

When they got to his office Joan hastened to the window.

"Damn!"

"I beg your pardon?"

"We must be on the wrong side of the building. I can never keep directions straight. Where is the tree?"

"What tree?"

"The big one that is squeezed between buildings." Rudy looked blank. "Never mind. Which way is the Radincki Museum?"

"Oh, let me think. Next to the side at the end of the hall, I believe. Yes, it is hard to keep directions straight in a town that is basically crooked. Well-planned in the layout, of course, oriented around the big Rynek. But what one expects should be right angles aren't quite, so it's easy to get turned around. One gets used to it. Why do you want to know?"

"I'll tell you in a minute. First, please show me the right side."

But the interior of the adjacent side of the building was entirely covered in offices, and Rudy had a key to none of them. He watched curiously as she scampered up and down the hallway trying doorknobs and peering through the small windows set into a few of the doors.

"I'm close. I'm close. I know I'm close," Joan muttered.

In the end, she sat in his office and told him the whole story while he sorted through his papers. It was a long story, and she had to reveal Adam's predicament. She did this reluctantly, enjoining secrecy. Rudy heard her through without interruption. Then he said,

"I am still in the dark about how finding a tree will help this situation. But there is something more important to consider. You say you plan to return this book, this diary, for Adam, because he is too ill or too paralyzed with guilt to manage it himself. You realize, Joan, that strictly speaking, you are abetting a small but not inconsiderable piece of wrongdoing. I realize Adam's intentions were innocent, but what he did was quite against the rules. Any scholar should know that. It's no wonder he feels guilty."

Joan was taken aback. She had not anticipated this admonishment from Rudy.

"Adam is a good person," she replied, seeking to match his solemnity. "This was one little mistake in an otherwise completely blameless career. He does not deserve to suffer for it. And he is suffering. Terribly. He has made himself ill with guilt and worry. Far more, frankly, than I believe this particular broken rule merits."

"Well, you may be right about that. But you are putting yourself at some risk in helping him out." Rudy stared down at his desk. "Is this something you owe to Adam? What is it, a price? A penance? Some kind of duty?"

She thought a moment. Rudy was still looking at his mail but his attention was almost palpably directed towards her. Finally she said, "It is, I think, a gift."

Rudy nodded. "I have to go and give a lecture, the last before the holiday break. Wait here for an hour. When I come back we'll see about finding your tree. I share this office with two other people. The university is always short on space. But we are close to the holiday and no one is likely to come in today. Make yourself at home. Peruse the shelves. Find something to read."

***

When he returned, Rudy found Joan leaning out the window.

"Good God, what are you doing? Be careful you don't fall. It's freezing in here. Come back in and close that window."

Joan wiggled back into the office. Her hair was blown about and her cheeks were red with cold. Rudy noticed how vigorous and eager she looked and wished he felt the same.

"I was trying to see what's beyond this side of the building. You were taking so long. It was more than an hour."

"My mind was, however momentarily, on my job. I had students to see."

"Do you feel alright? You seem kind of down."

Rudy, suffering from a well-disguised hangover, mustered a smile.

"Not at all. Just a bit preoccupied with work at the end of term. Let's look for this tree, shall we? And then you can enlighten me as to its importance."

There was a staircase at the end of the hall. They exited on the floor below and looked around, but again there were no windows that opened in the direction they sought. They set off down again, only to find that the door to the ground floor was locked.

"How frustrating!" exclaimed Joan. "It is as though the very place I want to see was deliberately sealed off!"

They went back up a floor and walked the corridors in search of another stairwell. With the upcoming holidays, the building was nearly deserted.

"It looks like most of my colleagues have left for the holiday already," remarked Rudy. "Lucky them."

"You're staying here? You're not going to Holland for a visit?"

"Not this year. My sons and their families will be away." Joan found herself pleased that he would stay.

A door opened at the end of the hall and a janitor appeared before them. "Excuse me, sir," said Joan. "Can you tell us where the nearest stairway is?"

Stupidly, she had spoken in English. Rudy repeated her question in Polish, and the man helpfully ushered them back in the direction they had come. To quell his puzzlement, they went down the stairs again, tiptoeing back up as his footsteps receded.

"He came from the right side of the building!" said Joan. "I mean the correct side. The one we want to see."

"I know what you mean. But he came from a cleaning closet."

"Yes, but on the right side of the building. Maybe we can see out the window."

"I doubt the closet has a window."

But there seemed nothing better to do. At the end of the hallway Joan grasped a doorknob and tugged open the cleaning closet. Rudy was right; there was no window.

There was, however, another door in the closet itself, a symptom of the architectural tinkering that had remodeled the building over the years. And behind this door, another stair, narrow and dark and beckoning.

Without hesitation, they headed down.

"I'm beginning to feel like Alice," said Rudy. "Or that bloody white rabbit. I hope we don't get locked in here. It could be a long wait for a rescue, with Christmas coming and all."

The stairs leading down became dirtier and darker as they descended, illuminated only by the odd window pane left in place after some remote period of renovation. Evidently this corner of the building was no longer in use, for when they finally reached what they judged to be the ground floor, they discovered that the door at the bottom had clearly not been opened for a long time. A large key was stuck in the lock, and it took Joan two hands to turn it. Resisting Rudy's offer of help, she put on her gloves to get a better grip and was finally rewarded by a protesting screech of metal as the lock released. A blockage of matted leaves had accumulated against the building. Rudy held the door while she knelt on the dirty floor and stuck one arm through the open crack to clear away the debris. Finally, the door opened wide enough to let them through.

"Tight squeeze, that," said Rudy, pleased that he was still slim and flexible enough to squash his way through. His mood was lifting somewhat.

They were in a narrow, overgrown space, an adventitious triangular courtyard bounded on one side by the wall of the Institute. The other two sides were formed by a short, jutting wing and a portion of the wall of the adjacent building. The two structures were so close that at the apex of the triangle they shared a drainpipe. In this cramped, neglected space, a huge tree grown wild and distorted in its confinement dominated the area. Its disgruntled roots heaved the ground into twists and crannies and made the footing uneven.

"My, my," said Rudy. "I've never been here. I had no idea what lay on this side of the Institute. Obviously it is untended." Dead weeds grew in choking brown clumps between the bricks of an ancient, disused terrace. "The Institute is a relatively new structure for this part of town, only about ninety years old. I guess this part was built when this tree was a mere sapling. Funny they didn't leave more space between the buildings."

Joan was moving around, looking upward rather than at her feet. She stumbled several times and Rudy caught her elbow and prevented a fall. He felt her grab his arm impersonally, as if hanging on to a railing. Was this what she thought of him? A mere convenience in the background, like a handle? But the grip on his arm warmed and strengthened, and he saw Joan's smile break through her anxious expression like the sun bursting from behind clouds. She pointed upwards, and his eyes followed her fingers to where a scrap of red could be seen fluttering in the winter wind.

"There it is!" she exclaimed, and flung her arms about his neck and gave him a quick hug.

Only after she had scampered home did he remember that she hadn't yet informed him exactly why the tree was so important for returning the diary. He went home thinking of that hug and her warm, clasping arms. Christmas was going to be a dreary time.

**

Joan did not tell Adam of her discovery. She merely assured him that she was confident that she would be able to return the diary, and quite soon.

Finding the window to the archive bathroom was a triumph in itself, but it hung two stories above the ground. Climbing the tree was the obvious solution—in theory. In fact, the lowest branches of the tree were still far above her head, and the limbs were worryingly thin at the point where they extended to the window. She left Adam happily sipping tea in bed and searched Beata's basement with a flashlight, casting about rather vaguely for equipment. Lawnmower. Flower pots. A broken chair. A rusty handsaw and a collection of screwdrivers. A length of old clothesline—which she took, thinking that a rope is always handy, though she was not entirely sure what for. Rather like hot water at childbirth. Why hot water? Who or what was to be immersed in boiling water when a baby is born? All the homilies about what one does in a crisis jumbled into her head: Tip a head forward for nosebleed, put it between your knees for fainting. In case of fire, crawl below the smoke. If a tornado comes, find a ditch. Unfortunately, there was no advice about breaking into large buildings. But despite the difficulties ahead, she felt a buzz of excitement. Surely with the window found, it was but a short step to enter.

"Your job now," she commanded Adam, "is to finish with the diary. Now. Because soon it will be back at the archives and you will be home."

Such words were tonic, and Adam returned to his desk with renewed strength. There were not many pages to go before he finished a clean copy. The old Adam might have excoriated himself with the thought that he had no right to profit from his malfeasance, but his guilt was all but burned out. With strong lamp and magnifying glass, he set about transcribing the text and carefully duplicating the little sketches that were drawn here and there in the daily log. His sense of kinship with Gorski returned, and though he was still weak, he found he could work at a slow and steady pace that was itself sustaining. Joan left him at work, Beata's clothesline under her arm.

39

The Payoff

"There you have it. Four thousand American dollars. Cash." Pawel slid a fat envelope under a menu and pushed it towards Bodie. "I leave it to you to divide fairly with your partner."

Bodie scooted the menu towards him, letting the envelope drop into his lap. He refrained from counting the money. Pawel was unlikely to cheat him in person.

"Thanks," he said flatly.

Pawel made as if to study his lunch choices. Bodie's waiting silence was a challenge. A decision had to be made. It could be postponed no longer.

"There remains the issue of this woman you say Keith is worried about," he continued. Bodie remained silent. "Has he seen her again?"

"Possibly. Probably in fact. Hard to say with him."

"Do you have a fuller description?" Pawel harbored one last hope that this woman was not the one he feared.

Bodie shrugged. "Medium height, slim. Dark or red hair. Keith sometimes says both. Mainly he talks about her eyes. Light green or blue. And dark eyebrows. He says she looks like the Queen of Diamonds."

"The what? A queen?" Pawel's royalist inclinations stirred.

"Not a queen really, that picture on a deck of cards."

"Oh, I see. Why diamonds? Don't all those queens look alike?" At least, Pawel thought, Keith doesn't know the Tarot. To have one of those dreadful figures come alive would be trouble indeed.

"Who knows? Diamonds for a queen maybe. Or maybe he's just crazy."

There was a silence as each pondered the image of a woman as a playing card. Then Pawel remembered the thin, dark brows and the pale eyes of the woman who had entered the archives. Like a hand just dealt, the hieratic image of the Queen of Diamonds appeared before his mind, her head turned towards him with a blank, accusing stare, and Pawel knew with sinking conviction that Joan was most certainly the saint pursuing the thieves.

"So," said Bodie, "what do you want to do about it?"

Pawel's heart beat against his ribs so hard it drove the breath from his lungs. Don't they say of murder that the first one paves the way for more? But although Pawel desperately wanted Joan to disappear, he didn't hate her the way he had Klementyna Kamynska. She did not stand as witness to his past. But she could undo all of his elaborate plans. Neither of his assistant thieves knew of the chalice or its purpose, and he didn't want Bodie to know just what kind of menace she posed. After a strenuous pause, he managed the nonchalant air he strove for.

"I believe she does indeed pose a threat—to you and to Keith," he said with grand dissociation. "It seems more and more likely that she witnessed your movements around the stolen painting, and that she saw something suspicious. Perhaps the unfortunate Keith was not careful." He hoped that Bodie's worry would make this invention seem likely. He concluded with a shrug. "So it is rather up to you to decide what to do. If it were I, well, it is better to be sure of her silence, don't you think?"

There, that was said. He had made no decision himself. Not in so many words. If Bodie engineered another death, it was on his own head. Pawel looked at him long and meaningfully. Bodie was expressionless, his eyes all but dead.

"So be it," Bodie finally said. The other man nodded.

They both noted that those nods said nothing explicit. Pawel thought: something will be done, but I will not be responsible. Another will bear the responsibility.

Bodie stayed and had a beer, thinking very hard about the stupidity of cowards. This time he would take matters into his own hands. And do it right.

40

Partners

"A what? A ladder? No, I have no need of such a thing."

Rudy was not pleased that Joan had dropped by unexpectedly. What had begun as a convivial gathering with colleagues the night before had ended with a private bout of despondency. He was shamefully aware of red eyes and the sour smell of his unwashed bathrobe. The whiskey bottle he had finished last night sat declaratively on the floor by the couch where he had fallen asleep.

Joan, used to seeing an invalid Adam in his bathrobe at all hours, was still taken aback at Rudy's disheveled state. She pretended not to notice anything amiss.

"Nothing to stand on at all? Nothing to help me climb?"

"Climb what?" Rudy moved to the kitchen and started making coffee. Strong and to his taste. Usually it drove away visitors.

"The tree, of course. The tree to the archive window. It's the only chance I have of returning the diary." Joan was shedding her coat and scarf. Obviously she intended to stay a while.

Rudy watched as the dark drips gradually filled the pot. The very smell of the coffee was beginning to sharpen his brain, although it did nothing to alleviate the headache thudding behind his eyes. He took two mugs and filled them. He did not offer Joan sugar or milk; the occasion demanded bitterness.

"Let me get this straight," he said taking a seat at the kitchen table so that Joan wouldn't go back into the living room and notice the rat's nest that had been his bed. "You actually intend to break into the Radincki Museum by climbing in a window."

"There seems to be no other way. I've tried every other possibility, but I can't find another entrance. I thought at first I could just take the diary in the front door, but the security screen is too thorough and they would likely find it. And I don't think I could just breeze in the way I used to. The museum staff, some of them anyway, are suspicious of me because of the questions I raised about the chalice. So the window is the last option."

Rudy took a sip of scalding brew. "How do you propose to explain your presence to the librarian when you suddenly appear in the archives from the bathroom without having first entered by the door?"

"Well, of course, I wouldn't go in until everyone else was gone. At night."

"At night. From a dark well between tall buildings. Buildings that will be locked at that hour, by the way, so getting into them will be a feat in itself. And up a tree. In a window. And then out again without arousing any of the guards posted at night. Are you quite serious?"

"It's tricky, I grant. But why not?"

"Well, for one thing, you are likely to break your neck falling. Not to mention your already injured arm. That window, as I recall, is quite high."

"My arm is quite a lot better." Joan wiggled her fingers and tried to look chipper. The feeling had returned to her fingers and her muscles were regaining strength. "Of course, I'll have to be careful. That's why I have this rope."

Joan held up the filthy loop of clothesline. Rudy eyed it sardonically.

"Oh good planning. Convenient for hanging yourself if you are caught, I suppose."

"There is no need for sarcasm." Joan dropped the rope and warmed her hands around the mug. "This coffee is terrible."

Rudy took an ostentatious gulp. "Sarcasm is precisely what is needed, Joan. Think about it. What you are planning to do has moved from the imprudent to the downright dangerous. I warned you before that you could get into trouble trying to return this journal. Well, now it appears you are willing to risk not only being apprehended but killing yourself. This is very noble behavior on your part, to do something so self-sacrificing for a man you love. And if you fall, maybe your eulogy will extol your courage on behalf of him. But your idea is fundamentally stupid. Tell Adam he just has to make a clean breast of it. Maybe the archives will be understanding and forgive him. Not guaranteed, of course. But surely this isn't worth risking your neck. How could Adam permit you to do such a thing anyhow?"

"He doesn't know about it. Not in detail, that is."

"Well, then." But Rudy had spent his energy on his declamation.

"Actually, Rudy," said Joan in a quiet voice, "Adam and I will not be staying together. We shall go our separate ways. I mentioned this before, or at least hinted at it. And now I'm sure."

"Really? Why?" Rudy looked at her more closely. "None of my business of course, but I thought, you know . . . I thought that you were committed to him."

"Not any more. Maybe not ever, really. And now, no, definitely not."

"Might one ask why?" Rudy's curiosity was piqued despite the headache. He felt an odd hope arise.

"I think," began Joan, and fell silent. "I have discovered, you see, that Adam is not the person for me after all."

"He displeases you then?"

"No. Or yes. It's kind of complicated."

"These things usually are."

"I suppose so. But to put it simply: we made a mistake. Not necessarily in coming here together but in assuming that we were suited for each other. That we would start a new life together. I know that now, and I expect he does too. I think he is too noble to make the break. Or maybe too indecisive, or too distracted with his problem. At any rate, it's up to me to do so."

As she tried to put her state of mind into words, Joan recalled that she had badly misjudged the source of Adam's worries, and as a consequence she really was not sure if he shared her feelings quite in the way that she had stated. But certainly, she herself was sad that their once promising match had come apart.

"But I can't leave him in this state, you see," she added softly. "He is ill and beside himself with worry. He is still a good friend. A good man. I promised him I would return the diary. So I must."

After a pause Rudy said, "I can see that." And all at once he could. There was a kind of nobility in Joan's gesture that cancelled out its foolishness. "And that is why you offer this gift, as you called it."

They were quiet together while the coffee cooled and they both made themselves swallow the black dregs. Then suddenly Rudy set down his mug with a clunk and sat up straight.

"You know, I might have just the thing for you after all!" he exclaimed. "Not a ladder, but much better. Wait here." And with his old alacrity he unfolded himself from the chair and disappeared into the back rooms of the flat. It took him some time to reappear, and now he was dressed and his hair slicked wetly back.

"My son left these three years ago after a trip to the Tatras," he said. "Turned out he didn't need them after all and his luggage was full. So he left them with me, and here they are, just waiting for you."

Joan stared at the items in his hands. "What are they?"

"Crampons. Straps that have grips for scaling cliffs. Should make short work of a mere tree trunk. Since your injured arm is still a bit weak, it would help to have some equipment."

"What do you do with them? How do you hold them?"

Rudy eyed the contraptions on the table and tried to imagine more precisely just how they would help someone climb a tree. The sharp points didn't seem to be aimed in quite the right direction. "You put them on your feet. Or, that was my idea, but now that I look at them the spikes don't seem very well placed for tree climbing, do they. Oh dear. I thought I had a solution." He dropped back into his chair, hangover returning.

"Oh, I get it now," said Joan. "These little points will catch in the bark and let me get up to the lower limbs. It isn't that far until I'll be able to grab onto a branch. I'm sure they will work!" Her voice was confident. "And my arm is better, much better. Thank you."

She waved her new found equipment enthusiastically. "There is only one thing more I need now, and you can help me with that too."

"What is that?" Rudy asked.

Joan smiled, and her smile was both invitation and summons. "A partner."

41

In Crime

If he were in it just for the money, Bodie would have walked away. A measly four thousand dollars. Of course, he wouldn't split it with Keith. But even so what did that sum buy? Certainly not another murder.

At the same time, he felt more vulnerable than he ever had in his whole villainous life. Should his part in the theft of the Leonardo panel come to light, it might reopen two other cases of art theft. They were not as widely reported as this one, but they were still open investigations. The more Bodie thought about it, the more it seemed that his dispatch of the inconvenient American woman was a matter of self-defense. Law of nature it was: self-preservation. He chewed this over long enough that he began to envision the deed with something like enjoyment. A greedy anticipation sidled in alongside his worry.

Keith would not be involved this time. He was still under the impression that Saint Gertrude was dogging his heels; he certainly would not cooperate in killing her. That young man needed more than anything to get out of here and forget about Poland, but he was crazily waiting for permission from his saint. Keith was seeing things: saints and angels and Christ himself with his upraised hand gesturing for God knows what. That picture, it had affected him too much. Bodie almost felt sorry for Keith, who now lived in fear of his own mind. Everywhere he looked he feared that Saint Gertrude might appear. And when she did not, he worried even more that she had abandoned him.

Bodie was an experienced thief, but he had never before taken a life. Unlike Keith, he wasn't stymied by the dread of doing wrong. He just wasn't sure how to accomplish the deed efficiently. Having traveled to Europe by plane, he had no gun and he didn't know how to get one here. The next weapon that occurred to his conventional imagination was a knife, but it was hard to stab someone so that the victim would drop dead silently and cleanly without spraying blood all over him. And then there was the question of transporting a leaky body to a hiding place in the middle of a city.

But he had hands. Big hands with long, strong fingers. And there was that river and its bridges. He could accomplish with greater success what Keith had fumbled. For the rest of the day, Bodie paced the streets and flexed his fingers, working up a conviction that he could kill with his bare hands. He rather liked that description of himself. And by Keith's account the woman's neck was slender. She didn't sound very hard to handle. He flexed his shoulder, still sore from its collision with the exhibit cabinet and weaker than usual. Even with this discomfort, it ought to be easy to dispatch someone like her—a lightweight, often walking alone with the river just waiting for her.

As his fantasies became more precise, it occurred to him that he was taking an unnecessary risk doing this alone. One man might kill easily enough, but two could plan the act more effectively. Keith's assistance was out of the question, but this Pawel character—weak but with a lot at stake. Bodie would enjoy seeing this sissified Pole, with his natty clothes and fancy jewelry, get his hands dirty. Permanently dirty, for murder doesn't wash off.

But first he had to induce Keith to identify Saint Gertrude for him. Or Gertruda, whatever it was. He now had a pretty full description, but he needed to see her in the flesh in order to identify his target precisely. Looking around for the Queen of Diamonds wouldn't get him anywhere.

42

Gathering Clouds

"Damn!!"

Joan slid roughly to the ground, the crampons swiveling around to her insteps.

"Keep your voice down. There might still be someone around," said Rudy as he helped her to her feet. "My son is a big man, and I'm afraid his equipment is rather large for your feet. Let's see if we can tighten them a bit. Did you hurt yourself? Is your arm alright?"

"I'm fine." Her wrists burned from scrapes where the gloves had been pulled back during her last descent, but she adjusted her cuffs to hide the marks.

The afternoon was dimming, and they needed to practice. It would probably be pitch black on the night they had chosen to return the diary. They had checked and found that there would be a moon, but neither was sure if its light would reach the narrow gap between the buildings. At the moment the weather was dank, and the large tree had an unpleasantly slimy feel, as though it were lightly greased.

"That's tight enough," said Joan. "I need some circulation to feel my toes. Let me try again."

They had fashioned the clothesline into a double-handled rope that fit around the trunk and caught like a tether in the rough bark. This time she made it nearly halfway to the lowest branches before sliding back. Rudy caught her clumsily. Her chin had scraped against the trunk and was bleeding in patchy strips. Rudy set her on her feet and shook his head. "Joan, I'm sorry. I really think this is not going to work."

"It has to! It has to work! There is no other way, and we are running out of time."

"Well, let's go back inside and get warm. We have to bandage you up a bit. Have a rest."

In the cold, Joan had not felt that her face was also scraped. She looked in dismay at the blood smearing her gloves.

The building echoed with their footfalls.

"Everyone else is sensibly at home preparing for the holidays," Rudy grumbled. Then he felt sorry for Joan and added, "Good for us, of course. Don't want company on this sort of mission."

In his office Rudy plugged in his electric kettle and assembled two cups.

"Extra sugar, don't you think?" he said brightly. "We need the energy."

On their next try, Joan got almost to the lowest branch before her grip gave way.

"Are we sure that the janitor's closet doesn't have a ladder?" she asked after catching her breath. Rudy, on whom she had made a soft landing, was quietly counting his blessings that he hadn't broken a hip as well as her fall.

"There wasn't one on the floor where we first entered the stairwell, but it wouldn't hurt to look again." He wasn't sure he would survive another attempt this evening, though he wasn't about to admit his aches. This effort with Joan was making him feel young again, and he didn't want to break the spell.

They looked around again in the echoing building. And when in the ground floor cleaning closet, larger and better stocked than the upstairs one, they indeed found a ladder, they stared at it with a sort of anticlimactic disbelief.

"All that time struggling to climb, and there was a ladder here all along," said Rudy. "It's a good thing these closets aren't locked. I'm a bit surprised at that, actually."

"It's just a step ladder, but maybe it will be high enough," said Joan. "Do you think we dare try it out now?"

"I haven't heard anyone in the building today. The janitors are usually around early in this particular building. I don't think they have a night shift."

Rudy tiptoed into the hall and listened to the silence. He returned and hefted the ladder. "Well, we might as well make the attempt now while there's still a bit of light outside."

The ladder was awkward on the narrow stair. By the time they got it out and propped against the trunk, it looked domestic and inadequate. Its top was still short of the lowest branches, and the tree's heavy roots and the uneven ground made it unsteady. It took them several minutes to find a spot where it would not immediately tip under Joan's weight. Finally, Rudy wrapped his arms around the tree from the other side and made himself a human tether, and all at once the tree surrendered. Joan cautiously ascended the rungs and stood on the top platform, her arms wrapped around the thick trunk. As she gained confidence, she extended one arm and grasped a branch. Bits of bark came loose from the scraping of her shoes, and they skittered down the trunk and landed in Rudy's eyes. Then he felt the pressure on the ladder lift.

"I'm up!" Joan whispered triumphantly. "And it's an easy climb from here to the window. We can do it! This is the way."

In the gathering dark he could just see her shape ascend to the branch by the archive window, and he held his breath as she slowly crept along its narrowing length. Her hand reached out and touched the sill, giving the red rag an experimental tug. Then she waved down and began to inch backwards. By the time she reached the ground her chin was bleeding again, but they both were smiling. Rudy gave Joan a congratulatory hug and was warmed when she readily clasped him back.

***

Adam improved in health and spirit. Gorski's text was still hard to decode, but as he copied the Polish text, he sketched in a tentative translation on the facing page, and his greater confidence yielded a more plausible narrative. There were still words to be figured out and idioms to decipher, but he could manage a more accurate translation when he returned home with the transcribed diary.

He was particularly taken with Gorski's little drawings, which he now thought might represent early notes for some of the famous fortifications that Kosciuszko had designed. He traced them with great care and precision, imagining already the illustrations that might accompany an article. He dreamed up a title: "Kosciuszko's Hudson fortifications: Notes on an Unknown Assistant." It would be a good way to introduce Gorski into the historical record. So confident was Adam that Joan would succeed that he saw his career bloom before him full of possibility and continuing promise. He did not permit himself to think of what would happen should she fail.

A breakthrough moment occurred late one morning when a series of pointed scribbles under a wiggly line rearranged themselves before his tired eyes to form a coherent picture, and three words of completely incomprehensible Polish suddenly resolved into French.

"*Chevaux de frise*!!" Adam shouted and jumped up to show Joan the little sketch of defensive armaments—named after horses but scarcely resembling them. They were harbor guardians: heavy spikes mounted on a submerged scaffold and concealed below the water's surface (the wiggly line) just deep enough to pierce the hulls of ships entering defended territory. Babbling with excitement, he searched the rooms of their flat twice before remembering that she had gone into town and he was alone.

He sat down again and made three more sketches, placing them in the transcribed text with the greatest exactitude he could manage. He imagined the caption for one of the better drawings: "Cheval de frise: after Gorski." Or no, maybe the armament was always plural: chevaux. He would have to check. Whichever was correct, the caption would be confidently followed by the manuscript's archival reference. For soon the diary would be back in its proper place for any future scholar to consult and to confirm Adam's discoveries.

***

"We're in luck, partner. She lives across the river and crosses that bridge every day."

The voice was so low it was almost a growl. Pawel was terribly startled. His head swiveled in the direction of the sound and he jerked away as from an attack, but he was too close to the curb and lost his balance. Bodie caught him and set him upright on the sidewalk, to all appearances a friendly gesture that saved the smaller man from a nasty fall.

"Nervous, are we?" he inquired, carefully smoothing the lapels of Pawel's black overcoat. It was artfully tailored with a tapering waist and wide epaulettes capped with little gold buttons. Bodie hated it.

"You! What do you want?" hissed Pawel. "Our business is finished! You should not accost me like this in public."

"Not quite finished," said Bodie. "Surely you haven't forgotten the final mission?"

Pawel's pulse was racing. There were impatient Christmas shoppers bustling around them, and he was jostled as they passed. "We can't talk here."

They retreated to a dark bar quite unlike the places Pawel preferred. Bodie prodded him to a seat in a far corner.

"Now," he said, "This woman. Keith's saint. I know who she is. It took me a while to pry it out of Keith. But yesterday afternoon his saint walked by. Thought Keith would faint. It was all I could do to keep him from throwing himself at her feet right there on the sidewalk. Fortunately, he noticed that she was with someone. Don't think it was her husband. Some older guy."

"So perhaps Keith is now disabused about her sanctified status?" asked Pawel, adopting a prissy, academic tone. "If he can be persuaded that he imagined all this nonsense about what he thinks she knows, then we can simply finish our business right now. It is most likely that he is mistaken about everything, is it not?"

"Not so fast. I convinced Keith that we should follow her for a while. Find a better place to approach her. He seems to think she has to give him permission to leave and go home. He's convinced of it, in fact. He won't leave until she tells him he can."

"Permission to leave Krakow? Why?"

"No clue. You can try and make sense of what he says if you want to waste your time. I've given up."

Pawel frowned. He made an impatient gesture as if to get up and leave, but Bodie put a heavy hand on his arm.

"The trek wasn't wasted, pal." He knew Pawel would resent the familiarity. "I know exactly who she is now. She lives on the other side of the river. This means that she crosses one of those bridges a lot. I've been thinking about it. The river served a purpose once, so I figure it can do so again. Consider the first time a rehearsal. This time we'll do it right. Neat, you know?"

Bodie was almost jocular. Pawel's eyes darted here and there in the room, wondering if anyone else could pick up on their conversation. But Bodie was being careful. He spoke in short, casual bursts around sips of beer. Pawel didn't like beer.

Bodie continued. "Keith got lucky with the fog. But we can't count on that. And there are a lot of people walking around this city. So your job—"

Pawel uttered a little squeaking protest at the thought of his job.

"Your job will be to go up to her when there aren't so many people around and keep her in one place on the bridge. Show her something maybe. She seems awfully interested in the museum. Maybe you could tell her about our little adventure there." A pause while Pawel wondered if Bodie were attempting a joke. "After all," he continued. "It won't matter what she knows now, because she won't know it long enough to tell anyone else. It would get her attention, wouldn't it?"

Pawel was sweating. Under his freshly pressed shirt he could feel his sticking plaster coming unstuck. The inept jabs he had inflicted on his chest were not healing quickly. A small trickle down his ribs could have been sweat or blood.

Bodie was enjoying himself. He noticed that the pale face of his companion was gray in the dirty light.

"All you have to do is keep her attention for a bit. And when the time is right and no one is looking, I'll do the rest. And the river will finish it."

Pawel didn't like the plan at all. Nor did he like Bodie's final words.

"I'll be in touch."

He left Pawel to pay for the beer.

***

Adam had reached the end. It came suddenly and so unexpectedly that he stared at the final page of text with incredulity. Foxing and ink stains from an overloaded pen had misled him into thinking that there were at least three more pages to transcribe, but suddenly he found that Gorski's account came to a halt.

Several lines below the last entry the handwriting changed. A larger hand, the letters carefully penned as if written slowly, finished the document.

As Adam began to copy them, their meaning dawned. He put his own pencil down and studied the final words in disbelief: a short paragraph followed by a new signature. He read them over and over, and now he had no difficulty translating the diary's last record.

Today I have lost a great friend. It burdens me to take the pen that was held in another's hand for all these weary months and to record the death of the author of this journal of war: Pan Andrzej Gorski, late of Warsaw and Paris, my companion for the last months of campaign. The fever has risen from the marshes near the river and several men have fallen ill. It is the misfortune of Gorski to be the first to succumb. I mourn his loss. He will be buried nearby, and I shall mark the grave. Perhaps in some happier time his family will travel here and carry his remains back to our beloved homeland, which by the grace of God will be free and whole once more. He was a brave soldier and a true patriot. May God take his soul on wings and heaven welcome him.

– Tadeusz Kościuszko

Adam sat stunned. His eyes filled with tears. He felt bereft. Gorski was dead.

Well, of course he was dead. More than two centuries gone. But in his absorption with the diary, Adam had thought of him as a living companion. Adam blew his nose and began to feel foolish. And then he told himself that a death is always a loss, no matter when it comes. Or when it is discovered.

He took his time copying the final text. The deliberateness of his writing was a memorial in its own small way, and he pored over it to be sure about the translation, which seemed something that should not be postponed. He had to be sure then and there exactly what it said.

So sad was he at Gorski's end that it wasn't until evening that it occurred to him that he had stumbled upon a hitherto unknown document in the hand of the great Kosciuszko himself, and that, short as it was, this final paragraph might represent the most significant discovery of his time in Poland.

43

On the Brink

The best time to return the diary, they decided, would be Christmas Eve. The bustling streets would empty as families gathered for dinner, and when the celebration of midnight mass commenced, the churches would siphon off those still about the town. What is more, on that particular night, the chances of anyone overlooking the obscure window of the Radincki Museum were close to zero. Beata would already have left to visit her family in Wroclaw and would not wonder when Joan went down the stairs and out into the night.

Adam was finally told the details of the plan to enter the archive. He was horrified. Recalling the drop from the bathroom window to the ground beneath, he had raised vociferous objections and tried to put a stop to the venture. It's dangerous, he protested. I can't let you take that risk. The thought of Joan falling in the attempt to rectify his own error was intolerable, and he strode around their flat objecting. He insisted that he would simply enter the front door with the journal as he had originally thought he could. With more bravado than conviction, he declared that if he was apprehended with a museum document in his possession, he would just take the consequences. Joan waited him out, repeating calm descriptions of the tree, the ladder, the proximity of the branches, and a protective sling that Rudy had fashioned from the remaining length of clothesline. It sounded very reasonable, if one put aside the illegality of it all.

"This is what I'm going to do, Adam," she insisted. "Think of it as a Christmas present. You wouldn't reject a Christmas present, would you? This is a finish to our stay here. Don't fight it out of some dumb sense of responsibility."

After a pause she added, "A sense of responsibility, I would point out, that is frankly just too late."

It was that censorious observation that brought a halt to Adam's resistance. It also brought a resurgence of such guilt and anxiety that he suffered a relapse of his malady and spent an uncomfortable half hour in the bathroom. It was as though his body were attempting to purge his wrongdoing with punishing cramps and diarrhea.

"At least then, let me go with you and help," he offered when the worst of the siege was over. Joan surveyed his white face and trembling hands and firmly insisted on going alone.

"Rudy and I have practiced. You have your part to play. Do it right and we'll be fine."

So with a heavy conscience he agreed. The archives would be open for only limited periods during the holiday season, and on the last possible day before the Christmas closing, he paid a visit to the library just as had been his former practice. He greeted familiar faces and acknowledged their smiles and welcomes, and he resumed his old place at the wide table by the window. There he worked quietly for several hours checking the translation of his transcribed pages and once more sorting through the boxes of miscellaneous materials. The latter was more for show than substance, as by now he knew exactly what each contained.

At the end of the day, he took special note of the wheeled cart that held the boxes of Gorski's documents. As was usual for materials under use by regular researchers, it was positioned at the end of a long row of shelves where it could be conveniently retrieved. He made a little sketch of the floor plan to give to Joan, counting rows of shelves and noting the placement of the heavy library tables. Then just before leaving, he visited the bathroom and double-checked the window: interior latch up; outer window barely ajar, tail of rag still firmly attached. As he left he bade the librarian good bye and wished him a Merry Christmas.

On Christmas Eve he would join the throngs at midnight mass. He knew what he would pray for.

**

Pawel reluctantly joined Bodie in the evenings, sitting miserably on a bench in a little park by the river waiting for their quarry. To their left rose the castle, magnificent on its hill, and before them the long bridge stretched across the water. Although Pawel thought she had a husband, according to what Bodie could glean from Keith, she usually walked alone. An easy target.

But she did not appear with the predictable regularity that Bodie had anticipated. For several nights they waited, and after three unsuccessful vigils in a row, Pawel began to hope that the plan to kill this woman would simply peter out and lose its necessity. Maybe, just maybe, she had returned to wherever she had come from and was out of his life.

Then one night just three days before Christmas they saw her. They rose at the ready, Pawel with trembling knees and a stomach full of dread, Bodie with the controlled eagerness of a predator. But then they saw that she was in the company of another woman and a man. Pawel recognized the latter from the Radincki archives. This was yet more confirmation — as if he needed any more — that Keith's saint was this very woman.

Bodie followed them, with Pawel a wretched dog trotting at his heels, until they entered a church. Bodie would have lain in wait, but the other three were there for a concert, and even he didn't want to linger outside in the cold that long.

"Same time tomorrow night then," said Bodie with no diminishment of purpose. "And then the next. One of these days she'll be alone."

Now it was Christmas Eve, and Bodie was already in position by the river.

***

Something more important, however, had captured Pawel's attention earlier that day. It had propelled him into action sooner than he had thought would be necessary.

Only he knew the true secret of the Bronislaw chalice. Even if Joan suspected something amiss at the Radincki Museum, she could not possibly know why anyone would want that particular object. Pawel doubted that anyone in Poland still shared the knowledge of its occult power. Of course there were the ancient stories about Bronislaw and his bridge of salt. But who now believed in the old rites, the sacred mineral of salt, and a demon who awoke at the year's end.

Also forgotten, however, was the fact that legends often grow around a core of truth. And the core of this truth, Pawel was convinced, remained intact: the chalice, the blood ritual, the salt, and — most of all — the Millennium. His heart beat fast when he thought of the impending New Year, the turn of the century, the turn of the next thousand years. Only on this propitious and powerful night would the powers of local magic and the universe's astrological forces converge at the apex of their greatest potency.

At the auspicious hour he would be ready with a carefully prepared potion: his own heart's blood, drawn when the new moon was but a sliver, pure Wieliczka salt, and a drop of the waters from the river, all mingled together in the silver chalice in whose curving embrace the magic would commence. As midnight began to strike, he would utter the ancient incantation. When the final bell tolled, he would drink the contents of the chalice in one imperative swallow.

And then — what would it be like, the power that restored his rightful place in the world? Would it be something he could see? Or would it be felt in his inmost being, a surge of strength, a sign of his dominion in the new Millennium?

A huge celebration was planned in the center of the city. Fireworks were a paltry rival for cosmic forces, but all the festivity would be a convenient cloak for Pawel's own activities. For many, the millennial turn would be tinged with apprehension. Some expected the end of the world. The more advanced of those predicted that Y2K would cause catastrophe. Pawel cared little for this petty technological concern. But his heart surged thinking of the moment when Pawel Meyer would finally be transfigured into the scion of a noble family, and he would at last be really and truly Pawel Radincki.

It wasn't impossible, he assured himself. His family line was traceable with only a few gaps. He had the elaborately branching family tree to prove it. And though in spots it might resemble a tangle of underbrush more than a noble oak, he still could boast a Radincki sitting on one of the twigs. To have his position acknowledged wasn't like wishing for something impossible like the ability to travel through time or to sprout wings or even to be able to turn base metal into gold. A simple wish to be recognized for what he truly was.

There would be skeptics, there always were. And Pawel had to contend with the fact that his link to the nobility was by means of a speculative paternity and illegitimate at that. Still, a boost from the powerful agency of the chalice was all he needed. He was so near his destination he could almost taste it. In fact, he would literally taste it. The potion in the chalice would likely be pretty nasty.

He had gathered the instruments carefully: He had the silver chalice, he had Wieliczka salt. He had collected his own blood. He had a pretty good sense of the location where the ritual would best be performed. He knew the incantation to utter at the appropriate time. All he needed now was to wait for the right moment. Therefore, it was quite important that his business with Bodie be concluded before the Millennium.

He was counting the days.

On the morning of Christmas Eve, he found himself idly wondering if the chalice had been used at the previous Millennium. It wasn't supposed to be that old. Unless, that is, one of the legends was true and Bronislaw had discovered it in a cave under Wawel hill. But probably its powers had only been unleashed in small doses on the New Year's Eves when the single years turned. Indeed, perhaps it was only effective at the turns of the centuries, when its powers would have been stronger. But now at the Millennium it would possess its greatest potency. In a mere seven days hence—

And then he had an awful thought.

At some point in the past, the length of the years had changed. Some pope or other had added a few days to the calendar. Maybe that had altered the New Year from the date it had been celebrated when Bronislaw had first invoked the power of salt. When had that occurred? And how many days were added? Three? Ten?

What if the old Millennium had already passed, and he had missed his chance?

The possibility was too terrible to bear. Pawel scrabbled through his small library, flinging books right and left, until he found an atlas. And then it wasn't difficult to discover the answer to his question: His suspicion was correct. The number of days in a year had been changed with the introduction of the Gregorian calendar in 1582. And with the change, calculation of the last day of the year had been moved. Pawel felt his blood chill when he noted the dates.

The year formerly ended not on December 31st the way everyone thought these days. The old Millennium would really arrive — or would have arrived without the interference of that meddling Pope Gregory — on December 24th.

On this very night.

Pawel's head spun. His skull felt carbonated, as if his very brains were swirling. He sat while the room whirled and tried to think. Would the chalice and the powers it summoned have taken note of the calendar adjustment? Or had he missed his one great chance?

Pawel fought a roiling confusion. Everything was falling apart. He had worked so hard and prepared so carefully, and now at the last minute his plan was coming undone. He heard a noise in the room and opened his eyes in alarm, only to realize that it was the sound of dry sobs erupting from his own throat.

Then all at once he was calm.

It was not too late. Whenever the real Millennium would arrive, he was not too late to catch its power. All he had to do was speed up his plan. He would conduct the ritual tonight, and if it worked, he would have seized the Millennium at its old turn. If it didn't, he would just wait until the last day of December as he had originally planned and do it again.

Really, quite simple. No need for panic at all. He would use half the salt, half the blood tonight, just in case. There was plenty. After all, magic substances need not be large to be powerful.

In fact—and this bestowed the final reassurance—he had remembered the calendar confusion just in time. This auspicious recollection was surely a sign that his quest was nearing its culmination. The powers that govern fate must have reminded him of the calendar, not wanting him to miss the opportunity of his lifetime. His destiny was surely at hand.

44
The Bridge

Adam was already sitting in church by the time Joan headed out. She carried Gorski's diary in a small backpack. Adam had nervously overseen its packing, and it was securely sealed in two plastic bags. She wore a jacket, jeans, thick socks, and a pair of Beata's hiking books borrowed on the pretext of climbing the Krakus Mound to greet Christmas Day.

The streets were nearly deserted. Yellow light from windows pooled patchily on the sidewalk, and from time to time she could hear muffled laughter from behind closed doors. As she hurried along the river path she could see dappled lamplight beneath the bridge ahead. She was a little early and hoped that Rudy would already be waiting at the Institute.

Across the dark river beneath a clump of trees Bodie paced. He was pleased at the absence of street traffic and cursed the thought that Joan might not appear, for it was a perfect night to do the deed. He thought he had recognized her husband earlier crossing the bridge into the Old Town, and he hoped that Joan might follow him to wherever one went here on Christmas Eve. Church maybe.

But where the hell was Pawel? Of all the times for him to decide not to show up. He couldn't stand cowards and their lack of responsibility.

There was a street lamp at the far corner of the bridge on the other side of the river. Bodie had stared at it for so long his vision was dancing. Suddenly he thought he saw movement. He blinked. And wonder of wonders, there was a person emerging from the dark. Someone was approaching from the path along the river. It was a single person, a woman walking alone. And as she crossed under the light he was fairly certain that it was Joan. Saint Gertrude. The Queen of Diamonds. Alone.

Perfect. He would meet her on the bridge and make short work of it. He flexed his fingers in their supple leather gloves.

But no, they were not alone after all. Hurrying footsteps sounded over his shoulder, and he turned and saw that a man was making his way rapidly towards the bridge from the town side. Bad luck; it looked like the two would meet in the middle and spoil his opportunity for a quiet kill.

Then he saw that the approaching man was Pawel. He was bundled up against the cold and carrying a little valise and looking anxiously up river. In four quick strides Bodie was by his side.

"Cutting it a bit close, aren't you?" he hissed. "But we're in luck. She is coming."

Pawel whirled and crashed painfully against the bridge abutment in his surprise. He had forgotten all about Bodie and their dreadful purpose. Belatedly it occurred to him that he should have chosen a different route to the river.

"Not now! I can't. I have something important to do!" he protested.

"Damn right you do. There she is. She's right in our hands! Quickly! Stop her where the bridge is high above the water, in the dark patch in the middle before she gets too close to the next light. Go now!" And with a paw like a hammer he shoved his reluctant partner forward onto the long bridge and dropped back into the shadows. Pawel moaned in protest, but Bodie was implacable. He seemed to have grown even larger in the darkness.

Pawel stumbled forward in helpless dismay. After so many propitious events, now that his hour was at hand everything seemed to be going horribly wrong. First was the near catastrophe over the date, which had made him hurry with his preparations. Then his lovely crystal vial of blood had leaked, and he had abandoned it in favor of an empty plastic aspirin bottle with a snap top. And with the calendar confusion he hadn't been able to arrange transportation to the place on the river bank that he had singled out as the most auspicious, so tonight he would have to jog just as far as he could along the water until he could hear the bells of midnight.

And now this horrid interruption.

Pawel drew a deep breath. Better get it over with. If he was quick enough, he could still get down to the business of the ritual. He didn't want to try the patience of Fate much further.

As Joan stepped onto the bridge, she saw a man approaching from the far side. She had first thought there were two of them, but that must have been a trick of the dark. The man was slight and carried a small bag. To be on the safe side, she crossed the street to the sidewalk on the other side of the bridge. Alarmingly, the man did the same. They were on course to meet in the middle. She began to feel vulnerable and was now sorry the streets were so empty. But really, he didn't look so threatening. Perhaps he would only ask for some money and be on his way. She prepared to wish him Merry Christmas and assembled the Polish greeting in her mind.

As they neared she was surprised to recognize the man as the one who had received the stolen painting. She drew an even breath and greeted him: "Wesołych Świąt." Her pronunciation was poor, but he ought to understand anyhow.

Pawel's voice caught in his throat. He clutched his bag to his chest. The precious chalice inside felt heavy and lumpy.

He could feel more than hear that Bodie was silently running on the other side of the bridge. He looked out over the water towards the uplit walls of the castle and its doubled image on the river and fished for some English words. "A beautiful scene, is it not?" he croaked. Joan followed his eyes and turned to regard the castle. Just as she should. So far, so good.

"Yes, very beautiful. It is one of my favorite views in Krakow." She wondered at the other man's shallow, rapid breathing. Perhaps he had been running.

She was still looking at the castle when she felt a presence behind her. A heavy smell and a closeness that should not be there. Before she could turn around, fingers closed at her throat, and she was lifted off her feet by the enthusiastic strength of an attacker. At first she froze with the surprise of it all, and then she kicked backwards and felt strong legs behind her, but they were impervious to her heels. She was startled more than frightened at first, for fear was taking its time to gather. Of all the difficulties she had prepared for, she had not anticipated a mugger. Her mind was still focused on getting the diary back in its archive, and she tried to protest that she had no money. And surely this other man on the bridge would come to her aid. Surely, he wouldn't run away. But the grip on her throat tightened. The pressure mounted slowly, as though her attacker were taking his time, relishing the moment. She twisted, and as her vision began to darken, Pawel's horrified face appeared in a narrowing band of clarity. But he stood quite still, his hands clutching his bag, and he made no move to help her. She grabbed at the choking hands and kicked again, and she thought she heard a laugh.

It was the laugh that unleashed her terror. The hands around her throat seemed bent on murder, and she sensed a single-minded urge to kill. Her diminishing vision was now full of red sparks, and her feet were kicking less in self-defense than with the uncontrollable reflexes of the hanged.

Then all at once the bridge rose up and hit the side of her face. She was on the ground in the middle of a lot of feet. Grunts and the sound of blows and words she could not make out through the roar of blood in her ears and the heaving gasps issuing from her throat. She scrabbled on hands and knees away from a melee of stamping boots. She leaned against the bridge rails and craned her head back, hoping for more air to reach her lungs, and from that position she could see Pawel inching backward from two men engaged in furious struggle. In the insane confusion of the moment she thought her vision had doubled. But there they were: two men locked in combat. She had never been so close to a real fight before. It looked stagey and improbable and emitted horrible noises.

She feared the larger man would triumph and return for her, for although he seemed to be injured, he was grabbing for the other with a rage that seemed more than defensive. The shorter man now had his hands up protecting his face from blows that gained in strength, and for a time he seemed to be pounded physically into the pavement like a nail slowly driven home. But then he suddenly leapt sideways toward Pawel and tore the valise from his arms. In a whirling roundhouse he struck the tall man across the jaw with the bag, and there was a heavy sound like metal meeting bone. He followed it with another blow from the bag, and another and another. One blow after another delivered with deep grunts of effort. The tall man clutched his shoulder, and one of the fierce blows caught him full in the throat and threw him against the bridge rail. He gagged and his eyes started from his head. And then, as if in slow motion, his body began to sag and tilt over the water. Another furious whack sent him over the edge, and with this last blow the smaller man lost his grip on the valise and sent it sailing into the dark. There was silence for a suspended moment. Then a thick splash was accompanied by a yelping wail from Pawel Radincki, who rushed to the side of the railing and then ran back to the riverbank without even a glance at Joan lying on the pavement. In the sudden quiet she could hear him slide on the slippery earth down to the water's edge.

Joan's vision was clearing. Her throat hurt but she could breathe. The cold air in her lungs tasted like heaven. She sat limply on the sidewalk and looked up at her rescuer. She thought she recognized him but was not sure. He approached and looked down at her.

"Can you forgive me now?" asked Keith.

Joan looked blankly at him. A strange figure, staring eyes and distorted face. "What do you mean? Forgive for what?" But her voice came out in patches and Keith could not understand.

"I've done all I can," he said. He started to kneel before her but then changed his mind. He extended a hand instead. Joan took it and unsteadily got to her feet. She felt the backpack shift against her shoulders and suddenly remembered its precious contents. Oh no, she thought. What if it is damaged. What if I tore it when I fell.

"I have to go!" she said, her voice returning. "I'm in a terrible hurry. But thank you. Thank you. You saved me. Thank you for saving me."

Keith clasped his hands in a peculiar gesture. "I'm sorry about the other one," he said. "I've prayed and prayed. Can you forgive me now?"

There was splashing by the shore. Joan turned and looked into the water.

"Who was that man?"

"A bad man," said Keith. The childish phrase uttered with such sincerity was chilling. "You should go. We are done now, aren't we? I can leave?"

She still didn't know what he meant, but there was no time to ask. The thought now rose that he might be another one to fear. His pleading eyes, slightly crazed, did not seem like those of a man who had simply intervened to save a strange woman from a mugger.

She backed away. "Yes. Of course," she said. "I am alright now. And I need to get somewhere. I am so grateful for your help. Thank you again."

The splashing continued.

"Go," insisted Keith. He looked down into the water where Pawel was now waist deep in fruitless search. "You should go before he comes back. I'll make sure he doesn't follow you."

A gibbous moon broke through the clouds, and Joan realized she must be late. She gave Keith a final, intense look. "Thank you," she repeated, and then turned and with a resource of energy she didn't know she possessed, she began to run.

Keith watched her retreating figure. Close up, she hadn't looked so holy, with her dirty face and the drops of blood welling out through the scratches. But he remembered that God works in mysterious ways, so probably saints do as well. He remained there a little while longer and watched as Pawel began to dive, coming up for gasping breaths and going under again. He looked like one of those swans dipping its head underwater for food. The water was cold. He wouldn't be able to keep it up very long. Keith thought he was looking in the wrong place if he expected to find Bodie. His former partner had fallen almost directly below him, but the other man was splashing around closer to the shore.

When the first woman went over the bridge, he was wracked with guilt. He would have given anything to have the clock turn back. Now as the disturbed water resumed its calm surface, he felt only relief. Bodie had not been a friend.

With her heavenly understanding, Saint Gertruda would understand that the one death cancelled the other. He would pray to her to make it so.

45

The Tree

Joan fled the bridge with focused intensity, barely aware of her bruises and scraped skin and the cold air searing her throat. As she sped further into the Old City, there were more people milling about on the street. They looked curiously at her, and she slowed her pace to an unsteady, trotting walk. Her breath was coming in ragged gasps, but she feared that if she stopped to rest, her legs would give out completely. By the time she made it to the steps of Rudy's Institute, a sharp stitch jabbed through her ribs, bisecting the contusions she could feel forming across her left side. Her injured elbow was aching. It was darker again by these buildings, recessed as they were from the street, and no light showed in the windows.

Black on black, Rudy's tall form separated from the shadow of the portico. He was anxious and irritated that she was late. But before he could speak he saw her face, and with a quick look around he opened the door and drew her inside.

"Good God, Joan! What happened to you?"

But Joan would not talk until he locked the door behind them and they were upstairs in his office, enclosed in a familiar space.

Her energy was spent and she could hardly walk, so he half-carried her up the stairs and settled her on his desk chair.

As her breathing calmed and she realized she was truly safe, the terror of the bridge washed up behind her with the force of a wake that lifts a slowing boat. She swallowed several times before she spoke.

"Someone attacked me on the bridge," she began, and then paused to get her voice under better control. She told herself she had no time to be hysterical. But before even one more word could be uttered, she burst into tears and sobbed too hard for speech.

Rudy removed the backpack and her torn jacket and wrapped her in his warm parka. There was a shabby armchair in a corner of the room, a donation from one of his colleagues who had moved house recently. He sat her on his lap and held her tightly, dabbing at her bleeding scalp with a paper napkin he found in the saucer of an unwashed tea cup. After a time that was hard to reckon the crying subsided, and he thought she might speak. But she was quiet—so quiet that he became alarmed. And then he realized that she had simply fallen asleep.

After Renata fell ill, many was the night he sat in her room and listened to her breathing. He remembered how to tell by the quickness of the air passing across her lips if she was in pain, or if she dreamed, or if her medicine held her locked in stupor. Joan's breathing was deep and even, occasionally interrupted by leftover sobs that caught in her throat and died away. He sat and held her for a time. Like a child. Like a lover when desire is spent. Outside the streets filled as churches discharged their Christmas worshipers, and then it was quiet again. Rudy sat very still. Whatever had happened, sleep was probably the best antidote. His foot was tingling from lack of circulation when Joan stirred and looked up at him with eyes blurry and confused.

"What time is it?" she asked. Her neck was stiff and her hair felt stuck to the side of her head.

"Almost one o'clock. You fell asleep for a while. Do you feel better?

"I'm not sure."

Joan got up and looked around as if bewildered.

"I need to wash up."

Rudy led her to the restrooms at the end of the hall.

"Please wait here outside," she asked. "Don't leave until I come out. Please."

She took a long time. He could hear water running. The clanking pipes might have attracted attention at another time, but he was sure they were alone in the building. When she emerged, her face looked more alert, and the hair that had been stuck together with drying blood was smoothed back and damp. She attempted a smile.

"Well, I guess we had better get to work."

Rudy protested. It was foolish for her to attempt the climb this late, especially after the shock of her attack. We can do this tomorrow just as easily, he said. On Christmas no one will be around and it will be light. But Joan was determined. Her calm persistence was intransigent.

"Really, it must be done now," she insisted. "I feel remarkably well. The nap did me good. My arm is only a little sore, really it's so much better than it was. Completely healed, almost. And by tomorrow I'll be stiff, and it will be harder to make the climb. Let's just phone Adam, though. He'll be worried."

Back in his office Rudy heard her end of the phone call and marveled at her ability to make up a plausibly calming story so smoothly. Evidently Adam himself had just gotten home from the midnight services and was frantic to discover that Joan was still gone. After many assurances made to the quacking inquiries emitted from the receiver, Joan hung up the phone.

"So tell me what happened," Rudy said.

Joan nodded but did not respond right away. She emptied the backpack and assembled the items she needed. The diary appeared to be undamaged, and after inspecting it she repacked it in the plastic bags. She smoothed out the paper that was Adam's map of the archive floor and studied it briefly before she spoke.

"I was alone on the bridge when I saw a man approaching me from the other side. At first I was worried because he seemed intent on intercepting me. And then as he got close I recognized him. It was that person who was on the news. You know, the one who the painting was mailed to."

"Yes, I remember. The one who has the same surname as the museum."

"I was nervous because I was walking alone. But he didn't seem all that threatening. Just odd. We talked a little while and looked at the castle. And then suddenly I felt someone behind me, and a man had his hands around my throat."

Joan shuddered hard and clasped her hands together. Rudy was quiet while she collected herself.

"It seemed like forever. I struggled but he was very strong. And you know what? That man Pawel, he just stood there. I hoped he would help me. At least make some noise or call for help. But he didn't."

"Perhaps he was too scared."

"Perhaps. But he didn't run away either. I think if he was just scared he would have run away. But he stood and watched."

"That's nasty." What else could one say?

Joan started to strap the crampons onto her boots, but she winced as she bent down and Rudy took them in his hands. "You're hurt. You shouldn't do this."

"I'm alright. It will be better if I move around. Nothing is broken, I'm sure." Joan suddenly realized that she was wearing Rudy's jacket. "What happened to my coat?"

"It's on the chair. It got a bit torn and dirty, I'm afraid."

"Oh, yes. That must have happened when I fell to the pavement. I was ready to pass out, and the next part is kind of blurry. But there was a third person, another man, on the bridge. I don't know where he came from. But he ran up and hit the mugger very hard. He saved my life. I'm not sure just how he managed to make him let go of me, because the first man was much bigger. And he was horribly strong." Another shudder at the memory of those hands.

Joan was frowning in the effort to clarify her recollection. "They fought, and the man who came to my rescue grabbed the small carry-all bag, that the Pawel person was holding. And he used it to hit the mugger. He swung it around hard and I could hear it connect. It must have held something heavy. Metal or stone, not soft like clothes. He hit him repeatedly, over and over. Finally he must have got a lucky hit, because the man who attacked me toppled over the railing and into the water."

Joan fell quiet. She seemed to be concentrating very hard at an image forming in her mind. Her eyes were fixed but she looked at nothing in particular. Her voice was slow and thoughtful as she continued the story.

"Then he threw the bag into the water too. Perhaps he didn't mean to. Maybe it just went over with the force of the swing. Anyhow, it was flung into the river. And then Pawel seemed to wake up. He kind of yelled and ran back the way he had come and down the bank to the water."

"Was he trying to rescue the first man?"

"I suppose so."

"Did you see him again?"

"No. I could hear a lot of splashing. But the man who saved me told me to leave before the bad man came back. That was his expression: the bad man. And then I remembered what we had to do and I ran. I didn't know how much time had passed. I ran very hard until I got here. And you know the rest."

Rudy studied Joan's face. She still looked pale, but now an aspect of intense puzzlement was replacing the distress. It was as though she were listening very hard for an idea that was slow to form.

Joan slowly turned. Her eyes widened as she looked at him and drew a long breath.

"Rudy. Rudy. I think I know what has been going on. All the pieces of the puzzle are coming together. I think I am beginning to understand how Pawel fits into what has been happening."

"How? What is it?"

Joan was still as a statue for a moment more, and then suddenly she smiled and picked up the clothesline and the diary.

"It's not entirely clear yet. Let me think just a bit more while we take care of this last little task, shall we? And then I'll tell you everything. But first, wait. I'm starving! Do you have anything to eat?"

Rudy laughed. He was having trouble keeping up with her changes of mood. "As a matter of fact, I do. Not terribly nourishing but it might give you some energy." He turned to a shelf and removed a flat, red box.

"Chocolates!"

"Yes. One of my students dropped them off. A holiday present of sorts."

Joan ate five chocolates and threw one away. "Sorry, I don't like nougat. Shall we go?"

Rudy did not point out again the folly of trying to break into the Radincki Museum after her ordeal. A double folly, in fact, since the break-in itself was an extravagant gamble. He marveled as Joan put on her own jacket. She stood straight, gathered their gear, and marched down the hall to the janitor's closet and the stair, where at the bottom the ladder stood at the ready. Her deep nap seemed to have filled her with strength. Rudy followed, remembering the resilience of younger days.

Despite her bravado, Joan had thought she would be scared to go up the tree in the dark. But she seemed to have spent all her fright for the evening, and in contrast to the terror on the bridge, this climb seemed a familiar escapade. Her body was sore and still a little shaky, but her mind was clear and full of purpose. Carefully, methodically, she mounted the step ladder as Rudy held it tight against the trunk. When she reached the lowest branch she clipped the tether of the makeshift sling to her belt in surety against a fall, though she was certain that she would not slip. Not now. Now she moved with the confidence of a cat. She adjusted the backpack across her shoulders and hoisted herself further into the tree.

Then it was as though the tree itself vouchsafed her passage. Higher and higher she climbed. The long branch that extended towards the bathroom window was the most tenuous part of the climb, and she inched along it on her stomach, wincing at the bruises on her ribs as they pressed against the rough surface. The bough bent under her weight and gave a little protesting creak, and then she was within reach of the rag tied to the window. It took two or three tugs to pull it open, for she dared not shift her weight too much. And then there was a bad moment when it caught against the branch and had to be persuaded further outward so she could hoist herself onto the sill. A brisk push against the inner pane, hands gripping the upright center bar of the casement, one more heave, and she was draped across the stone sill and half into the archive bathroom. The branch whipped upward as her weight transferred to the sill, and she felt a little encouraging spank that sent her the final distance.

She was in.

She unhooked the tether, gave Rudy a little wave from the window, and removed her shoes. It wouldn't do to leave a trail of loose bark and mud to pique anyone's curiosity.

She opened the bathroom door cautiously and felt the large space beyond loom before her. It had a maw-like quality that was almost menacing, but she stood quietly in the dark until the room got used to her presence. With a pen light she checked Adam's map and counted the shelves until she found the cart loaded with boxes of Gorski's materials. It even had a card with Adam's name on it taped to the front. She lifted the lid of the top container and set it aside. She removed the diary from its two plastic bags and placed it gently into the box. Then she replaced the lid, silently, softly, as if putting a baby to sleep.

After all that effort, the actual return of the diary seemed almost too easy. Such a simple transfer from one place to another, accomplished in a moment. She paused to breathe deeply and to sense the space around her with a kind of wonderment. For a moment she savored the sheer excitement at being someplace she did not belong. But then weariness began to rise, and she retreated back to the bathroom.

She put on her shoes and used the little flashlight to check the floor while she swept up the dirt and bark that she had tracked in. Getting back on the branch was awkward. Joan began headfirst and then retreated back into the bathroom, realizing that facing away from the building she would not be able to close the windows. So she exited backwards, twisting around to see where she was going and ignoring the hissed directions from Rudy below. At last she lay again along the branch, and though it bowed beneath her weight, she could just reach the inside window to pull it shut. She had to scoot beyond the rag-tagged outer pane before she could shove it back to its original position, and the last few inches had to be accomplished with a series of little jerky pushes. Not perfect, but good enough.

By the time she reached the ground, her legs were too tired to do anything but fold up under her, and she sat propped up by the side of the building while Rudy unhitched the safety tether and restored the ladder to its proper place. She started back up the stairway on hands and knees. Rudy locked the lower door with the rusty iron key and left it as they had found it days before.

Joan was too fatigued to go home, so they went to Rudy's nearby flat. She stood in a shower nursing her bruises until the hot water ran out, and Rudy phoned Adam, who had been pacing the hall in fits of anxiety. Adam flung on his coat and ran to Rudy's flat at a speed that rivaled his high school track records, though by the time he arrived, Joan was fast asleep on a little pull-out cot wrapped in a plaid flannel bathrobe and covered with a quilt.

Adam stood over Joan's sleeping form and made as if to touch her.

"She is exhausted," said Rudy. "It has been a difficult night, but successful. Your diary is back at its proper home. And you should know that your lady here has been quite heroic."

"I never should have let her go," said Adam, both relieved at the diary's dispatch and remorseful at the danger he had occasioned.

"We have lots to talk about," said Rudy. "But it can wait until morning. Here's an extra pillow. You can have the couch."

Adam was sure he could not sleep, but the sounds of the others' slow breathing gradually lulled him. So many feelings competed for attention — relief, embarrassment, shame, guilt, the remnants of fear — that they canceled one another, and he dozed half-aware until morning.

46
Final Pieces

The bells ringing from the church towers awakened Adam early, but Joan slept hours longer. When she awoke she was so stiff that she needed another hot shower before she could move her muscles.

She was glad that Rudy had already told Adam of her encounter on the bridge. It had taken on a surreal quality that she didn't want to revisit for a while. There was time enough to come to terms with her brush with death. When Adam tried to put his arms around her she winced at the pressure against her bruises and he let go.

They sat with large cups of Rudy's potent coffee and an unexpectedly lavish spread of cheeses, fruits, and breads.

"I forgot that I had laid in a store for a little Christmas Eve feast," Rudy said, looking rather sheepishly at all the food. "I had the idea that we could finish our business in time for a bit of celebration. But then it slipped my mind, what with everything else that happened."

"It's even better for Christmas breakfast," said Adam. "Thank you. Thank you both again. I can't tell you how grateful

I am. And how sorry that my blundering put you in such danger."

Adam had been expressing gratitude and remorse more or less continuously.

"Well, let us toast to a job complete," said Rudy, raising his coffee cup. He resisted the impulse to suggest a breakfast brandy.

"Na zdrowie!" said Joan.

Rudy poured more coffee from a freshly brewed pot. "Now that we are all safe and sound and gathered over breakfast, I'd like to know, Joan, what you figured out last night. Remember, you said you had solved a puzzle. That you knew what was going on. But you fell asleep before explaining."

"What do you mean?" asked Adam. "Do you mean what was going on when you were attacked?" He reached for Joan's hand. "I am so sorry," he said again.

"Not exactly," said Joan. "Though maybe that can be fit into the picture too. Here is what I think. This cheese is excellent, Rudy. Thank you. I am really hungry." She was eating voraciously, despite the fact that her bruised neck was sore when she swallowed. She wanted to erase the feeling of those hands.

"There is no rush," said Rudy. "There is plenty of food." He watched in awe as half a cheese round disappeared.

"Yes, of course. Sorry. There. I'll stop for a bit."

"Catch your breath," said Adam.

Joan put her fork down and took a slow drink of coffee. Then she cleared her throat, wincing.

"Are you sure you don't want to see a doctor?" asked Adam. "Your neck is beginning to show bruises." Purple smudges were emerging where Bodie's fingers had gripped. Joan pulled the collar of Rudy's bathrobe higher. She shook her head decisively.

"No. Positive. I'm fine. Sore, but fine. Now, here is what I have been trying to patch together." Joan pushed her plate back and set her elbows on the table.

"I think that several things have been going on, and that we all became peripherally involved in them without knowing it. Maybe me especially, but all of us in one way or another. The pieces of the puzzle that I've been trying to put together are the theft of the Leonardo painting, its return, the missing silver chalice, and the man Pawel."

"What missing chalice?" said Adam. "Who is Pawel?"

Joan looked at him with a combination of fondness and irritation.

"Well, I did mention it to you several times, but you weren't feeling well. I mean the thing called Bronislaw's chalice that is in the Radincki Museum."

"Oh yes, I remember. We read the label together."

"Right. And I've been trying to convince the museum that the object they now have on display isn't the one I saw at the beginning of autumn."

"I thought they didn't think it was all that important," said Adam, as fragments of recollected conversation surfaced.

"That's true. But the fact remains that whatever was in that display case earlier is not the same thing that is there now. I have almost convinced Andrzej that I'm right."

"Andrzej?" said Adam, thinking of Gorski.

"Go on," said Rudy.

"So anyway, even if the chalice isn't a valuable item, it was stolen and a substitute was put in its place. It is not a perfect replica, but it wasn't likely that anyone would notice the change, at least not immediately. However, I spent a lot of time in that room and took a liking for the items there. And I remembered what it looked like. I even drew a picture. No one could have anticipated some tourist would do that. It might have been years before the substitution was detected. In fact, it might never have been discovered at all."

Joan's voice was beginning to falter. A timer dinged in the kitchen and Rudy bustled away, returning with hot rolls.

"If you take a spoonful of honey," he advised, "it will soothe your throat." He held out a laden spoon dripping gold. Joan obediently swallowed.

"Yuck. Too sweet. But that does feel better. Thank you."

"And switch to tea. It will be better for your throat." He had a pot of herbal tea steeping. These domestic remedies were unexpected, but after all, Rudy had raised two children. After several hot swallows, Joan continued her speech.

"There is so far nothing but timing that links the chalice to the theft of the painting. But I think—in fact, I have been trying to convince Andrzej—that one famous and valuable object was stolen to deflect attention from the theft of a less important one."

"That seems rather excessive," said Adam. He figured he would find out who Andrzej was soon enough. "It doesn't seem valuable enough to go to such risk, does it?"

"Only to someone who perhaps also believes that it is worth stealing for another reason," said Rudy.

"Exactly!" Joan said.

"What additional reason?" Adam was feeling sidelined. Joan and Rudy were now speaking intently to one another, almost as though he weren't there. But under the circumstances, he could hardly complain about being left out.

"There is a legend attached to the Bronislaw chalice," said Rudy. "We looked it up a while ago. The chalice is supposed to have the power to summon a demon if you fill it with salt and some other stuff and utter the right mumbo-jumbo. This ritual raises some kind of local genie who will grant wishes. But only at certain times of the year. Damn, I can't remember the whole story."

"Certain times of the year! That's it!" said Joan. "It grants wishes at the New Year, at midnight when one year turns to the next and a demon wakes up."

"Wow," said Adam. "It must be a killer at the Millennium."

He had spoken half-jokingly in the effort to insert himself into the flow of conversation. But Joan grabbed his hand and squeezed it.

"Yes! That must be it, Adam! Which explains why all of this has happened now! Think of the urgency. It's almost the New Year. And not just an ordinary new year. Not just even a new century—but the mark of the next thousand years!"

"Conjuring a demon at the Millennium," mused Rudy.

"Makes my worries about Y2K sound downright reasonable," said Adam, pleased to have contributed something.

There was quiet for a while as these ideas settled around them. Rudy went to a cupboard and found a bottle of brandy. He poured it into his coffee without apology. Adam reached for the bottle and added some to his own cup.

"I'm still not clear about the connection of the chalice to the theft of the painting," Joan eventually said. "But here are some possibilities. If we assume that the person who stole the painting did so really in order to take the chalice, then he is also the person who returned it."

"That certainly makes sense," said Rudy. "Not a very efficient plan though. Once you successfully steal a valuable painting, why give it back? Unless, that is, you never really wanted it in the first place."

"But if you want one thing, and you can break into a big museum and steal two things," said Adam, "why bother with both? Why not just take the one?"

"Exactly," said Joan. "And that is why Pawel is an important piece of this puzzle."

"Who?"

"The man who received the painting when it was returned, the one who was on the news."

"Right. I keep forgetting his name."

"What would he gain from stealing and giving back the painting?" asked Rudy.

"Good question," said Adam. "If he really wanted the chalice, he could have just snuck in and taken it, and no one would have been the wiser. But to take a work by the most famous artist in history just calls attention to the theft."

Joan got up and began to pace, with a stiff limp at first, then more easily as her muscles relaxed. The coffee was singing through her blood and she felt electrified.

"The answer to that is exactly what began to occur to me all of a sudden last night. A bunch of things fell into place, probably because he appeared on the bridge. Why was he there? He has to fit in someplace. So we can figure out why he might have taken the painting if we also figure out what he got from the attention of receiving it back."

"Well, it was the attention itself he got first of all. He was on the news," said Rudy. "His name! It wasn't just he who was on the news, it was the name of the person to whom the painting was addressed."

"Pawel Radincki!" They all spoke the name at once.

"But he denied the connection!" said Rudy.

"Maybe that was strategy. Plant an idea and see it grow up later."

"I just realized something else too," said Adam, pleased to be able to add another piece of information. "Where did you first see this man, Joan? Apart from the television. Had you seen him before?"

"No, I don't think so. Although now that you mention it, I might have seen him once or twice in the gallery. Maybe in the very room with the chalice in fact. Why?"

"Because I've seen him myself. He comes into the archives. And he works sort of secretively on a paper that looks like it could be a genealogical chart. He looks at reference books in the reading room and then takes out the chart and adds a name or two. I didn't connect him with the painting until now, even though he did look kind of familiar. He has one of those faces that are easy to confuse with other people."

"Who is he really?'

"No idea," said Rudy. "But I'll bet we can make a pretty good guess as to who he would like to be. And why he wanted the chalice."

"How pathetic," said Joan. "Is it really possible? He wants to raise a demon at the Millennium to make him into a real Radincki. Maybe a prince. Or a count, whatever. You could almost feel sorry for him."

She took another spoon dripping with honey and washed it down with brandy. Hot tea, more brandy. And the thrill of discovery.

And then a chill of recognition.

"You know," she said, "this puts the attack on me last night in a different light." She sat down again, her legs suddenly weak.

"Why?" asked Adam.

"Pawel," said Rudy. "He was part of it. He didn't come to your aid because he was in league with the attacker. Oh my lord, Joan! It was a deliberate attempt on your life!"

"What?" Adam sat bolt upright and his coffee sloshed into the saucer.

"And the man who I thought was just a mugger was in fact . . ."

"Targeting you."

"What? Why?" Adam had lost the thread again.

"Which means that he must have been in on the theft too."

"But why would they want me dead?" asked Joan. "What did I do?" Fear rose. A mugger would have been purely bad luck. The wrong place at the wrong time. But a planned attack . . .

"I don't understand anything!" said Adam. "Would someone please explain what you mean?"

"It's what you just said a minute ago, Adam," said Joan, turning to him. "You have seen Pawel in the archives. And now

I think I've seen him elsewhere in the museum too. Suppose he noticed my interest in the chalice. Oh!"

"What?"

Joan had on her sibyl look again, scrutinizing her own memory.

"The man who saved me last night. Who came to my rescue on the bridge. I thought he looked familiar, but I was too scared to think about it. But I just remembered something. Once when I was in that room with Andrzej, we were looking at the chalice. And that man came in. I'm almost positive now that it was he. He looked terrible, like he had been in a fight. And he saw me and ran away. I didn't think anything of it at the time because I was too occupied with the chalice. But I think—I think that he too must have been part of the theft."

"But he is the one who rescued you."

"I know." Joan put her head in her hands. It felt ready to burst with so many racing thoughts. She was trying to recollect the terrible scene on the bridge. Her memory was simultaneously confused and vivid.

"He asked me to forgive him. He asked me if we were done. Or something like that. It didn't make any sense at the time. And it doesn't now either. There is something we still don't get. Another missing piece." She raised her head and looked intent. "But it will come clear. I know it will. We must be very close to the truth."

"Not a very pleasant truth, Joan, if the attack on you was planned," said Adam.

"What did he mean? Why should you forgive him? And for what?" asked Rudy. "He saved your life. What is to forgive? Did he speak to you in English?"

"You know, actually he did. That hadn't occurred to me. But he did. With an American accent. He asked me to forgive him for the other one."

"The other one . . ."

There was silence, but they all came to the same terrible conclusion at once.

"He must have meant another woman he killed. The guard. I knew her drowning wasn't an accident." This piece of the puzzle slid into place with a terrible fluidity as Joan recalled the image of Klementyna pulled from the river. "And if he meant her, then I must have been saved by a murderer."

"One act to save a life to expiate the act that took a life. It makes a certain sense," said Rudy.

Dread crept into the room.

Adam broke the silence. "You might be still in danger, Joan. The man might come for you again. The one who fell into the river. Don't you think you should go to the police?"

Joan thought: I refuse to be scared again.

"Not yet," she said. "I think I'm safe. I thought that Pawel ran down to the water to rescue the attacker. But perhaps he didn't. Maybe he wanted to make sure that he stayed under."

The room was quiet under the weight of thought and too warm now from the kitchen oven. Rudy crossed to the window and pulled it slightly open, letting the cold air of Christmas enter. They could hear the hejnal bestowing its familiar tribute from St. Mary's steeple.

47

Loose Ends

The archives were open briefly between Christmas and New Year's. Adam paid his last visit and took a final look through the boxes that had occupied his mind for so many months. He also examined the bathroom. A few small twigs had fallen under the sink, and a smear of mud on the windowsill required a wipe. Otherwise there were remarkably few traces of Joan's dramatic entry. He looked down from the window at the ground, said a private thank you to the tree, and latched the inner window firmly.

He kept his eye on the entrance, hoping that Pawel might appear so he could make a report to Rudy and Joan and sustain that sense of purpose they had shared on Christmas Day, but only one other scholar arrived that morning, and he left quickly.

He spent two hours checking over his transcription. He turned the fragile pages of the diary one by one, corrected the spelling in his notebook here and there, added to the drawings he had copied. He spent a reverent minute rereading Kosciuszko's farewell, and then he gently closed the journal and inserted it back into its ancient oilcloth wrapping.

As the closing hour grew near, he said goodbye to the archivist and thanked him for all his help. There were handshakes and expressions of mutual appreciation. And then at long last he showed him Gorski's diary, devising a little story about finding it in the envelope that had seemed just part of the archival box. He even gestured to the remains of the envelope, omitting just when he had found it and wondering if anyone would think to ask. But the librarian was thrilled that a document from those dusty boxes was so important, and he raised no question about exactly when Adam had made the discovery. Adam now suspected that a simpler, more straightforward method of return would have worked just as well, and that his panic had been inflated and foolish. He filled in the form requesting that a microfilm copy be made and sent to him, a request he should have initiated weeks before. Perhaps someday copies would find their way into the American archive where he had first discovered Gorski's misfiled letters. Perhaps the diary would eventually be scanned into a digital file the way some archives were now making their holdings available. That would be convenient for scholars of the future, assuming anyone else would ever be interested in one obscure Pole in eighteenth-century America.

Despite the trouble he had caused for himself, Adam did not envy those future scholars with their easier access to old texts. For a while the diary had been his. He had traced the ink with his fingers and smelt the leather of the binding. He had copied it with pencil and pen, just as Gorski had recorded the events of his short life. It was back in its repository now, and who knew if it would ever be read again. But he was glad to have held it for a brief time in his hands.

***

Keith was surprised when he went through Bodie's things to discover a large cache of money. He pocketed the additional dollars without guilt. Maybe Bodie had been holding out on him. But it didn't matter now. No amount of money could compensate for what he had been through. And Bodie would not be returning to claim what was his.

Even more surprising was the discovery of two passports bearing unfamiliar names. Keith didn't have a chance of passing himself off as a Frenchman, but he retained the Canadian document and thought that if he grew a beard the picture might resemble him sufficiently in an emergency. He did not intend that such an emergency ever arise, however. Keith was a reformed man. His soul had been saved in the nick of time, and he would ever after pray to Saint Gertruda, just in case she still kept an eye on him.

***

"Miss Templeton! Joan!"

The Sukiennice was so crowded and noisy that Joan did not hear Andrzej calling her at first. Her muscles were still sore and she walked slowly. Andrzej appeared at her elbow.

"Holiday shopping?" he inquired.

"Oh hello," said Joan, smiling at his sudden arrival. "Just a little. I haven't bought any souvenirs to speak of yet. Mainly I'm taking a walk."

Andrzej looked doubtfully at the sleet falling in the Rynek. "Not the best day for a walk. Come have a coffee with me. I have something to tell you."

He produced a giant umbrella, and they made their way to a restaurant on the corner, an old-fashioned one with wallpaper traced with flowers, a high ceiling hung with brass chandeliers, and a piano covered with a lace cloth. Single long-stemmed roses twinned with sprigs of holly decorated each table. To celebrate the season, they changed their coffee orders to mulled wine.

"I want to tell you something in confidence," said Andrzej. "You've told me that you might write an article about the chalice, but you have to promise that you won't publish it yet."

Joan crossed her fingers under the table. "Okay."

"My colleagues checked more on the Bronislaw chalice. In fact, I think they were more interested in your claim than they said at first. And they checked to see if weight was recorded when the museum first put the chalice on display."

Andrzej savored the pause as the waiter placed the spiced wine before them and fussed with spoons and napkins. Joan smiled, for she knew what was coming.

"And guess what?" Andrzej continued. "The weight recorded in 1926 when it was acquired is different from weight of the object now in the case. The original chalice was recorded at almost a kilo. That is quite heavy. And the new one weighs only about 700 grams. So you were right. The chalice now in the museum isn't the one that was there before."

Joan nodded. "Yes. I knew it." But she did not say it with the triumph that Andrzej expected.

"Joan," he insisted, "You can't make this a story. I wasn't supposed to tell anyone, but I thought you deserved to know. We have to find out the truth before anything is said. Promise me."

"I agree," said Joan. "But I think that the truth is going to turn out to be much more complicated than we first suspected. Because I now have something to tell you."

And over wine, followed by sandwiches and then more wine, she told Andrzej what had happened the night before Christmas. In the middle of her account she extemporized to omit her illicit entry into the museum archive. She had been, she claimed rather vaguely, on her way to join Adam at a late Christmas party.

At first Andrzej was disbelieving, then rapt, then excited. And when she finished with the account of the attack on the bridge, he was appalled.

"Joan, this is terrible. I thought you did not look so well. You limp a little. Have you told police?"

"Not yet. Actually, I wanted to talk to you first. But as you can see, the investigation of the chalice and its disappearance really needs to be sped up."

"I understand. There is danger if we don't get to bottom of this."

"The bottom," Joan corrected absently. "I promised you just now that I wouldn't write a story about the substitute chalice. At least not yet. But you know, Andrzej, the story will come out. And frankly, I would like it to write it myself before I leave for home in a few months."

Andrzej reluctantly nodded and sighed. "Yes, I knew you would. Now there will have to be formal investigation soon." She did not insert the missing article.

Instead she said, "Well, the informal investigation is already underway, and as you can tell, we have made much progress. I truly believe we are on the trail of the truth. And if you join us— Rudy and me I mean, because Adam is going home—it will progress even faster. Will you help? Please? There are lots of loose ends to wrap up."

Andrzej hesitated, struggling with competing allegiances.

"Please," said Joan again. She held out her hand.

After a short pause Andrzej beamed and shook it firmly.

"Agreed!" he said, "I will enjoy this." He held her hand a little longer and added, "You have been sometimes annoying, you know, Joan, with your stubbornness and your reporting. And your grammar. But I am pleased to be part of your team."

48

Millennium

In the dark before dawn of December 31, 1999, Joan kissed Adam goodbye. They stood together at the window in the yellow light of the kitchen, and he put his arm around her waist and held her lightly against his side as they watched the taxicab creep around the corner and pull up outside their flat.

"Safe trip," said Joan.

He descended the stairway slowly, and she heard him fumble as he picked up the heavy bags on the landing. There was a click of the latch and an updraft of cold air, and then the door closed again and he was gone. From the window she watched as the driver loaded the suitcases into the cab. The trunk closed with a dull thump, the only sound in the dark. Adam turned and raised his hand. His face was a pale smudge looking back at her as the cab drove to the end of the street and turned along the riverbank.

There was a fog rising from the river.

Adam settled himself in the seat, his briefcase heavy in his lap. As they drove away from town the fog grew denser, filling the flat fields with its presence and smudging the trees to shadows against shade. The headlights of the cab lit the road and diffused along the frozen edges. When things are dimly seen, they might go on forever. It was eerily quiet. Perhaps the driver was going too fast, but Adam did not worry. His typical cab habits—a clutch of the seat backs, feet pressing brake-like against the floor—none of these were present. Now there was only the ride.

The flat land passed swiftly, the road directionless in the murk. If he had been put out of the cab at this point, Adam would have had absolutely no idea which way to turn. This is trust, he thought. Ride with a stranger in a fog. It was as though he were adrift on an empty river, letting the slow current take him to his destination, as it inevitably would. He was relaxed, and while it would never be correct to call this man fearless, for the present Adam was without fear.

The transcribed manuscript and his notes were tucked inside the briefcase in his hands, and he thought of them now with a kind of mortified pleasure. His narrow escape had left him with such relief that the torturing guilt had all but disappeared. It reminded him of a description he had once read of an adventitious cure for syphilis: the high fever of malaria sometimes killed the resident spirochete, leaving the patient, if he survived, free of a disease that had dwelt in his body for years. Just in this way had his intense anxiety burned away the guilt. He embraced the unpleasant comparison. Thanks to Joan, thanks to Rudy, thanks to his own peripheral task, his small academic niche was secured. It was enough, and he was grateful. He had survived the illness, and he would live with whatever scars it had left.

Last night he had hardly slept. Every hour he checked the clock for its progress toward morning, at last switching off the alarm before it rang. He thought he could leave without waking Joan, but she too was awake. They had come together, and although they would leave separately, she rose to bid him goodbye. She made him coffee and cut its bitterness with the last of a jug of milk. Their final moments together were taken up with: Are you sure you have your ticket, and is your passport in your pocket, and is there anything you forgot to do. At last they ran out of words and let the quiet dark take over.

Their more important conversation had taken place earlier. It was Joan who first had said the words: Adam, I am staying here. Our time together is over. I think you know that. He was not surprised. He nodded and only said Yes, I know. They had sat together in the kitchen with a candle on the table, watching the wick burn long and the wax slowly overflow. It was a sad finish but not a bitter one. In some ways, they were better friends now than they had been as lovers.

He was on his way home, flying on the disputed ticket that had so worried him earlier. The weather prediction was cold but fair, no delays were expected, and he figured he'd beat the Millennium by a couple of hours. Adam thought of Joan watching his departure from their kitchen window, the yellow square standing out against the dark and receding as he drove away. He would miss her, but it was a relief to be leaving alone.

***

As the Millennium turned, Pawel Radincki motored slowly down the Vistula. His boatman faced backward; he guided the tiller and sipped vodka as he watched the fireworks rocket up from the Rynek and fill the sky. He would have preferred to be with friends in the celebrating crowds, but the man in the bow had paid him well for this night trip.

Pawel's ring gleamed in the light from the square lantern he held. The amber stones seemed to mock like the eyes of a tiny demon, and he pulled on his gloves. The boom of the distant fireworks sounded against his ribs like the drum of a huge heart. The little slashes on his chest had picked up a flaring infection after his fruitless dive into the river, and his skin prickled and burned. He ignored the pain and told himself it was his heart on fire. In penance. In hope.

There was still a chance.

With unsteady hands he dribbled a handful of crusty Wielitzka salt in an uneven loop around his narrow seat. The thrum of the engine drowned out his voice as he chanted the old words over and over. From time to time he cast more salt into the water and scanned its rippling surface. With each cast he gestured to his shoulders and his torso, describing the circle of the salt demon. Every now and then he took a grimacing sip from a little white bottle. The boatman, tugging at his own bottle, figured they were both celebrating.

Somewhere beneath the boat there lay the Bronislaw chalice, caught in the frigid muck of the river. For several desperate days, Pawel had paced the riverbank, venturing twice into the water when he thought he detected the shape of his little bag among the weeds. But he had to face the dismal fact that it had escaped him, and now as the world cycled into its next thousand years, there remained just a tiny chance of uttering the right words over the chalice at the moment that the boat passed over it, of casting the salt in just the right pattern so that, in slow solution, it could do its magic in the deep current below.

In fire I bloom. In water I flow,

Originally he had hoped to spend this night beside the great walls of the abbey at Tyniec, but Bodie's interruption had prevented him from reaching his chosen spot. Pawel still shuddered at the horrifying image of his valise flying into the Vistula. The heavy chalice would not have drifted very far. He had hired the boat for the entire night and intended to go up and down the water as long as he could. He had brought a blanket, and the boatman seemed content with the warmth of his drink.

As the bells tolled midnight and the sky exploded in light, a breath of wind blew out the candle in the little lantern. Feeling the powers gather round him, Pawel continued his incantation by the light of the millennial celebration.

In blood I abide and avail.

***

Rudy and Joan leaned comfortably together under a heavy wool blanket. They were not the only ones who had determined that the hillside of the cemetery would afford a good vantage for the fireworks, but the others had chosen their spots at some distance.

Rudy had lit a small brazier at their feet. It had taken him the better part of an hour to get the coals burning securely. Fortunately, the wind was at their backs, and small skirmishes of breeze were blocked by the gravestones. He had brought a set of candles in glass lanterns and salvaged a few leftovers from All Saints Eve. It is difficult to be entirely cozy in a cemetery, but Rudy felt at home, and Joan, in turn, was his guest. She snuggled against him, sharing the blanket.

"I have something for you," said Rudy. He handed Joan a small, square package loosely wrapped with creased Christmas paper. "You can read it on your way home. If nothing else, it should help you sleep."

Joan unfolded the paper, wishing she had brought a present for him. Instead, she handed over a bottle of champagne topped with a crimson bow. He set to work removing the foil.

"Spinoza's *Ethics*?" said Joan. It was hard to read the title in the candlelight. "Is this from your library?"

"Yes, one of the several volumes I had. This one doesn't seem to be marked up. It's not new, of course, but I thought you'd find it a suitable memento of your time here. I don't expect you'll read it, not the whole thing. It's hard going. But it's worth it if only for the final sentence."

"Thank you," said Joan. She riffled the pages of the book, liking their feel. Many hands had turned these pages. She located the last lines and tilted the book towards the candles. She smiled and nodded as she read: "*All things excellent are as difficult as they are rare*. Oh true. Very true. Thank you." She closed the book. "But it won't be airplane reading for a while. As I told you, I've decided to stay in Krakow for another few months."

"Still trying to untangle your mystery, I suppose? I hope I'll be permitted to continue as your assistant."

"I hope you will. In fact, I insist that you do. Beata is letting me stay in the flat for less rent, which is nice of her. And I'll have a story to write, once we figure out for sure what happened with the chalice."

Rudy slipped his arm around her shoulders and gave her a light squeeze.

"I'm glad you're staying, Joan. We can ride out the end of our times in Krakow together. I'll be leaving too at the end of this term. Back to Holland."

"Really? After all this time?"

"Yes, really. It is time. Probably it is long past time. But frankly, my dear, I wouldn't have missed the last few months for anything."

She leaned against him. Their bodies together felt warm and solid. Rudy said something in a low voice she could not hear, and she asked him to repeat.

"I was just thinking about time. And timing. It is a pity I was not born twenty years later. Or thirty. I feel we might have made something of it."

"We might still yet," Joan said. "Just with less time. Doesn't your favorite, Marcus Aurelius, say that all present moments are the same?"

"Does he?"

"I thought you said so. That a long life and a short one come to the same end. Doesn't that mean that a short time together can be as valuable as a long time?"

Rudy liked this interpretation. "Something like that, I guess. Our sort of situation is not his particular lesson, but why not turn it to good use? He is one of the philosophers of the past I would have liked to have known."

A blaze of light shot into the sky. Overhead the fathomless dark gave way to a riot of sparks.

"Speaking of time. Here comes the Millennium! Ring in the new!"

The tombstone of Renata Vander Lage served as a convenient table. Rudy gave it a brief caress before laying a cloth across its rough surface. The pop from the champagne cork made a domesticated little bang amid the rocketing explosions erupting from the Rynek, filling the sky and reflecting in the streak of river below. Their two glasses were more than chilled in the night air.

"To the next thousand years," said Rudy.

"To the next four months," said Joan. "And to all the present moments we're allowed."

They raised their drinks in solemn salute. Champagne bubbles broke across the shimmering surface of the wine, and their glasses filled with tiny lights as the jubilant sky exploded. Below them the river was netted with matching glitter as it made its steady course northward to the sea.

49

The River

Beneath the bridge crowded with revelers the dark water hides a terrible bounty. The river will not give up its secret until spring, at which point the branch of a submerged tree, rotting for years, will finally snap. Pawel's valise, weighted by its heavy load, might have stayed lost forever snagged in the branches of the drowned tree. But that tree also holds the body of a man, and soon the gases gathering in the tissues of his bloating flesh will bulge and inflate the skin until they overcome the grip of the cold and buoy his body to the surface. Onlookers will recoil at the grisly sight, then wonder at the bag he still holds in his arms. They will guess that it was clutched so tightly that it has mingled intimately with his very skeleton, for one protruding arm bone, shedding its cover of flesh, is threaded through the handles. After the authorities remove the grim remains and separate the man from the debris entangling him, they will wonder even more at the contents of the bag, which the Radincki Museum will have an interesting time explaining.

Joan will write her story.

Acknowledgments

My first visit to Krakow was in 1994, and in the four visits that followed I was amazed to see how rapidly the city was changing. Readers familiar with this area will notice that many of those changes have occurred since the millennium, including the archaeological excavation of the area under the Rynek where Joan and Rudy have coffee, the introduction of carriage rides for visitors, and the conversion of some of the riverbank where Pawel and Bodie lurk to a parking lot for tour buses. I hope that I have captured the feel of Krakow at the end of the last century, despite the tinkering of the city map that this story required.

This book is dedicated to my husband, David Gerber. In 2004, he and I enjoyed an association with the Jagiellonian University, and I taught a class near Rudy's invented institute. We lived in the area where I have placed Joan and Adam's flat, and our treks to and from the Old City inform my descriptions here. We spent happy and interesting times exploring Krakow and its environs, and I thank our many hosts for guiding us around and sharing their affection for their home and its complicated history, particularly Dorota and Michal Prazalowicz, Jan Lencznarowicz, Zofia Golub-Meyer, and Beata Polanowska-Segulska.

Deserving special thanks is my faithful reader, Barbara Andrews, who patiently read through many drafts of this novel and offered such helpful advice. Lynn Hasher suggested productive revisions to a much earlier version, for this book was long in the making. In addition, I am grateful to Regina Grol for advice about Polish and its uses in personal address; and to Rob Samborn for information about Y2K.

The two quotes from Marcus Aurelius come from G.M.A. Grube's 1983 translation of *The Meditations*, Hackett Publishing Company.

About the Author

Carolyn Korsmeyer is both a novelist and a philosopher. She is especially interested in how the senses and emotions are engaged by works of art, themes prominent in three of her philosophy books: *Things: In Touch with the Past, Savoring Disgust: The Foul and the Fair in Aesthetics,* and *Making Sense of Taste: Food and Philosophy.* She is keen to explore the ways that fiction can revive lives from long ago by engaging the reader in the sights, sounds, smells, and tastes of the past. Her first novel, *Charlotte's Story,* imagines the life that Charlotte Lucas (of *Pride and Prejudice*) might have had after her hasty marriage.

Details about her work can be found at her website:
www.carolynkorsmeyer.com.

Note from the Author

Word-of-mouth is crucial for any author to succeed. If you enjoyed *Little Follies*, please leave a review online—anywhere you are able. Even if it's just a sentence or two. It would make all the difference and would be very much appreciated.

Thanks!
Carolyn Korsmeyer

We hope you enjoyed reading this title from:

BLACK ROSE
writing™

Subscribe to our mailing list – *The Rosevine* – and receive **FREE** books, daily deals, and stay current with news about upcoming releases and our hottest authors.
Scan the QR code below to sign up.

Already a subscriber? Please accept a sincere thank you for being a fan of Black Rose Writing authors.

CPSIA information can be obtained
at www.ICGtesting.com
Printed in the USA
BVHW070742280922
648127BV00004B/14